"This Prince of yours," he said confidentially, "shares with me the same name, similar coloring, and we are of an age. The only difference is that he is dead, and I, you see—I am alive."

"That you are," she said, feeling a trifle feverish.

"So, my little dreamer, why don't you simply put this vivid imagination of yours to use, and pretend I'm he? I would so like to fulfill your fantasies, and perhaps," he murmured, "exceed them."

"It won't work," she forced out breathlessly as he edged closer and deliciously closer still.

"Why not, my darling girl?"

"Because." She faltered. "You kiss like a pirate."

"Not always," he whispered, smiling a little at first when he kissed her. The dizzying pleasure of it parted her lips slightly, then he lingered, breathing her breath, giving his own to her. . . .

By Gaelen Foley
Published by The Random House Publishing Group

THE PIRATE PRINCE
PRINCESS
PRINCE CHARMING
THE DUKE
LORD OF FIRE
LORD OF ICE
LADY OF DESIRE
DEVIL TAKES A BRIDE
ONE NIGHT OF SIN
HIS WICKED KISS
HER ONLY DESIRE
HER SECRET FANTASY
HER EVERY PLEASURE

THE PIRATE PRINCE

Gaelen Foley

BALLANTINE BOOKS • NEW YORK

A Fawcett Book
Published by The Random House Publishing Group
Copyright © 1998 by Gaelen Foley

Excerpt from *Princess* by Gaelen Foley copyright © 1999 by Gaelen Foley

Published in the United States by Fawcett Books, an imprint of The Random House Publishing Group, a division of Random House, Inc., New York, and simultaneously in Canada by Random House of Canada Limited, Toronto.

FAWCETT is a registered trademark and the Fawcett colophon is a trademark of Random House, Inc.

ISBN 978-0-449-00247-6

Printed in the United States of America

www.ballantinebooks.com

First Edition: September 1998

OPM 19 18 17 16 15 14 13 12 11 10

To Eric, who saved me.

Thanks also to my dad, sea-captain extraordinaire, for guidance on matters nautical.

Not all the water in the rough, rude sea
Can wash the balm off from an anointed king.
                                              —SHAKESPEARE

❧ CHAPTER ❧
ONE

May 1785

He took a faceful of sea brine, flung the stinging salt water out of his eyes with a furious blink, and hauled back on the oars again and again with all his strength. All around him, the swirling, bucking surf smashed itself in silver plumes of foam, drenching him as it sought to dash his longboat against the shark-tooth rocks guarding the cave. Arms and shoulders burning with the strain, he held the boat steady by sheer bloody-mindedness until at last, with a barbaric cry of exertion, he fought his way past the towering, jagged boulders. Passing under the low arch of rock, he ducked his head as his longboat glided into the cavern's mouth.

Meanwhile, leagues behind him on the moonlit bay, seven ships waited at anchor.

Once under the pitch-black granite dome, he wiped the sweat off his brow with his forearm, slowly catching his breath. He lit a torch, for there was no one to note his invasion now but the legions of bats hanging and screeching and fluttering overhead. Finally, he maneuvered the longboat to the landing and jumped off onto solid ground.

Fifteen years.

It had been fifteen years since Prince Lazar di Fiore last set foot on Ascencion.

Almost half his life, he mused, or this underworld existence that was no life at all.

He stared at the soft, sparkling sand beneath his scuffed black boots, then crouched down on one knee, scooping a fistful of it into one sun-browned, rope-callused hand. With a bitter, faraway expression, he loosened his grasp and watched the sand slip through his fingers as easily as everything else had.

His future.

His family.

And, with the dawn, his soul.

The sand whispered to the ground until all that was left in his hand was a hard, black little rock. This, too, he let fall.

He wanted none of it.

He stood, shrugging the shoulder strap of his sword back into place. The wet leather had been chafing his chest for an hour now, vexing the tender strip of skin where his black vest fell open. He took another swallow of rum from the silver flask hanging on a thin kid strap inside his vest, wincing as it fired his belly, then he put it away again.

Lifting his torch, he looked around the cavern until he spotted the entrance to the secret underground tunnels. They had been hewn from the mountain centuries before exclusively for his family. Strange to think he was the last one alive who would ever know that they truly existed, he mused, and were not just another legend of the great House of the Fiori.

When he reached the rough-cut entrance to the tunnels, he thrust his torch in ahead of him warily, peering into the shadowy gulf. It was damned claustrophobic in there for a man accustomed to the open seas.

"Ach, get on with it, quake-buttocks," he muttered aloud just to break the ponderous silence.

He forced himself in.

The black walls of the secret passageway glistened with trickling water and slime by torchlight. Shadows cast by the flame made fantastical shapes that writhed across the sharp-knuckled fists of rock. Beyond the sphere of his torch's glow, all was black, but somewhere far above him, he knew, his enemy was congratulating himself at a ball he had thrown in his own honor.

Lazar could barely wait to wreck the party. Soon the tunnels would admit him inside the sealed city walls, under all of Monteverdi's painstaking efforts at security.

After half an hour's laborious hike up the steep grade, the tunnel branched, the left fork leveling out while the right continued upward until, he knew, it reached the cellars of Belfort, the fallen castle on top of the mountain.

He would like to have seen the old place, but there was no time for sentimentality. Without hesitation, he took the path to the left.

At last cool tendrils of fresh air trailed against his cheeks, and the upward slant of black ahead became a diamond-dusted midnight blue. The torch hissed as he extinguished it in a small, primordial pool collecting water from the leaking walls. In darkness, he crept up to the tunnel's narrow exit.

A formidable macchia made up of thorny vines and weeds hid the cave entrance from the outside. His heart began to thud as he picked his way out of the brambles, trying not to make any noticeable rift, until at last he stepped out into the clearing. He slipped his curved Moorish knife into his belt, moving slowly, welling with a kind of wonder as he emerged. Unaware he was holding his breath, he stared about him.

Home.

Everything was tinged with silvery moonlight. The terraced fields, the olive orchards, the vineyards, the orange grove on the next hill. Fine, earthy fragrances ribboned through the night breeze to him. And here, behind him, the solemn old Roman wall still stood, its great stones hoary with moss, protecting the heart of the kingdom as it had for a thousand years. Memory sighed through the chinks in the rock.

We are the cornerstone, boy, we, the Fiori. Never forget. . . .

He took a few, faltering steps forward, surrounded by the music of fields, of crickets and frogs, with the soughing of the surf in the distance. Just as it had been forever.

His heart wrenched, and for a moment he closed his eyes, tilting his head back, remembering all too clearly things he could not bear to face again.

A cool breeze crept over the landscape, stirring the leaves on the vines until the whole orchard, the citrus grove, the grasses, murmured to him like the voices of beloved ghosts sweeping out of their haunts to greet him, lost generations of dead kings and queens. They rose and floated in spires above him, urging him on with ghost whispers, *Avenge us.*

Yes. He opened eyes that suddenly blazed with muted pain made into rage.

One man alone was to blame for stealing the life that should have been his. He had a score to settle, by God, and that was the only reason he'd come. He had no further business in this place. *Signore* the Governor had seen to that. But now the don would pay.

Aye, legend said it was not on Sicily, not on nearby Corsica, but here on this isle that the ancient tradition of *la vendetta* had been born. Monteverdi would soon come to know it.

The waiting, the scheming, the biding his time for a full fifteen years, would be over. By dawn he would have his enemy in his grasp to mete out to him the measure he deserved. He would slay his kin, take his life, lay his city to waste.

But the most exquisite torment must come first.

The traitor must suffer as he had suffered. The blood justice he had hungered for, for so long, would be complete only when Monteverdi stood by in chains and watched him snuff out the life of the one creature he loved best in all the world—his innocent young daughter.

When it was done, Lazar would sail away, and he would never lay eyes on his kingdom again.

Even if it broke what remained of his heart.

* * *

Hands clasped behind her back, a polite, attentive smile fixed by willpower on her face, Allegra Monteverdi stood in the ballroom with a small group of guests, wondering if anyone else could tell that her fiancé was slowly getting drunk.

It was rare for the governor's right-hand man to succumb to intemperance, or any other vice for that matter. She was merely glad he wasn't being loud or sloppy about it—but then, the Viscount Domenic Clemente was incapable of doing anything with less than impeccable grace and elegance.

Must have had a spat with the mistress, she thought, eyeing him askance as he stood talking with some ladies, and emptying his wineglass again.

With detached admiration she noted how his pale gold, lightly powdered hair gleamed in its neat queue under the crystal chandeliers.

The wine was having an interesting effect on him. *In vino veritas*—in wine, truth, the old adage said, and she was curious to catch a glimpse of the inner man the polished viscount hid, for their wedding was just a few months away and she could not escape the feeling that she still did not know him at all.

Furtively, she studied the man whose children she would bear.

When Domenic noticed her gaze, he excused himself from the ladies and crossed the room to her with a cool smile.

Rather than turning him sentimental, the wine brought out an edge in him, Allegra thought. There was a sullen, pouting tilt about his mouth. The crisp, aristocratic angles of his face became sharper, and his green eyes glinted like the points of emerald blades.

Arriving at her side, he flicked a speculative glance over her body, and bent to kiss her cheek.

"Hello there, beautiful." He smiled at her blush, brushing her bare arm with his knuckles, the Mechlin lace of his sleeve tickling her.

"Come, young lady. You owe me a dance," he murmured, but just then the guests' conversation grabbed Allegra's attention.

"Rabid dogs, I say," one venerable old gentleman declared, speaking loudly over the music. "These rebels! Hang 'em all, if it's the only way to make 'em mind."

"Hang them?" she exclaimed, turning to him.

"Whatever is the trouble with the lower orders these days?" his wife complained, a persecuted expression on her doughy face while blue diamonds dripped from her neck and earlobes. "Always complaining about something. So violent, so angry! Don't they see if they were not so lazy, they'd have all they need?"

"Lazy?" she demanded.

"Here we go again." Domenic sighed. Beside her, her betrothed bowed his head, covering his eyes with one hand.

"Quite right, my dear," the old man endeavored to instruct her. "As I always say, they need merely to put their backs into their work and stop blaming everyone else for their troubles."

"What about the latest round of taxes?" she replied. "They haven't bread to put in their children's mouths."

"What, taxes? Oh, my!" the fat lady exclaimed, peering at her through her monocle in a mixture of puzzlement and alarm.

"There is talk, you know, of a peasant uprising," another lady told them in a confidential tone.

Allegra drew breath to explain.

"Darling, please, don't," Domenic murmured. "I am so weary of smoothing ruffled feathers all night."

"They will kill us all if we don't watch 'em." The old man sagely nodded. "Like rabid dogs."

"Well, pay them no mind," Allegra said gaily. " 'Tis only starvation makes them cross. Would you care for some cakes? A marzipan? Some chocolates, perhaps?" Eyes sparkling with anger, she gestured one of the footmen over, then stood back and watched them feed like high-priced pigs.

Coiffed and powdered, bewigged and brocaded, her father's guests cooed over the exquisite display of confections, sweets, and pastries on the servant's silver tray and began consuming them, powdered sugar sprinkling down the front of their satin finery.

Domenic looked down at her with a long-suffering expression. "Darling," he said, "really."

"Well, it's true," she tartly replied. These elders of the *ancien régime* were past reforming, their heads hopelessly muddled under their white wigs, their hearts shriveled like dried prunes. The spirit of the age was change—bold youth—glorious new ideals! Their kind would be swept away like dust.

"How about that dance?"

She couldn't help but smile at him. "You're just trying to distract me so I won't speak my mind."

He gave her a slight, narrow smile in answer and leaned down toward her ear. "No, I'm just trying to get my hands on you."

Oh, dear. Definitely must have quarreled with the mistress. "I see," she said diplomatically.

Meanwhile she noticed the doughy duchess whispering to the woman beside her. Both women sent pointed looks her way, eyeing the green-and-black sash she wore with her high-waisted gown of frothy white silk.

If they didn't comprehend her gown in the new pastoral style inspired by the ideals of democracy, then the fact that she was wearing the green-and-black must utterly, she supposed, confound them.

She lifted her head, unwilling to be intimidated. Perhaps no one else in this room gave a fig whether or not the peasants were starving outside the palace walls, but she did, and if the only voice she was permitted to give her protest was the wearing of the old Ascencion colors, she would do it and be proud.

She had taken the idea from the glamorous and savvy salon

hostesses to whom Aunt Isabelle had introduced her in Paris. They wore red-white-and-blue sashes to express their sympathies with the American Colonials during their war with England. Upon arriving here six months earlier, Allegra had adapted the practice to suit Ascencion's situation, but here, she found, women with political opinions were frowned upon, especially when those opinions ran counter to the established government in power.

Her father's government.

"Governor!" someone cried pleasantly just as the man of the hour came ambling into their midst.

While her father was greeted by a chorus of cheers, Allegra tensed, knowing he would be displeased with her if he, too, noticed her green-and-black sash.

On second thought, she told herself, why worry? Papa never noticed anything she did.

"*Salute,* Governor! Here's to another fifteen years," the guests chimed, raising their wineglasses to him.

Governor Ottavio Monteverdi was a brown-eyed man in his middle fifties, of medium height, still rather fit except for a respectable paunch. Though his manner was always slightly tense, he handled his guests smoothly, seasoned by decades of civil service.

He nodded thanks to one and all in his restrained way, then nodded to her and glanced up at Domenic.

"Congratulations, sir." Domenic shook the hand of his future father-in-law, the man whom he was being groomed by the Council to one day replace as Governor of Ascencion.

"Thank you, my boy."

"Are you enjoying your party, Papa?" she asked, touching his shoulder fondly.

Instantly his posture stiffened. Chastened, Allegra lowered her hand in embarrassment.

At Aunt Isabelle's cozy, elegant house in Paris, where she had been raised for the past nine years since her mother's death, everyone was demonstrative of family warmth, but here she was still trying to learn that displays of affection only made Papa uncomfortable.

Ah, he distressed her so, this nervous, gray-haired stranger, she thought sadly. Such a tidy, meticulous man, held together by the tenuous knowledge that all the odds and ends on his desk were in their exact, proper order. After the thrill of finally getting to live under the same roof with her one remaining parent, she found her father only wanted to keep his distance from her, she supposed because she reminded him too much of Mama. She felt his suffering, though he never spoke of it. Somehow she had to reach out to him. That was the reason she'd gone to such lengths as his hostess to make his civic anniversary a happy occasion.

He offered her a tense smile, but when his gaze homed in on her green-and-black striped sash, he froze, paling.

Allegra turned red but offered no excuses. Domenic withdrew, leaving her to fend for herself this time.

Her father gripped her arm at once and turned her aside. "Go to your room and remove that immediately," he whispered harshly. "Damn it, Allegra, I told you to burn that thing! If you were anyone but my daughter, I could have you jailed for insurrection."

"Jailed, Papa?" she exclaimed, taken aback.

"Have you no sense? Your little show of rebellion is a slap in the face to the whole Council and to me!"

"I meant no insult," she said, marveling at the intensity of his anger. "I'm only expressing my opinion—I *am* still entitled to my opinion, aren't I? Or have you made a law against that, too?" She wished she hadn't said it the moment it slipped past her lips.

His brown eyes narrowed. "Would you like for me to send you back to Paris?"

"No, sir," she said stiffly, lowering her gaze. "Ascencion is my homeland. I belong here."

His grip eased. "Then mind when you are under my roof, you will follow my rules, and while you are on Ascencion's soil, you will abide by Genoa's laws. Charitable efforts and good works are all very well, but I'm warning you, lately you have been verging on acts of open civil disobedience, and I am losing patience with it. Now, go change that thing, and *burn* it!"

With that, he turned away, his whole demeanor metamorphosing back to that of the pleasant host. Allegra simply stood there, stunned.

Jail me? she thought, watching her father exchange the usual social blandishments with the cluster of guests. *He'd never jail me—surely!*

Domenic glanced down smugly at her as if to say, I told you so.

She turned away from him with a scowl. "I'm going to my room. I've got to *change* my sash," she muttered with furious sarcasm. She was certainly not going to burn the royal colors of the Fiori.

"Allegra." Domenic captured her wrist softly.

She glanced up and found him watching her, his gaze strange with that too-keen focus, his eyes the overpowering green of the steamy woods after a hard summer rain.

"Your father's right, you know. Perhaps he doesn't appreciate your intelligence and your spirit as I do, but I agree with him completely that your youthful fervor is . . . well, let us say misguided. Get it out of your system now, because I won't tolerate it either."

She glared up at him, a tart rejoinder on her tongue, but by force of will she swallowed it. If she was truly going to serve her country, she needed to marry Domenic. She could put up with his mistress, his smooth condescension, his belittling of her work disguised as harmless teasing. She forced an obedient smile instead, biding her time, promising herself she would teach him some respect once they were wed.

"As you wish, my lord."

Gratification flickered in his green eyes.

"Go upstairs, my pretty bride," he whispered, tracing her bare arm again, though Papa was still standing right there. She blushed, glancing over to see if her father had noticed, then she looked back up uncertainly at Domenic.

He was getting quite drunk, she thought, noting the empty wineglass in his hand.

"Go," he urged her softly. There was something predatory in his slight smile as he nodded toward the door.

Furrowing her brow, she turned and walked away, wary, puzzled, and still stewing about his high-handed manner. *Youthful fervor is misguided,* she thought, mentally mimicking his condescending tone.

She stopped to check on the chamber orchestra in the corner. The musicians were presently taking a short break and tuning their instruments. She praised their performance and cheerfully reminded them to have something to eat before the night was done.

In the hallway, she breathed a sigh of relief at the feel of the cool draft wafting along the marble floor. Rather than go up to her room directly, however, she went down the dimly lit servant hall to the kitchens. The ovens had finally cooled, but the familiar smell of garlic roasting in olive oil always hung in the air.

She reminded the weary staff to package the food left over from the party for the pension houses and orphanages she regularly visited, then she ordered a portion brought to the jail, though she knew Papa would be angry if he found out.

This done, she turned to leave, but something made her pause. She crossed the kitchens to the wide supply door, which had been propped open with hearth bricks to admit the cool night air.

Silks billowing softly in the languid breeze, she came to stand in the doorway, where she gazed down longingly at the

square. The festival she had designed for the rest of the populace was gradually winding down.

Oh, she yearned to go out there and be with her countrymen,
with their rough-and-tumble ways, their loud laughs, their
sparkling dark eyes. Perhaps they were crude, she thought, but
at least they were genuine.

Over the centuries the mixed blood of Greeks, Romans,
Moors, and Spaniards had created a breed of southern Italians
as volatile and intense as the hot, rugged land they inhabited.
Ascencioners were considered even more dangerous than the
shiftless Corsicans, but to Allegra they were warmhearted,
robust, and passionate, hopelessly romantic as they fed themselves on old stories and dreams, such as the legends of the
great Fiori. She loved them, just as she loved this strife-ridden,
poverty-stricken island situated like a clod of manure about to
be kicked by the boot of Italy.

True, she mused, the winds of change blowing a bold new
age into the world had yet to riffle a curtain here, but she intended to use her position as the governor's daughter and the
future governor's wife in service to her country, no matter how
insufferable both men were.

She would be their conscience.

Then perhaps one day, she thought, with proper loving care
Ascencion might finally begin to heal, for the loss of the royal
family, and King Alphonse in particular, was a wound from
which the island had never recovered.

Nor did Mama.

From this vantage point, Allegra could hear lively music and
see some of the performers, a man breathing fire, acrobats. She
smiled, seeing a few young couples dancing the fiery, whirling
Sicilian dance called the tarantella, and shook her head to think
of the dull, decorous minuets in progress in the ballroom.

With a wistful smile, she gazed at the rows of colored
lanterns hanging over the square, each a candle lit to her faith
that surely the warring classes and families and factions could

set their differences aside and let there be peace, if only for a few days.

She lifted her gaze higher to the starry onyx skies, then closed her eyes as the balmy breeze caressed her cheek. The Mediterranean night was pure seduction, worlds away from the cold and drizzle of Paris. It whispered to her senses, luring her with hints of jasmine and pine and the faint scent of the sea.

It made her think of *him*.

The one even Domenic could never compete with, the one who lived nowhere but in her heart, in her fantasies, perfect and impossible as the utopias she envisioned.

Her secret Prince.

His name was Lazar, and he came to her in her dreams. Prince Lazar was a knight and a scholar, a warrior and a rogue; he was everything and nothing but moonbeams and fancy.

Actually, he was dead.

Yet there were those who claimed he was alive, somewhere, somehow. . . .

She opened her eyes again, saddened, yet smiling at her own foolishness. She gazed up at the full moon lounging on her cloud like a vain golden queen.

When there was a shift in the mob below, Allegra saw that the bishop had come out and was walking about, shaking hands with people here and there, trailed by his eternal retinue of pious widows, deacons, and nuns. Seeing them, she decided all of a sudden that she was going to go down there and say hello.

She was not a prisoner in her father's house, after all, though she often felt like one. Papa and Domenic could not control her every move, she told herself in defiance. Surely she need not take her bodyguards just to go chat for a few moments with dear old Father Vincent.

Without a backward glance, she left the wide doorway, startling the kitchen staff.

No one would question her if she acted as though she knew

what she was doing, she thought as she marched off, heart
pounding. At first she walked away from the house, then she
picked up her pace, crossing the landscaped lawn toward the
tall, spiky wrought-iron fence that surrounded the front section
of her father's property. Beyond it was another fence made of
men, blue-uniformed soldiers who lined the perimeter of the
palazzo.

Allegra strode faster, every step filling her with rising tension, almost a desperation to escape, as if she would suffocate
under all the hypocrisy and greed if she remained inside the
palazzo one minute longer. She was almost running by the time
she reached the edge of her father's property, her face flushed,
heart racing.

Most of the soldiers knew who she was, of course, and
would surely find it highly irregular for the governor's daughter to leave the palazzo unattended, but she reminded herself these men were trained to take orders. If any of them
questioned her, she would make some excuse and put him in
his place if necessary. Somehow she would brazen her way
past them.

As it turned out, the task was easier than she'd hoped.

Perhaps in the darkness they didn't realize who she was,
merely thinking her one of the guests. Trying to act perfectly
natural, she went out the small side gate. Here the wrought-iron
fence met the ten-foot wall that surrounded the back of the
property and the garden.

All nonchalance, while inwardly her heart pounded, she
passed the men and made her escape into the cobbled side
street, unquestioned. She was so amazed she had succeeded
that she wanted to throw her hands up and shout, *Freedom!*
Instead, she hurried the short distance down the narrow, shop-
lined street until she arrived at the square.

Pausing breathlessly under the cluster of palm trees that
graced the corner of the piazza, she stared about her in joy,
barely knowing where to go first.

She glanced toward the young couples dancing the scandalous tarantella, then looked toward the bishop.

It occurred to her that if she went straightaway to say hello to Father Vincent, one of those shrewd, hawk-eyed widows of his coterie was sure to ask where her chaperons were.

Perhaps, she thought, she could steal just a peek at the sinners before she rejoined the saints.

Skin tingling with the seduction of the Italian night, she followed the sound of the wicked, irresistible music.

With lethal grace, Lazar stalked through the olive orchard toward the twinkle of lights that was the small, new city the usurpers called Little Genoa.

It would be charred ruins by tomorrow, he thought with a narrow smile.

He checked his rusty timepiece by the light of the full moon as he walked. It was midnight now. His first priority was to break into one of the two heavily guarded gate towers. He wasn't exactly sure how he was going to do it, but he trusted he'd figure something out. He slipped the fob back into his small vest pocket, content that he had two full hours for the task. At precisely two o'clock, he would open the massive gates, allowing his men in to storm the city.

When he reached a field of tall, waving grasses, he could smell the bonfires, hear the distant music of the governor's anniversary feast where all those marked for death were gathered.

He narrowed his eyes as he gazed toward the square. The Genovese nobles were attending the ball in the gleaming marble palazzo, he knew, but it appeared Monteverdi had opened his coffers to provide the common folk with a more rustic festival in the piazza.

Bloody hell, he thought. These people were going to be underfoot. God knew he would not have one hair harmed on any Ascencioner's head. He concluded that if the festival crowd was still there at two in the morning, he'd find some way to clear the square. He was rather resourceful when it came to creating chaos.

He walked on, intent on sizing up the gate towers.

As he neared the crowded square, once more Lazar brooded upon the prospect of being recognized, then he brushed off the idea as absurd. Nothing remained of the swaggering boy he had been. After fifteen years, his people could not be expected to know him. Besides, Ascencion thought him dead. And for all practical purposes, he reflected with a morbid sort of humor, Ascencion was right.

When he reached the square, he faltered as he gazed about him, almost without the heart to go on, for it was exactly like the festivals his mother used to delight in arranging. He smelled the traditional foods, heard the old songs the guitarist was playing for a small crowd at a nearby fire, earning his coin. He stared at the peasant faces of the fun-loving, earthy souls who had loved his father so well and who might have been his own subjects, if not for Monteverdi's treachery.

It was strange even to think of it.

He took a few lost steps onto the warm flagstone, his soul in shreds as he stared about him, certain he was caught up in another aching dream of his childhood. The anguish of it he had borne so long made him want to lie down and die.

From the corner of his eye, he noticed two young girls looking at him, pretty creatures with flowers in their long, unbound hair, ruffled aprons, and bare feet. The dark-haired beauty ran a hot gaze down the length of him, while the blonde hid behind her, peeking at him shyly. He turned toward them with a raw sense of relief, for nothing eased his suffering like the feel of a woman's soft arms around him, the taste, the smell, the welcome of the female body.

But he held himself back, making no move toward them, even though, voyaging here from the West Indies, he had been weeks at sea.

No, he thought a trifle bitterly, he could numb his mind in a debauch of wine and unbridled sex later. There were always willing women to be found.

Tonight all that mattered was destroying Monteverdi.

He looked resolutely away from the girls and walked on, prowling silently through the crowd. Here and there people eyed him, especially his weapons, but they quickly looked away when he met their furtive glances with a stare meant to intimidate.

At last he reached the far end of the square. Hitching a thumb in the front of his black cloth belt, he sauntered with seeming idleness toward the gate towers.

The two towers were as high as mizzenmasts, squat, fat, and bulky, with slick stone sides and a few unglassed windows. Between them, the formidable city gate stretched two wagon widths across, nearly two feet thick, of solid wood reinforced with iron. God knew Monteverdi took every precaution with security, for all the good it would soon do him.

He counted twelve soldiers outside, and Lord only knew how many were inside. He considered climbing up onto the gate itself and going in through one of the windows or setting a fire or causing some other distraction that would bring the squadron inside charging out to restore order. Of course, it might be amusing simply to bang on the door and challenge them all single-handedly, he thought wryly. Fifteen, twenty to one? It had been a while since he had faced those odds. Perhaps he should brush up on his skills.

He stopped nonchalantly to pet a stray cat, all the while keenly eyeing the west gate, when he noticed one of the soldiers peering belligerently at him.

"You there! Halt!"

Lazar looked over with an innocent expression as the plump sergeant started marching toward him. In a glance, Lazar picked out the large key ring jangling from the man's belt.

One of those keys surely opened the iron doors that gave access to the towers, he thought.

The little red-faced sergeant stomped over and glared up at him. "Hand over those weapons! No arms inside the city walls tonight. Governor's orders!"

"I beg your pardon," Lazar said politely. Straightening up to his full height, he held the purring cat in his arms, scratching it under the chin.

"How'd you get past the guards? Everyone was searched at the gates! Weren't you searched?"

Lazar shrugged.

The little man narrowed his eyes. "Young man, you'd best come with me for questioning."

As the sergeant moved around to his side, Lazar watched him curiously, but when the little man reached to take away his guns, Lazar felled him with an elbow in the face.

He looked down almost regretfully at the unconscious man lying belly-up on the ground, another mere tool of the corrupt Council. He couldn't blame these men for soldiering for Monteverdi if it gave them a living. When a man got hungry enough, he would serve any master, as he himself well knew. The cat jumped out of his arms and vanished into the shadows. Bending down, Lazar took the sergeant's key ring and strolled back to the square, one thumb hooked idly in his belt as before.

Biding his time, he watched everything around him, especially Monteverdi's dozen or so mounted guards patrolling the edges of the piazza. One was riding a giant black horse that did not like the crowd. Perhaps he could spook the big, fiery animal, Lazar thought. That would give a few dozen people a good scare and allow him to begin clearing the crowd that way.

Nah, he thought.

He riffled through the twenty keys on the sergeant's key ring, realizing belatedly there had been no point in stealing it. They'd drill him full of lead before he had time to figure out which keys opened which locks. He was going to have to find another way, but he kept the keys just in case, jangling them idly in his hand as he strolled through the crowd, keeping an eye out for something he could safely set afire.

Meanwhile, he pondered Monteverdi's guilty conscience. The Governor obviously lived in terror, for there was absolutely no reason for so many soldiers and so many guns to mind a crowd half made up of old ladies, such as the two walking so vexingly slowly in front of him, blocking his path.

Just then he noticed a stir in the mob ahead. Excitement surged through the crowd, and the people shifted to make way for someone's approach. He felt an inward pang, half expecting to see Father come striding along, what with the way the people had suddenly become so animated.

He heard someone say it was the bishop.

He was about to move away when one of the old ladies in his way exclaimed, "Beatrice, look! There's the governor's daughter with Father Vincent. Such a lovely, good-hearted girl. Reminds me of myself when I was twenty."

The remark stopped Lazar in his tracks. He went very still, then forced himself to look at her just so he would be prepared tomorrow.

He saw her, and his heart sank.

He picked Allegra Monteverdi out of the crowd as easily as a diamond cast upon a pile of rocks, though she was still twenty feet away. She was bending down talking to a group of peasant children. She wore a white, high-waisted dress of an airy, delicate material. She had a slender, elegant figure and chestnut-colored hair in an upswept arrangement, and as he watched her for that instant, she burst out laughing at something one of the children said.

He looked away, heart suddenly pounding. He closed his eyes for a second, hearing that laughter like clear silver bells.

So she is not an eyesore. So what? he snarled inwardly. She was still a Monteverdi.

She was also, he realized suddenly, the perfect means for getting him into the gate tower. Indeed, as his hostage, she could prove invaluable. No one would dare get in his way if he had her in his power.

She was moving freely through the crowd, he saw, narrowing his eyes as he watched her. All he had to do was slip in close to her and persuade her to come with him, using soft words or weapons, whichever sufficed.

But instead of going after her at once, he held back, torn. He did not want to touch her.

He did not want to talk to her. He did not want to smell her perfume or see what color her eyes were. He didn't want to go near her at all.

The plain fact was that he had never killed a woman before. In fact, he had a grandiose sort of rule for his own conduct, in that he refused to kill in front of women. He could not imagine any sin worse than destroying one of those creatures whose wondrous bodies could make new life, but his duty required it. He had come here to destroy Ottavio Monteverdi, and the traitor's punishment would not be nearly complete until he knew how it felt to stand by and watch one's family massacred before one's eyes, helpless to stop it. The daughter must die.

When he saw a group of soldiers moving into the crowd from the direction of the alley where he'd left their unconscious sergeant, he realized he might soon have no choice. Self-defense might swiftly require it, for Monteverdi's supply of soldiers appeared inexhaustible. If Lazar allowed himself to be captured, he risked the lives of the thousand loyal men waiting for him just outside the city gates.

No, he thought, it was going to be torment, but he could spare himself no such nicety of feeling. Allegra Monteverdi would be his human shield.

His mind made up, he began stalking her through the crowd. Keeping a wary distance, he looked first for the bodyguards she would surely have on hand to protect her. He scanned the crowd around her, but for all her father's paranoia, it seemed Miss Monteverdi had not bothered to bring her guards out with her.

Interesting.

Following her, he decided to approach her from behind and at an angle. Continually he glanced at her over the heads of the peasants and townsfolk that stood between them. He saw her leave the children, stopping to talk with people here and there. Everyone seemed to like her, a fact that struck him as remarkable, for the Ascencioners hated her father, the petty dictator.

Drawing ever closer, he watched her wander to the triple-tiered fountain in the middle of the square, her hair brilliant under the colored lanterns. When she half turned to reach her hand out under the arc of water, Lazar saw her in profile. She curled her wet fingers around the nape of her graceful neck, letting the water cool her. Tilting her head back, she closed her eyes for a moment, savoring the water on her skin in the heat of the night.

Something in her fleeting rapt expression instantly fired every male instinct in his blood.

Stay away from her, the hardened anger in him warned, but he ignored it, tilting his head slightly as he watched her in increasing fascination.

It was at about that moment she began to sense she was being followed.

God, she was easy to read, he thought, amused. Her sudden apprehension was obvious in the way she stiffened, paused, looked around her just like a wary little cat.

Lazar leaned into the shadows of the wine seller's stall as Allegra cast a worried glance over her shoulder, then turned toward the sound of some music near the edge of the square. She hurried off in the direction of the bonfire, where the guitarist was playing the old ballads. Lazar followed, sauntering along, perversely enjoying the thrill of the chase.

The peasants here lounged around the fire, swigging from

bottles of the local wine, exchanging jokes and lewd stories, while the fat bard paused to count the few, grimy coins strewn in his battered guitar case.

As Miss Monteverdi stepped up to the fire, Lazar approached slowly, very slowly. He found himself seized with an awful curiosity to see her face in the light, the face of this innocent whose life he would take, whose death would consign to him, finally and irrevocably, as a force for evil in the world.

The ragtag bard hushed the waiting crowd and began plucking his guitar strings.

She was staring into the flames almost pensively while Lazar rounded behind the small crowd, watching her all the while. He slipped into position behind some people directly across the fire from her.

Gazing at her, he watched the firelight twine itself in gold through her hair and tinge her ivory skin with wine-pink light, like the allover blush of a woman's skin during lovemaking. As the slight breeze moved her skirts around her like fine silken sails, the firelight suggested to his practiced eye the long, beautiful legs and slender hips the silk concealed.

What a waste, he thought ardently. And a virgin, too.

Allegra Monteverdi had a childlike smattering of buttery freckles and large, expressive eyes, honey brown, with lashes tipped in gold. Though she had been raised in decadent Paris, as his spies had told him, the pristine air of the convent school still surrounded her, and that glow of untouched purity enticed something dark in him.

There was a fineness in her bearing that commanded his instant respect, a gathered, focused grace that made her shine, and already he had no idea how he was going to pull the trigger when the time came.

He only knew that he would. He had failed his family fifteen years ago, but he would not fail them this time.

As her gaze traveled over the group around the fire, the people standing in front of him walked away. The movement drew her attention, and before Lazar had time to slip away, she saw him.

Her stare slammed into him.

Her eyes flickered, widened slightly. Her lips parted on a quick intake of breath. Her glance took in his weapons, his all-but-naked torso, then flicked up to stare at his face.

Lazar did not move.

He was not sure he could have if he tried, for he saw her lovely face illumined by the golden glow of the fire and by another, brighter fire within—her spirit.

Her expression changed, so lucid, so transparent. At first she liked what she saw, it seemed, but seconds later fear set in, and she began to withdraw, staring at him as if she sensed his intentions.

Lazar never moved.

Before his eyes, the girl backed away, whirled around, and fled.

⇥ CHAPTER ⇤
TWO

For a long moment, Lazar could only stand there at the fire.

He lowered his chin, rubbing his mouth. Then he adjusted the black silk skullcap he wore to complete the look of the murdering outlaw—he had cultivated it well to keep his victims properly terrified. It had certainly worked on Allegra Monteverdi.

Do not go after her.

Those eyes. *My God, those eyes,* he thought.

He stepped toward the fire and crouched down, uncertain how to proceed. He uncorked his flask, ignoring the curious glances of the people around him, and took a long, long drink. He could not get the image of her face from his mind.

That light. He would snuff out that light from the world. He resolved to make it painless for her and, lowering his head, blamed a sudden sense of nausea on the rum.

When he glanced up again, the old, frail farmer on the other side of the fire was staring at him as if trying to recall some dim fact from his senile brain. That steady, searching gaze made Lazar uncomfortable.

"Hey, *paisan,*" one of the peasant men said to him with a sideward wink. "Governor's girl caught your eye, did she?"

He stared at him.

"Go get her, man!"

"Ho, ho, that's asking for the gallows!" another declared, laughing.

"She's a pretty piece," a thin, hungry-looking man said, then looked evilly at the others. "Maybe we ought to send Monteverdi a message tonight."

"I'd be interested in that," another mumbled.

"Are you mad? He'll stretch all your necks!" a robust fisherman scoffed.

"So what? He means to hang all of us sooner or later," the first retorted.

Others took interest.

"Count me in for a turn!"

He was well familiar with what he heard in their voices, and he did not like it. Allegra Monteverdi was the pivotal instrument of his revenge, and he would not have these hard-eyed fellows interfering. He stood, straightened up to his full height, and rested one hand idly on the hilt of his sword, the other on the butt of his pistol.

They looked up at him as if they expected him to charge off, leading the way.

"I don't think so, boys," he said in an amiable, quiet tone.

"No?" the shrewd one demanded.

He shook his head.

"We do not rape women on this island," he said, daring a challenge.

"Since when?" one exclaimed.

"She's a Genovese!"

"And who do you think you are?" the smart one scoffed. "King Alphonse, come back from the dead?"

Before the fellow knew what hit him, he was flat on his back with Lazar's sword point under his chin.

Around the fire complete silence fell.

"You will leave Allegra Monteverdi alone," he commanded them softly.

The old farmer suddenly spoke up. "He does look like King Alphonse!"

Lazar froze. He glanced over at him swiftly, fiercely, and for a moment the old man looked into his eyes.

"Santa Maria," a middle-aged peasant woman nearby breathed, blessing herself with the sign of the cross as she stared up at him.

"The legend!" whispered the guitar player, gaping at him as though he were the bloody Ark of the Covenant. "It's true! He is—"

"No," Lazar said sharply.

"But—"

"You're blind," he said coldly to them. "Leave me alone." He sheathed his sword and abandoned them, stalking off after his prey, heart pounding.

He searched the thinning crowd, ignoring the hammering of his heart, refusing to consider how stripped he had felt by that old man's mad-prophet stare and his idiotic remark. He looked nothing like Father. He *was* nothing like Father. He hadn't a noble, self-sacrificing bone in his body, and he was damned glad of it.

Stupid girl, he thought as he searched the crowd, angry now. Why the hell had she come waltzing out into this volatile crowd anyway? Where were her guards?

He saw her by the fountain in the middle of the square and followed, intent on catching up to her quickly, for after that conversation by the fire he didn't know what some of these radicals might dare.

Watching her, he focused his unsettled mind on the loose, sure swing of her hips as she walked, until he caught himself wondering how those long legs would feel wrapped around his flanks, that ivory skin moist in a silken sweat beneath him, that gold-streaked chestnut hair spread out upon his pillow, spilling through his fingers—

He thrust the images from his mind in self-disgust, unwilling to appreciate anything Monteverdi in origin.

He quickened his stride, intent on his pursuit of her, but he was twenty paces behind her when she ran straight into the arms of a tall blond man.

Lazar paused abruptly, arching one eyebrow. He sauntered toward the couple on a roundabout course, keeping to the shadows.

At first the smartly dressed man seemed angry at her, gripping her by the arm above her elbow and using his considerable height to loom over her, but quickly Allegra pointed toward the fire, no doubt telling him all about the half-wild killer who was stalking her.

Ah, her hero had come out to save her, he thought in dark amusement as he watched the blond man scan the crowd for him. *Must be the fiancé.* He knew about their betrothal, of course. He had done his research well for this night.

He disliked Lord Domenic Clemente on sight, but when the blond man waved a few of the guards over and began dispensing orders, no doubt to find and arrest *him*, Lazar heaved an irritated sigh.

All the while Miss Monteverdi hung close to her fiancé, watching the crowd fearfully as if she expected Lazar to leap out at her like a monster. When the soldier marched off to do his lordship's bidding, Clemente laughed easily and drew his frightened bride into his arms, showering her with gallant reassurance.

Curling his lip in disdain at the lovebirds, Lazar shot a glance out over the square, swiftly assembling his course of action. He noted that the soldier on the pawing black horse was not far away, then he looked back at the happy couple, scowling. The fiancé was leading her by the hand back alongside the palazzo—making off with *his* hostage.

For what? he wondered. A lovers' tryst?

His eyes narrowed as he saw Clemente caress her back.

All right, Miss Monteverdi, he thought, now you've annoyed me.

* * *

"But Domenic, they're enjoying themselves! There's no need to clear the square," she protested, wishing belatedly that she hadn't told him, for he had instantly started managing things, as usual.

Now, in her fright, overreacting to what was surely just her fervid imagination at work again, she had ruined the festival for everyone.

"Nonsense. It's past midnight. These people should go home," Domenic replied matter-of-factly, tugging her by the hand like a child caught in mischief. He led her along the shadowy side of the palazzo, back toward the walled garden.

She heaved a sigh but gave him little argument, still privately absorbed in the vision of that beautiful, half-wild savage with the piercing midnight eyes.

He had frightened her, yes, with his deadly-looking weapons and his bold stare as if he could see through her clothes, but she had never seen anything like him before.

Magnificent ... *beast*, she thought with a shiver as she recalled that powerful bare chest, that ridged belly the very firelight seemed to caress, and all that golden skin, which must feel like velvet to the touch.

Staring at her, insolent as you please, from just across the fire, she mused.

That hostile, hungry stare had left her so flustered and out of sorts that when Domenic found her, she couldn't think of any good excuse to explain her rattled state, so she just blurted out the truth—a dangerous-looking man had been staring at her and possibly following her.

She wished now she hadn't said a word.

What if the stranger had not been following her as she feared, or if his intentions had not been unfriendly? She knew the especial brutality of her father's soldiers. There had been such fierce pride in that hard, chiseled face, it pained her to think of the humiliation the stranger would suffer.

Now, because of her, he was going to be dragged away in

front of all the people, that untamed spirit caged, his powerful body beaten into submission. There was something in his dark eyes that haunted her even now, a strange, enigmatic blend of melancholia and hunger and rage. Why had he been staring at her like that?

She didn't know. She only knew that as soon as she could get rid of Domenic, she would go to the guards and make sure that they weren't too rough with him and that they were fair when they questioned him. Once they determined what he was up to, she would find out his name. Then, provided he wasn't a threat, she would make sure they let him go.

Domenic's words jerked her out of her thoughts.

"You, young lady, I am tempted to turn you over my knee, and, as for your guards, I'm going to have them court-martialed for having failed so completely in their duties—no, better yet, flogged," he declared as he took out his own set of keys to her father's house and opened the garden gate. "I'll have them flogged."

"Don't be absurd. You'll do no such thing," she retorted. "How can you even suggest anything so barbaric?"

He paused and looked down his pointed nose at her masterfully, one fist cocked on his hip. "Allegra, you don't seem to understand. If the rebels managed to take you hostage, they could make your father do virtually anything they wanted. If I hadn't come after you, who knows where you'd be right now?" He held the gate open and, with a polished, sweeping gesture, indicated for her to step in ahead of him.

She could feel the keen gaze of his forest-green eyes on her, scrutinizing her as she brushed by his lean, athletic body. She took a few steps past him into the garden, then turned back to him suddenly.

"Domenic," she said, "how *did* you know I had gone outside?"

Locking the gate from the inside, he paused, but said nothing.

"When I left the ballroom, I meant to go to my room. . . ." Her voice trailed off.

He turned to her, smiling. "You caught me."

He dropped the key neatly into his waistcoat pocket, then sauntered toward her, his blond hair a silvery-gold shade that sparkled in the moonlight as he approached.

She glanced a trifle nervously toward the palazzo, then back up at him. "Papa would not approve," she said uncertainly, though she knew full well Papa thought Domenic walked on water. Domenic had become the son Papa had never had.

"Don't worry," he said smoothly. "I locked the veranda doors, dismissed the servants from the back rooms. I even told the guards to take their places elsewhere. You see? I took the liberty of ensuring we'd have perfect privacy."

"What for?"

"Tut, tut, so suspicious." He took her hand and led her past the dimly glowing garden lantern under the laurel tree. He plucked one of the blooms, gave it to her, and, smiling in the shadows, maneuvered her back against the slim tree trunk.

She held the flower awkwardly, neither wanting it nor knowing what to do with it as Domenic ran his hands lightly up and down her bare arms.

"Come, Allegra. We are going to be man and wife. You're going to have to get used to my touch, you know." He caressed her cheek with the backs of his fingers.

"What a perfectly vulgar thing to say," she murmured, blushing as she turned her face away. "Isn't that why a gentleman keeps a mistress?"

"When a man has a wife as beautiful as you, trust me, mistresses are unnecessary. Tonight all I want to do is kiss you. That's not too much to ask, is it?" His strong hands molded around her shoulders in a firm but gentle caress. "You may find we are more compatible than you have yet suspected."

"I fear you have had too much to drink, my lord."

"Not until I drink from your lips will I be sated," he whispered.

"That was well rehearsed. Did you practice it on your mistress?"

He laughed. "I've gotten rid of her, Allegra. Darling, you and I have been engaged for over a month. A man's entitled to kiss his betrothed."

"I am not comfortable with this."

"You will soon be exceedingly comfortable. I assure you." He sounded very sure.

"Oh, all right," she muttered.

He laughed softly again. Then, holding her gently, he lowered his lips to hers. It was not unpleasant, she admitted reluctantly to herself as she waited for him to be done. A long moment passed. He barely moved, brushing his lips against hers.

"Very sweet," he whispered. He began to kiss her cheek and lower, her neck. His embrace tightened, pulling her up slightly onto her toes.

Hesitantly, Allegra slid her arms around his neck and looked at the starry sky through the laurel tree's flower covered branches, wondering how long this was going to take. She liked Domenic, there was no question, but when she dared close her eyes, she thought only of *him.*

Her Prince, who would never kiss her, because he was not real. Ah, well. She didn't particularly like the idea of any real man pawing her.

Her betrothed began nibbling her earlobe oh-so-gently. That felt rather tolerable, she thought, opening her eyes again, alarmed by the pleasure, even more alarmed when Domenic slid his hands low down her back, inching toward her backside.

She squirmed against him, pushing against his chest. "I think that's enough."

"Not nearly enough," he murmured, a roughened note in his voice. This time when he kissed her, his mouth was hard and hot, his hands holding her in place. He was pressing her back against the tree so hard with his body that she felt the hilt of his dress sword pressing against her.

Then she realized he wasn't wearing one.

Oh, dear. She braced both hands against his shoulders.

"Domenic, stop," she began, only to have him thrust his tongue into her mouth when she parted her lips to speak, both his hands cupping her face.

She had no idea what she was to do.

This is absurd, she thought.

Drunk or no, he was too smart not to see that all she had to do was tell her father about this and the engagement would be over—

She froze.

Of course he knew that. Suddenly she was seized with a diabolical realization. Domenic knew perfectly well she was determined to marry him for his position; therefore, he knew that, do what he may, she would *not* tell her father.

"You shouldn't have gone out to the square, darling," he breathed raggedly against her skin, his grip rough. "There are men out there who will insult you, take liberties." She heard ripping silk as he pulled at her dress and thrust his hand inside, cupping her breast.

"Stop!" She tried to pull away, but he held her against the tree.

One hand lightly bracing her by the throat, the other on her breast, he moved back to smile slightly down at her, green eyes glittering. "Go on, scream. I dare you. Your punishment will be all the sterner when I have you in my house."

"Punishment?" she breathed, wide-eyed.

"It is a husband's right, you know. But as long as you're my good little girl, you'll have nothing to fear," he whispered, kissing her again, if his assault could be called a kiss. "What's wrong?" he asked when she refused to respond, tilting his head as he gazed down at her.

She stared up at him in amazement, still unable to believe it was happening. Surely the straitlaced, impeccable Domenic, the golden boy of the Council, would never do anything like this. But when his grip tightened gently on her throat, she had to accept that it was real. She gritted her teeth, summoning up all her self-possession.

"Get away from me this instant. You are drunk."

He smiled in his all-knowing way. "You want to use me— why can't I use you? That's what marriage is all about, isn't it?" He kissed her again ruthlessly, nudging her legs apart with his knee.

She fought to turn her face away. "I won't marry you!" she gasped out.

"Darling," he panted hotly, his tone perfectly reasonable, "when I've spilled my seed inside you, you'll have no choice."

She drew a breath to scream as loudly as she possibly could, but he clapped a hand over her mouth with a low, chiding laugh.

"You cannot beat me, you see?" he said pleasantly. "Oh, I shall enjoy mastering you, Allegra. There are so few worthy challenges in life."

Abruptly he turned as if someone had tapped him on the shoulder.

Allegra gasped to see the savage stranger from the bonfire standing right behind him. He towered above Domenic, hands on hips, his feet planted wide in black boots and gaiters above the knee. He was armed to the white flash of his teeth, his shoulders a yard wide, his black vest parted by his aggressive stance, revealing every smooth inch of his muscled chest and chiseled belly.

"Pardon me for interrupting," he said politely, his voice deep and commanding, "but I distinctly heard the lady tell you no."

She caught a glimpse of glittering midnight eyes, then the stranger grabbed Domenic and threw him. Instantly he put his own body between her and Domenic, his broad back to her clad in an expanse of black leather. The long, silky ends of his skullcap trailed down his back, billowing slightly with his graceful walk as he stalked toward Domenic, wielding the most barbaric-looking knife she'd ever seen. The knife twirled lightly in his grasp as he adjusted his grip.

Domenic looked from the stranger to her, to the knife, as he backed away, panting, his blond hair tousled.

"Friend of yours, darling?" he asked, shooting her a cold glance.

"A good friend," the stranger replied affably before she could answer. "A very good friend."

Domenic's angular face took on a look of furious understanding. "Oh, now I see. Now I know why you're always running off to your filthy peasants!" he spat at her, looking the man over from his skullcap to his boots.

The stranger's answer to his derision was a big, booming laugh, merry and wicked. The sound actually made Allegra smile a little, shaken though she was. With trembling hands, she righted her dress as best as she could, but Domenic had torn it two or three inches at the neckline. She clutched the ripped edges closed and thanked Providence for sending the mysterious stranger to rescue her before anything worse happened.

"Allegra," Domenic began, "I am shocked and disappointed in you—"

"Don't be jealous, mate. I only had her six or seven times."

Her jaw dropped. She snapped it shut again as she realized he was intentionally trying to enrage Domenic. *Clever rogue.*

"You slept with this man?" Domenic nearly screamed at her.

"And three of my brothers," he assured him. "She wore us all out. The girl's insatiable."

"Now, that is quite enough," she cut in indignantly.

"I'll kill you," Domenic told him.

"All by yourself?" he asked sweetly. "Maybe you'd better call a few guards."

Torn between outrage and relief, Allegra didn't know whether to go over and kick him or laugh, but she had to admit his taunting was doing the trick. If her former fiancé had any sense, he would take this chance the stranger had given him to save face and go storming back to his mistress.

But, she discovered, Domenic was too full of liquid courage tonight to take the easy way out—or perhaps there was something to his reputation as a fine swordsman.

Uneasily she watched him pull a jeweled dagger from inside his coat.

The stranger merely smiled and gave his big knife a nimble flick from one hand to the other.

Now that she saw him in action, she was not surprised he'd evaded the guards Domenic had sent. She couldn't imagine how he had gotten over the garden wall, either. Then again, he didn't look like a man who would let anything as trifling as a ten-foot brick wall stop him.

The only question was why he had bothered to save her.

"You're the one who was following her," Domenic growled. "You never slept with her."

"Well, yes," he admitted, "not yet."

She snorted. Arrogant heathen.

Folding her arms over her chest, she leaned back against the tree with an irresistible sense of satisfaction. So, she mused, he had been following her. She knew it. But why?

"Allegra, go into the house. This ruffian is obviously with the rebels."

"You locked the doors, my lord," she said. "Remember? Besides, I don't think he is." She looked him over. "No one in the square knew him."

"Miss Monteverdi, don't go anywhere, please," the stranger cajoled her. "When I saw you, I sought a proper introduction, truly I did—"

"Ha," she replied.

"But his lordship here interfered before I was able to procure one. Bet you're glad I persisted, eh?" He tossed her a beguiling grin that quite took her breath away.

"Allegra," Domenic said tautly, "go and shout for the guards to arrest this scoundrel, or what's left of him when I am through with him."

"For what crime, my lord?" she asked.

"Trespassing."

"That hardly seems fair—considering."

"Do not contradict me," Domenic snapped, never taking his eyes off the stranger, his dagger glinting in the moonlight as the two men circled in fighting stance.

"He is not trespassing," she said. "It is my house. I shall say I invited him. Don't worry, Domenic. I think if he wanted to kill you, you would be dead already."

The stranger belted out his jolly laugh again. "How now, do I hear a compliment for my lowly self? Now I shall fight for you all the more fiercely, my lady. Apologize, villain, or I shall be forced to deal harshly with you," he commanded her betrothed in a thunderous tone full of a humor Domenic failed to appreciate.

Allegra rolled her eyes, charmed in spite of herself, while Domenic's eyes narrowed to slits of glittering green.

"Get out of here," she told the man. "They will hang you."

"They won't have time," Domenic declared, and charged at him.

Allegra watched in distress, desperate that no blood be shed but knowing that if she called for the guards to pry them apart, only her misguided rescuer would end up punished for his gallantry, and at this point she rather felt Domenic deserved a thrashing.

Who on earth is he?

Wearily she lifted her hand to her forehead, watching the

two cut and slice at each other and slam each other about, dueling, it seemed, for her honor.

Aunt Isabelle would have been so thrilled for her.

But gazing at the spectacle, all she could think was that here was yet more proof that her plans for peace were a waste of time. It could almost make one wax philosophical on the brute nature of man, but she was so tired from hostessing the ball and organizing the festival that all she wanted to do was go up to her rooms to sleep and let the two fools knock each other senseless. Nevertheless, she remained, flinching every time their blows connected.

The soldiers were bound to hear the fight soon. She had to stay so she could explain that the Ascencion man was only trying to help because he'd heard their struggle. She couldn't have them chopping off his lovely head.

For a moment she studied the stranger by the dim orange illumination of the garden lanterns. He was arrestingly good-looking, with a broad, elegant forehead under his skullcap, and finely etched brows, charcoal black, with a devilish flare at the outer corners. Beneath the poignant sweep of inky lashes, his large, soulful eyes were as black as the night sea. He had a proud, Roman sort of nose and the rugged square jaw of a born conquerer, but his lips were full and sensual, made for kisses and telling pretty lies.

He grinned again with that mad, wild glint in his eyes as Domenic slashed at him, whirling easily out of the way to grab his arm, flipping the viscount onto the grass as if Domenic weighed nothing.

"Are you through yet, or am I going to have to hurt you?" the stranger asked politely.

"Hurt him," she muttered.

Domenic climbed to his feet, his face an icy mask of rage. "You will die for this, Ascencion dog," he told him.

"For this? Why, this is nothing," he growled, launching at him.

Within the next few minutes, Allegra began to worry. The duel grew fiercer, but even when she decided to go for the guards before either man really got hurt, she remembered the garden gate was locked. Domenic had the key.

"Won't you both please stop it," she began.

The stranger cast her a brief glance as if to make sure she wasn't going anywhere, but it was a mistake. Domenic darted in at him, swiping at him with his dagger. Allegra gasped as the dagger sliced across the stranger's left arm at his biceps, cutting his smooth, golden skin. Blood ran instantly from the wound.

Laughing softly, Domenic backed away. "Have at you," he said smugly.

"Well, how do you like that?" the stranger murmured in surprise, peering down at his arm. When he looked up from the wound, his gaze was like a lightning bolt. "Rather stings," he said slowly.

They stared at each other. Allegra was suddenly terrified.

She saw that if she did not take control of the situation at once, he would kill Domenic, and, as a result, he would hang— two young men dead because of her.

"That's enough, both of you," she ordered them firmly, though her voice shook. "Sir, I will get you a doctor. Domenic," she said, holding out her hand as she went toward him, though she was frightened of how perfectly sinister he looked with that bloody dagger in his hand. "You've proved your point. Now, give me the keys, and remove yourself from this house."

Domenic tossed her a cold, cruel smile, pleased with himself. "I'll deal with you later, darling. First I've got to finish with this insolent . . . filth."

Even as Allegra cast the stranger a fearful glance, he hurled his knife away, staring at Domenic through narrowed eyes. The big, curved knife struck deep into the soil, shuddering where it landed.

Domenic looked at the leather-wrapped hilt jutting out of the ground, then at him.

"Now, my friend," the stranger said softly, cracking his knuckles, "you have annoyed me."

Allegra stared at him, riveted with awful fascination. Domenic raised his dagger, bracing himself for another round, the stranger's blood staining his hand and the Mechlin lace of his sleeve.

There was a second of silence, stillness, all action suspended by the power of the stranger's burning black predator stare. Allegra could not look away.

Then he attacked.

Without warning, he leaped at Domenic, tackling him into the flower bed by the garden wall. He tore the dagger out of Domenic's hand and cast it aside. Allegra cried out, running to the pair as the stranger began to beat Domenic so brutally she thought he would kill him.

"Stop, stop," she pleaded, not daring to get too near the powerful recoil of that right arm.

After four or five blows, Domenic's face was half covered in blood.

"That's enough!" she shouted.

Still fighting him, Domenic made a wild grab for the pistol in the stranger's holster. The stranger knocked his hand away. Domenic's stray grasp instead clutched the trailing end of the man's skullcap, and it came off, revealing a head startlingly shorn to a coarse black stubble like that which roughened his face.

The barbarian snarled at him and grabbed Domenic's hand. With one deft, awful blow, he slammed Domenic's hand against the brick trim of the flower bed, breaking his wrist. She actually heard it snap.

She gasped in horror, covering her mouth with both hands as Domenic let out a short, piercing scream, then stifled it back in pride.

"Oh, you're a tough one, are you?" the stranger muttered, then knocked him out cold with one final, massive punch across the face.

Wide-eyed, Allegra stood there in shock, both hands still clapped over her mouth.

As if ashamed of his shorn hair, the stranger quickly fixed the skullcap back upon his head with one hand, an absurdly vulnerable gesture in contrast to the fierce, chiseled menace of his face. Meanwhile, blood was running in rivulets down his arm.

Slowly Allegra lowered her hands from her mouth. "Is—is he dead?" she whispered.

"No, he is not dead," he growled as he began searching Domenic's pockets. It appeared the stranger was going to rob him right before her eyes, but instead he merely took out the keys to the garden gate.

When the stranger swept to his feet beside her, she found he towered over her by at least a foot. The man was as big as a gladiator. She had to tilt her head back to look up at him. All of a sudden, with Domenic unconscious, no one else in sight, and the walls of the garden hemming her in with this hard, bloodied man, she could not comprehend why she had trusted him for one second.

He stared down at her, his black eyes sparkling like a wintry, star-filled sky. Slowly he walked toward her, every rippling muscle limned by blue moonlight. It was pure instinct that made her back away, though his voice was soft seduction.

"And where might you be going, my pet?"

She whirled to run. He grabbed her by the waist and hauled her back against his granite-hewn body with a low, mean little laugh.

"No, no, *chérie,* I've earned you now." He held her with a grip that was far abler and more powerful than Domenic's. "You should have listened to your fiancé."

"Who are you?" she demanded, her voice shaking with terror.

He lowered his head over her shoulder. "Prince Charming," he whispered. "Ain't it obvious?"

She fought, kicked, punched, but it was useless. Without a word, he marched across the garden, all but dragging her by the wrist. Terrified, she pulled and pulled, fighting to free herself, but his grip was like an iron manacle.

"Let me go! Here—take my jewels," she tried desperately. "They're diamonds and emeralds. You can have them. I won't tell anyone about you. Just go—"

He laughed at her. "Ah, Miss Monteverdi, some men can be bought. I'm not one of them."

As they crossed the grass, he swooped down with lethal grace to retrieve his knife, then slipped it into his belt with such nonchalance, she marveled that he did not open his own side. He stopped to unlock the gate and threw it open with a bang, making no effort to be silent. She clung with both hands to the lattice of the iron gate, but he pried her free.

"What do you want with me?" she cried.

"Just be calm and do as I say."

He seized her by the waist and tossed her up onto a big stamping, snorting black horse that might have come galloping straight out of Hell in answer to his whistle, except for the regiment's insignia emblazoned on its saddle pad. She barely had time to wonder what had happened to its former master.

Before she had quite gained her balance, the stranger was swinging up into the saddle behind her.

My God, he is kidnapping me. She couldn't believe it. Domenic had been right all along.

The stranger was one of the rebels.

When she realized this, it took away some of her immediate terror, because she knew he could not harm her, or else Papa would never meet his faction's demands. Therefore, she was safe, more or less. She forced herself to be rational.

Normally she would never have approved of such extreme measures, but maybe a rash act like this was the only way to make Papa and the Council listen to the people. Maybe her abduction would ultimately bring about the higher good of Ascencion.

With that thought, she decided to cooperate, not that he was giving her much choice.

Yet her heart sank, because she knew for certain the bold rebel would hang. Even if she came back home unscathed, Papa would have him hunted and killed for his part in this. And if her father didn't, Domenic surely would.

"Hold on to me," he ordered as they heard the first shouts of the guards.

She obeyed, slipping her hands around his hard, lean waist under the black vest, his warm golden skin like velvet-sheathed marble under her hands, slick with a fine sheen of sweat. He shifted her against him, pulling her onto his lap with one hard arm around her stomach, then he wheeled the horse onto the road leading away from the city. He gathered the reins in his other hand and clucked to the horse, giving its sides a light kick.

The next thing she knew, they were racing off at a gallop.

⊰ CHAPTER ⊱
THREE

Monteverdi's daughter sat sidesaddle in his lap. How he had been cast in the role of her rescuer, Lazar had no idea. He only knew he had been cut because she had distracted him, and he was not amused.

Nor was he amused that her pleas had caused him to spare Clemente, nor presently was he amused at the way her slim body rocked lightly, rhythmically against his. Nor by the flowery scent of her hair beneath his nostrils, nor by her silken hands almost caressing him as she changed her snug hold around his waist.

He got the distinct impression Miss Monteverdi might be enjoying her own abduction. He scowled over her head. It would not do. She was supposed to be afraid of him.

There were twenty or thirty mounted soldiers in hot pursuit of them about half a mile behind, but Lazar was glad. For one thing, the more soldiers who followed in the wild-goose chase on which he was about to lead them, the fewer would be left behind to man the gate towers.

For another, the chase kept his mind off other things, such as the way his prize victim shifted her soft derriere in his lap, or the tear in her dress that gave him an unfettered view of her virginal cleavage.

When he saw the ancient oak that bowed out over the road, he pulled the black horse to a halt, cocking his head.

"Why are you stopping? They're right behind us!" Miss Monteverdi cried.

"Shh!" He listened.

No. Farther. He whipped the horse into action again, went only about fifty strides, then stopped again, listening.

"Damn it, it's around here somewhere." He drove the animal back to the tree.

There, yes.

"Give me one of your hairpins. Now," he ordered her as he leaped off the horse and reached up for Allegra.

He tied the reins over the horse's neck while she swiftly pulled out an emerald-studded pin, long hair tumbling over her shoulders in the moonlight. In the distance, through the trees, he could see the soldiers on the road, swiftly approaching. He took the pin and wove it through the horse's saddle pad so the end of it pricked the animal's hide. The horse protested violently. Lazar slapped the big animal on the rump, and it bolted angrily down the road.

He grabbed Allegra by the hand and ran with her into the thicket on the side of the road, ducking branches, tearing through briers. He leaped over a large fallen log and helped Allegra over it, then pulled her down with him onto the leaf-packed ground behind the log, for her white dress would give them away easily if the soldiers looked into the woods.

They lay side by side, she flushed and he panting, like lovers after an afternoon of vigorous sex. She watched him, wide-eyed. He lifted a finger to her lips in a hushing gesture, but oddly he didn't sense any intention on her part to scream for help.

He stared warningly into her eyes as two squadrons thundered past on the road, chasing the riderless black horse. Their horses' hooves drowned out the distant rushing murmur of the waterfall. Still holding his hostage by her delicate wrist, Lazar scanned the road in the direction of the city, for he guessed reinforcements could not be far behind.

"Come on."

They got to their feet. Her soft, slender fingers linked through his rough, callused ones, he led her through the dark, fragrant woods, following the sound of the waterfall. He was satisfied they were out of danger once they crested a small ridge, for now the road was no longer visible. With their every step, the sound of the waterfall grew louder.

When he heard her little cry of pain behind him, he turned to find one of her long tresses snarled on a thorn. He drew his knife and moved to cut her free, but she gasped.

"Don't you dare!"

He looked down at her in surprise. She glared up at him in rebellion.

"Kidnap me if you must, but you will *not* chop off my hair!"

He stared down at her, barely comprehending how she could fret about something so trivial at such a time. But when he considered what he was going to do to her at dawn, he was overcome with guilt and thought, *This is the least I can do for her.*

Gently, he unwound her hair from the thorn. She stood there, patiently waiting. Then he became aware that she was staring at him again, her face tilted up to his, bathed in moonlight. He tugged the last knot free and turned away.

"Thank you," she said, blushing a bit. "Now. What is your name?"

"Come on, no questions," he grumbled, annoyed by her managing tone. This time he held her hand a little more loosely, all too aware of how soft her skin was, until at last they arrived in the clearing, where the waterfall spilled into a large pond.

He turned to find her watching the moonlight sparkle on the water.

"You could act a little scared, you know," he muttered.

"I'm scared," she assured him.

He stared at her, itching to taste that pretty mouth where an impudent smile tugged.

I cannot possibly take this creature's life, he thought. Then he remembered Father, how they had fallen on him like dogs on a wounded bull, stabbing him again and again right before his eyes, cut Pip's throat as if he were a yearling calf, his little brother only eight years old.

Abruptly Lazar turned away, kicking off his boots.

"Going for a swim?" she asked.

In reply, he stepped into the pond, yanking her in behind him, his boots in one hand, her wrist in the other. She gave a little shriek of protest, but the water was not deep—only up to his thighs, her waist.

"Where are we going?"

He ignored her.

They waded across the pond to the waterfall, where he set his boots upon the rock. Allegra stared in fascination as she came in close enough with him to see the cave entrance the rushing water concealed. He climbed out of the water onto the rocks and turned, on one knee, offering her his hand. She took it, and as he pulled her up, drenched and dripping, from the water, lust hit him low in the gut full force.

Oh, for God's sake, Fiore, why didn't you carry her?

Wet white silk clung to every curve of her very female form, he discovered, and the full moon's brightness only made the effect more magical. Once she'd gained her feet, he immediately checked his rusty fob.

How much time did they have? It was a quarter past one. Not enough time.

Growling at himself, he put the thing away. Even if he had a week, he was not going to make love to this woman. He was not even going to think about it. Perhaps he was a disgrace to his family, but he wasn't that far gone.

Besides, what kind of twisted fiend could think of seducing a woman he intended to kill in a few hours' time? But was it right that such a lovely creature should die a virgin?

You evil bastard, he said to himself.

He glanced at the yawning black mouth of this branch of the tunnels.

"Come on," he grunted, refusing to see her beauty or to gaze at the moonlight shining through the outline of her dress, where he could see every long, elegant line of her legs, all the way up to the apex of Aphrodite's mysteries.

"Why are you taking me in there?" she asked, finally showing she had sense enough to be at least a little afraid.

"To feed you to the bears," he muttered. "Hurry. I haven't got all night."

"Is your faction waiting in there?"

"My what?" He turned around.

She stepped closer to him, gazing up earnestly at him. "You're not going to leave me with them, are you? People are angry at my father, and I—I should feel so much safer if you were there."

"Safer?" Bewitched, he stared down at her.

She glanced up shyly at him, a brave smile on her lips as she brushed a billowing lock of hair behind her ear. "I know you wouldn't let them hurt me. You already saved me once tonight."

Lazar stared down at her as understanding slammed through him. She trusted him.

Agonized, he realized the conclusions Miss Monteverdi had drawn about his motives, and it came to him why she was cooperating so nicely.

Oh, his spies had told him all about the little patriot's democratic leanings, picked up from the new philosophers in the salons and cafés of Paris. Allegra Monteverdi was a regular champion of the people. He knew all about her charity projects and her efforts to save the world—as if to atone for her father's sins.

Don't give her false hope. She deserves to know the truth, he thought, but he found he could not bring himself to tell her.

What good would it do to let her spend the final hours of her life in a state of panic and hysteria? he reasoned. He didn't want her to suffer any more than necessary. It was her father he wanted to suffer, not her. No, let her grasp the seriousness of her situation by degrees, he thought. It might be easier on her that way.

God knew it would be easier on him.

She was gazing up at him with wide eyes full of hope and trust mixed with fear.

How could that heartless fiancé of hers look upon such innocence, he thought, and think of rape? Aye, do more than think of it. At that moment, he decided to send men out after Clemente—he would hunt the viscount down and kill him for what he'd done to her.

Maybe that would help ease his own conscience a little.

For a moment, Lazar reached out and cupped her lovely face in one hand with a sense of ineffable sadness. By the happenstance of lineage, destiny made them enemies. If to this day he were some decadent, idle Crown Prince—for he had no doubt Father would still be alive, just turning sixty— and if Allegra had followed as lady-in-waiting to his little sister, Princess Anna, just as her mother, Lady Cristiana, had once attended his mother, Queen Eugenia, who knew? Perhaps he'd have made a conquest of her and been the one to instruct her in the arts of love.

"Come, *chérie*. We've little time," he said, his voice a trifle hoarse. He took her hand and led her into darkness.

The rebel was an enigma, Allegra thought as he guided her slowly into a cave that was even darker than his midnight eyes. After having seen him beat Domenic so brutally, she never would have thought his large, warm hands could be so gentle, untangling her hair from the thornbush and presently steadying her as they went.

"There should be a torch and flint here somewhere," he murmured, leaving her to search for them. She couldn't see anything, but she could hear his movements, feel his warmth.

"Who are you?" she asked, her voice echoing strangely in the dark.

"There's no need for you to know."

"What am I to call you?"

"Whatever you please. It doesn't matter."

"It does to me."

"Why?"

She shrugged. "Civility."

"Sorry. I'm not much for that," he muttered.

Their voices echoed into the cavernous gloom, making her realize the cave was much larger than she'd thought.

"What are your demands?"

His growl told her she wasn't allowed to know that either.

"What is this place?"

She heard a frustrated sound of male exasperation. "No more questions! Do you want me to put a gag on you?"

"No."

She heard the snick of flint on steel and saw a few sparks against the blackness. One of them caught, and as a few moments passed, the tiny flame grew, consuming the torch. Slowly it illumined his sun-bronzed face, his burning dark eyes and flared brows, the narrow planes of his cheeks. She wondered if she should be afraid of him instead of fascinated, but no man with so jolly a laugh could be cruel at heart, and his hands were so gentle.

She wondered if he would put them on her as Domenic had.

"You won't tell me your name, then?"

"I will if it will put an end to your questions." He smiled like a devil over the spreading flame. "My name is . . . Humberto."

"Humberto! No," she laughed. "Humbertos trip over their own feet."

He slid her a mischievous look. "Paolo," he suggested.

She shook her head. "Never. Too bland."

He blew lightly on the torch, watching her. "How about Antonio?"

"Possibly." She stared at the pout of his lips as he blew on the torch again, sending it into searing flame. "You swagger like an Antonio. But if you were a true Antonio, you would never have told Domenic I was insatiable. No Antonio would ever admit that he had left any woman unsatisfied, even if it was a lie."

"I didn't say you were unsatisfied, only that you wanted more." His eyes danced.

"Your name is not Antonio," she insisted.

"Come along, *chérie*. We have a rough two miles before us."

"Two miles?" she echoed, gazing into the darkness ahead.

When he lifted the torch, she realized they were walking into the very bowels of the earth. She stared into the blackness ahead, incredulous, for she knew instantly what it was.

"The Fiori tunnels," she whispered in awe. "Antonio— Humberto—how did you ever find them?"

She took the torch right out of his hand and walked ahead of him, staring about her in disbelief.

"You seem amazed, Miss Monteverdi," came his deep voice from behind her.

"I thought these passageways were just a legend!" She turned back to him, suddenly grave. "Oh, we should *not* be in here."

"Why not?" There was something strange in his eyes, a hard, glittering darkness within the midnight.

"These tunnels belong to the Fiori," she said in a reverent, emphatic whisper.

He shrugged. "They're dead."

"Show some respect!" she said, quickly blessing herself.

One charcoal brow shot up. "It's just that I don't think they'll be using them anytime soon."

Bracing one fist on her hip, she turned to him and gave him

a severe look. "*Tell* me you haven't shown your whole faction these tunnels."

"Er, no," he replied dryly.

"It's a good thing. They should stay a secret." She walked to one of the tunnel's walls and ran her hand down the sharp, black granite, knowing it was the closest she would ever come to touching *him*. "Poor Lazar," she sighed.

"What did you say?"

She glanced at him, and something in the determined set of his shoulders, the proud angle of his chin, made her stare, and for a moment she almost thought—

But no, that was impossible. It was just her overheated imagination again. No one could survive a jump two hundred feet into rocky, shark-infested waters, especially not a boy of thirteen. Just because they had never found his body did not mean the legend of the lost prince was anything more than that—a legend.

Like these tunnels? she wondered.

The rebel walked over to her and lifted the torch roughly out of her hand. "Let's get on with it, Miss Monteverdi," he muttered.

He said her name as though he hated it.

Lazar marched along, sulking over the fact that it never even occurred to Allegra who he might be. He did not want her to know yet who he was—he was saving that revelation for her father, but when she failed even to wonder at the possibility, he found himself annoyed.

How the hell did she *think* he knew about the tunnels? Was it so very hard to believe that he might be the son of King Alphonse? At the same time, his own indignation, or perhaps wounded vanity, left him cynically amused.

Halfway through their march, he heard another little cry of pain behind him and turned back to discover that Miss Monteverdi had contrived to twist her ankle.

Suspiciously he went to where she had plopped herself down on the wet, rocky tunnel floor and was holding her ankle in both hands, rubbing it, tears in her eyes. He was certain she was feigning until he glanced down at the satin dancing slippers on her feet, already reduced to ribbons by the trek. Her white silk stockings also were torn and snagged and stained. Slowly he lowered himself to one knee before her.

"What happened?"

"I tripped," she cried, as if it were his fault.

He handed her the torch.

"Let me see." He brushed her fingers away and examined her ankle himself, disregarding her little, fussing noises of protest, running both hands down the graceful curve of her limb. When he pressed gently with his thumb on a spot in front of her ankle bone, she sucked in her breath in pain. She looked up at him, still biting down on her plump lower lip.

He moved back and looked down at her thoughtfully. She had been quiet since they had gotten under way, but now he could see that her endurance was beginning to wear thin.

It had been a rough night for her, he supposed. Near-rape, abduction, being chased by soldiers, dragged into a pond. Now she'd turned an ankle, and there was worse to come. Far worse.

He uncorked his flask and offered her some rum.

She looked at it and him in disdain, then reconsidered and took it. She raised it to her lips and took a wary sip. He chuckled when she burst out coughing and spluttering.

"Terrible!" she choked out, her honey-brown eyes watering. She covered her mouth with her hand and shot him a look of reproach.

"It will dull the pain." He stood, offering her his hand. "Come on, my little captive. Up you go."

He carried her piggyback the rest of the way. She held the torch, lighting his path. At first he was annoyed by the way she directed and chided him incessantly, warning him to look out for small pits in the floor of the tunnel or reminding him to avoid the clusters of rock here and there in his path or to bend down where the granite teeth jutted low above them. Eventually he got used to it.

What he couldn't get used to was the feel of her arms around his neck, her legs around his waist, her slender thighs secured firmly in both his hands. There was something barbaric in carrying a woman off this way that pleased him inordinately. Her dress was still wet, and the damp material clung to her limbs and to him, conducting her body's heat to his skin with mesmerizing intensity.

Every time her breath tickled his ear, it seemed to him less and less likely that Miss Monteverdi would emerge from the other side of the tunnel still a virgin.

And yet he had to kill her.

With every step, he brooded upon this fact and was beginning to feel strangely split off from himself. Since the earliest planning stages of his vendetta, Allegra Monteverdi had been just a name on paper to him, an object to be used to achieve a desired result, not a thinking, feeling, wondering creature with sweet, silvery laughter and freckles on her nose.

She hummed softly at his ear as he took the turn to the exit he had used before. She interrupted his silent war with himself, making conversation to pass the time.

"Thank you for saving me from Domenic," she said, "even if it was only because you wanted to kidnap me."

"Do you love him?" he heard himself ask.

"No." She sighed as she laid her head down on his shoulder. "Is there a lady you love?"

"Aye."

"What does she look like?"

"She has three decks, three masts, and the finest-built stern a man could desire."

"A ship?" she exclaimed. "Oh, you are a seafarer. Of course! I see now." She gave him a little squeeze around the neck, and he smiled in spite of himself. "You are a native Ascencioner, but you've traveled. I can tell by your accent."

"Very good, Miss Monteverdi."

"If I'm not mistaken, you are highborn, too."

"My father was a gentleman," he conceded, the understatement of the century.

Due to the fact that he'd been martyred, King Alphonse was being considered by the Vatican for sainthood.

For some reason Lazar hoped he didn't get it, but he would probably never know. The cardinals wouldn't rule on it for another thirty-five years, and Lazar had no intention of living that long.

"Am I too heavy for you?"

"Certainly not."

"Does your arm hurt very much? It looks as though it has stopped bleeding."

"It's fine."

"Where are you taking me?"

"You'll see."

She was quiet for a minute. He could almost hear the little cogs and wheels whirring in her brain.

"Can I ask you a question? Something Domenic said when he was being so awful still preys on my mind. You're a man—you might be able to make sense of it."

He shook his head to himself in exasperation as she proceeded before he could tell her to shut up.

"You see, Humberto, the main reason I wanted to marry Domenic is because he is going to be Ascencion's next Governor."

Don't bet on it, he thought. "They say power is an aphrodisiac."

She gasped. "What a shocking thing to say! But that has nothing to do with it."

"Of course not."

"I mean it," she said seriously. "I thought as his wife I could have some impact on the affairs of Ascencion, try to temper the injustices, ease the people's suffering."

"Admirable."

"You know what they say," she whispered, a teasing note in her voice as she set her chin on his shoulder. "Behind every great man is a great woman."

He paused to shrug her higher up onto his back. "Sorry, but I doubt your fiancé will ever be a great man."

"Ex-fiancé. I certainly will not marry that cretin now! I don't know what I'll do," she mused. "Maybe join the convent."

He cringed to hear her talk about her future when he knew she didn't have one.

"Anyway, Domenic claimed he was justified in what he wanted to do to me because he said I was using him. I never wanted to use him!" she exclaimed. "I never thought about it that way. Was I unkind? Was I wicked for wanting to marry him to serve the common good? I mean, I think Domenic wanted to marry me only because of my father's position. You see? I am confused. What do you think of it all, Humberto?"

"What do you think of it, Miss Monteverdi?" he replied quietly. "Your opinion is the one that matters."

She was silent for a long moment. "I don't know, but I feel guilty now."

"That's what he wanted you to feel, *cherie*."

She laid her head on his shoulder once more, almost snuggling against him. "Humberto? No one has ever defended my honor before."

He said nothing.

Maria . . .

The first thought that wandered into his cloudy brain was that he wanted Maria, his mistress, loyal and obedient as a spaniel. Maria knew how to take care of him better than his own mama. He tried to open his eyes, but only the right

worked. The left was swollen shut. His head was full of cob-
webs and stars and fire.

Flowers towered over him in the dark. Marigolds loomed.
The trumpet heads of daylilies peered down silently at him like
the faces of worried women. For a moment he was uncertain
where the devil he was or how he had come to be there.

Then he remembered.

Domenic Clemente dragged himself up, panting through his
mouth, for his nose was not operating properly either. Still
rather stunned by those half-dozen sledgehammer blows to the
head, he stood looking around him for his wits, weaving on his
feet slightly just as three guards came running into the garden.

"My lord!"

"You are hurt!"

"Brilliant deduction," he growled, shaking off the steadying
arm of the nearest man with his left hand while he kept his agonized right wrist close to his chest. "Miss Monteverdi?"

"He took her off on that horse he stole. We've got two
squadrons after them right now."

"We'll bring her back in no time, sir. Don't you worry! We'll
have 'em by morning!"

"Bring me that man," he ordered them in a low voice. "He is
mine."

"Yes, sir!"

One of the men found Clemente's dagger nearby and gave it
back to him. Domenic put it away.

"You," he ordered one man, "fetch the governor to meet
with me at once in his office. And you," he said to the other,
"get me the best surgeon in Little Genoa. And you," he said,
nodding to the third, "see that my carriage is ready within half
an hour."

He needed Maria. As soon as he told his story to the dimwit
governor and got medical attention, he was going to the little
country house where he kept her. Maria would lick his wounds
and soothe his bruised pride for him.

As for Allegra Monteverdi, prim little bitch, she was just going to have to rely on her father to rescue her. He'd done his share.

That black-eyed devil kicked your arse, you sniveling, pathetic weakling.

Snarling at the thought, he tried to put himself back into some order, dusting the soil off his rumpled clothing, raking his left hand through his hair as he made his way into the palace. As he limped down the hall toward Monteverdi's offices, avoiding the guests, giving the gawking servants cruel looks to make them mind their own business, he brooded on the perilous question of whom the governor would believe if Allegra told her father that he'd tried to have a little fun tonight with his frigid daughter.

Not that there was any harm in what he'd done. He'd only been acting in Allegra's best interest, after all, so their wedding night wouldn't come as so much of a shock to her. Monteverdi must be made to understand that he, Domenic, had merely been trying to protect the girl from that insolent lout.

Who was that man? If he was one of the rebels, which he had to be, why didn't he have the coarse, peasant accent? Why had he called himself Allegra's good friend? The ruffian had teased her as if the two were old friends.

Perhaps he'd had his brains rattled loose by those blows, Domenic thought, perhaps he'd had too much to drink, but something just didn't fit.

If Allegra had obeyed him and called for the bloody guards as he'd commanded, none of this would have happened. Hell, it was her own damned fault she'd been abducted. He had done his best to protect her, but she had been so uncooperative, why, it was almost as if she'd wanted to be abducted.

An astonishing realization hit him full force.

She knew that man. Of course she did. Just as the rogue had idly said—*a friend, a very good friend.*

Allegra was one of the rebels.

Domenic stood motionless in the hallway, staring at nothing as he tried to absorb it. Of course.

She was a traitor.

All her little displays of rebellion—her wearing of the old Fiori colors, her disrespect for her father and for him, her childish arguments with the guests over matters she knew nothing about—he'd never taken any of it seriously.

She had set him up. This abduction was a hoax. She wasn't in the slightest danger—she was merely playing along with the rebels to bend her father and the Council to her will. And she had been using him, toying with him all along.

Even more furious than before, Domenic stalked to Monteverdi's dark-paneled office, went straight to the liquor cabinet, and fumbled with his left hand as he attempted to pour himself a whiskey.

"Damn it." He went back to the doorway and bellowed down the hall for a servant to do it, and to light a few of the candles as well.

When the room was brightened and the servant handed him a tumbler of whiskey, he glanced in the mirror over the mantel and stared at himself with his one working eye, barely recognizing his own handsome face, now a mangled, prune-colored mess.

No wonder everyone had been gawking at him.

Instantly, he promised himself revenge on that rebel dog—no swift, simple hanging but a slow, lingering torture. And as for Allegra, who had dared try to make a fool of him, she would be sorry. Very, very sorry. He would have vengeance on her, too, but somehow he would have to get around her father.

He knew Monteverdi would never bring Allegra up on charges, the same way he had never brought his wife up on charges when she had found out the truth about the Fiori murders. Oh, coming up under the close tutelage of certain Councilmen, Domenic had eventually been made privy to the whole secret story of what happened to Lady Cristiana

Monteverdi. Allegra's mother had been eliminated before she had been able to take her story to Rome, as she had been secretly planning, but since her death had been made to look like a suicide, her husband was never the wiser. The governor had been too besotted with her to keep her in check.

Likewise, he thought, Monteverdi would use all his power to protect his little girl, even if she was a rebel turncoat.

Perhaps she *should* be spared, Domenic thought, an evil twist coming over his half-swollen mouth. When he looked down at his wrist, puffed up to twice its normal circumference, he decided there and then, if his right hand had to be amputated because of this break, he was going to uphold their betrothal. Then, as her husband, he could take his vengeance on her every night for the rest of her life.

The rebel never took her to his faction. Instead, he took her back to Little Genoa.

The city was dark and deserted now except for pockets of guards who roamed the streets or gathered in the empty square. There was a mood of tension in their sharp calls, the piercing toots of the sergeant's whistle, the sound of marching boots and pawing horses.

Everyone's looking for him and me, she marveled as her captor led her along the shadows of the old Roman wall toward the gate towers—into the very lions' den, it seemed.

On the one hand, she felt guilty for cooperating with her captor so willingly, as if she had turned against her father and joined the rebel side herself. But what choice did she have? She could not fight a man a foot taller than she and twice her weight, in pure, solid muscle.

Her stomach felt strange, kind of quivery and sick, when she thought about what they'd do to Humberto when they caught him, especially when they saw her ripped dress—ripped by Domenic—but they would think he had done it. The soldiers would take retribution on his whole village and no doubt do to the peasant girls there what they would assume he had done to her. Then the men of the village would blow up a garrison or set up an ambush of the soldiers and do horrible things to the men they caught. Retribution upon retribution upon retribution, vendetta piled on vendetta, back and forth ceaselessly, she thought wearily.

Considering the fact that Ascencion was a Catholic country whose Savior had told men to turn the other cheek, Allegra could never fathom why the medieval custom of vendetta infected all Italy like a disease, a fever of madness. The islands were plagued with it worst of all, Sicily, Corsica, and Ascencion. Though King Alphonse was all but worshipped here, no one seemed to remember or care that he had made a law against the practice twenty years earlier.

Glancing toward the palazzo, she saw that all the windows were still bright. She wondered what Papa was going to have to say about all this. She only knew he would not let the news of her kidnapping leak out among the guests.

Domenic had probably been discovered by now and carried in to see the doctor, she thought. Probably had told Papa a lot of lies about how it all happened, making himself appear blameless, then staggered back to the mistress.

Near the gate towers, the rebel turned to gaze down at her in silence for a long moment, with a strange, feverish look of pain in his dark, soulful eyes. He stared at her so long, she thought he was going to lower his beautiful mouth and kiss her. Instead he drew her into his arms, turning her gently so her back was pressed close against his front. Then he slid his left arm around her belly. Still she did not protest.

"Allegra," he murmured, and she trembled at the deep, hungry heat of his voice. She closed her eyes as his fingers lightly brushed her neck, smoothing all her hair forward over one shoulder. The accidental caress made her fleetingly so weak she had to lean back slightly against him just to keep her balance.

When she did, he paused. She could feel his restraint in every powerful muscle that surrounded her.

"Does your ankle still hurt?"

"Just a little," she whispered breathlessly.

He was very still, and then he caressed her deliberately. All her awareness seemed focused where he put his fingertips on the side of her neck just beneath her ear, running them lightly, slowly down the curve of her neck to her shoulder.

Her skin felt acutely sensitive and soft wherever he touched her, as if it were newly made silk being unfurled for a master weaver's touch. She shivered uncontrollably and felt his pulse quicken in answer against her body. His mighty heart raced, and she ached to know his real name.

His fingers rounded her shoulder, coming down the back of her arm to her wrist. When he slipped his fingers into her hand for a moment, she clasped them lightly.

"Allegra," he breathed, "I am so sorry for what I must do."

"It's all right," she murmured, eyes closed, her head against the taut, supple cushion of his breast while she drifted in the spell he'd cast on her. He removed his callused fingers from her gentle grasp, trailing his hand up her arm.

She was still savoring the feel of him against her when she heard a small, metallic click.

She opened her eyes just as the stranger lifted the silver muzzle of a pistol and set it against her temple, gentle as a kiss.

She froze in his arms. "What are you doing? Oh, dear God."

"Easy, *chérie*," he said as he walked her out into the open toward the tower door. "Just be still, do as I say, and nothing unpleasant will happen."

Men saw them and ran toward them, but Lazar ordered them to stay back. They obeyed.

"Now, knock on the door," he murmured to her. "When they answer, announce yourself."

She didn't move.

"Allegra."

"I can't," she squeaked. "I'm too scared."

"You can do it, *chérie,*" he said, staring down the nervous soldiers.

"Stop calling me that! How can you call me that when you've got a gun to my head?"

She began to cry. He told himself that was good; it would add to the effect. But it made him feel desolate.

"I hate you for this!"

"Come on, honey. You can do it," he said softly. "I'm not going to hurt you. We have to get these soldiers out of the way, that's all."

"D-do you promise?"

"I swear," he whispered.

"A-all right." Her whole little body shaking against him, she stepped forward and pounded on the massive, iron-bolted wooden door that sealed the tower. She seemed tiny in front of it, a detail that clenched his heart somehow. He pulled her immediately back into his half embrace before she had time to contemplate escaping, but she merely winced at placing her full weight on her ankle. Instantly they heard men's voices on the other side. She announced herself in a quavering voice.

"How could you do this to me?" she whispered. "I never did anything to you. I would never hurt anyone."

He believed it. His heart twisted like a horse with a bullet in its gut.

When she closed her eyes again, apparently straining for calm, he examined her extraordinary gold-tipped lashes. "If it's any consolation, I would sell my soul to make love to you," he murmured.

"I wouldn't have you! Not in a thousand, million years!"

"I think you would," he said.

"Oh, God, I hate you so."

"Good evening, gentlemen," he addressed the soldiers in a taut, amiable voice. "Miss Monteverdi and I would like all of you to step outside. Come out quietly, with your hands in the air."

In minutes, he had emptied the small garrison, bolted himself and Allegra inside the tower alone, and further secured the door by wedging the coarse table against it, scattering the colorful playing cards the soldiers had abandoned mere moments ago.

"You are mad!" the girl screeched at him, throwing up her hands. "Do you realize you are going to hang? The minute you walk out the door, you're a dead man!"

He tossed her a grin. "How sweet of you to care." He holstered his pistol, then grabbed her hand, pulling her up the circling flight of stone steps, two at a time.

The air in the tower was close and old, the walls damp. They reached the garret slightly winded. He looked around at the little room perched high atop the tower, overlooking the sea. It was bare but for a crude wooden table with benches pushed back carelessly and a few lanterns, still lit, that hung from iron hooks.

He blew out all of the lanterns but one, preferring to work mostly by moonlight so as to deny the soldiers an easy target if they started shooting.

In the center of the room was the big crank for the east gate. The wheel was the culmination of an elaborate system of chains and pulleys that operated the gate. He released Allegra's hand, stalked to the center of the room, and put his shoulder to the crankshaft. It would take two or three men to turn it with any dexterity, but he was just going to have to do it himself.

Allegra stared at him, white-faced and strangely still. At the first great groaning of the gate, she jumped.

"Who are you?" she demanded as he threw his weight against the shaft—and promptly burst open the cut on his arm.

He muttered a foul oath and stepped back to find blood spilling from the cut afresh.

"Rip off a strip from your dress," he ordered her. "I have to wrap this damned cut, or I'll never get the gate open."

"Why are you opening the gate?"

"Just do it," he said with acerbic sweetness. He took out his flask of rum and poured a generous draft onto the wound, cursing under his breath at the sting.

Allegra suddenly turned and bolted out of the garret.

"Get back here!" he bellowed. "Damn you, woman," he panted. His arm streaming with blood mixed with rum, he dashed after her.

In a few moments, he had her slung over his right shoulder and was carrying her, kicking and punching, back up the stairs. He threw her down onto the table, snapped the kid strap off his flask, and hobbled her with it, binding her ankles with a sailor's knot she would never figure out. She was cursing him in a convent-school girl's version of black oaths all the while.

"Brute! Liar! Murderer! Get away from me! You are bleeding on me," she growled, staring up at him mutinously.

"Give me this," he muttered, tugging at the satin sash around her waist. "Should do the trick."

"No!" she gasped, grabbing it with both hands.

He stared down at her. "No?"

She clutched the sash. "No. You will not blot your disgusting blood on *this*, Mister No-Name!"

He narrowed his eyes at her.

"Look, Miss Monteverdi. My arm is bleeding because of your precious fiancé, from whose, you may recall, I rescued you."

"Remind me to thank you for that the next time you put a loaded gun to my head!" she shouted, gesturing at her temple.

"Oh, you are a vexing chit. I was not going to shoot you. Besides, my gunpowder got wet coming here—it probably wouldn't even have fired. Now, give me this—it's just a piece of cloth."

"No, it's not!" she roared.

He snapped it out of her hand and walked over to the lantern, unraveling it. Just as he was about to clean his wound with it, he realized what it was.

He stopped, staring at it. He held the length of satin up to the light.

How had he failed to see it until now?

Chills ran down his spine.

The green and black. The colors of the Fiori.

Heart pounding, Lazar looked over at her. "What the hell is this?"

She lifted both eyebrows and gave him a nonchalant shrug.

"I asked you a question."

"Why should I tell you anything when you won't even tell me your name?"

He raised the ribbon in his fist. "Why are you, a Monteverdi, wearing the colors of the Fiori?"

"None of your business."

"Actually, it is." He turned fully toward her, hands on his hips, ignoring his bleeding arm. "Tonight you were hostess at a ball for Ottavio Monteverdi, with half the Genovese Council present." He lifted the satin. "And you wore this."

She thrust up her pert chin. "So what if I did?"

He stared at the brazen, unrepentant creature with a kind of awe. Then he stared down again at the satin in his hand, barely hearing the rest of her barrage.

". . . But you know what? I don't even want to know your name anymore. I don't want to know a single fact about you. You are the most uncouth, uncivilized, un—"

Suddenly Lazar was overjoyed.

He crossed the garret to her in three steps, took her face between his hands, and stopped her insults with a jubilant kiss. Instantly her sweetness fired his senses, and he slipped his arms around her, gathering her closer with a low groan of heady pleasure.

Allegra Monteverdi could not have imagined at that moment how happy she had just made him. He could not *possibly* kill her now. She had given him an unassailable excuse to spare her.

All sailors were superstitious, and as far as he was concerned, that green-and-black sash was as good as a sign from the afterworld. No, he would torment Monteverdi some other way. Allegra would live.

He would take her under his protection and, praise God, straight to his bed.

Oh, he was going to turn her into a goddess of sensuality, he thought, tasting her soft lips like cherry wine. He would spend the passage back to the West Indies instructing and enjoying her.

Beyond that, well, he'd figure something out. He only knew he'd be personally responsible for her, because by morning her father, her relatives, and her vicious betrothed would be dead.

He shivered with desire when she slipped her arms around his neck and began tentatively kissing him back.

Oh, yes, she belonged by his side. They were bound together by her father's crime. By morning they would be the sole survivors of their respective clans.

For this reason, he decided there and then to tell her his true identity, something he never confided to his women. This situation was entirely different. And perhaps he wanted, finally, to tell someone.

His heart pounded as he kissed her lips apart, wetting them with a slow glide of his tongue that made her moan softly. It would have been so easy to linger here, exploring her, but he held himself back in anticipation of those long nights at sea. Placing one final chaste kiss on her lips, he released her gently and pulled back, smiling at her dazed expression.

He smoothed her hair back behind her ear as he watched her

sit there with her eyes closed. Then he drew her softly against him and laid his cheek against her hair.

"Allegra, I have something to tell you."

He took a breath and held it, pressing his eyes shut tight for a moment, praying she would believe him, telling himself he was mad to trust her this way.

"I am Lazar," he said. "I survived."

She did not move.

Warily, he inched back and looked down at her face. Her gold-tipped lashes flicked as she opened her eyes and stared up at him.

"Lazar?" she repeated, searching his eyes. "Prince Lazar di Fiore?"

He nodded.

She stared.

Then she laughed in his face.

≈ CHAPTER ≈
FOUR

It was not exactly the reaction he'd been hoping for.

His hopes fell and splintered into a thousand pieces. He should have known.

"Never mind," he growled as he moved away from her. Wrapping his lacerated arm tight in the length of satin that bore his family's colors, he returned to fight with the crankshaft.

"The lost prince, eh?" she said gaily behind him, a bitter note in her laughter. "Humberto, your lies just keep getting better."

"I don't lie."

"You are not Lazar di Fiore," she said after a moment. "Look at you."

"Why don't you just use a dagger, Miss Monteverdi?" he muttered, sweat streaming down his face from his exertion.

Behind him, she hopped off the table and walked by tiny steps, her ankles hobbled, toward the window. He eyed her darkly as he worked. If she was going to call for rescue, she was out of luck. In moments, the raid on Little Genoa would begin.

At that thought, he decided to keep her locked in the tower until he was through with her father and ready to set sail. She'd be safe in here, and the less she knew about the morning's events, the better.

"What are you doing?" he asked.

"I'm getting out of here, away from you—Your Majesty!"

she said furiously. "You are not Lazar di Fiore, you are *not*!"
She lost her balance and tripped but caught herself against
the stone windowsill. She stopped abruptly, staring down
at the road where, he presumed, his men were now visible.

She whirled around, wide-eyed. "What's going on?" she
demanded in a whisper. "Who are you?"

"I told you," he said wearily. Halfway done, he locked the
crankshaft into place to give his arm a break and joined her,
pointing to the bay and the road. "The day of judgment has
arrived, Miss Monteverdi. You see?"

The first ranks of his men were but a quarter mile away. He
could just make them out. He felt a surge of pride at their
silence as they approached, in spite of all their numbers. Carried not a single torch among them. Good lads.

There were two hundred in the first wave, handpicked for
their skill in close combat. These were the veterans who could
be trusted to stick to his instructions even in the heat of battle.

There would be no repeat of the Antigua horror this time, he
assured himself. The men would not go berserk. Not on Ascencion, by God. He trusted he'd made it sufficiently clear to even
the most dim-witted of his men that whosoever committed any
infraction of the rules would be shot.

Order was everything.

Antigua had taught him that.

After the first force swelled into Little Genoa, the rest of
his men would follow shortly in three successive waves of
two hundred each, with two hundred kept behind in skeleton
crews to man the guns and mind the lookout. Genoa was only
fifty miles across the bay and had a powerful fleet with well-
trained men. He calculated it would take the ships six hours
to cross the bay in response to the first boom of cannon fire
over Ascencion—but he and his horde would be long gone by
the time the navy arrived to find the Governor's administra-
tive compound up in smoke.

"Oh, my God, it's an uprising," she whispered in dread, then looked at him. "You're leading the peasants to overthrow my father. You've brought them here to murder us in our beds, and you're using the legend of the lost prince to make them follow you!"

"Wrong." He scooped her up off her feet and carried her back to the table, setting her on it. She seemed too stunned to object. "What's this legend everyone keeps yammering about?" he asked as he went back to the crankshaft. He figured if he could keep her talking, she might stay out of mischief.

Her face was white, her dark eyes glazed with shock. "You know perfectly well," she said in a toneless voice. "The wish of these poor, brokenhearted people, that Prince Lazar didn't die. That somehow he survived when the highwaymen cornered him at the cliffside and made him leap into the sea. That he has grown up in hiding somewhere and one day will return to take Ascencion back from the Genovese and restore the reign of the great Fiori."

For a long moment, Lazar stared at her, incredulous.

"That is pathetic," he spat.

Angrily he hauled upon the crankshaft, and, inch by inch, the huge eastern gate swung open.

"That poor boy's murder was a tragedy," she declared, impassioned. "If you were a true patriot, you and your petty factions would never exploit his death and our people's hope just to seize power for yourself!"

"I have no interest in power," he muttered.

His arms were shaking with exertion by the time he locked the great wooden handle into place, his left arm burning and bleeding afresh through the satin, but his heart leaped.

Right on time, Little Genoa was open, vulnerable.

Monteverdi was in his hands.

"You're a fraud," Allegra was whispering. "You're not my Lazar."

He looked over. "*Your* Lazar?"

"Nobody's ever going to believe in you. You're no prince."

"How do you think I knew about the tunnels?"

"You just *found* them somehow, just another trick, like when you stopped me from calling for the guards by acting charming! Oh, you're clever enough, but you have no conscience, none at all, and no respect for the Fiori or Ascencion or me or anyone—"

"Silence," he said curtly.

"—not even for yourself. You're a fraud."

He stalked over, half tempted to slap her, but she shut her mouth, glaring up at him in mutiny.

"You're right. I am no bloody prince. I never said I was, if you recall." He climbed up onto the rough, large table and slowly pushed her onto her back as he straddled her. "I only told you my name, since you were so bloody curious about me, Miss Monteverdi. And since you are so *very* curious, my clever Miss Monteverdi, let me tell you just what I am," he snarled, inches from her face. "A sea captain. An exile. A pirate, Miss Monteverdi. And your new master."

At that moment, the cry that rent the air as his men poured through the gates was like nothing Allegra had ever heard.

The pirate was atop her on the table, staring down at her like a ravenous wolf, as the wave of sound rose around them. She thought the demons of the underworld must have broken down the black portals of Hell and come whirling out to ravage the mortal earth. Thunder rolled down from the sky and exploded on the rocks outside the city walls, shattering the dawn.

She stared up at him, aghast. "What have you done?"

"No time for talk." Swiftly he removed himself from her and picked her up again. Carrying her in his arms, he went quickly down the circling stairs. In the room below, he set her in the corner, her ankles still tightly bound together, one slightly sprained.

"You have nothing to fear," he told her, looking evenly into her eyes. "You will not come to harm. I swear it on my mother's grave. But I charge you, Allegra, do not open this door for *anyone* but me. My men make your father's soldiers look like schoolboys. Do you understand?"

She nodded, wide-eyed, tempted to throw herself into his arms and beg for his protection. Fortunately for her pride, she remembered in time that she loathed him.

He gazed at her for a minute, then gave a sigh and brushed her hair behind her shoulder. He leaned close and kissed her on the forehead, his lips warm and firm.

"You look terrified. There is nothing to fear, *chérie*. This tower has a good, fortified wall. You'll be safe. Mind you, stay here on the lower floor. Don't go upstairs. That roof won't hold if it's hit. I'll come for you when we're done shelling the city, sometime after daybreak."

"Come . . . for me?" She stared at him. "You mean to take me prisoner, don't you?"

His narrow smile was smug. "My dear Miss Monteverdi, I already have."

With an arrogant laugh for her angry huff, he stole a kiss from her lips, then drew his dreadful curved knife and charged up the steps to leave, she supposed, by way of the window. The gate was high enough so that he could probably jump onto its wide top and climb down from there, where the soldiers would not be expecting him.

For a long moment, she sat there in the dark corner, simply stunned.

Then her daze of astonishment cleared in a sudden firing of pure survival instinct.

Your new master?

"Not bloody likely," she muttered under her breath. She stared about angrily at the stone walls of her prison. She had to get out of this tower.

If she hurried, she could still get back into the palazzo before Papa's men sealed it against the enemy, but with her ankles bound in the inscrutable sailor's knot, she was all but helpless. She had already tried untying the knot, to no avail, while Lazar had worked at the crankshaft. Now every minute was precious. She scanned the room, trying to spy any object she could use to cut the soft leather thong while her bones rattled with each exploding shell.

"God, I despise that man," she whispered to the room, knowing even as she said it that dislike was not the only thing she felt toward him, especially after that drugging, claiming kiss. There was also exhilaration, anger, exasperation. *Passion.* This so-called Lazar was the most intensely alive person she had ever met, but if he continued at this rate, he wouldn't be for long.

She did not know if she believed his story of piracy. She still felt it was a peasant uprising, but at least it was better than his claiming to be the lost prince. He could not know what a tender nerve he'd struck in her when he'd said that. People could not come back from the dead. She knew that all too well.

She wanted, needed, her perfect Prince to stay safely where he belonged, inside her head, where he could never hurt her or leave her or die. But how had he known about the tunnels?

No, impossible! She refused to believe it.

He could have found them as a boy playing in the woods. He was a fraud—look at what he'd done to Domenic! The man was an animal.

For one thing, the real Lazar was dead, but even if he wasn't, her Prince would not take his kingdom back this way— stealing in like a thief in the night, putting guns to women's heads. He would come home to a fanfare of trumpets, clouds of rose petals strewn in his path. He would come in a golden ship, dressed in richest finery, with the pope and all the crowned heads of Europe to give him their backing.

That pirate rogue was—why, he was a barbarian, that's what he was.

Her searching gaze homed in on an apple one of the soldiers had been eating. Sticking out of it was a small paring knife. She hobbled over to get it and, after sawing at the knot, freed herself with a cry of victory, though the cords were still wound about her legs in two leather anklets. She jumped up, not wasting another moment.

Grasping her weapon in her right hand, she raced up the steps to view the situation and to pick out the safest path to the palazzo. She couldn't believe what she saw when she looked down upon the square. The artillery fire burst over the city in flashes of wild color, reds, yellows, and vivid blues against the black sky, while the shock of the cannons rocked the earth. She stared with one hand over her mouth in disbelief.

The city square was in chaos, each man for himself, everyone running for cover amid the parti-colored clutter of yesterday's festival. She could see people getting trampled and reserve soldiers ill from last night's drink scrambling out of the magazine in hectic disorder, trying to organize themselves against the barbaric invaders. She couldn't see Lazar anywhere.

She shrieked when the lantern crashed from the iron hook to the pounding floor beside her, then she clamped her jaw shut. Her nerves felt stretched as tightly as violin strings, near snapping if they hadn't already. On shaking legs, she crossed the garret to look out the window on the other side.

Down in the bay, seven ships barraged the city. She could not be sure, but by the flashing light of artillery, those appeared to be black flags flying from their masts. Orange light flashed amid the hazy white clouds all along the ships' wooden flanks as they fired again and again.

She fled the garret room and ran down the steps, almost falling down them in her fright. With all her strength she wrenched the table by degrees away from the door, and after fighting back every stubborn lock on the massive tower door, she burst out into the chaos.

Ignoring her sore ankle, she bolted for the palazzo and made it all the way to the steps, but there she found she was not the only one who sought safety inside. There was a crush at the main entrance as a wave of fear-crazed people fought to swarm in while dozens of guards struggled to hold them back, seal the doors, and secure the palace. She screamed to be let through, but she could not make herself heard above the deafening roar, and none of her father's men noticed her. She ran to the wide kitchen door where she'd left the palazzo hours ago, but it, too, was bolted, as were the third and fourth doors she tried.

With mounting terror, she bloodied her hands pounding on the last door on that wing, her voice frantic in her own ears as she shouted, "Papa! Papa!"

Her own father had locked her out. She couldn't believe it.

Answering shots sounded much closer as the soldiers finally began to work the cannons on the city walls, and Allegra realized she should have listened to Lazar. She walked in defeat to the edge of the square and stared at the gruff, weather-browned men who were everywhere, bare-chested, swinging weapons of all kinds at her father's soldiers, even great, cruel-looking clubs.

They didn't look like any Ascencion peasants she'd ever seen. They didn't fight like them, either.

Her fingers tightened on her paltry weapon. She could see no other solution but to return to her fortress in the gate tower. Lazar had said she would be safe there. She scanned the crowd for him and did not see him.

Jesu Christi, what if he'd already been killed? Who would control these wild men of his then? She could not bear to think about it yet. First she had to get back to the tower. It meant submitting to her fate as his captive, but it was better than dying, and if he chose to be gentle, why, she might even enjoy herself in his bed, she thought rather hysterically, for she had certainly relished his kiss.

She had not gone a dozen steps when her bodyguards came rushing out of the chaos to her defense, along with a few other soldiers. She cried out in thanks, for she had never been so happy to see anyone before in her life. They surrounded her in a protective ring, weapons outward.

"Donn'Allegra, we've been looking everywhere for you! What are you doing out here?" Giraud cried, but he did not expect an answer, for he instantly had greater matters with which to contend.

In their dashing blue-and-gold uniforms, the guards were immediate targets for the enemy. They strove to fend off the sudden swarm of pirates on all sides.

Surrounded by the clash of weaponry, Allegra screamed when the sweat or spit of a pirate flicked upon her skin like the first drizzle of storm rains. The great wretch swore at Giraud and opposed him. The brawny guard put a swift end to him. Her mind went blank as she stared at the ragged crimson gash of the pirate's torn throat and his bulging eyes.

They had only gone perhaps five steps when handsome young Pietro was run through.

"Jesus!" he yelped, falling to his knees.

Allegra stared at her big, familiar guard in astonishment as he looked down at the sword buried in his chest. She covered her mouth with both hands in horror, not even noticing when her little knife slipped from her grasp and clattered to the ground.

She looked over her dying bodyguard's head at the one who had done this to him, saw the giant scimitar steeped in scarlet, heard the hearty cry die on the brute's lips as he stared back at her, his sweaty face filling suddenly with an altogether different passion.

He had a dark mop of mangy, ragged hair, beady eyes beneath a heavy brow, and he loomed half as big as Gibraltar. Appalled beyond thought by his eager leer, she took an unconscious step backward.

In that moment Giraud was wounded.

"Milady!" he gasped.

"No!" She grabbed for him even while his right arm faltered. She covered her face with both hands as he was struck again and died with an anguished curse while a crowd of the brutes fell upon the last, valiant man standing by her.

Rough hands seized her. She would not look. She was going to die, but she did not want to see it coming. *Dear God, please just let it be swift.*

"Well, well. What 'ave we here?" came a deep, garbled voice while the cannons deafened them all.

She uncovered her ashen face and looked up to see the giant who had run poor Pietro through. She was filled with instant, burning hatred that for a moment conquered terror.

"Either kill me as we stand, or take me to Lazar! God curse you forevermore!" she added with uncontrollable savagery.

The pirate threw back his thick head and laughed. " 'Tis a hellcat we've got 'ere, Andrew McCullough, and a lady, to boot!"

"Take me to Lazar," she said through clenched teeth, hoping indeed that was the name by which his men knew him.

"Feisty lass! Now, why should I do that? Maybe old Goliath ain't as bonny a man as the Cap, but I got me own virtues!" he cried, grabbing himself between his legs. "It's finders keepers with the Brethren!"

She shrank from him as the big pirate bent his shaggy head, looming closer.

"Aye, pretty, methinks we can find a few uses for you aboardship." He reached for her.

To his mates' delight, she succeeded in stumbling a few steps from him before another easily caught her and held her. Slowly, defiantly, she raised her gaze. The stench of his rotten-toothed breath filled her nostrils. She refused to breathe his foul air until black explosions burst silently across her field of vision. For a moment, she feared she was going to faint.

Her head began to swim as his big dirty hands clamped around her waist. There were smatterings of blood on his ragged shirt.

Her bodyguards' blood.

The two smiling, manly fellows who had followed her around on her errands like big, lovable dogs.

"Come to Golly, pretty," he rumbled, a bestial light in his eyes.

She fought furiously, to no avail, as the pirate hoisted her over his sweaty shoulder and carried her out of the square.

At six in the morning, Lazar leaned against the white frame of the open window. He was in the drawing room of the governor's palazzo, gazing out to sea. Taking the island had been as simple as he'd known it would be, for his plans had been flawless. All had come off easy as a harlot's frock. He had even sent three of his meanest men out to capture Domenic Clemente so he could die with the others, but for some reason he felt bloody odd.

The moment had come. The lads were delivering his arch-enemy into his hands. He had dreamed of this since he was thirteen years old, but it did not feel the way he had always imagined. There was none of the rising scarlet glory he knew in the thick of the fight or in the leap from ship to ship, sword in hand, or in battles against black gales at sea a hundred miles from any port.

His men knocked at the door and, at his word, brought in the governor. Lazar took one look at his prisoner, and his uncertainty bled to misery. *Damn it to hell.* In the lapse of fifteen years, the archfiend of his nightmares had become a tired old man.

The sailors threw the don to the marble floor of his own drawing room. He cursed as he went sprawling in a clanking knot of chains and manacles. "You will never get away with this! The navy will be here at any moment! I'll see you hanged from the highest tree!"

Monteverdi glared at the men as he climbed stiffly to his feet. He untangled his chains with the dignity of a man used to public address, but when his gaze swung across the room to Lazar, he went motionless.

Staring, Monteverdi turned the sickly white of overcast skies.

"That's right, old man, your sins have come home to roost," Lazar told him with a soft, bitter laugh.

He wished right then that Father could have been there to see his old adviser. What a joke, that this little ferret should have found the means to bring low a man half as big as a mountain, with a mind as keen as the gleaming, ancient broadsword of the Fiore kings, Excelsior, which just an hour earlier Lazar had recovered from the city's treasury, along with the crown jewels and the other royal heirlooms.

He dismissed his men with a firm nod.

As he considered the many ways he'd thought of over the years to begin this conversation, he took a casual stroll around the large, bright drawing room. With each moment he kept his silence, he could sense the old don's fear mounting. It was most gratifying.

In a fortress on the Barbary Coast, he'd learned all the tricks of intimidation from His Excellency of Al Khuum, who had a flair for such things. Aye, his two-year sojourn in the bad place was not the least of the favors for which the Governor would pay today.

While Monteverdi watched his every move in dread, Lazar took down a dusty leather-bound book from one of the shelves and fanned idly through the pages, then found a fine box of cheroots on the writing table and helped himself to one. After lighting it with the expensive automatic tinder lying nearby on the desk, he turned his attention to his enemy.

"Before you start lying, or attempt to pretend you don't know who I am," he said, "let me just advise you that I have your daughter. It would be prudent to cooperate."

This took the governor off his guard. "Where is she? Where is Allegra?" he demanded shakily.

Lazar gave him a slight, evil smile and turned away to watch the curtains wave over the window in the sea breeze. "In my keeping, never fear."

"What have you done with her?"

"Not half yet what I intend. My compliments, Governor, on your sweet little girl. Delicious breasts, a mouth like silk, and the tightest little ass." He closed his eyes for a moment, feigning an expression of remembered bliss. It had the calculated effect. "Exquisite."

"What do you want of me?" Monteverdi whispered in a choked voice.

"First I want to hear you say you know who I am."

Monteverdi was quite gray in the face. "But it's not possible," he croaked. "The boy is dead. Killed—by highwaymen—dreadful—"

"Highwaymen, eh? That *is* the official story, isn't it?" This work was getting easier as the memories returned. He puffed upon the cigar and looked down at the bald spot on the top of Monteverdi's head as he circled him. "We both know better than that, old man. I've come to collect my pound of flesh."

"Not possible. You're a fraud." He clutched at his chest. "Your creatures told me you are a pirate—called the Devil of Antigua."

"But it was not always so. Say it, Monteverdi. Admit you know me. Remember, I have Allegra."

The don stared up at him.

"My God," he whispered, "you are Alphonse's elder son, Lazar. You have your mother's coloring, but you are his very image." Monteverdi suddenly gulped. "Your Majesty, I am innocent—"

Lazar laughed. " 'Your Majesty?' The king is dead, Monteverdi. You and the Council saw to that."

"I am innocent."

"You don't seem to understand how painful I can make death for you. You are not a man accustomed to pain, are you?

You've had a soft life. How well you've done for yourself," he remarked, gazing about at the sumptuous drawing room, "feeding off the carrion of the great Fiori. Fifteen years as governor, eh? Very laudable." He exhaled a puff of smoke and looked away, unable to stomach the sight of the man.

"I am innocent!"

Lazar smiled blandly. "I tire of hearing you say that. All I really want to know is why you did it. I have asked myself that question a thousand times. You were a member of his cabinet, one of the six men he trusted most. He was good to you. He trusted you. As did my—mother." He checked himself before he wavered.

Monteverdi searched the floor, then his shoulders sagged. He shook his head. "They were going to do it anyway. I could not have stopped it."

"So you agreed to help."

"Once the dons of the Council brought the matter before me, if I had not cooperated, I, too, would have been killed."

"Why did they choose you?"

He shrugged. "Most of my family is Genovese. Genoa was all but bankrupt," he said heavily. "Not even the revenues from Corsica restored the industries."

"Those old men are lucky they're dead. You—you're not so lucky." He slid Monteverdi a look. "Your crime is the worst one, anyway. You sat at our dinner table. You rode to the hounds with him. You taught me how to play chess. You were our friend, and you sold us for the slaughter. Didn't even try to warn us—"

"Enough," he choked out. "I'll tell you why. I did it for my wife. My beautiful wife, who was in love with him," he whispered.

Lazar stared at him warily.

He remembered her clearly, the beautiful, sad-eyed Lady Cristiana, his mother's closest girlhood friend and her lady-in-waiting.

"I loved her, oh, more than a man should ever love a woman," he said with quiet, futile passion. "But I could not make her stop loving him."

Instantly Lazar suspected a trick, for Monteverdi was a proven liar. "So when I bed Allegra, I'll be tupping my half sister, eh?" he taunted, approaching him. "Do you seriously think that will deter me?"

"Allegra is my daughter," he said frostily. "Only in her heart was Cristiana an adulteress. She was a pious woman, and she loved Eugenia too much to act on her feelings for Alphonse— and of course, your father was never known to stray." He lowered his head. "Cristiana fell into a deep melancholia after they died—"

"Died?" He suddenly grabbed Monteverdi by his cravat, lifting him off the ground above him. *"Died?* After they were butchered by your hirelings, you mean!" he roared.

Lazar threw him to the floor and stalked to the door, intent on leaving before he killed the don with his bare hands. Monteverdi had not suffered enough yet to receive such a swift and merciful death.

"Nothing you can do to me matters," the man on the floor sobbed out behind him. "None of it matters."

"What is that supposed to mean?" Lazar paused at the door, turning around.

"Cristiana found out what I'd done—"

"Did you have her killed, too?"

"No! God, no," he wrenched out. "She suspected all along, but somehow six years later she realized the truth. She sent Allegra to her sister in Paris, and one day when I came home, my too-beautiful, highborn wife had blown out her brains there, in our home, where she knew I would be the one to find her. And a note saying she had done it for shame of me."

He hung his head in his hands and sobbed, shoulders shaking.

Lazar stared at him, realizing the man was already tortured beyond anything he could have devised.

"Please do not harm my daughter," he whispered without looking up. "She is a good girl, and she has suffered enough."

Lazar was silent for a moment. "You are a failure in every imaginable way. Do you know that, Monteverdi? Do you realize you promised your only daughter to a man who even tonight tried to rape her?"

He looked up, white. "What?"

"Your Lord Clemente—I redressed the situation," he muttered with a wave of his hand.

"No, no." He bent his head, weeping softly. "Allegra, my little one."

"I am taking her under my protection," he said, "for her sake and for Lady Cristiana's, not for yours. Then only one survivor shall remain from both our families."

Still prostrate on the floor, the governor looked up at him in sudden horror, apprehending at last the full scale of his vendetta, understanding now why Lazar had timed his revenge for this celebration, when all of Monteverdi's kin were gathered under his roof.

"The House of Monteverdi, like the Fiori, shall be no more," Lazar said softly. "Though I carry out this deed, the blood is on your hands."

He walked out and slammed the door behind him as the governor's wailing and pleading began.

Lazar found himself strangely moved as he walked down the sterile halls of the palazzo to retrieve his lovely prize from safekeeping in the tower.

Poor kitten, he thought sadly. How empty her young life must have been. A mother left devastated by the death of her friends. A lying coward for a father. He could just picture her as a lonely little girl in this big, marble palace devoid of love, pawned off on relatives in a city where she didn't even speak the language. At least for the short time he had had his family, they had been close-knit and happy—Father and Mother, him, Phillip—otherwise known as Pip—and little Anna, who had been only four years old at the time of her murder.

Not for Monteverdi's sake but for hers, he decided to let Allegra see her father one last time to say good-bye as he had not been allowed to do. In any case, then she could hear from Monteverdi's own mouth that Lazar was indeed who he claimed to be, not a fraud.

In the white, breezy foyer, he called a few men over to update him, standing out of the way as the Brethren carried out treasure after treasure, looting the palace with the methodical efficiency he'd taught them.

Captain Bickerson, of *The Tempest*, reported the ships' holds were near capacity. If they loaded up much more, they'd pay for it in speed. The lookouts still saw no sign of the navy.

"Excellent. And Clemente? Has he been taken?"

"Er, not yet, sir. We ain't found him yet. He's run off, hiding somewhere in the countryside, but we'll get him," replied Jeffers, the tough ex-convict he'd put in charge of the task, along with his equally hardened partner, Wilkes.

"Get more men on it. Time is short. I don't want him getting away. I have faith in you, Jeff," he added darkly.

"Right," the hulking man answered with a nod.

"If for some reason you don't catch him before we set sail," Lazar added as an afterthought, "you and your men stay here until he's taken care of, then follow us." He clapped him on the shoulder. "I'll make it plenty worth your while."

"Aye, sir!" the man said, a sparkle of greed in his eyes as he went off to do his bidding.

"Now, then. What of the governor's kin?" Lazar asked. "Are they all accounted for?"

"Aye, Cap," answered Sullivan, captain of *The Hawk*. "Six-and-forty of 'em. They're all in the magazine jail, just as you instructed."

"Good. Take them to the ramparts of the eastern wall, where the cliffs drop down to the sea. Line them up there."

"Aye, sir."

Lazar paused for a moment, head bowed. "Sully," he added, "get me twelve men with rifles up there, too."

The Irishman started to laugh. "Aye, sure, ye're not losing heart, are ye? Why, ye was all piss 'n' vinegar a week ago to pop 'em each yourself—"

Lazar lifted his chin and met the man's eyes with a frosty midnight gaze. Sully's laughter stopped abruptly.

"It is merely a matter of convenience."

The Irishman swallowed his joviality. "Aye, sir."

Lazar threw his cheroot to the ground, crushing it under his boot heel on the white marble floor, grouchily admitting to himself that Sully was right. Last week he had vowed to put a bullet personally into each Monteverdi head. A mere three days ago he was as hungry for their blood as the ghosts in his memory.

He had a sinking feeling that his growing sense of unease, almost reluctance, sprang from the unbalancing effect the girl was having on him. He was about to render her as alone in the world as he was, but he could not afford to feel guilty for it.

No, the hell with her, he thought, irked. If she had any sense, she would thank her lucky stars he saw fit to spare her at all.

He stalked down the steps of the palazzo and had gone only a few yards into the busy piazza when he heard a shout. Suddenly he saw a man running toward him, waving his arms. Instinctively he reached for his pistol and took aim.

"Halt," he said.

The man stopped and threw himself to the ground, hollering something into the cobblestones. Two of the mates came running a step behind and hauled the man up from the ground, each taking an arm. Lazar furrowed his brow, holstered his gun, and walked over to the fellow hanging limp in his men's grasp.

"Who's this?"

"Says he's your servant, Cap."

"I am! I must speak with you, sire. It is imperative!"

"You're a lunatic, you are," said the other pirate as he gave his arm a rough tug. "He ain't your bloody sire."

When the squat, tattered fellow peered worshipfully up at him, Lazar found it was the same fat, greasy musician from the previous night's bonfire.

"Oh, you again." He sighed. "What is it?"

The man seemed to be trying to keep his eyes fixed humbly down, but at the question, he looked up at Lazar with a quick, imploring gaze.

Understanding dawned. The guitarist wanted to join them. They picked up strays everywhere they stopped, brave, wayward lads who longed for adventure, dreamers chasing gold, and desperadoes running from the law. This one looked like the last category. In a heartbeat, however, Lazar realized just how far from the mark his assessment was.

"We are gathering outside the walls even now, my liege," he told him, a zealous light in his beady eyes. "Your people are coming from all over Ascencion to hail you!"

"*What?*"

Abruptly the man fell to his knees, shoving his face down to the cobbles. The two pirates looked down at him in bewilderment, then at Lazar.

"Praised be God for this day, Your Majesty!" he cried. "May the sun shine on your reign forever!"

Lazar snapped out of his utter astonishment when the two pirates started to laugh. The blood drained from his face.

"He's loony!" the first cried.

"Your *Majesty*?" roared the other. "He's foxed! Conversin' with Pharaoh, him!"

Swift as a panther, Lazar crouched down by the Ascencion man. "Get up," he said in a low, deadly voice. "Who are you? Who sent you?"

The man looked up. "No one sent me, sire! I am Bernardo of St. Eilion, on the south coast. I am a musician. I've kept their hope alive for you with the stories and legends, sire." He bowed his head. "My father fought with Alphonse on St. Teresa's Day. I know we will see such glories again, sire, and even greater triumphs to come, now that Your Majesty has returned. You have crushed the Genovese foe!"

Lazar knew only that he was numb. Beyond that lay something akin to terror. How the hell did they know who he was?

Was this some kind of joke?

It might have been funny had it not had the potential to explode in his face like a faulty cannon. His men had no idea would never believe—that he'd been born a prince, while the mule-headed Ascencioners refused to see the obvious fact that he had become a pirate. There was no prince left in him.

His men continued to guffaw and poke gibes at the poor, pathetic bard, who in turn shot them indignant glances.

"Forgive me, great sire, but these knaves do not show Your Majesty proper homage. If I may be so bold, I would serve you with far greater respect—"

"Er, Bernardo," Lazar began. He propped an elbow on his knee and scratched his jaw, at a loss.

"Yes, my liege?"

"I'm afraid there's been a mistake. Whoever it is you've taken me to be, I can assure you I'm not he." He shook his head, hating himself with every cruel, casual word. "We're pirates, you see, and we're looting this place. We'll be leaving shortly."

His countryman stared up at him. "My liege?"

He shook his head. "Merely 'Captain.' I'm sorry. I can see this meant a great deal to you."

Shock, horror, and betrayal made the bard's fat face even uglier. His look cut to Lazar's heart. Bernardo shook his meaty head in staunch refusal. "No, sire, no!"

"I'm afraid your wish has clouded your vision, my friend," he said softly. "Surely you can see that I'm no king."

"No, you are Alphonse's son! You are his very image! The legend is true!"

"Legend!" He laughed, amiable as ever, as if these words were not a dagger in his heart. "The only legends of me are the ones that nannies in the West Indies tell misbehaving children to get them to mind." He shook his head. "Ach, you people were always daft."

"Sire, why you deny the truth of who you are, I cannot say, but I know what I know. You are Alphonse's son, the rightful heir of Ascencion's throne, and our king!"

The two pirates laughed uproariously. Lazar smiled stiffly at them. "Aye," he said, "I'm king. Aren't I, lads?"

"King o' the sea!" the first hiccupped.

"King o' thieves!" the other said with a grin.

"Nay, Prince o' Darkness——"

"And we're his loyal subjects, ain't we, William?" the first howled.

Lazar regarded Bernardo with a cold smile amid the lads' antics.

"You see?" he said quietly. "That's the way of it." He nodded to his men. "Get him out of my sight." He walked away even before they had picked the squat man up off the ground.

An inconvenience merely, he told himself. The Ascencioners would survive as they always had.

Like rats.

"Vendetta," he assured the shades of the slain Fiori, but just now they were silent.

He strode across the square toward the eastern tower and the open city gates. Yards away, however, he froze.

The door he'd left secured was hanging open.

He knew even before he ran inside and tore up the steps to the garret that Allegra was gone. Moments later, he crashed back out into the square, stalked to the center, and leaped up onto the stone rim of the fountain. He fired his pistol into the air, getting his men's attention. All motion in the piazza came to a halt.

Sweat streaming down his face, he roared at them, "God damn it, where is she? Which of you scurvy bastards took *my woman*?"

⊰ CHAPTER ⊱
FIVE

Allegra had found a place on a low shelf between two sacks of grain. The shelf above her gave her a roof, and, in this little hole in the wall, she curled up and sincerely willed herself to die. After carrying her onto the ship, Goliath had been so thoughtful as to leave her a lantern with the assurance that there were no rats in *this* storeroom. He had locked the door and left then, for she was a sure thing while the lure of more booty still called.

He had said he was going to marry her. She knew that wasn't what he meant. He was the foulest, most uncouth creature she had ever seen, and she hoped she was dead by the time he returned. She tried not to ponder the thought of his hamlike hands on her, for to think of what he was going to do to her filled her with such unstoppable horror, she felt the edges of her sanity fraying in earnest.

She heard hard, swift footsteps in the companionway and felt a new surge of panic. She stuffed herself deeper into her hole in the wall. In a last-ditch effort she even blew out the lantern. Better rats than Goliath.

Her ears were ringing from hours of cannon fire just over her head, but it seemed, distantly, that an angry voice was calling her name. She could not remember having told Goliath her Christian name, but that was of little consequence as she heard doors being slammed all down the passageway.

Suddenly the door burst open. Her breath heaved impossibly fast.

"Allegra!"

She realized the very hem of her dress was hanging over the edge of the shelf. She yanked it in. Wild-eyed, she covered her mouth with her hands to keep from crying out. There was silence, then slow footsteps sounded in the little storeroom, one, two, three. She could not help the terrified, tiny sound that overflowed her lips.

The man who had come for her bent slowly down. She saw his eyes, sea black, furious and gentle all at once as he gazed at her. She stared at him, not daring to move.

"Oh, sweetheart," he said sadly. Lazar held out his hand to her. "Come out. It's all right now, *chérie*. Come out of there," he coaxed her.

At the soft, civilized tone of his voice, what was left of her composure shattered. There was no strength in her, nothing left. She began to cry without holding back.

He reached into the hole where she was and gathered her up. She spilled resistlessly into his arms and clung to his hard shoulder as to a lone rock in an angry sea. He cradled the back of her head with his big hand and held her to him like a babe. She breathed in the scent of him as she sobbed, rum and sweat, smoke and leather, gunpowder, blood, and the sea. She wanted to be back in her convent school, in bed by nine, Mother Beatrice dousing the candles. She wanted no part of this man, but it was too late. The smell of him was deep in her lungs, on her skin, in her hair.

"Shh, *chérie*," he was saying softly as he walked slowly up and down the dim passageway, rocking her gently and murmuring soft, kind nonsense. "Poor baby, you're all right now, sweetheart. I've got you now," he whispered, and she knew it was true. He had her now.

She was his captive.

She realized by the red glow behind her eyelids that he had

taken her out into the sunshine. Somehow he had climbed up the ladders of the companionways without her even realizing it. He was so strong. Too strong. She burrowed her face closer against his neck.

"There you are, my brave girl," he murmured. "I need you to tell me exactly what happened so I can decide how painfully Goliath deserves to die."

She shook her head, never looking up. *No more death.*

"Allegra." He paused. There was murder in his voice. "Did he rape you?"

She shook her head again, refusing to talk.

"Did he hit you?"

She nodded, yes.

"In the face?"

She opened her lips against his salty skin to answer, "Stomach."

"Are you badly hurt?"

She didn't think so. She shrugged and held him tighter, refusing to open her eyes or loosen her arms' tight hold about his neck. "I still hate you, but please don't put me down yet," she whispered.

He chuckled sadly, softly in reassurance.

She felt his stride change as he walked with her in his arms. She heard creaking noises, and she sensed their entry into shadow again. When he spoke again, his voice was deep and unbearably gentle.

"You can look now, angel. You're in my cabin, on my ship. You're quite safe here. My friend will look after you until I return—John Southwell, of England. He's a gentleman, used to be an Anglican priest, in fact. Just call him Vicar—everyone else does. I trust him as I trust myself, *capisce*?"

She kept her eyes screwed up tight as she clung to him.

"Oh, Lazar," she whispered on a breath that was dangerously near a sob, "please don't leave me again. I have never been so frightened in my life."

He squeezed her tighter for a long moment, then she felt him set her down on a deliciously deep mattress, but he didn't put her out of his arms.

"*Chérie,* I have things to do," he said softly. "Get some sleep. You've been through hell. We'll talk later. I promise."

"Is my father all right?"

"He's just fine."

"May I see him?"

"No, *chérie*. You stay here and rest."

She still didn't want to open her eyes. She had a feeling she was in his bed, her head cradled on his pillow. Her mind protested at the situation, but exhaustion, practicality, and her instinctive sense of safety in his presence were forces too powerful for mere propriety.

At last she reluctantly opened her eyes and found herself gazing straight up at him. She was instantly absorbed by the vision of his bronzed, chiseled face just above hers. Lazar had removed his skullcap, and she saw that his close-cropped, jet-black hair was thick and velvety. She could only stare. By daylight he was the most beautiful creature she'd ever seen, even though she knew now what he was.

Goliath's witless henchman had told her that on the other side of the world, Lazar was known as the Devil of Antigua— the cursed, the damned. Slayer of innocents. Burner of cities. Feared even among the Barbary corsairs, who called him *Shaytan* of the West, the Devil of Antigua feared neither God nor man, it was said. His vessel was a sleek seventy-four-gun warship called *The Whale*.

The Devil of Antigua was evil incarnate. It was common knowledge.

He was gazing down anxiously at her, a world of feeling in his soulful, chocolate-brown eyes. There were flecks—no, rays—of gold in his irises, she saw in wonder. He caressed her cheek with one fingertip, then tucked the fine linen sheet over her.

"Goliath is about to pay a very dear price for what he's done to you," he whispered a trifle hoarsely. He leaned down and pressed a kiss to her forehead. "You will stay here and rest, and this time do not disobey me, for I won't have you getting into any more scrapes. I fear you have used up all your rescues." He offered her a warm, crooked smile.

She reached up and hugged him to her, just to keep him a little longer, for he made her feel so very safe. His laugh was rich and soft as he returned her embrace.

"There you are, now. No one's going to hurt you or frighten you anymore, Allegra. You place your trust in me, *capisce*? I'm going to take very good care of you," he whispered as he petted her hair back. "Be a good girl till I get back." He leaned down to kiss her on the cheek, pausing to whisper by her ear, "*Then* you may be as naughty as you please."

To her amazement, her stomach fluttered at his words. After all she had been through, he still knew exactly how to make her newfound desire stir. She watched him rise with natural grace and stride toward the cabin door.

Ah, she loved the way he walked, she thought with a sigh, that warrior strut.

There could be worse fates than to be held captive by such a man, she thought in exhaustion. Perhaps her sojourn as his hostage wouldn't be so bad. Clearly, after having rescued her twice now, he would not hurt her. It would only be a day or two until Papa amassed the ransom he would demand. She'd probably be ruined, true, but at least she wouldn't have to marry Domenic or any of Papa's other tedious Genovese lords.

She looked around at the elegant space he called home, a large, bright cabin that gleamed with a colorful array of polished woods. Whoever he was, the captain had good taste, she thought, but for all its offhand luxury, the cabin displayed little of the orderly spit-and-polish she'd have expected of a mariner's quarters. Everything looked as though he expected an elaborate staff of servants to materialize at any moment and clean up after him.

His berth, where she lay, was a giant bed built into the bulk-head, but it had a cozy feel, tucked behind deep-blue velvet curtains, which were presently looped back behind the two carved pilasters. The bed linens were rumpled, and a red satin blanket was kicked into a ball near the corner of the mattress.

A large leather storage trunk stationed at the foot of the berth was piled high with a careless mound of his clothes. A fine satinwood washstand with claw feet was nearby, nailed to the floor.

In the center of the cabin, a comfortably faded medallion rug of dark blues and reds adorned the polished wooden planks. Upon it stood a massive mahogany desk cluttered with books, half-furled scrolls and navigational charts, a pair of brass dividers, a table globe, and a sandglass. There was one pon-derous oak armchair, upholstered in a dark wine brocade. On it, a tattered orange cat missing the tip of one ear was absorbed in the task of licking its paw.

Spanning the bulkhead opposite were cherrywood lockers to hold the captain's belongings, and bookcases with etched glass doors, but the back wall of the cabin comprised the stern of the ship and was lined with beautiful diamond-shaped windows, some with brightly colored glass. In the center of this wall was a narrow door leading to a balcony beyond and all the wide green sea.

Lazar had paused in the doorway and was holding a low-toned conversation with the man who stood there, staring up at him as if he had sprouted two heads. This, she gathered, was John Southwell, or Vicar, the friend he had mentioned. She turned onto her side and studied him sleepily, sinking ever deeper into Lazar's sprawling goose-down mattress.

Vicar was a lean, distinguished-looking older gentleman with a book tucked under one arm, long, gray-white hair pulled

back in a neat club, and small spectacles perched on his aristocratic nose.

"Monteverdi's daughter? I—I am speechless!" he exclaimed.

"Well, look at her," her captor murmured, glancing in at her.
"She's priceless. What else was I to do with her?"

Vicar swept off his spectacles and tucked them neatly into
his breast pocket. His deep-set, silver eyes were keen and penetrating as he glanced over at her.

Allegra's toes curled with pleasure under the light sheet. No
one had ever called her *priceless* before.

The small, intimate smile Lazar gave her from across the
cabin pulled a sigh of contentment from the depths of her
being. At her sigh, Vicar turned and stared back up at Lazar in
what appeared to be utter disbelief.

Lazar turned back to Vicar, still slightly smiling. "Give her a
small dose of laudanum to help her sleep, and see that she
doesn't get into mischief."

"As you wish," Vicar replied, shaking his head to himself.

"Are you a pirate, too, sir?" she asked with as much grace as
the question garnered.

Lazar chuckled while Vicar stared at her, taken aback.

"My dear lady, no!" he replied with an urbane chuckle. "I've
been the Devil's prisoner now for, what, eleven years?"

"Prisoner," Lazar scoffed. "Don't mind his ploys for sympathy, *chérie*. He's a wily old frigate bird. I can't seem to shoo
him away."

Lazar told her that Vicar had been a professor at the Oxford
University, in England, before their paths crossed. That sounded
very interesting to her, but she was too tired at the moment to
give a fig.

After Lazar had gone, Vicar stood in the doorway, staring
at her. Then he marched over to her side and thrust out his
right hand.

"Miss Monteverdi, I would like to shake your hand," he
declared.

"Oh? Why?" she asked, acquiescing with a sleepy smile, too tired to move any other part of her body.

Vicar crouched down to her level next to the bed. "Somehow you have bewitched our young captain, Miss Monteverdi. I don't know how—divine Providence, I daresay, but oh, I have been waiting for something like this to happen for the past ten years! He might at last be free of this *obsession*!"

"Lazar has an obsession?" she asked idly, eyes closed. "Oh, with ladies, I suppose you mean. Yes, he is quite the charmer."

"No, indeed, Miss Monteverdi, his obsession is with vengeance. Now, you must come at once. There is no time to lose!"

She dragged one eye open and regarded him skeptically. "Huh?"

"My dear lady, what would you dare for the people you love?"

She eyed him warily, her head too heavy to lift from the pillow. "Is this some scholarly dialectic, sir? For I haven't slept in twenty-four hours—"

"No, no, it is a matter of the utmost urgency! Miss Monteverdi, Lazar is a man balanced on the very razor's edge between good and evil. You may be the only one who can reclaim him before he is lost forever!"

It took several moments for Vicar to explain what Lazar intended, and then Allegra still did not entirely believe it, but enough of the pieces fit to dissolve her fatigue in a rain of cold fear.

Calmly Vicar assured her that if she did not act at once, her whole family would die at Lazar's hands for the sake of some vendetta the pirate had against her father.

"What wrong did my father do him?" she cried as she jumped out of his berth. Knowing Papa's dictatorial ways, she found it all too easy to believe that Papa had dealt Lazar some terrible injustice.

Vicar pursed his lips for a moment, then took pity on her. "His family was murdered. Your father was responsible."

She froze, staring at him. The most horrible thought of her life flashed through her mind, striking nausea into the pit of her stomach.

What if he *was* Lazar di Fiore?

Could the rebels' worst public accusation against her father be true—that Papa had betrayed King Alphonse?

Never could she believe such a thing, never.

"Who is he, Vicar?" she whispered hoarsely. "What was his family that my father destroyed?"

"I am not at liberty to say, my dear. Lazar will tell you what he deems best in time. For now, I fear you must make your decision blind."

There was only one way to decide. "Let's go!"

They went. As they ran, she wondered briefly why Lazar had chosen to spare her, but the answer required little thought. She realized now it had never been his intention to ransom her, not if he planned on leaving her whole family dead. The very thought made her skin cold with dread.

Your new master . . .

"I have been against this vendetta from the start," Vicar said as they scrambled up the companionway and out over the broad decks of his warship. "I have tried to show him there is no justice in such total, massive revenge, but he refuses to listen! Maybe he will listen to you. It is primitive, uncivilized! If he does this thing, it will destroy him."

She started down the gangplank, but Vicar clamped a hand around her arm. "Wait."

She turned back, wild-eyed. "What is it?"

His silver eyes were cool, forceful. "If you fail, he may execute you along with them."

She flicked the warning off impatiently. "Where are they?"

"The magazine."

In moments, they were running down the dock. Vicar

shooed the ruffians off the latest-arrived wagon, and the two of them climbed up into the driver's seat. He drove the wagon at a breakneck pace all the way up the winding road to Little Genoa and through the gates Lazar had opened last night.

Allegra flung herself down from the wagon before it had barely stopped, running across the square, each step jarring her hurt ankle through her tattered slippers. Lazar's pirates watched her pass. None dared make a move to stop her, all having been warned not to touch her.

Surely he wasn't Lazar di Fiore. She knew her father was not a good man, but she couldn't believe anything so horrible of him. Nor, surely, was the stranger capable of anything so evil as a mass execution. Even after the brutal way he had beaten Domenic, he had held her so gently, tucked her into his bed so tenderly. But as she tore past the Poseidon fountain, she gasped to see them dragging the dead body of Goliath over the flagstones toward burial somewhere, a trail of blood left by the gunshot wound in his head.

Then a bit of movement up on the eastern wall caught her eye. There was a crowd of people coming out onto the high, windy ramparts of the city wall from the side door of the formidable garrison. She saw the outlines of women and children among them.

"God, no," she breathed. *Don't let me be too late.*

It took forever to cross the piazza to the immense magazine, but at last she was stumbling up the three stone steps, through the open door, and into the atrium. She paused for only a heartbeat. She had never seen the inside of the magazine before. It was deserted. She did not want to wonder what had become of all the gallant blue-coated guards. Panting with exertion, she looked right and left. She spied a stone staircase at the end of the corridor on her left and ran for it.

She lost her footing on one of the steps and scraped her shin, but she kept going and at last came to a little door at the top of the steps. She opened it to the eastern rampart of the wall. She stopped in the shadow of the doorway, staring in disbelief.

Papa was there. All her relatives were being herded against the battlements that overlooked the cliffs. Across from them, a group of men with guns was milling into order.

And at the far end of this group stood a giant black silhouette, massive arms crossed, a curved blade at his side. The long ends of his silken skullcap waved slowly in the breeze behind him.

⊰ CHAPTER ⊱
SIX

High on the eastern ramparts, the sun was hot, and the breeze was swift. Sully was ordering the men into firing-squad position when Lazar caught himself studying his victims.

Damn it, you idiot. Never look at the faces.

Captain Wolfe had taught him that much when Lazar had been barely sixteen. With a low growl of anger, he turned away to look out at the sea, but already the image of a big-bosomed matron and her stout little lad in togs and strings was imprinted onto his memory forever, along with that of a skinny Monteverdi grandfather with a square white beard who was shouting, in an utter Italian fury, at his weeping kin to die with some pride.

Lazar let out a long breath that was just a trifle unsteady and reached for the flask of rum in his vest, but it was no longer there. He remembered he had used the strap to hobble Allegra.

The Monteverdis began chanting the rosary with one quavering collective voice. Lazar listened for only a moment, then turned away with a growl. It had been a long time since he'd heard the sound of prayers.

He looked at his own shadow looming black over the flagstone. His men awaited his command, their guns cocked. The Monteverdis seemed prepared to die, each on his knees, eyes cast heavenward—except for the governor, who knew the futility, Lazar supposed, of prayer in his case.

He called the order for the men to bring up their guns.

Reminded himself he could bear this, he could live with this. He had done, and would undoubtedly do, worse. This was his duty, his penance, and if they hanged him for it one day, well, the truth of it was he had no business being alive anyway, did he?

He drifted a moment, unanchored, remembering the night his world ended.

Everyone waited. Somebody sobbed. The wind scored his cheeks invisibly with tiny blades of sand.

He did not like this duty, but he had lived when he should have perished. Only a river of blood could wash him clean now.

"To ready," he said, hard and black, broken and charred, as the castle on the mountaintop.

The guns were leveled to the men's shoulders in a spiky line.

"God curse you forevermore!" the governor uttered, shaking with his malediction like a sun-dazed Ezekiel.

Lazar met his glare evenly, felt his mouth go into a slight, cruel smile. Cursed? he thought. *If you only knew.*

But something held him back from giving the order, coward that he was. He had the vague sense that he ought to get that baby out of there, and the old woman on the end. He turned to the sea, a part of him somehow imploring the deep. He saw a dark speck on the horizon that was no doubt the Genovese flagship.

Mawkish idiot. Get on with it.

"Cap?" he heard Sully ask from a vast distance.

He did not answer. He listened to the wind. No message came, only the howl in his head of ghosts craving blood. He wanted it to be over. He wanted peace.

Then he did not have to speak to Sully. The flick of his eyes out to sea, then down to his own blood-speckled hands, was signal enough.

"Right," said the other captain with a nod.

It was a comfort, his men's loyalty. How well they knew his mind. His brethren.

"Readyyy!" the Irishman sang out.

Lazar raised his head and looked. It was his deed, after all. He would not turn away like some tender woman who couldn't bear to watch the death scene of an opera. Stiffly he turned.

"Aaaim!"

It was at that moment he saw the apparition in the doorway.

Dressed in sepulchral virgin white, long hair billowing in the draft, she stood in the gloom of the magazine's shadow. The heavy stone doorway framed her like a sarcophagus. Her unfathomable eyes were stricken wide with horror, disbelief. Then she broke out, floating silently, swiftly, blindly before the line of guns before anyone could stop her. They would riddle her body with lead.

He roared her name and plunged down the line to meet her. Distantly he heard Sully shout, *"Guns down!"*

He reached her, the impact of her running body, slender and lithe, slammed against him. She punched him hard in the chest at once and screamed unintelligible curses. He captured her by the arms, wanted to give her a good shake to bring her to her senses but feared to break the delicate bones. He started speaking softly to her whatever nonsense came to mind, but that trick wasn't working this time. She ripped herself out of his arms and dropped to her knees. She threw back her head, exposing the pretty white line of her throat.

"Do it if you have the courage, you skulking thief," she snarled, a tigress cub cornered, possibly dangerous but probably not.

He looked down his nose at her, pretending scorn to hide his bafflement. He was going to thrash Vicar well. Of all the damned nuisances.

"Pray tell, do what, little fool?" he asked with far more self-possession than he felt.

"Cut my throat!" she cried savagely. "But I promise you, do not dare leave me alive if you destroy my kin."

He felt the edges of his resolve curl slightly with nausea at her ferocity. She was pure and young, and bloody well ought to have swooned a long time ago. But, typical Ascencioner, she was born to fight.

"Do it, damn you!"

"I'll box your ears, that's what," he muttered. He yanked her to her feet, dimly aware of her father wailing to her. They both ignored him.

"I will not permit you to do this, Captain—whatever you call yourself, Lazar," she said, shaking. The light in her shining eyes was near madness.

"You can't stop me," he said. "I'm sorry."

Her hands balled into pretty fists. She brought them up against her rosy cheeks and pressed her knuckles in until she made white blotches. Her eyes were frantic. She refused to look at him. She looked only at her relatives.

Her voice broke. "Why? Why? What have we done? What is our crime?"

"Surely you can see this is vendetta," Lazar said quietly.

"But the vendetta is outlawed!" she shouted, shoving uselessly at his chest, as if he were a dolt and now all was solved. "King Alphonse made that law twenty years ago!"

He shook his head at this absurd point. As if he didn't know. Too much kindness was what had gotten Father killed. "It is my duty."

"To kill my family?" She sobbed, a wild laugh. "What duty is that? You've taken everything we own! Isn't that enough?" Her eyes, the rich color of mahogany, filled with tears as she stared up at him. "You said I should trust you!"

He gazed down at her, mute and strangled, unable to fit words to the jumbled nets of wretchedness within him. "Allegra."

Her only reply was a blink that made the tears well over and run down her cheeks. The defenselessness of the picture she made enraged him inexplicably all at once. He reeled away, then back to her, in exasperation.

"Why don't you ask your precious father, then? Go on! Tell her, old man! Tell her what you did. Tell her who I am! Tell her how you turned traitor and sold my father and all the Fiori to the Genovese!"

She looked over at Monteverdi, eyes round. "Papa?"

Monteverdi was turning an odd shade of greenish white as he backed against the wall.

"Papa, say something!" she said brokenly.

The governor's eyes darted from Allegra to his staring kin, to Lazar and his men with rifles.

"Admit it," Lazar said, "and I will let these children and these old ones go."

"Papa?" she nearly screamed.

Before the old don said a word, Lazar already saw that Monteverdi was coming unhinged. Now that he was being asked to state the truth before witnesses, he was going to deny it.

"Daughter, I am innocent. I have never seen this outlaw before in my life!" he declared.

Lazar laughed, though his heart thumped with anger. He thrust Allegra into the Irishman's arms. "I don't have bloody time for this. Sullivan! Lock her in my cabin, have Vicar give her the goddamned laudanum, and see that she doesn't harm herself."

It was her father who shouted when she wilted out of Sully's arms and fastened herself around Lazar's knees. He looked down in bewilderment at her crumpled form on the flagstone. She lay nearly prostrate before him, her tender lips nigh at his boot.

"*Jesu Christi,*" he began, recoiling from her. For he, the Devil of Antigua who feared neither God nor man, felt himself beginning in the furthest reaches of his mind to panic.

"Take me instead," she murmured over and over.

I was planning on it, obviously, he thought acidly, but silenced with awe and nausea at her sacrifice, he could not bring himself to say the words.

"Allegra Monteverdi, get to your feet!" her father bellowed from the edge of the wall. "I'll die a thousand deaths before I'll see you thus!"

She did not seem to hear.

Lazar bent down to lift her away. She captured his hand, began plying it with pleading kisses, smoothing soft lips over every coarse knuckle and whispering mercy and pleas. He watched her, transfixed, staring down at the burnished streaks of gold in her coppery tresses.

Her tears moistened his skin, giving water back to the dried flecks of blood so that they ran red again, mingling salt. He reckoned she must taste it, the blood of his killing. If she did, she gave no sign.

She raised her eyes to his, silver tears clumped on the tips of her lashes. "Please," she said in a strangled whisper, "let them go, Lazar. Take me instead. I'll do anything you ask. I give you my word."

God, he wanted to yield to her.

And that he would betray his parents a second time—run away again because this duty was too hard for him—filled him with rage. He felt cruelty gathering inside him, a pitiful last defense against the crumbling of all his resolve before her.

"Anything, eh?"

She closed her eyes like an angel and nodded fervently. A low, piratical laugh bubbled up from him like molten tar. He took her chin between his thumb and fingers and glowered down into her eyes.

"And are you worth so much?"

She opened her eyes with new fear at this. She sat back on her shapely haunches in surprise.

"You have no idea what you ask." Anger came over him in one rising gust. He released her face roughly and straightened to his full height. "Are you such a prize that you can replace what I've lost? My mother, my father, my home? My future? My pride?" He barked, a jackal's laugh. Wildness was coming unleashed inside of him. "Can you get me back these things? Can you bring my father back from the dead? Take you? What are you? You know nothing of it—God damn it," he choked out.

Pacing away on legs that quaked beneath him, he jerked the skullcap off his head and wiped the sweat from his brow with a savage pass. He gave her a burning glance. "I've made concessions enough for you already. They die." He opened his arms wide in a vast, sarcastic shrug, the symbol of his existence. *"Mea culpa."*

She did not move or speak. She merely stared at him, pale, the wind and the morning sun rippling through her long, gold-streaked hair while her dark eyes searched his. She looked exhausted and unnervingly wise.

"Then I must choose, too." Unsteadily, she climbed to her feet and walked to her father.

Lazar slumped his shoulders and looked at the sky, letting out an exasperated exhale. He did not try to stop her.

She stood with the governor as the others knelt. She lifted her chin, seeming to gather strength from the finality of her decision. In a moment she forced a slow, cold, collected smile. She held out her hands, palms upward like a stone grotto Virgin, making a mockery of his shrug.

"Go on, Captain. It is your duty."

He stared at her, and she stared back, flaunting her courage as if she knew his deepest secrets, and it hit him that she, a pampered slip of a girl, would stay with her kin and die, while he, a hero's son, had fled and lived to become a curse to all who crossed his path, a curse, aye, even to himself.

He stared at her, at a loss. He could not tear his gaze away from her ruthless beauty forcing him to face the truth. The ghosts in his head howled for blood. But, for the first time, he saw that he was not here for their sake.

No, it was the killer in himself that craved revenge—the avenging monster that had sprung, phoenixlike, from the ashes of the ruined princeling, as if the wound done him was so deep there could be no mending it. There could only be equal death for death. To savor this day, he'd stayed alive at any cost, even at the cost of his soul.

But when it was done, what in the name of God would be left him?

There would be no farm, as he sometimes daydreamed, no fields of crops, no homemade wine. It would never happen, and he knew why. When he finished here and saw his men back safely to the West Indies, he meant to do it. There was a silver bullet he kept in his desk especially for the occasion.

The high winds raked at him. No one had the power to stop him now. All he had to do was say the word.

Stricken, he gazed at Allegra. For the first time in his life, he had no idea what to do next.

Her crystalline composure shattered him. She searched his eyes with soft anguish, accusing, yet ready to forgive, making him unbearably human, not an impervious angel of wrath, but a man—and helpless—for he had no defense against those trusting honey-brown eyes, and the satin tremor of those rose-petal lips.

The world wavered. Something was rising in him, a flood tide he could not stem, a cup he could not drink from, more unbearable than shame. Shame, rage, anything but this. He would drown in inconsolable grief. Everyone he'd ever loved was dead, and he was always going to be alone. He knew it.

"Lazar," she called out softly.

He looked for her through the rising tide. The sound of her voice steadied him. She looked deeply into his eyes with a calm that calmed him, a strength that fortified him.

He drew a breath. He held it.

Then he did not look right or left. He did not want to see his men, who could only remind him of this beast, this thing he had become. He did not stop to consider. He kept his gaze and all his battered soul fixed on her, a star above his storm. Then his voice came, a strangled whisper.

"Let them go."

⚜ CHAPTER ⚜
SEVEN

His men looked around uncertainly at one another, but Lazar stared only at her. Her relatives began shoving away, and still Lazar gazed at her, looking utterly lost. Allegra stared back at him from across the sudden chaos, fresh tears in her eyes.

"What about the governor, Cap?" one of the men asked. "Him, too?"

Lazar didn't seem to hear.

"Hold him," the Irish captain muttered for him, gesturing.

One of her relatives tried to take her hand, but Allegra shook off the pulling grasp. She didn't even turn her head, as if in a heartbeat all her loyalties had changed.

It did not matter who he was, in this moment. He was just a man with gentle hands, a wonderful laugh, and more pain in his midnight eyes than anyone should have to bear alone.

Steadily, she walked to him through the fleeing crowd, and when she reached him, she slipped her arms around his waist, laid her head against his chest. His arms came up around her, and he was clinging to her, his face half buried in her hair.

She could hear his heart racing as if he was terrified, could feel his big body trembling with inward pain. She spoke soft words to him as he had to her a short while earlier, telling him he had done the right thing, that everything would be all right.

"Allegra," he breathed as he shuddered, "I cannot let you go now. I cannot be left with nothing."

She paused, not knowing how to respond, when suddenly she felt him tense in her arms. He swiftly lifted his head.

"Stop him!" he shouted.

She turned around, but Lazar's arms held her back when she saw Papa standing on the precipice, where the wall dropped hundreds of feet to the rocky sea below.

"You spineless bastard! Get down!" Lazar thundered, pulling out his pistol and aiming, though he didn't shoot. "You'll not cheat me!"

"Papa, no!" Allegra screamed when horror gave her back her voice. She began fighting to get free of Lazar's hold, but he would not let her go.

"Fine. You win," Monteverdi said heavily to Lazar. He ignored the men clutching at his clothing. "You've turned her against me, just like her mother."

Allegra gasped. "No, Papa, never!"

Lazar's arms tightened around her. "Easy," he murmured to her. "He knows his crimes. It's his decision."

Monteverdi looked down from his pedestal there, gazing brokenly into her eyes. Tears filled his eyes. "Forgive me," he said. He turned around slowly, facing the sea.

Allegra heard herself pleading. "Papa, don't! No, please, Papa, I love you, please don't do this, I can't bear it—"

He turned away, and it seemed he only leaned.

Then he was gone.

Allegra screamed, lunged toward the place on the wall where her father was no longer standing, but Lazar held her back, grasping her by the shoulders. With a broken cry, she turned in to his arms, weeping her heart out against him, scarcely aware of his silence as he wrapped his strength around her.

Within an hour of Monteverdi's suicide, they were under way, pouring down the road to the port, scrambling into their loaded ships, leaving columns of black smoke billowing to the sky over Little Genoa behind them. The great portion of the hot, humid day was taken up by a skirmish with a few Genovese warships that had arrived too late.

Now it was eventide. A fiery gold sunset bloomed ahead of them, spanning the western horizon, and *The Whale* wafted toward it on white clouds of sail, unscathed by her fight.

Lazar let the men relax.

They sat down on the decks and reclined in the rigging as he addressed them from the quarterdeck, raising his voice over the snapping of canvas and the soughing of wind. He praised the valiance and discipline of the whole company, noting a few individuals who had fought especially well. Nothing was said about Goliath, whom he had executed shortly before the episode on the wall, precisely as he had promised to anyone who broke the rules.

He gave no excuses for his change of heart before the Monteverdi clan nor offered any explanation for the presence of the girl. He was relieved when no one asked about it. The lads had what they wanted, which was the gold. Looking around at their sweaty faces, he supposed they figured that in the past he'd always shown good sense as their captain and therefore must know what he was doing now.

If only he did.

He had no idea what he was feeling and was not sure he wanted to know. All he could seem to think about was the tearstained, grief-stricken girl who lay, drugged and sleeping, in his bed. His consolation prize, instead of massacre. He still could not understand what had happened to him, what she had done to him up there on the wall. She moved him in a way few creatures ever had. This made her unutterably dangerous.

He knew what he had to do, and he fancied she knew it, too. He was going to go down to his cabin and exact his price for showing mercy.

She would pay with her virgin blood, and he did not intend to be particularly gentle. It was the only way he could see to regain mastery of the situation after the way he'd laid his will at her feet.

In the weeks to come, he would make good use of her. He had never taken a virgin before—he had never wanted the headache—but in Allegra's case the idea held a certain charm. He would make her his plaything, his completely, until he tired of her. When he grew bored with her, he decided, he would present her as his sister or cousin or some such thing and marry her off to one of his acquaintances in his other life, in Fort-de-France, on Martinique.

He would see she was well taken care of, at least that she had some decent husband, not like that bastard Clemente, who would soon be finished off by Jeffers and his lads. With her Paris upbringing, the Creole gentlemen planters would go mad for her. She'd fetch him a handsome price.

But first, he thought idly, *first* he would teach her precisely how this world used beautiful creatures with noble young souls. He would ruin her innocence, because he could not afford the way it moved him.

After a few moments of congratulating the company on their fine work and telling them the totals of the booty taken and what each share amounted to, he rewarded them with the barrels of good Ascencion wine taken from the governor's cellars, then left them to their antics.

He slipped through the hatch to the mid-deck and wandered to his cabin, opened the door, and paused for a moment to gaze at the girl curled up in a ball in his berth. She was a mess. Her hair was a tangle, her white silk dress torn, stained with black powder, her face puffy from crying. Why, then, was she the most beautiful thing he'd ever seen?

He closed the door quietly behind him, ungirded himself of his weapons, and pulled off his vest, glancing at Allegra from time to time in speculation. He went to the washstand, where he poured some tepid water from the jug into the porcelain basin, then leaned over and splashed his face and neck.

He ducked his head to look in the small round mirror, running his hand over the soft black spikes bristling up from his scalp. Just a month earlier he'd had a fine, rich, jet-black mane past his shoulders, only to be forced to hack it off when *The Whale*'s resident lice had had the audacity to jump from the lowly sailors' heads to his.

So much for vanity, he thought with a sigh.

He picked up his ivory-handled straight-edge, dipped it in the water, and commenced the pleasant monotony of shaving, wondering at his own procrastination, delaying Allegra's ravishment. He wished she would wake up and fight him, hurt him a few more times with her stubborn denials of his identity. He had never taken a woman against her will in his life.

Of course, it might not be entirely against her will, he admitted, smiling slightly at the memory of how he had coaxed her into returning his kisses up there in the tower.

As he stirred the water idly with the straight-edge, he paused to wonder if he should hide the thing when he was through using it, in case his little captive took it into her head to cut his throat for ruining her life, much as Monteverdi had ruined his.

Ach, who cares? he thought. She'd only be doing him a favor. He didn't think she'd do anything so bloody anyway, especially when to kill him would leave her at the mercy of the crew. She wasn't stupid.

He scraped the straightedge deftly along his throat, then came around over the edge of his squarish chin. At length, he rinsed his face, then stripped nude to give the rest of his body a brisk scrubbing, glancing occasionally at Allegra, because her reaction to the sight of her first naked man would no doubt prove amusing.

But she remained fast asleep even after he had donned fresh clothes, soft buckskin breeches and a loose-fitting shirt of fine-woven white lawn. He sauntered to the bed and sat down on the edge of it near her.

"Wake up, little kitten," he called softly, petting her pale, silken shoulder, bared through a tear in her dress. He leaned down and kissed the shoulder.

She did not stir. He frowned, wondering how much laudanum Vicar had given her. He felt her brow, but she did not have a fever. No, he concluded, she was merely exhausted.

Well, he preferred her awake when he took her maidenhead. He rose, standing over her, hands on his hips as he looked her over. She appeared to have been through a war.

"*Chérie,* you will not *do* in such a state," he told her.

Allegra slept on.

He sauntered back to the washstand, lifted out the porcelain basin, and changed the water, perfuming it with some of his cologne in a mysterious impulse to cover her in his scent. He returned to her side with the water and the softest washcloth he could find, and he sat down.

He took his time undressing her, ignoring his slowly thickening arousal and the fantasies that whispered through him as he easily rid her of her ruined dress. She lay full-length on his bed now, clad only in her chemise. He stared down at her, sorely tested as he studied the curving lines of her slender, elegant figure.

She was limp in his arms as he slipped the straps of the chemise from her shoulders. He wiped her tearstained face first, and she stirred a little, but then she merely nestled against his lap when he placed her head on his thigh.

"What am I going to do with you?" he asked in a barely audible murmur as he rinsed the cloth, stroking her white throat and chest, rounding her shoulders, taking his time as he traced the lines of her slender arms with the wet, scented cloth.

He rinsed it again, swallowing hard at the sight of her exposed breasts, the nipples like soft, peach-flavored candies. He worked the ivory satin of her chemise lower, to her navel, where he paused just to gaze at the creamy expanse of her flat belly. He laid his hand on her stomach, where she'd said Golly had punched her.

Punched her.

Incomprehensible.

"Poor baby," he whispered. She really was just a baby. How young twenty was, he thought. Eight years his junior, and a virgin. He caressed her cheek, then rinsed the cloth again. He was surprised when she moved a little in her semiconscious state.

"Lazar," she whispered, loosely clutching at a handful of his shirt. She made a sound like a tiny groan of pleasure, then drifted still again.

Her whisper left him sitting there, momentarily blinded with desire.

"Oh, Christ," he breathed, closing his eyes, his mouth gone dry. He could not resist the temptation. He leaned down and grazed her lips with his own as he cupped her breast softly in his palm, feeling the nipple harden under his touch.

Give her to somebody else? Do you seriously think you could ever share her?

He ignored the inner question, willing her to stay asleep as he stroked her sides and belly, explored the other breast. He kissed her throat, barely parting his lips.

She moaned again, shifting slightly in his lap, arching instinctively for him. Lazar stared at her, forcing himself to be still. Only his heart pounded, and his erection throbbed.

He sat up again and reached for the cloth, pressing it to his own brow, but the water did little to cool him. Staring, he cast it aside. Finally he pushed the material down over her hips, revealing the dark, silky tuft veiling her femininity.

She slept, but he found her senses were awake to him. He ran his fingers slowly through the tiny curls between her legs and stroked her, closing his eyes in ecstasy to feel her wetness lave the tip of his middle finger.

Exquisite.

He opened his eyes again and watched desire play across her face while her hips lifted slightly for his softest caress. He did not push inside but waited for her to seek it, and when she did, he slid his finger into her deeply, holding his breath because she was so beautifully tight. He watched her round breasts heave, while her moaning breaths led him deeper into a trance of sensuality. When he rested his thumb ever so lightly on her rigid nub, her eyes barely opened. He met her drugged, heavy-lidded gaze, wet and hazy with longing.

Her eyes closed again, and he withdrew to slide the satin chemise down over her thighs, his mind made up to have her at once. He stood to pull the chemise the rest of the way off her, and that was when he saw the leather cords, still bound about her slim ankles from when he had hobbled her earlier in the gate tower.

He stopped abruptly, taken aback.

He touched one white ankle and saw the redness of the chafed skin, like a rope burn.

Allegra suddenly turned onto her side again and curled up into a ball as if it had been nothing but a strange dream. She began breathing normally, both hands tucked under her cheek.

He stared at her gold-tipped lashes fanned against her freckled cheek, thinking how she looked absurdly like a little girl.

"Jesus, what am I doing?" he whispered. He stood there for a second, wanting her as he had never wanted a woman before, but he couldn't do it. Not this way.

Somehow he turned himself around and paced away from the bed, heart pounding. He crossed his arms over his chest and glanced back at her hungrily, eyeing the soft curves of her backside, but he kept his distance until guilt adequately overcame his lust.

He went to his armoire, pulled out a soft linen shirt like the one he had on, and returned to the bed, dressing her in it. He cut the leather cords from her ankles. He meant to leave her in peace then, but he couldn't bring himself to go.

Instead he lay down behind her, molding his body around

hers while he held her close against him, his right arm around her waist. They fit together as if they had been made for each other.

She let out a pretty sigh of contentment, nestling against him, and though the wriggle of her derriere against his groin was torment, he gave in to a slight, weary smile as she slept on. His smile faded, however, when he admitted to himself that— all his useless vaunting aside—he had no right to her, no right to any of this.

Bold, noble Miss Monteverdi had made her oath in the heat of the moment to save her family, but it was him she had saved, in truth. He had no right to hold her to her reckless, selfless vow, but he *would* hold her to it. He locked his arms around her as if she were his life raft and swore to the Heaven that hated him that he was never letting her go.

The hell with giving her away. Ever.

She was his now. He had brought her into his exile, carried her off like Hades with his springtime goddess, an unwilling bride to share his sufferings—not that he had any intention of marrying her. For reasons he could not explain, he needed to make her see that what he'd become was never what he'd intended. She must understand he had suffered.

He nestled his face in her streaming hair. It smelled of smoke and gunpowder now, but the scent of flowers was still there, very faint. Then he petted her silky hair back from tickling his nose and asked himself a simple question. Honestly, was it so imperative to regain mastery of the situation over this defenseless girl? He was secure in his own strength, and she was surely terrified. Need he break her for the sin of stopping him from doing something that curdled his blood in the first place?

For many long moments, he considered the question as he listened to Allegra's breathing and gently caressed her hip.

He had lived the past fifteen years of his life fueled by hate, ridden by death, with no other purpose than revenge, and look, he thought, what it got him.

Nothing.

If he had gone through with it—wiped out all those lives— he would have felt just as empty as always. And yet, lying here with Allegra, he didn't feel empty at all.

The knowledge did not frighten him, though perhaps it ought to. He felt as though she'd cut him free from a millstone that had been tied around his neck so long he'd forgotten it was there.

He could feel something profound happening inside him, deeper than arousal, surer than all his fears, could almost feel his life charting a mysterious new course for him. All he had to do was let it happen. He was not even sure he had a choice, so certain it felt inside him, a sea change.

Everything he'd been living for had just ended. She had ended it for him in an instant, but it did not feel like an ending to him.

Perhaps, he thought as he held her warm body close, a new voyage in his life had just begun.

⚜ CHAPTER ⚜
EIGHT

Allegra leaned against the rails, staring out to sea. The day was hot and overcast, the waves the gray-green of tarnished copper, and her whole world was as unsteady as the rocking deck beneath her feet. She was pondering the weighty fact that her life was over.

She was alone in earnest now.

How could Papa have done this to her? she asked the sea over and over again, brooding. Surely he had known that after Mama took her life nine years ago, another suicide was the one thing she could not bear. Disbelief had left her numb, and grief exhausted her, but now the raw, broken feeling of loss was beginning to give way to anger. At least the anger held a spark of life in it.

Until this morning, she had been too devastated to assess her situation or to think about the future, but she was beginning to feel her strength return, and, as the captive of a notorious pirate, God knew, she would need it.

All her efforts, all her principles, all her high-flown ideals—all for naught. The victress of the people had become the plaything of a man, she mused bitterly. A man who stood for everything she despised—vendetta and violence, crime and trickery.

She could even have believed he was the Prince except for one small problem: he had boarded his ship, lifted his anchor, and sailed away from Ascencion.

No, he was a pirate, and she was his captive, and what a perfectly absurd situation in which to find herself.

She scowled down at the waves.

Really, she was much too sensible for this sort of thing, and back on Ascencion, she had work to do.

She caught Lazar's scent on the humid breeze a moment before he appeared beside her. She had come to know that scent, that warmth, and the rhythm of his breathing when he slept.

He said nothing, only folded his arms on the wooden rail and joined her in staring at the sea. Neither looked at the other.

Two mornings now she had awakened in his arms, but beyond the admitted comfort of his embrace, he kept a respectful distance while she grieved. When she cried about Papa during the night, though she tried not to make a sound, he stroked her hair and her back, never saying a word, simply giving her his soft reassurance.

His kindness frightened her. She did not trust him.

"The sea is a vast and lonely place," he mused in a low voice.

"Strange words from a pirate," she replied in a tone like a small steel knife.

"Allegra." He sighed. "Don't judge me when you know nothing about me."

"I know plenty," she said in cold, quiet tones.

"I'm not going to hurt you."

But I will bleed for you, won't I?

She turned and looked up at him, feeling as though she were seeing him for the first time.

Why, the man looked practically civilized. When had he donned a cravat and waistcoat? she wondered. His clothing was in impeccable taste even by Parisian standards. He was bareheaded under the leaden skies. His black hair made his eyes look black, too, beneath his long, heartbreaking lashes.

He glanced down almost hesitantly at her, distress in his

marvelous, warm eyes. "I am worried about you, Allegra. I don't want to see you lose yourself in grief."

"I shall be cheerful, then, to amuse you," she said, looking swiftly at the waves again to mask her panic at his gentle concern.

"That's not what I meant," he said softly, gazing down at her.

She refused to look at him. His animal beauty unnerved her, especially after that sinful fantasy born of laudanum—that he had undressed her, slipped his warm, callused fingers inside her—but it was his undemanding patience, his careful, determined gentleness, that terrified her most.

If he had raped her, it would have been simple to hate him. Why it was not simple already, she could not guess. He had stolen everything she owned, burned down her home, torn her away from her family, made havoc of her formerly bright future. He had ruined her, and he had dared, *dared* claim to be her beloved Prince.

She didn't know who he was.

He had destroyed her life for no apparent reason but his own selfishness and his wanton lust for destruction, and soon he would make use of her body. Her heart, her mind, her inner self, were the last things she still owned, and she vowed he would not have them.

He was subtle, trying to conquer her with soft words, comforting touches, and that haunted look in his eyes that seemed the very answer to her loneliness, but she refused his every attempt. She did not trust him, this thief, this fraud, and she did not trust herself around him.

He sighed again, studying his hands where they rested on the rail. "Soon we'll pass Gibraltar. May run into a fight there. The Atlantic crossing should take about a month, depending on the winds."

"May I ask where we're going?"

"You may ask anything you want, *chérie*. The West Indies. Home."

She bit her lip against the urge to point out that it was certainly not home to her. "What if I don't want to go to the West Indies?"

"Where do you want to go?"

"Ascencion."

He forced a patient smile. "Tell me anyplace else you want to go, and I'll take you there on a holiday once I've concluded my business with my, er, colleagues."

"A holiday." Allegra studied him dubiously, refusing to fall for this lie. "Perhaps it's time you told me exactly what it is you want of me, Captain."

She refused to call him Lazar.

He merely gazed down at her for a long moment. "Allegra," he said, "I am not going to hurt you."

She folded her arms over her chest as she stared up at him, feeling small with the way he towered over her. "Too late."

"Be fair. You haven't heard my side of the story yet."

"Nothing you can say will bring my father back to life."

"I did not kill him, Allegra."

She clenched her arms more tightly as her lower lip began to tremble.

"You scared him out of his senses. That's the only reason he would do such a thing. It's the same as if you had pushed him off the side yourself. Don't touch me," she said swiftly when he reached toward her face.

He touched her anyway, cupping her cheek. "I am not the one to blame. But you must come to that realization on your own. I'm not going to force you to face the truth about him, or about me." He lowered his hand. "I took all the files and official documents from the governor's office, so when you are feeling up to it, perhaps you'll wish to look through them. Then maybe you'll see that your father was not . . . ah, a nice man."

"I know he wasn't a nice man," she said through clenched

teeth. "But that doesn't mean he betrayed King Alphonse, and that does not mean you are the Prince."

"I'm not going to argue with you. You'll find the truth on your own, in time," he said gently. "I'm not going to force you to do anything you don't want to do. Do you understand?"

She tore her gaze from his, refusing in the nick of time to be enticed by his efforts to make her drop her guard. "Do you realize I have nothing now? What am I to do? I have no one."

"You have me."

She gave a bitter laugh and looked at the sea.

"I will take care of you."

"To be sure."

He gazed down at her in distress. "I know how it feels. I lost my family, too."

"Yes, I know, the great Fiori," she replied caustically, swiping away a tear before he saw.

He studied her, at a loss. "Don't you remember how it was between us that night when we were in the tunnels? We were getting along fine until I told you my name. Why is that?"

"We were getting along fine until you put a gun to my head!" she shouted.

He shook his head. "You knew I wouldn't hurt you."

"I knew no such thing! You're a madman! There's no telling what you'll do!"

He arched one brow at her, then glanced over dryly at his men, a few of whom had turned, in curiosity, at her outburst. "I told you, you have nothing to fear from me. If you will try to trust me a little, I believe we can get along together quite suitably."

"I will never trust you." She clenched her jaw, for even as she said it, she knew it was not entirely true. He still inspired in her an illogical sense of safety. But she sealed her lips and avoided his gaze, refusing to soften toward him. Everything she'd lost was his fault, and she could not, would not, believe he was her Prince.

He searched her face with a deep gaze, alight with promises. "I have not forgotten how you stared at me through the fire, Allegra, and how you welcomed my kiss."

"That was before you made my father k-kill himself!" she wailed.

"You know that is a lie. I won't disguise the truth—yes, I wanted Monteverdi dead, with good reason. In fact, first I wanted to kill you and make him watch. That's the sole reason I followed you in the square that night and ended up saving you from Clemente—I had no interest in you but as a pawn in my revenge, but then . . ." He faltered. "I just . . . couldn't."

She stared up at him. "Is this supposed to reassure me?" she asked incredulously.

"I'm merely trying to be honest and show you, you have nothing to fear from me anymore." He looked impatiently at the mast. "I know you don't understand. I don't understand it myself, but somehow you have changed everything."

He shot her a searing look, then lowered his head.

"You are mine now. Understand that. We are bound together by your father's crime, whether either of us likes it or not. But I will not hurt you, Allegra. I swear it on my mother's grave. The graves of the great Fiori," he muttered in sarcasm as he stalked off, brushing past her.

In baffled silence, she turned and watched him go. She gazed at the powerful expanse of his wide shoulders and his lean, tapered waist as he marched off in princely affront, descending down the hatch.

He was a fraud. He was not Lazar di Fiore.

Her father had not been a traitor to King Alphonse all this time. And Mama had not killed herself over something that had been all Papa's fault.

Lazar walked into the stateroom adjoining his cabin, an airy space that served as both dining and sitting room. Vicar looked up from his book when he slammed the door. Lazar paused by the door for a moment.

"I am going to strangle her," he announced, and then he walked over to the liquor chest and poured himself a brandy.

Behind him, Vicar chuckled. "Ah, rejection. A new experience for you, eh, my boy?"

Lazar tossed back his drink and turned to face his grinning tutor as Vicar whisked his spectacles off and tucked them in his breast pocket.

"She hates me."

"Welcome to the world of mortal men."

Lazar regarded him dryly. "Truly, I am undone by your sympathy." He sighed, looking down into his empty glass. "At least she's out of bed."

"She has begun to rally?"

"With a vengeance."

"Good," the older man said, nodding. "Try to be patient with her, lad. She needs to be angry for a while. It would be unnatural if she weren't."

Lazar gave a bored, one-shouldered shrug and set his empty glass down. "I liked her better when she was drugged." He moved impatiently toward the porthole, scowling. "How do I deal with her, Vicar? I feel as though I can do nothing right with her."

The Englishman merely laughed.

"Why do you sound so delighted?" he mumbled, staring out the porthole. "You enjoy seeing me suffer?"

"Immensely. I have never seen a woman get to you this way."

"What way?" Lazar studied the waves, wondering when they had become so blue. In the sky, there were the most wonderful clouds piled in the west where columns of sunlight had begun to pierce through the morning's overcast.

"I say, Captain, is your hearing bad?"

"Hmm?" Lazar turned and looked inquiringly at Vicar, who shook his head at him in amusement.

"I just asked if you recovered the family heirlooms you sought in Little Genoa's treasury."

"Ah, yes!" Lazar exclaimed. "Just a moment. I'll show you."

He went into the cabin, unlocked the safe, and withdrew his father's ancient broadsword and some of his mother's finer pieces of jewelry. Lovingly he examined the necklace of diamonds and purple amethysts, which had matched the color of her violet eyes.

Vicar admired the fortune in jewels, then Lazar unwrapped the long package swathed in sackcloth.

"Excelsior," he said in a hushed voice.

He grasped the hilt of the mighty broadsword and slid it from its jeweled sheath. The wide, double-edged blade gleamed gold. The sword was even heavier than a cutlass. He gave the precious sheath carefully to Vicar to examine it, then took the hilt in both hands, arms straight and low.

"The first king of the Fiori, Bonifacio the Black," he told Vicar, "cut down the invading Saracens with this sword. A couple hundred years later, the French Crusaders who built the original keep at Belfort tried to take over the island. That time it was King Salvatore the Fourth who put down the insurrection. This blade beheaded twenty rebel knights."

Vicar shook his head in wonder.

"Ascencion, you see, has been invaded by practically every people on the face of the earth. Most have left their mark one way or another. Although originally," he added with a crooked grin, "it was a penal colony of the Roman Empire where the most dangerous criminals were sent to live out their lives in hard labor in the marble quarries."

Vicar chuckled. "Your earliest forebears."

"I'm afraid so."

Planting his feet in fighting stance, Lazar swung the blade

experimentally from side to side, giving it a light flick at the extremes of the arc so that it sang through the air.

He was awed by the feel of it in his hands.

"When I was a boy, I couldn't even lift it," he said. "It made my father seem to me all the more like a god."

He remembered that the old reports he'd collected had stated that Excelsior had still been in Alphonse's hand when his body had been found at the scene of the slaughter. For a moment Lazar was silent, and the sword lowered in his grasp until its deadly tip touched the worn Persian rug.

Just as they reached D'Orofio Pass, Mama gathered little Anna, sleeping, on her lap and sat back against the velvet squabs. "My!" she said. "How that sea tossed! Thank heavens we all are safe." The words had barely left her lips when the first shouts sounded.

"Lazar?" Vicar said as if from a great distance.

They came out of nowhere, guns and knives. Father, shouting orders at the guards, barreled out of the carriage with Excelsior drawn, and for a moment the masked men were afraid of him.

He remembered that look on his father's face, his sudden stillness, as the king realized before anyone else did that they all were dead. Father turned his head and looked him in the eyes amid the chaos all around them.

Survive, he said, and hold the line.

He obeyed, fleeing as fast as he could just as the first one swung out with his knife at Alphonse while another dragged his little brother, Pip, from the coach and killed him right before his eyes, cut his throat. He had stood there staring for a second, frozen with cold horror, then Father bellowed, *Run!*

So he did.

Ran and ran with bile in his throat, heard the guards and the footmen and the ladies-in-waiting die like animals behind him. When he made out his mother's screams, he stopped and turned back, but then they came crashing after him through the briers. He fled through the lightning and storm, forgetting in his terror that he headed straight toward the sea cliffs. . . .

Presently, as Lazar held the royal sword that had been in his family since the Dark Ages, he was filled with so strange and uncanny a premonition that he had to put the weapon down on the polished dining table.

"Excuse me," he mumbled to Vicar, then went into the cabin and out to the sea balcony beyond, beneath the overhanging stern. He braced both hands upon the railing and lowered his head, his eyes shut tight.

A part of him was still a bewildered thirteen-year-old waiting to wake from the nightmare. A part of him was still running.

❧ CHAPTER ❧
NINE

The sailors were seized with terror at this and said, "What have you done?"

They knew Jonah was trying to escape from God, because he had told them so.

Allegra sat in the stateroom, reading the Bible by the strong, gold light of afternoon, seeking solace in the ancient, holy words.

Jonah replied, "Take me and throw me into the sea, and then it will grow calm for you. For I can see it is my fault this violent storm has happened to you."

Yahweh had arranged that a great whale should be there to swallow Jonah; and Jonah remained in the belly of the whale for three days and three nights. From the belly of the fish he prayed to his God; he said: "You cast me into the abyss, into the heart of the sea, and the flood surrounded me. All your waves, all your billows, washed over me." And I said: "I am cast out from your sight. How shall I ever look again on your holy Temple? The waters surrounded me right to my throat, the abyss was all around me. The seaweed was wrapped around my head at the roots of the mountains. I went down into the countries underneath the earth, to the peoples of the past. . . ."

Allegra bowed her head, closed her eyes, and prayed for guidance. There had to be some reason Heaven had placed this benighted man in her path. She asked God for discernment so she could make out the truth in the baffling dilemma the pirate captain presented.

"Praying for deliverance from the Devil, madam?" a deep, familiar voice inquired.

She looked up to see the Devil of Antigua sauntering across the stateroom toward the cabin. The air of effortless command in his walk, the power in his broad shoulders, the self-assurance in the very angle of his chin, made her feel all the more keenly the powerlessness of her captivity, and she chafed against it. Surely not once in any of her salon conversations about liberty had she ever imagined she would lose her own.

Closing the Bible, she watched her captor pass. He looked very much the grand sea captain in his dark blue waistcoat, the sleeves of his shirt bright white, a neat and efficient cravat tied around his golden throat. She listened to him moving about in the adjoining cabin, wondering what mischief he was up to now.

"I might point out, Miss Monteverdi," he called absently, "that you were the one who begged me to take you, in exchange for sparing your family. As I recall, you swore to do anything I asked—anything at all. I believe those were your exact words. I have been remarkably lenient so far, don't you think?"

She paled, wondering if he was implying his patience with her had come to an end. She did not regret her oath, but it would have been much easier to bear up under her word of honor if Papa had not nullified it.

With a lone tremble that ran the whole course of her body, she decided to go in there and get it over with. She would state her protest, but she would not fight him. Mind made up, she rose, smoothed her dress, and walked to the cabin. Was there any way, she wondered, to prepare oneself mentally before being ravished?

She stood in the doorway, watching him sort through his desk. The captain did not pay her the slightest mind. He certainly did not look like a man maddened with ravening lust.

Suddenly suspicious, she decided to carefully probe his mind, try to learn what plans he had in store for her. "Captain," she said calmly, "I would speak with you."

"I'm honored," he replied without looking up from his search through a drawer.

She opted to begin with roundabout good grace, though it was difficult to be civil to him.

"How is your arm?"

He cocked his head, instantly on his guard. "Healing clean."

She studied him, wondering why he should seem so wary of her when they both knew she was the one at his mercy. Maybe she held some advantage she had not realized. The prospect filled her with sudden hope.

Crossing her arms, she leaned against the doorframe. "Captain, I pride myself on broad-mindedness, but I realize what you said is true. I haven't been fair to you. I apologize. I have been—out of sorts." The words rather stuck in her throat, but she continued. "I am still ignorant of your motives, but I understand it cost you dearly to abandon your vendetta against my family. I would like very much to hear your side of the story, as you asked."

"Well, that is all very generous of you, I'm sure," he said as he straightened up and examined a quill pen, "but I've decided my side of the story is of no consequence, so"—he looked up with a bland smile—"never mind."

This took her by surprise, though she did not know why it should when the man seized every possible opportunity to vex her.

"But I am prepared to listen without judging, as you requested."

"Ah, but I no longer wish to tell you, Miss Monteverdi. You will dine with me tonight in the stateroom, now that you are up and about. Eight o'clock sharp. And after dinner, well." He cast her a very wicked, lazy smile. "We'll see if you're good on your word."

She stared at him, paling. "You said you wouldn't force me."

"You don't believe anything else I say, so why would you believe that?"

She looked about her as her heart began to pound, realizing anew she was completely at his mercy. She didn't know whether to flee screaming or start taking off her clothes.

He laughed at her. "I'm joking. Would you stop looking so terrified? Come, I want to show you something." He took her hand and led her across the cabin to the balcony. At the threshold, she hung back, looking anxiously toward the spindled banister.

The swaying of the ship was obvious here, up and down crazily against the steady, distant line of the horizon.

"Upon my word," she uttered, a trifle seasick at the sight.

"Come and look."

"No, thank you, I-I'll stay here."

"What's the matter?"

"I can't." She swallowed hard. "I'll fall in."

"Fall in?" he asked quizzically. "The water?"

She swallowed hard. "I can't go near the edge."

"By all means, Miss Monteverdi, if you fell in, I would dive in and save you without hesitation."

She lifted her apprehensive gaze from the blue-green waters to his bold grin, forgetting her anxiety to notice how his snug waistcoat flattered his powerful chest and the narrow angle of his waist, sun glancing off every gold button.

"But I've used up all my rescues," she said in dismay.

"Nonsense. Only for that twenty-four-hour period."

When he started toward her with a devilish twinkle in his dark eyes, she shrank from him, sure he meant to pick her up and hold her out over the edge, just to terrify her. It was just the sort of thing he would call fun. But he stopped, probably warned off by her sudden pallor.

He searched her face, her eyes, then his gaze skimmed over her hair and came to rest on her lips, lingering there until she licked them self-consciously. Then she saw the naked hunger in his eyes, and she knew it was only a matter of time.

For now, he turned himself away with a resolute look and went to the edge alone, resting his elbows on the rail as he gazed down at the water, the wind billowing through his loose white sleeves, sculpting the white linen against his muscled arms.

"Dolphins," he said, pointing idly.

"Really?" She stood on her toes in the doorway to the balcony, trying to see them, for she was fond of the merry creatures, but it was no good. On the other hand, his casual stance gave her the most appealing view of his compact bottom.

She forced herself to quit staring. It suddenly seemed acutely unwise to ask him to elaborate on his plans for her. If she opened that topic now, he was sure to give her a firsthand demonstration, and she did not think she could bear it.

The most prudent solution she could discern was to accept his earlier offer of friendship, neither to anger him into handing down some dreadful punishment nor to give in to the seduction she felt in his every glance.

If she was very careful, she thought, she could balance safely on the fine line between extremes until she found some way to extricate herself from this predicament, or until he grew bored with her.

Yes, she thought, she was good at being careful. She had never liked extremes.

"What was it you wanted to talk to me about?" he asked, never turning around.

"I did not want to talk so much as to listen," she ventured.

"How wise you are, Miss Monteverdi," he remarked, sounding not sarcastic for once but thoughtful and distant, even a trifle melancholy.

"My mother always said there's a reason God gave us two ears and one mouth."

"Ah, yes, Lady Cristiana. Beautiful woman," he said. "I once put a toad in her reticule."

Her eyes widened. "How do you know about that?" she demanded.

He looked over his shoulder at her for a long moment, then turned judiciously away in a cool show of reproof.

She furrowed her brow, then brushed the question off. He had already proved himself resourceful and intelligent. If he had found the ancient Fiori caves, he could easily have unearthed a few stories of the Crown Prince's boyish practical jokes. Obviously he had done his research well for his imposture.

He addressed her in an aloof tone, his back to her. "You seem to have reached certain conclusions about me, Miss Monteverdi, but I am willing to overlook them due to the great shock you've had. Only let me ask you a simple question, my dear. You're a clever young woman. You should know the answer in a trice."

"Yes?"

"If I am a charlatan, and my aim was to use this pathetic legend of the so-called Lost Prince in order to seize power on Ascencion, why on God's earth did I leave the island when my alleged goal was accomplished?"

She opened her mouth to reply and discovered she had no answer.

He turned around, one brow lifted high. "Hmm?"

Primly she lifted her chin. "I do not know. You probably realized you couldn't get away with it. I'd say the fact that you *did* leave proves all the more that you are *not* the real Prince."

He folded his arms. "How is that?"

She scoffed. "Obviously, the prince would never abandon his people when they needed him so much, when they were poor and hungry and suffering all manner of oppression. He would do everything he possibly could to help them."

"What if he had already examined the situation and found he could do nothing and so decided not to get involved?"

"Then he would be as selfish as you," she neatly replied.

"Mmm. What if he saw no point in trying because he knew no one would believe him?"

She shook her head. "That would not happen. His people would know him at once."

"What if something so humiliating had happened to him during those lost years that he just . . . couldn't show his face?" he murmured.

"Then he would be a coward."

He let out a short, miserable laugh as he stared down at the dolphins. "I confess you are too clever for me, Miss Monteverdi. You have an answer for everything."

"But no son of Alphonse would be so. There were no cowards among the Fiori." She turned her gaze away impatiently from his broken, downcast stare. "May we change the subject, Captain? I cannot like your hoax."

He turned to her. "Why are you so, shall we say, *passionate* about the Fiori, Allegra?"

She shrugged and gazed up at the clouds. "King Alphonse and Queen Eugenia were my mother's dearest friends. Myself, I even went to play with Princess Anna when I was very small, though I barely remember her."

A pained look passed over his handsome face and quickly vanished.

She furrowed her brow and continued. "You see, I grew up on Mama's stories of life at court. She told me so much about the Fiori, I feel as if I knew them all personally, especially the Crown Prince. That is why you cannot fool me."

"Especially him? Why?"

She smiled fondly to herself as she looked down at the planks. "I suppose it's because I always tried so hard to be good and obedient, and he was an irrepressible rascal. The stories Mama told me about him just . . . thrilled me. I was always so careful never to be naughty, but Prince Lazar could get away with anything."

"Really?" he said skeptically.

"Oh, yes." She chuckled. "According to Mama, the boy went out of his way to be impossible at all times."

"I'm sure it was just high spirits," he said indignantly.

"And . . . I guess I always wondered what it would be like to have a big brother, as Princess Anna did," she added wistfully, shooting him a rueful smile.

He stared at her without a word.

"So, you see?" she said. "I know all about the real Lazar di Fiore, and, trust me, he was nothing like you."

"What else did your mother tell you about this precious young martyr?"

"I'm certainly not going to tell you! I will not help you impersonate him."

He cast her a bland smile full of silken threat. "Indulge me."

She decided it was not perhaps so wise to defy him under the circumstances.

"Well, she said he was a good son. He loved his mother very much. Queen Eugenia's nickname for him was Leo. He had many, many friends, and he was betrothed in childhood," she said thoughtfully, "to one of the Austrian Habsburg princesses."

"The bulldog girl," he murmured.

"I beg your pardon?"

"It was Nicolette—the youngest. But never mind that."

"Yes, of course, Princess Nicolette!" she exclaimed. "I just read about her debut ball in the newspaper Aunt Isabelle sends me from Paris. It was a lavish affair." She sighed. "I wonder who she will marry now. They say she is a great beauty."

"To be sure. Please, continue."

"He liked to play practical jokes on people. Hated to study. He was an outrageous braggart, but charming enough to get away with it. An excellent shot for a young boy, and"—she considered for a moment—"according to Mama, he was known to delight in teasing young ladies until they broke down in tears."

"You're right. That sounds nothing like me."

She was silent, unconvinced herself until she shoved the doubt angrily away. She refused, *refused,* to be drawn in by his game, because if she believed he was the real Lazar, she would have to accept that Papa had been a real traitor. She could not bear even to think of it.

"Well, I can certainly assure you, whoever you are," she declared, "if Prince Lazar *were* alive, he would certainly not be sailing about in a pirate ship, terrifying people."

He studied her in amusement. "Why is it that you blush when you speak of him?"

She lifted a hand to her cheek, taken aback. "I am not blushing."

He smiled. "Oh, yes you are."

He began sauntering toward her, and she could tell by the way he was looking at her all of a sudden that he knew. He'd guessed.

The devil.

"I seem to recall your referring to him in the tower as 'my Lazar.' Why is that?"

She blushed deeper red as he prowled slowly toward her with a mischievous twinkle in his eye. "I did no such thing."

"Do I detect a little schoolgirl's dream tucked away in your most secret fancy, my sweet?"

"I have no idea what you're talking about."

He gave her a fond, chiding look with a hushing motion, a finger to his lips, as if he wouldn't dream of telling her secret.

"I must come clean with you, Miss Monteverdi. You have found me out. I am an imposter, just as you said. I am merely an outlaw of the seas, looking for something different to do to amuse myself. The coup didn't work out the way I'd planned, but it's of little consequence. I still made off with the treasure."

"Yes, I know. You took all my father's gold."

"That's not the treasure I mean." Meaningfully, he lifted her hand and kissed her knuckles.

She blushed, refusing to be beguiled by his flirting. "Well, I'm glad you finally decided to be truthful with me. Thank you for respecting me at least that much."

"Miss Monteverdi, my respect for you knows no bounds. To me, you are on the highest pedestal."

"What lies you speak." She shook her head as she studied him skeptically. "So, you thought you'd go from being a pirate to a prince, eh?" She fought the urge to smile at his dashing cockiness. "Nothing like starting off small. But you are an Ascencioner, aren't you? Your accent."

He nodded.

"And I was right," she continued, encouraged. "You are the son of a gentleman?"

"Indeed."

"Obviously you are well educated."

He gave her an ironic bow. "Vicar has much to do with that."

"Well!" She folded her arms over her chest, greatly satisfied to see that she had been right all along. Knowing she had seen through him from the start made her feel much more equipped to deal with him. *But how had he known about the tunnels?*

And why had the sight of her green-and-black sash changed his whole demeanor that night?

"What am I to call you?" she asked.

"I'm sure you can think of all manner of select epithets, but my name actually *is* Lazar."

She puckered her brow, about to protest.

"I was, er, born a few months after the prince—I was named after him," he said. "My parents were staunch royalists."

"I see." A bit too warmed by his dark-eyed gaze, she looked away to study her hand where it braced her against the wood.

She had to admit his explanations made sense, but he had given in much too easily. It was almost as if he had cast the whole issue aside just to tell her what she wanted to hear. The pain she'd seen in his eyes that day on the wall had certainly been real.

"No wonder you couldn't bring yourself to execute my family," she said, attempting to prod him into revealing more, "considering your vendetta was all a hoax. They all might have died for your whim."

His eyes flickered with amusement as he declined to rise to the bait. "Do you know why I spared them, Allegra? Because you asked me to. It pleases me to do what you ask."

She blushed and muttered, "You are mad."

"Now then," he said. "About this fantasy of yours."

"For heaven's sake, do not speak of it!" She saw he could barely stop himself from laughing at her.

Oh, she loathed him.

He approached her once more, his midnight eyes dancing with mischief. Mere inches away, he braced his hands on the lintel above her, hemming her in. She watched him warily.

"This Prince of yours and I," he said confidentially, "we share the same name, at least, similar coloring, and we are of an age. The only difference is that he is dead, and I, you see— I am alive."

"That you are," she said, feeling a trifle feverish.

"It is a distinct advantage, you must admit. So, my little dreamer"—he lowered his right hand and traced a design on her shoulder, sending shivers down to her toes—"why don't you simply put this vivid imagination of yours to use, and pretend I'm he? I would so like to fulfill your fantasies, and perhaps," he murmured, "exceed them."

She had to admit his eyes sparkled exactly like her Prince's as he lowered his lips coaxingly toward hers.

"It won't work," she forced out breathlessly as he edged closer and deliciously closer still.

"Why not, my darling girl?"

She stared up at him as his big hands moved around her waist and drew her body gently against his. Somehow she could not stop her hands from sliding up his lovely chest.

"Because." She faltered. "You kiss like a pirate."

"Not always," he whispered, smiling a little at first when he kissed her. He brushed his lips over hers, back and forth, with a silken caress as soft as a butterfly's wings. The dizzying pleasure of it parted her lips slightly, then he lingered, breathing her breath, giving his own to her.

He moved on. Weaker every second, she held perfectly still as he kissed the corner of her lips, her cheek, her brow. When his lips grazed her ear, he paused to whisper to her.

"I have a fantasy, too, *chérie,* of a beautiful girl who saved my soul. What would I not do for her?" He lowered his head, and for a moment he just stood there, drawing his smooth, clean-shaven cheek up and down gently against hers, but she could feel the turmoil inside him.

"What is it?" she asked, cradling his head against her. "What ails you, my friend?"

A tremor moved through him at her caress. He kissed her throat, her ear. Lightly he gripped two handfuls of her hair as he burrowed his face in the crook of her neck. "Help me, Allegra," he whispered. "I am so unhappy."

She stroked his weathered cheek and held him. "What would you have me do?"

He paused. "Love me."

Neither of them moved, and then she trembled.

Her strength fled. Her eyes closed, and she leaned back against the doorframe, waiting for him to consume her, knowing it had been her fate from the moment their eyes had met through the fire. She clung to his shoulders as his lips skimmed her throat.

"Love me," he murmured, running his hands slowly down her sides to her hips and back up again. She felt his fingers take down her hair and sift through its length, heard him whisper that it was like silk as it fell softly against her neck and shoulders. Her ivory combs were in his hands, then she heard them drop to the floor. When the ship rocked, the combs slid right over the planks and fell to the bottom of the sea, but she did not care, for he returned to taste her lips. He lingered against her mouth once more, unmoving, breathing her, letting her simply feel the enormity of the magic between them.

By sheer force of will, she pulled back, senses reeling. She turned her face away from him. "No, no, I do not want this. I cannot do this," she breathed, heart hammering.

"Do what, *chérie*?"

She withdrew from all his tenderness, pressing her head back against the doorframe in wordless distress.

"What can't you do?" he asked softly, stroking her neck. "I will help you."

She dragged her gaze up to his, at a loss with so much sweetness from this man she was determined to despise, this beautiful, troubling criminal who had planned to kill her.

"I cannot go near the edge," she whispered, her gaze pleading. "If I fell in—it is so deep—I cannot swim."

He lifted her hand and pressed a kiss into her palm, for a long moment simply gazing down at her as if there was so much he wanted to say, he didn't know where to begin.

He shook his head.

"I would still save you," he said.

Then he gave her back her hand and quietly left her there on the balcony, alone with all the vast and empty sea.

❧ CHAPTER ❧
TEN

"She's in love with me," Lazar announced, strolling to the canvas shade under which Vicar sat writing in his logbook. The older man looked up.

Lazar took one of Vicar's cheroots out of the silver box and lit it from the nearby lantern he was working by. He straightened up again and puffed, relishing the moment.

Vicar checked his watch, then stared up at him. "Two hours ago I believe you said she hated you."

"Oh, she hates me, all right."

"Beg pardon?"

Lazar lounged back on the capstan, watching his men at work and feeling rather smug. "I am in competition with myself," he said slowly, "for the lady's heart."

"I wasn't aware it was her heart you were after." Vicar made a final notation, then snapped his logbook shut. He looked up at Lazar, one silvery brow lifted.

"I am not an utter barbarian," Lazar said indignantly.

"Are you telling me your intentions toward Miss Monteverdi have become honorable?"

"Of course not."

"Oh," Vicar said in dry disapproval. "Very well. I will rise to the bait," he grumbled. "How are you in competition with yourself for the same woman?"

With a slow, lazy grin, Lazar examined the cheroot. "Miss

Monteverdi harbors a secret fascination with the dead crown prince," he said. "She loves him and hates me."

"I see." Vicar began laughing quietly and scratched his head. "What are you going to do?"

He exhaled a smoke ring, considering, then watched it vanish. "I've decided to let her go on seeing me as the Devil of Antigua for now."

Vicar watched him with a keen light in his eyes. "Why? Surely you could bed her faster if you simply convinced her you are the last of the Fiori."

"I know." Lazar nodded, then gazed up at the sails. "But it was the only way I could put her at ease. And . . . would you think it very strange if I said I want her to want me for *me*? Not for my namesake, not for some romantic ideal . . . I don't know." His voice trailed off as he frowned toward the horizon.

"I suppose it would gratify any man's vanity to win the desire of a woman who has every reason to detest him."

"It has nothing to do with vanity." Lazar shot him a scowl, then turned away. "It's just that—well—can you imagine how disappointed she's going to be when she realizes the truth?" he burst out angrily.

"Disappointed?"

"Do I look like anybody's prince to you?"

Vicar was patiently silent.

"How keenly she makes me feel the discrepancy between what I am and what I might have been," he said softly at last, gazing down at the cheroot in his hand. Then he rolled his eyes, disgusted with himself. "Figures only *I* could give myself serious competition for a woman," he muttered.

"You're not that bad, Fiore." Vicar chuckled. "Not as bad as you might have been, anyway, if I hadn't come along to keep you in line. Perhaps you should tell her about some of the obstacles you've faced. Put things in perspective for her."

"I don't want her pity," he grumbled, brow furrowed in

thought. "The problem with Allegra is that she wants to be safe."

"That seems natural enough."

"Not in the sense you mean. In that regard, she's as safe as houses, as you always say, and I think she's finally starting to see that. I mean . . ." He frowned at Wallace, who was having trouble with the topgallant's backstay. "I have no bloody idea what I mean."

Restlessly, Lazar got up from the capstan and perused the decks as he smoked, making sure the men were looking lively at their tasks.

"Fantasies are always safer than reality," Vicar remarked, watching him in his keen way.

"Except when they trap a healthy, desirable young woman inside herself, where nobody can hurt her! She won't trust me."

"How can she, at this point?"

Lazar shrugged.

Both were silent for a moment. Vicar looked up suddenly from his idle study of the planks. "I say, Lazar, are you falling in love with her?"

He stared at Vicar for a long moment. "Don't be absurd," he replied.

Vicar scratched his temple, gazing back at him, looking fascinated and equally bemused.

"Bloody hell." Turning on his heel, Lazar stomped off to take over the wheel from the helmsman, desperate for any work to do.

Allegra spent the rest of the afternoon writing a letter to Aunt Isabelle, telling her not to worry herself into illness. The pirate captain who had carried her off was a wicked man, to be sure, but he would not do her any outright violence, she wrote. He could even be somewhat civilized when he chose.

She didn't tell about how softly he could kiss or how gentle his hands could be.

Next she wrote to the matrons of the pension houses and orphanages she sponsored, with instructions to carry on without her until she could devise a way to return. As she wrote out detail after detail of who would need what, the homes to which food should be taken, which children needed checking in on, like little Tomas, whose father was a brute, and her favorite angel, little blind Constanzia, and how the DiRosas were faring after their barn had burned down, she realized with some astonishment how much of a load she had been carrying. It was another reason to resent the Devil of Antigua for having taken her away from the people who had come to rely on her. She even doubted she would be given any opportunity to send her letters, but at least she was prepared.

She took a long time at her toilette, readying herself for this dinner the captain had ordered her to attend. It was a silly thing to do for a meal that would no doubt consist of hardtack and cider, but the ritual of dressing was such a familiar part of existence, it made her feel as if there were some semblance of her old life left.

She selected a peach-colored satin Watteau, still amazed by the fact that Lazar had ordered all her personal effects from her chambers to be brought aboard his ship. He was a most thoughtful and considerate cutthroat. There was a whole storeroom on the mid-deck filled with her clothes, stuffed and smashed haphazardly because his brute men had done the hasty packing. She was happiest to have the irreplaceable mementos, such as the miniature portraits of her family, and Mama's jewels.

Standing before the satinwood washstand in Lazar's cabin, she brushed out her hair, endlessly mulling over his words. The mere memory of his whisper sent a shiver through her limbs.

Love me.

What an absurd thing to say. Only he would say such a thing. Of course, he had meant it only in the strictly physical sense, she realized. A reckless outlaw asking for gratification of his overindulged appetites.

A lost prince, her heart whispered, *asking me to help him find his way home.*

She ignored the inner whisper with a will, carefully pinning up her hair with topaz-studded ivory combs, singing old Ascencion folk songs quietly to herself as she worked. She chose an easy coiffure, for she was not an *artiste de mode* like her Parisian maid, Josefina.

Dressing in the voluminous gown without her maid's assistance was no easy feat, either, but at last she had front-laced her stays the best she could and arranged her creamy flounced petticoat so that it peeked out demurely at the open front of the gown. Crossing the cabin with a few light steps, she twirled a bit, joyous to feel human again. But when she checked the time on her pocket watch, she saw she had an hour to wait.

She heaved a sigh and paced the room.

How boring life at sea was, she thought. How could a man of action like the captain stand it? No wonder he was unhappy. He was wasting his life, throwing away his potential, she fretted. A man like him—strong, clever, charismatic, and bold—why, what could he not do successfully, if he put his mind to it? With all his strengths, he could make the world a better place if he tried.

Ah, but men were so foolish. She pushed away a memory of Papa.

Obviously the captain enjoyed getting himself into trouble, but why would anyone choose a life of crime, outside of everything decent and upright? Why hadn't he done something productive with his life?

She wondered for precisely three seconds if she could reform him, then laughed at herself, declining such a foolhardy challenge. No doubt scores of women had already attempted it. She wondered how many women he had taken captive before, how many women had slept in his arms in that deliciously soft bed, been kissed that way out there on the balcony until they clung to their senses by the barest thread.

The memory of his sweet kiss evoked such an ache of longing in her that she walked hesitantly, silently to his locker and opened it, looking at his clothes. She touched a scarlet jacket hanging on a peg, running the soft material slowly between her thumb and forefinger. She caressed a striped satin waistcoat of black and dark blue, closing her eyes again, remembering the feel of him against her.

Love you? Beautiful savage, if only you could love me, she thought wistfully. *If only I could tame you, just a little.*

But that wasn't going to happen, and she must not for an instant deceive herself into hoping otherwise. This man was made for living dangerously and breaking hearts, she thought sternly, and she had barely mended her own in all the lonely years after Mama's death. She never wanted to feel again that overwhelming loss and grief, which was, she knew, the only thing Lazar would ultimately give her. But oh, he knew how to make himself hard to resist.

The door creaked behind her while she was still examining his wardrobe. She froze, knowing she was caught.

The door slammed.

"Oh, for God's sake, woman, have pity!" He groaned. "Setting off your beauty is no way to keep me at bay, *chérie.*"

She turned around in the midst of a furious blush. "I only wanted something to do." She pointed toward the armoire. "I meant to see if you had anything that needed mending."

He smiled as he sauntered toward her. "Just my heart."

"What a rogue you are," she murmured, turning away, more scarlet still.

He snatched her fichu away so quickly she did not even see his hand reach out.

"Give that back!"

"There will be no modesty on this ship."

"Captain, I demand—"

"Ah, ah—what is my name?" He inhaled the scent of her perfume from the gauzy cloth.

She glared up at him in staunch refusal, jaw clenched. "Give it back."

"But I've cut myself again," he said with a pout. "I need a bandage."

She folded her arms over her chest, tapping her foot. "Oh? Where?"

"My heart, I told you. You've cleaved it in two. It is bleeding."

"You *are* a devil."

He tossed the fichu at her. "So they say."

And then he began undressing.

She gave a shocked, haughty sniff of disdain and marched toward the door, heart pounding in her effort to ignore the effortless seduction in the languid way he slid the untied cravat off his shoulders.

"I wouldn't go out there looking like that, if I were you."

She halted, stealing a glance over her shoulder. "Why not?"

"You'll cause a mutiny. I'm not joking. You'd better stay here with me. Where you'll be safe," he added with a wicked lift of one flared brow.

She turned around, folding her arms again, the fichu still dangling from her hand. "So you may flaunt your muscles at me?"

"Precisely. Come. Help me choose what I shall wear so I might look the part of your proper escort for the evening."

"There is nothing proper about you."

"Indeed. Aren't I refreshing?" he drawled.

"What is a pirate doing with a collection of fine evening clothes, anyway?" she asked suspiciously, unable to resist the temptation of his playfulness.

"Very good question, my clever captive. I often go ashore on my travels to pluck the varied fruits of the world's cities, you might say. When I do, I prefer to be received as a gentleman."

"And this works?"

"Never fails."

"What cities have you been to?"

"All of them."

"What do you do ashore?"

"Well, let's see. I always go to the opera, of course."

"To look at the ladies."

He cast her a cocky half smile. "I am one of those who actually listen to the music. Shall I take you to an opera, *chérie*?"

She shook her head just to be contrary. She adored the opera, the more gut-wrenching the hero's tragedy, the better.

"You don't like opera, and you call yourself an Italian?" he scolded. "What do you like to do?" He reached for her hands and placed them on the top button of his waistcoat.

Her acquiescence to the task was automatic. "To argue."

"I gathered that," he said dryly as he watched her efficiently unbutton his waistcoat. "What do you like to argue about?"

"Oh, anything. Ideas. Politics. Religion. Philosophy. The rights of man."

"And woman?"

She glanced up at him. There was something deliciously wicked in the way he said it.

"It is not a joke, Captain. There are those who feel ladies should be allowed a wider scope for the exercise of their faculties—a more practical education, greater opportunities to contribute to the world. Don't you feel women deserve at least some of the rights men enjoy?"

"I have always been a great proponent of a woman's right to erotic pleasure," he purred, gazing down at her, eyes dancing.

She poked him in the chest, catching on at last to the delight he took in being deliberately shocking. "I was speaking of the right to own property, for instance, or the right to legal recourse against a husband who takes his role as disciplinarian too much to heart."

She forced away a grim memory of Domenic.

"My, how frightfully high-minded you are! A true visionary. I'm afraid I'm made of baser stuff." He sounded bored with her already.

She flushed. "I would not say I am particularly high-minded. I merely try to be aware of what is going on in the world. A new age of freedom is upon our civilization, Captain—but you would know nothing about that, would you? Absorbed as you are in your vendettas and your pleasures—"

Oh, why did she take every opportunity to insult him? she wondered as soon as the words left her lips and she saw his faint wince.

Lazar drew away from her, and she stood there, staring after him, not knowing what to say in her regret—not knowing why she even *should* regret. She watched him shrug off the waistcoat and drop it on the floor. He pulled his shirt off over his head as he walked away.

"Captain," she began, "I didn't mean—"

Suddenly she gasped. He whirled around quickly, hiding what she'd seen, then lowered his gaze, scowling at the floor.

"You may go now, Miss Monteverdi. The men won't mutiny. I lied," he muttered.

"Lazar," she said softly, "let me see."

He merely stood there as she walked toward him, the shirt still hanging in his grasp. Her gaze devoured the splendor of his golden skin, muscled chest and arms, his belly carved with flowing ridges. *Beautiful man.* She could scarcely believe she'd slept in his arms for the past three nights without ravishing *him.*

With a wordless growl of forbearance, Lazar turned, showing her his back. She flinched just to see it. Someone had once flogged him within what had to have been an inch of his life.

Scourged him.

Brutalized him. The crisscrossing scars had healed into a tough, leathery mesh that spanned his back in a gridiron design, a complex, miniature earthwork like those that boys made in the dirt playing war with toy soldiers.

His chin was high, his eyes wary but proud. "Are you going to swoon with revulsion?" he asked in a tone of biting irony.

"No. Does it hurt you?"

"Of course not."

"Can I touch it?"

"You'd want to?" Still bristling, he obviously longed for a reprieve. But perhaps not entirely.

She laid one hand on his back, running her fingers up to mold against his scarred right shoulder blade. She felt the tingle low in her belly when he responded to her touch with a sound under his breath that was almost a moan.

"Who did this to you?" she asked in a hushed tone.

"'Old Cap'n Wolfe wielded the whip," he said with forced lightness. "But indirectly speaking, it was your father."

She frowned. "Who is Captain Wolfe?"

"Was. The pirate king," he said in a voice edged with razor sarcasm. "The man I once served."

She glanced up at him, but he continued looking straight ahead. "It's hard to imagine you serving any man."

"Let's just say I owed him."

"For what?"

"No, Allegra."

She fell silent. "This should never have happened to you," she said sadly, tracing a long, pale furrow that cut from his shoulder on a diagonal down toward his left hip.

"It was my own stupid fault," he growled. "I volunteered for it."

"What do you mean?"

"Vicar was inspired one day to argue with the old sea dog about sparing some prisoners whose families had no money for ransom. Even you, Miss Monteverdi, would not have argued with Raynor Wolfe."

"You took a beating for Vicar?"

The wide, powerful shoulders lifted again in a shrug. "He wouldn't have survived it."

" 'Twas a very noble thing to do."

He remained silent.

"You should not be ashamed of these scars," she said softly, her caress mournful across his ravaged hide. "You should be proud."

"God's truth, you are the strangest woman I ever met," he muttered. "If you think I bore it in stoic silence, you are mistaken. I screamed my head off and cursed that Dutch bastard with every blow. It was only hatred that kept me alive."

"Of my father?"

"And God."

"Do not say such a thing!" she breathed, sending up a mental prayer assuring the heavens he did not mean it.

There was a long silence as she drew her fingertips lightly down his spine. He shivered a little.

"Allegra," he said, "I do like the way you touch me."

Her heart suddenly pounding, she stepped closer to him, sliding both her hands around his waist to caress his bare chest and belly. She placed a whisper-soft kiss on the middle of his back, then another.

She couldn't believe she was doing it, but she couldn't seem to stop. She held her breath, eyes closed, as she laid her cheek against his ravaged back and explored him, every warm, hard line of his torso, the smooth, golden skin like softest kid, the massive arms. She reached up to stroke his neck and touched the velvety softness of his short black hair.

When he tilted his head back as if in surrender to her touch, she heard the soft sound that escaped his lips, heard his heart pounding inside his body. He stood obediently even when she brought her left hand down to savor with her open palm the hard, sinuous line of his lower back's curve, flowing downward into the lean muscle of his buttock in tight, dark blue breeches. There was something about the taut power of him that was beautiful to knead and stroke.

"Do I please you?" he asked in a heated murmur.

"Oh, yes," she breathed.

He turned around and gripped her, curling his hand around the back of her neck. When he leaned down, this time she welcomed his kiss, tasting his brandy on her tongue. He must have felt her hunger, for he crushed her against him, coaxing her lips wider apart with an onslaught of hard, driving kisses, his tongue lunging deep into her mouth.

He drove her back firmly two steps, pinning her against the hard surface of his locker, where he kissed her endlessly, running both his hands down her sides to her hips. Now when she touched him, his skin was hot. She could not believe she'd had this effect on him.

She pressed both palms against his bare chest, trying to temper his response, but he was too strong. He would not even let her turn her head to draw a breath but moved with her however she tried to escape, kept kissing her. She could feel every long, unforgiving line of his lean, powerful body pressing against her.

As the moments passed, she began to feel almost faint, not simply overpowered but on the deepest level overwhelmed, until all she knew was the taste of him and the stroking of his large, hot, trembling hand upon her neck, her shoulder, and downward over her chest, unfastening the ribbons of her gown with one hand so deftly she was astonished.

"Allegra," he whispered as he tugged the last ribbon free. "God, I want you."

Her knees went weak at the sound of pure male need. She kept her eyes pressed closed while her senses and her emotions rioted around a core of desperation. He clasped her buttocks, hauling her up closer against him, as if to make sure she felt the solid heft of his erection jutting against her stomach.

She wrenched her face away. "Captain, please—"

"I have a name, God damn it. Use it."

"You said you wouldn't force me!"

"Say my name. Say it, Allegra, or I'll take you right here."

"Lazar," she choked out.

"Again."

"No!"

He laced all his fingers through her hair with wild, sudden tenderness. "Again, Allegra. Give it to me."

"But you're not—"

"Please," he whispered. Abruptly, his kiss went gentle, so soft and sweet that she shuddered at the reprieve. His thumbs traced her cheeks with feather-soft twin caresses while he held her face.

Against her own volition, his kiss made her ache with its sweetness, his tongue slowly stroking over hers, intoxicating, confusing her. She felt herself starting to crumple. He began winning her over with his poignant gentleness until she could no longer brook her own need to touch him.

He went motionless at her uncertain caress upon his chest. He drew back a small space to watch her run her hand hesitantly over the ridges of his stomach, upward through the lightly furred area between the swells of his breasts, to curl finally behind his neck.

When she looked up into his eyes, she was frightened, but she knew she wanted him.

With a pained expression, Lazar closed his eyes and leaned his forehead against hers. He let out a long, shaky breath.

"Allegra, for the love of God," he said quietly, "tell me who I am, because I can barely remember myself anymore."

She went very still, her arms around his neck. Whoever he was, the despair in his voice sent cracks all the way down to the foundation of her defenses. Just for a moment, she was weak enough to want him to be, to pretend—he'd suggested it earlier himself—just to fantasize. . . .

Her heart was pounding, and his full lips were lingering upon hers when she gave in.

"Lazar."

He wrapped his arms tighter around her waist. "Oh, yes. More," he breathed with a soft, heady groan.

"Lazar." She tilted her head back further and reached deeper for his hungry kiss as she stroked his chest, so solid and real. So dangerous.

"Lazar," she whispered. "Lazar."

He lifted her softly and carried her to his berth, kissing her all the while as he rested her on her back. He lowered himself atop her, covering her with his big, powerful body, his weight deliciously crushing her. He propped himself on his elbows on either side of her head, gently framing her face with both his palms.

"Don't be afraid," he whispered. He kissed her slowly, tenderly, stealing every breath she took as he parted her bodice and caressed her breasts. The way he touched her made her feel strangely fragile, melting and soft beneath his hard, gentle power.

She was not sure when she became aware of it, but there was something unbearably right about the feel of him lying between her legs, a growing search for something he had that made her body undulate beneath him with a will of its own. She heard herself groan aloud.

"That's right, honey," he whispered. "Feel it. What do you want? I'll do whatever you want."

His movements answered hers completely, the symmetry of it shocking, yet rich with bliss. Each pressing contact of him riding her rising hips back down again filled her with a sense of joy that became increasingly barbaric. Each time, sweet anguish. Each time, *why him? why now?* until it didn't matter anymore. She ran her hands down his sides, clutching his lean hips, guiding him precisely against her in a rhythm that rolled faster with each heartbeat. He gave her willingly, generously what her body asked.

When her very mind seemed burned with the flames of her desire, he lifted back, sliding her skirts' flounces up past her knee, over her thigh. She dragged her eyelids open and looked up at him. He was staring down at her with an expression in his eyes she could not fathom, a dark tenderness. Closing his eyes, he lowered his head to kiss her for a moment, then it was just like her laudanum dream. He paused, panting, eyes closed. Then he stroked her, once.

She was amazed by her own teeming wetness. She could feel it on his fingertips. She looked up at him dazedly, took in his subtle expression of pleasure, the concentration on his chiseled face, then she closed her eyes with a groan when his finger dipped slowly inside her.

He lowered his head and kissed her lips softly as he slipped two fingers together inside her, so gently, while the pad of his thumb stroked her most delicate center. He began to move, luscious, deliberate. She caressed the flexing muscles of his arm, for a moment only lying there, letting him use his expertise to touch her as he willed, drifting with pleasure as he lowered his head, nibbling along her neck toward her earlobe.

"Feels good, hm, *chérie*?" he whispered.

She was too bedazzled by the sensations he was giving her to answer, but his low, velvet laugh told her he knew. He whispered to her like the voice of fantasy itself until she began arching hungrily for him once more with his every stroke, rising to meet his touch.

"Don't fight it, sweetheart. That's right. Let it take you."

She clung to his shoulder as her ragged breathing turned to gasps.

Now he was silent, swept away as she was, every particle of his attention focused on giving her increasing pleasure. He lowered his head and kissed her breast, licking the nipple slowly with the tip of his tongue.

He opened his eyes and gazed boldly into hers. His skin was flushed to sun-warmed copper; his lips were full and pliant with kissing. He gave her a half smile like a satyr before dipping his head to flick his tongue over her hardened crest again.

Hand between her thighs, he extended his little finger deftly to caress her deep in the cleft of her backside, and she gasped at the unexpected shock of pleasure while he took her breast into his mouth, suckling hungrily, consumed with passion.

"Yes, oh, yes," she breathed urgently, arching her head back against the pillow. "It is sublime."

Something was building.

She clamped his head to her breast while she rode his touch in an ever-wilder frenzy. His fierce kiss became painful on her breast, so she drew him up again to her mouth. She knew he possessed her completely when she heard his voice at her ear, a deep, soft whisper of command. She would have done anything he asked.

"Scream for me, *chérie*."

But she could only give a gasping cry, as if she were in pain. *"Lazar."*

He let out a trembling breath. "I want you so much." He almost stopped, and she could not bear it. She clutched his shoulders, moaning.

"Oh, Lazar, oh, please."

At his answering groan of helpless need, the first wave of pleasure rose to drown her, sweeping over her, wave after wave. She held him tight, her arms around his neck, as she convulsed around his soaked hand. It was the most vulnerable moment of her life, and he did not fail her. Cries of bliss tore free from her throat, but something deeper than joy welled as tears behind her closed eyes, slid down her cheeks.

He caught them on his lips, and still her body pulled for him, desperate, writhing with demand, until she had milked his fingers of every drop of pleasure in them.

She lay there, unable to move, so deep was her relief, her sense of wholeness, healing. Gently he moved his hand away, and she could feel at once the swollenness of her own flesh. She marveled at her galloping breath, her racing pulse, the warm, slightly bruised ache of satisfaction between her thighs.

Eyes shut tight, his big body shaking, Lazar wrapped his arms around her and held her, murmuring to her that she was the most beautiful thing he'd ever seen. It seemed a lie, but she could not entirely disbelieve him. There was something in the way he said it.

She kissed his cheek, feeling enervated but complete somehow, and strangely, blissfully close to him.

"Oh, Lazar," she sighed, too spent even to shake her head.

He said nothing, laying his head on her chest. She raked her fingers through his short, soft, jet-black hair and caressed his back, closing her eyes to face the unreasonable knowledge that at this moment she felt closer to him than she ever had to anyone, this scarred stranger with tragedy behind all the sparkle in his eyes, this outlaw who could see he was a born hero if he would only try.

He had such sweetness in him.

Holding him, she wondered if it was already too late for her. *You have me,* he'd said earlier, and it appeared she did—for the moment—but oh, she thought, squeezing her eyes shut tight, it terrified her. The edge she feared was racing up entirely too fast. She prayed, as if heaven could stop the sliding of her heart into his sea, *Please, God, not him. Anyone but him. He is too dangerous for me.*

He was a pirate and a rake.

He would die young, well before he wised up and pondered the revolutionary notion of loving one woman. If that calamity ever befell him, she was quite certain he would not choose her, his enemy's plain, prudent, tediously moral daughter.

He was a criminal. He had destroyed her life. They said

he was evil incarnate, this wild, irresistible rogue who was weaving himself into her fantasies, and somehow she'd been falling from the first moment she'd laid eyes on him.

Whoever he was.

⚜ CHAPTER ⚜
ELEVEN

Everyone sees what you appear to be, few feel what you are, and those few will not dare to oppose themselves to the many—

The chime of the clock broke into his reading. Domenic Clemente looked up.

Two in the morning.

He set his well-worn edition of Machiavelli lovingly aside and stood. With a leisurely stretch, he left the villa and strolled out for a bit of night air to clear his head.

One week earlier, Little Genoa had been sacked and burned, Monteverdi had flung himself to his death, Allegra had been kidnapped, and he had come to power. The island had been in constant chaos since—fires, riots, wars of villagers against soldiers. The guests from the anniversary feast, as well as most of the Genovese nobles, had bundled up their families and fled.

With his having come into the governorship with a broken wrist, a black eye, and no fiancée, the crisis that fell into his lap was made all the more complicated by the rebels' efforts to seize power.

The funny thing was, Domenic mused, he had captured a few rebels, and, with a little torture to persuade them to talk, all had admitted that the man who had carried out the destruction of Little Genoa was not one of their own. No one from any of the existing factions knew him or could explain his whirlwind of destruction, nor his disappearance.

It was beginning to look more and more as though the black-

eyed ruffian who had abducted Allegra was in fact not one of
the rebels of Ascencion at all. Poor little Allegra had never
been a traitor, as he'd first thought.

Domenic was most contrite.

He was sick of his mistress again, and he wanted his fiancée
back. Indeed, his reputation depended upon his showing that
he could protect Allegra and avenge her by bringing to justice
that ruffian who had kidnapped her.

Pistol in his left hand—for he didn't dare leave the house
unarmed anymore—his right forearm splinted and hanging in
a sling against his chest, Domenic wandered down to the stable
to say hello to his fine Arabian horses. When he stepped back
out into the glistening dark, he heard someone following him.

He paused for only a moment, and then he smiled to himself
and kept walking.

About bloody time, he thought. He was ready. He'd been
ready for a week now. Too ready. Since the night he had realized he was being stalked, he'd been going half mad with
waiting.

Hellfire, how many assassins had that black-eyed savage
sent after him? He'd already killed one, but the man had died
before Domenic could interrogate him.

Before him rose the hulking shape of the elegant villa. Two
lanterns on either side of the grand entrance gleamed their cozy
welcome, but he didn't need their light. Nighttime had always
sharpened his senses. He heard, or rather felt, the man stealing
up cautiously behind him, still several yards away. He smiled
to himself as he played the tantalizing game of waiting for the
precise moment to turn the hunter into the hunted.

He whistled a slow minuet and admiringly held up the
smooth silver muzzle of his pistol, which gleamed in the bright
pallor of the moonlight. All his awareness was trained upon the
shadow stalking him. Lucky for him, he was an equally good
shot with his left hand.

When he heard the soft, deadly click of a gun being cocked,

he whirled, pistol in his left hand, and fired into a man-shaped pool of shadow, dropping the mercenary like a quail a second after the man had squeezed the trigger. The bullet whizzed past his head. Domenic's eyes widened with thrill as he felt the hot breeze whir by, harmless. He heard the gasp as the body fell. The gun clattered down onto the pebbled drive. He ran toward the enemy, the weight of his pistol swinging as he ran, propelling him eagerly forward.

He came upon his gasping victim, seized him, and dragged him into the light.

"Who is your leader? What is his name?" he demanded.

The man didn't want to tell him anything. Domenic shook him with his left hand.

"Tell me!"

"Devil," the big thug rasped, grimacing as he clutched his streaming chest.

Domenic paled.

"What do you mean, you filthy wretch?" he demanded, hauling him upward by the collar.

"The Devil," he whispered.

"He is not the devil," Domenic scoffed. "He is a man. He bleeds."

The man looked almost surprised, then laughed at him, his eyes glazing with the first flutter of death's wings around him. He wheezed and shuddered.

"Don't you dare die yet, you son of a bitch. I want answers!"

But in the next moment, the mercenary was quite hopelessly dead.

He shoved the body away in disgust. Good God, now he had blood all over him.

"The devil," he repeated. "Satan? Beelzebub?"

It was better than the story spreading like wildfire among the rioting peasants, that that black-eyed savage was none other than Prince Lazar di Fiore, come back from the dead.

Believing they'd caught a glimpse of the last surviving Fiore, the people already hated him, their new governor, even more than they had hated the old one. But the Viscount Clemente was not a man to tolerate any insolence.

It was enough of an insult to have to conduct the island's business from this country house, because that ruffian had burned the governor's mansion to the ground.

Cleanup was still going on down in Little Genoa and would probably take another two months, about the same length of time his doctor had said it would take his wrist to heal. At least, thank God, there had been no need to amputate his hand.

Domenic kicked the body, bellowed for his servant, and stomped back into the villa in a foul humor. When his servant came flopping out of his sleeping closet, Domenic slapped him and sent him out to get rid of the body.

Attack me again, he thought urgently, staring out at the dark landscape. Next time he'd be sure to take them alive.

He would get to the bottom of this. Prince or no, by God, he would not give up his power to anyone now that he had finally achieved it. But he could not defend himself against this mysterious enemy until he captured the men sent to kill him.

When he learned his foe's identity, why, he thought, that black-eyed savage was going to be sorry he had ever set foot on Ascencion.

Lazar assigned himself to the night watch, knowing that if he lay beside Allegra tonight, he would not be able to stop himself from making love to her. Since the previous afternoon's exquisite torment, his frustration was extreme, and the last vestiges of the sulky crown prince in him took the denial with ill grace.

Presently dawn was hatching, a glimmer of gold cracking open along the dark egg of the horizon. He was leaning against the wheel, bored, tired from having been up all night, and restless, with nothing to do but plan possible strategies on when, where, and exactly how to bed Allegra.

It was better than brooding on the knowledge that they were about to cross the zero longitude, dead north of Al Khuum. It was the closest to that place he ever cared to go again. He pushed it out of his mind.

The night had been warm, but it was cooler now. Humidity haloed the moon, waning just past full. Lazar wondered if Allegra was sleeping, if she had missed him beside her. Then he growled at himself. What the hell was wrong with him?

He could not recall ever having reacted so idiotically to a female before, aside from one infatuation with the savvy older woman who had relieved him of his virginity at sixteen. By now he could barely remember her face. In the ensuing years, he'd had women all over the world. In his quest to forget his demons, he'd become something of a connoisseur of female flesh, but what he felt toward Allegra made his past exploits seem uncomfortably shallow, and he could not remember even one about whose opinion of him he could care less, so long as they had spread their legs for him.

He still barely understood what perverse impulse had driven him to hide his true identity from her on the sea balcony yesterday, almost as if he were ashamed of something.

She would have started believing him if he'd stuck to the truth, he thought. Only, to his chagrin, he was not eager to have his little captive sit in judgment on him and tell him how miserably he was failing to live up to the great Fiore namesake.

All he wanted to do was bed her and hopefully get her out of his system, because his preoccupation with her was beginning to alarm him. He assured himself he would grow bored with her soon.

On the other hand, he was beginning to wonder who among his Martinique friends was worthy of her.

At dinner last night, after their interlude, she had spent the whole meal blushing and staring down at her plate. He had watched her from across the white expanse of the tablecloth like a starved man, contemplating the idea of sweeping Emilio's five-course meal off the table and taking her right then and there. Vicar had sat there, vastly amused, meanwhile, turning his head back and forth like a spectator at a match of lawn tennis, delighting in Lazar's misery and trying valiantly time and time again to make polite conversation.

If Lazar was unprepared yesterday for her first, shy touch on his disgusting, gnarled back of all places, the unfolding fire of her passion consumed him. She was fierce yet sweet, demanding yet pure, her sexual enthusiasm artless and unmasked, hiding nothing. She had wanted him, welcomed him into her arms, between her legs, and the knowledge filled him with such absurd joy, it was almost satisfaction enough.

Why? he wondered.

She wasn't the most beautiful woman he'd ever pursued, at least not in the ordinary sense. She was the offspring of his enemy, and he worried that to feel this way toward a Monteverdi was a direct insult to his family. But she was brave and honest, and her idealism made her seem to him so naive, so vulnerable, that he ached to keep her safe.

Something in her clear, contemplative gaze mystified him. There was a quality of wistfulness in her eyes that moved him, a secret, sad wishing for something that repeatedly drove him to make an idiot of himself just to see her smile.

He had never deflowered a virgin before, but he would smooth the path before her as he led her over the threshold from child to woman. *His*. Then she would be his, he thought, as he'd known she must be from the first moment he'd seen her there by the firelight, little lost kitten.

Tears, he thought, still awed. For those moments, she had let him inside of her in a way that was infinitely better than crude penetration.

She had yielded her passion beautifully, but he would continue to move slowly, coaxing her to give up all the treasure of her trust to him, the one thing in the world no pirate thief could steal.

"Hello," said a soft, hesitant voice behind him, breaking into his thoughts.

He turned around in surprise and saw her lithe silhouette approaching across the quarterdeck.

"Well, here comes my kitten," he said broadly, casting her a sleepy smile. "You're up early."

"I have coffee for you." She moved toward him carefully because of the ship's slight swaying. "Here's a piece of biscotti, if you're hungry. You'd better take it," she said hastily, making a little sound of pain that told him she had just spilled the coffee on her fingers. "I couldn't find the sugar, just the cream."

He stole a kiss as he took the clay mug from her. "*There's* sugar enough for me."

"You are such a flirt," she mumbled.

He smiled over the steaming coffee, sensing her blush in the gray half light. He decided to push his luck. "Biscotti?" he inquired.

"Here." She held out the small plate toward him.

He looked at the wheel in his left hand, the coffee in his right hand, then gave her his best smile. "Would you mind terribly, *chérie*?"

"Oh," she said, flustered again, but she took the thick slice of hard almond bread and carefully dipped it in the coffee, then slowly lifted it for him to take a bite.

He wanted to laugh aloud at her demure hesitation.

She looked at the sails and cast about nervously for a topic of conversation. "My, what a wonderful supper last night! Your Emilio is a fine chef."

"Glad you approve," he said as he finished chewing. "He attended the di Medici school in Tuscany. I am fondest of Italian cuisine." He wished he had a free hand to give her backside a meaningful pinch when she turned to examine the mizzenmast.

"I confess I am astonished at your gourmet tastes," she said.

"We hedonists take our pleasures very seriously. Bite?"

She turned back to him and repeated the process, dipping the biscotti into the coffee. Her fingertips were dangerously close to his mouth this time. There were a few moments of companionable silence between them as he sipped his coffee, and she gazed up at the limp breeze moving the expanses of sail above them.

"How beautiful your ship is," she mused.

He said nothing for a moment, watching her. She turned back to him with wonder sparkling in her eyes.

"Come," he said suddenly. "You shall steer her."

"Me?"

"You, Miss Monteverdi."

"But I don't know how to do that!"

"I'll teach you." She fed him the last bite of biscotti, and he nipped playfully at her fingers, then switched his coffee into his left hand, propping his wrist against the wheel's spindle. With his free hand he drew Allegra in front of him to the wheel.

"It's simple," he told her. "Just hold here."

He arranged her soft hands on two of the spindles at ten and two o'clock. This left his own hand free to wander down her hip, but he snatched it back at the last minute, stepping away from her.

It would be expressly unwise to go groping at the girl now that she was finally starting to trust him. He went over to lean against the curving top of the hatch and watched her as he drank the coffee.

"Am I doing it?" she asked in amazement. "Is this right?"

He chuckled. "You're an old salt."

She lifted up on her toes as she peered at the open sea ahead, her face alight with a grin.

"Next you can tar the deck," he suggested.

"Lazar!" she scoffed, then hastily amended, "I mean Captain."

He smiled to himself at her accidental use of his name. "Mind that iceberg."

She looked over and gave him a delicate snort.

Aye, he thought. He was getting to her.

Though she only stood at the wheel for about a quarter hour before the helmsman came on duty to take over for Lazar, steering the huge ship was a thrill Allegra knew she would never forget. She marveled at Lazar's trust in her not to wreck it, and was so pleased that she allowed him to watch the sunrise with her, which was the reason she'd dressed and come above so early.

Presently the captain was insisting that the best view was to be had from the crow's nest, the tiny platform precariously balanced on the very crest of the mainmast. It had to be a hundred feet in the air above them.

"There is no way you're getting me up there," she declared, but when he smiled at her that way, he eroded her fears to nothing, like the salt sea smoothing the furrows of ancient shells. She might still have refused him in her terror of such heights, but then he dared her.

"Dares are for children," she replied crisply.

"Quake-buttocks," he said softly.

She narrowed her eyes. "We'll see who's a coward!"

The next thing she knew, she was climbing the ladder, and he was right behind her, swearing on his honor that he was not looking up her dress.

He had made her take off her shoes, because the satin would be too slippery on the rungs and ropes. Her bare feet clung to the hemp, and she found herself surrounded by huge white sails that billowed gently and made soft, rhythmic sounds like the flapping of angels' wings.

She forgot her fear in wonder and excitement. She had never watched a sunrise at sea before, nor shared her most sacred ritual with anyone.

The climb was not easy, but the trick was to keep looking upward, she found. Once she was past the mid-top, looking down at the deck made her nervous, though Lazar's presence helped her feel safe. She hurried so they wouldn't miss a moment of the sky's new-flung glory.

Terror struck when she reached the crow's nest, a round platform with nothing but a low bar to hold on to. Once more Lazar steadied her until she hugged the great pine mast. She had not expected to feel as though she were riding the pendulum of a gigantic, upside-down clock. She gripped one of the wooden racks nailed to the mast. Lazar explained that these were for rifles, because in battle sharpshooters were stationed there. She barely heard.

"I don't think I can get down again," she whispered in wide-eyed dread.

He told her not to worry as he vaulted up beside her, cavalier as ever. He moved to hold her, but she stared, stricken, into his eyes.

"Don't touch me. I'll fall!"

He lifted his hands away in token surrender. "As you wish."

They faced the east. Feeling the loveliness of the breeze up here above the sails and seeing that her life was perhaps not in as much immediate dire peril as she'd thought, she forced herself to relax a bit and settled more snugly against the mast.

Lazar turned to her and caressed her knee. "Are you all right now, *chérie*?"

She nodded. "Sorry. I guess I am a bit of a quake-buttocks after all."

"Not a chance. You called the Devil of Antigua a skulking thief to his face. Most men would never dare."

She cast him a glance that was part gratefulness at his attempt to bolster her courage, and part wince at the memory of those terrible moments on the wall.

He gazed at her for a moment, then leaned toward her and offered her a chaste kiss on the cheek. "Good morning, Allegra."

She put her head down, blushing fiercely. "Good morning, Captain."

He seemed to fight the smile upon his lips, assuming a businesslike air. "Now then, on with your ritual. Tell me what is so important about this sunrise." Dangling his legs over the side, he laid his hands one atop the other on the low rail, then rested his chin on them.

"One morning when I was seven, my mother woke me up very early and dressed me and took me to a hilltop near our house. We watched the sun rise, and I remember that she cried."

He turned and gazed at her in silence, the growing light sculpting one side of his chiseled face in an orange glow.

"I didn't understand anything at the time, but over the years I've pieced it together," she explained. "I was five when the Fiori were killed, and I think Mama had been grieving for them all that time. Should I not speak of my family to you?" she asked suddenly.

"Your father paid his price," he replied. "Go on. I like to hear about your life."

"My father tried to comfort Mama, but"—she paused— "they were never close. I'm sure he had no idea how to cope with her grief. Not just her friends but her whole existence had been destroyed. For years she was like a woman in a trance. Her health was poor. She never went out. She cried often and paid me little enough mind."

He touched her knee again, caring warmth in his eyes.

"Oh, I don't mean it in complaint. I had an excellent nurse," she said hastily, smiling through the faint pang.

He tilted his head, gazing at her.

"I believe that on the day we watched the sun rise, my mother finally overcame her loss. She saw that she still had some semblance of a life, still had a child who needed her. She turned to good works after that and slowly built up her health again. After Mama made up her mind to live again, at least until her next fit of melancholia, she possessed an aura of strength. Calm, steady poise."

"Like you."

She was taken aback. He smiled at her.

"She must have been remarkable," he said.

"When she was well." Allegra nodded, too choked up suddenly to answer and afraid that if she spoke at all, she would cry out to him, *Why did she leave me? What did I do wrong?*

"And we are watching this sunrise, I take it, because *your* whole former existence was destroyed. I destroyed it," he said as he met her gaze, "and now you must forge a new beginning. Is that right?"

She nodded slowly, looking into his eyes.

After a moment he turned back to the eastern horizon. "I'm glad you've decided there is hope."

"There is always hope," she said automatically, swiping away a tear, then bitterly added, "unless you take your own life. My mother and father both gave up, Captain, and for that I shall never forgive them."

He was silent for a long moment. "Sweetheart, have you ever wondered if your mother's death wasn't suicide? After all, your father had a lot of enemies."

She turned to him, round-eyed. "What are you suggesting? That she was—murdered?"

He only stared at her with a steady, searching gaze.

"Lazar, if you know something I don't, you must tell me."

He shook his head, reaching out to brush her cheek with his knuckle. "All I know is that the world is a darker place than you suspect, little one. I don't think your mother would have willingly left you alone in the world, no matter how unhappy she might have been over the death of King Alphonse."

She turned away. "I don't want to talk about this anymore."

"Why not?"

"Because she did leave me on purpose, Captain. She abandoned me to join her friends in the grave. She didn't want me, and my father didn't want me, either. That's why I was pawned off on my aunt Isabelle, and, by God's grace, I was loved. But that doesn't mean I ever felt I belonged. Now, if you don't mind, may we change the subject?" she said stiffly. "Your family, for instance." She decided to see if Vicar's explanation for his vendetta matched Lazar's own story. "How did you lose your family?"

Lazar was silent for a long moment. "They were murdered."

She closed her eyes. "I am so sorry."

He barely shrugged.

"When did it happen?"

"Eons ago. Yesterday." He shrugged. "I was a boy. You know the story, Allegra," he said with faint, self-mocking bitterness. "D'Orofio Pass, on the night of the great storm. Ten minutes past ten o'clock, June twelfth, 1770."

She stared at him. "I don't understand. Yesterday you said you were a pirate."

He did not meet her gaze but stared straight ahead while the breeze sculpted his shirt around him. "You be the judge, Allegra. What do you see when you look at me?"

She stared at him, motionless. "You are quite seriously telling me you are King Alphonse's son?"

For a few minutes there was silence as he simmered with an inward, brooding stare toward the horizon. Allegra awaited his reply with heart pounding, trying to read in his face any sign of the truth.

"It doesn't matter who I am," he said at last. "I'm just a man, and you're a woman. That's all that matters between us."

"If God put you on this earth to rule and protect Ascencion, so help me, it matters a great deal." She stared at him. "If you are he, you cannot deny your destiny and leave your people to suffer. You cannot defy God's will."

"There is no God, Allegra."

She lifted her eyes to the bleaching sky and let out a long breath, holding her exasperation in check.

"If you are he, why did you have us leave Ascencion?"

Lazar sat there, inscrutable, utterly remote.

She tried another tack to test him. "How did you get away from the highwaymen?"

"They weren't highwaymen. They were trained assassins, your father hired them, and it was just dumb luck." He stared intently at the rising sun so long she thought it would blind him. "No," he said. "No. It was not luck. My father gave his life so I could escape. Would that it were not so," he added in a low voice.

"Oh, now, don't say that," she murmured softly, reaching out to touch his arm, but he pulled away, staring toward the east. She shook her head at him in distress, not knowing what to believe. "How I wish there were something I could do for you."

"Sleep with me," he replied, never breaking his stark, forward stare.

"That is not the answer."

"It is for me."

"Well, look at you!" she burst out. "Whoever you are, you are a lost soul! Why don't you seek a proper answer to what ails you? Look at this life of yours! You are strong and smart and brave—why do you settle for so little? You could have so much more—"

His low, cold laugh cut off her words. "Clever, high-minded Miss Monteverdi. There is that scorn again. I'm coming to know it well."

"Scorn? What are you talking about?"

"Your scorn for me, my haughty little captive. Your contempt. That's why you wouldn't let me make love to you."

Her jaw dropped. "Impossible man! Is that your conclusion? What am I to say to you? It is not scorn I feel for you; it's terror!"

He finally looked at her.

"Terror?" he demanded, then scowled. "No."

"Yes, you terrify me! Pardon me if I am not eager to give myself to a man whose intentions toward me range from murdering me to seducing me, perhaps getting me with child, then casting me off in a strange place with nothing and no one to turn to! I'm sure it would be very nice for the moment, but one of us must be sensible here! You terrify me," she went on recklessly, "because you are so selfish and wild and so hard to resist. I am not a toy for your amusement! My life is not a game! I have feelings. I have rights. I have a heart!"

He shrugged. "You made an oath."

"Yes, but what choice did you give me? What would anyone have done in my place?" she demanded. "What would you have done?"

"Why, I'd have run away, *chérie*," he said, a terrible, black note in his voice. "I'd have let them perish and saved my own skin."

"No, you would not."

He turned on her. "Ah, but I did. That's precisely what I did, and there's your prince for you."

Her eyes widened.

He looked away again at the sea. "You're not terrified of me. You're terrified of letting yourself care for me, and I can't say I blame you. People who love me usually end up dead. But you see, I'm not going to give you any choice. You belong to me now whether you like it or not."

"I don't like it, not one bit!"

"Try to escape," he suggested coolly. "Go ahead. See what happens. Give me one excuse to take what I want from you, even if it is against your will. I want you that much. Too damned much." He turned without warning and kissed her, flattening her back against the pine mast.

Instantly, she was petrified—she knew she was going to fall to her death, break her head on the deck a hundred feet below, all for his kiss, which made her senses reel. Lazar did not give a damn, obviously. His mouth consumed hers with relentless, fiery passion.

"And are you terrified now, Miss Monteverdi?" he asked roughly, but he did not permit her to answer. His hard, angry kisses shoved her closer and closer toward an inward edge. His need invaded her, ever deeper.

She would not fall to him. She gripped the rails, dizzier and dizzier. Her stomach plummeted with desire, her fingertips tingled for the velvet of his golden skin, but she refused to touch him.

The paradox of it! she thought wildly. The perfect knight of her fancy, transformed to a demon lover she could not escape.

Extreme, intense, dangerous man. He was dangerous in more ways than she could fathom, and her body was trembling for him, for his hands, for his kiss—she craved his very lawlessness.

Lazar pulled back, panting. "Now tell me that's not the answer."

She couldn't say a word. Her mind was frayed. He steadied her against the mast as he released her. For a moment she pressed her head back against the rough wood, closing her eyes in an effort to regain her senses.

Watching her, he let out a soft, bitter laugh. "Aren't you glad I spared your life?"

She gazed at him, trembling faintly, then she looked off toward the southern horizon as she forced out a long, furious exhalation.

They sat, not touching, as the sun rose.

⊰ CHAPTER ⊱
TWELVE

What a damned debacle.

He wished he had never laid eyes on her. He supposed he might have seen this coming had he been using his head, instead of other regions of his anatomy, in his dealings with Allegra Monteverdi. Now his involvement with her was all tangled up with his groin and his solar plexus, and he did not know what to think.

He hated self-doubt above all things. It was so much better not to give a damn, just to be dead inside. How dare she try to tell him his duty?

It was early evening. Nothing glorious had happened after the sunrise. There were no new beginnings, nor did he want one. God's truth, he should have forced himself on her the first day and been done with the wench, he thought in disgust.

Lazar wandered over to his sea trunk and dug around inside for a shirt among the haphazard order of his clothes, then sought comfort from a bottle of fine French sherry, pouring himself a generous draft. He meandered out to the balcony to stand in the shade of the stern's gilded overhang, where he watched the frothy V of his ship's wake perpetually unfolding.

It was cruel of her to torment him so, he decided in a full royal sulk. She was picking away at old scabs so they bled afresh.

She had touched off a war inside him, and today the first shots had been fired, the moment she made him admit aloud for the first time in his life that Father had fought off the killers long enough for him to escape—had sacrificed himself—under the presumption that Lazar, his heir, would survive and hold the line.

Not survive and—what had she said?—*go sailing about in a pirate ship, terrifying people.*

You cannot deny your destiny, she'd said.

Watch me, he thought, and took a drink.

This morning up there on the crow's nest, she had made him admit to himself, if not to her, that he was reneging on his father's dying wish. On the destiny to which he had been born, and the duties and responsibilities for which he had been groomed until the age of thirteen, when the world ended.

He was exactly the things she said he was.

He was a coward. He was a vain, selfish desperado, living a pointless life of no use to anyone. He hated her for having seen the truth and could not fathom how she'd done it. She was just a baby, after all. Formidable kitten. Clear-eyed angel. He resented her for disturbing the familiar peace of his misery. She had no right. She was a Monteverdi, for God's sake. She annoyed the hell out of him, and he wanted her so badly he was almost blind with it. He had to have her.

Soon.

Lord, the physicians said it was unhealthy to live with this inward vortex of pent-up lust curling in his belly like a serpent of flame.

Damn, he needed sex. No. He needed her, but after this morning's argument, satisfaction looked all the further away. If Miss Monteverdi scorned him for piracy, she would never forgive him for what he was in truth, a prince who had turned his back on his people. He could never explain to her why he could not return to Ascencion. It was a secret he would take to his grave. Pointless even to think about it.

It was all bloody pointless, and it hurt like hell.

He glowered at the bright sea in mute rage and nearly finished the bottle of sherry, drowning his pain in the numbness and indifference it bestowed. Half an hour later, he was drunk and glad of it.

An excellent drink, he thought slowly as he slouched back into the cabin and sat down in the armchair with a sense of exhaustion. It was so much wiser to take nothing seriously.

He leaned his head back against the chair, his mind full of the bad place.

His brain grew clouded and strange whenever he thought of Al Khuum. Every memory he had of the place came back to him through an opium haze, for Malik had found the perfect way to make his most troublesome slave stay put.

Get the boy addicted to opium. Brilliant.

Strange thing was, sometimes he still craved it. He curled his lip in self-disgust with a bitter, forward stare, then finished the last swig from the bottle and held his head in one hand.

He noticed how the lengthening afternoon shadows were full of curious colors, maroons and olives, deep purples, earth browns. The bedraggled ship's cat perched on his desk, peering at him curiously with phosphorescent green eyes.

"What do you bloody want?" he asked it.

The cat ran, sensing his black mood.

He shut his eyes, his skewed mind full of Al Khuum, zero longitude. Zero hope.

How pretty it was, high white arches, brightly colored tiles, lovely hell, the splash of the alabaster fountain—a relief just to hear it in the endless desert afternoons. The muezzin's eerie warbling calling the faithful to prayer, and the silken, gliding music of the oud in the cool pitch of night, Malik's pistol at his temple, forcing him to his knees.

A shudder racked him, and he squeezed his eyes shut more tightly against the memory.

What Allegra would think if she knew what really had become of her beloved young prince, he thought, a crazed, slight smile flickering over his dry lips. He wished he still had his signet ring, for he'd have loved to shove it down her throat.

He'd had actual proof once, proof of his high birth. Long, long ago.

His signet ring with the onyx lion rampant, whose eye was a ruby taken from the hilt of Excelsior, in ancient Fiori tradition. The setting had been left empty on the sword so that when it was his turn to ascend to the throne, it would be replaced, the design made whole again, and in the years to come he would have taken a jewel from the hilt of the broadsword and set it in a ring for his heir.

But the circle had been broken.

His ring, the last vestige of his real self, had been stolen from him, along with his faith, his pride, his self-respect. Sayf-del-Malik, who was called the Sword of Honor, now owned it, a trophy of the boy prince his corsairs had fished out of the sea, half-dead, and brought to Al Khuum.

No matter what it cost him, he was never going back there.

Allegra let out a sigh and wearily rubbed the back of her neck, noticing that the lantern was burning low. In her quest for the truth, she had spent the day, as Lazar had suggested, in the cramped, dim storeroom, poring through boxes of the dusty files he had stolen from her father's offices. Over the past few hours, she'd learned more about the stranger who had been her father than if they had both lived out the rest of their natural lives on Ascencion, seeing each other every day.

She didn't much like what she found. It was salt in the wound so soon after his death to learn that Papa had been taking bribes, diverting funds, and sending dozens of alleged young rebels to jail or execution on scant evidence.

These discoveries certainly strengthened Lazar's claim that Papa had indeed betrayed King Alphonse to gain wealth and position for himself and had hired assassins to carry out the bloody task, men he had later hanged for the very crime he'd paid them to commit. In this light, Papa's suicide practically seemed an admission of guilt.

But how could she wrap her mind around the thought? And how could she accept that her fierce pirate captor was none other than the true lost prince of the great Fiori?

Lost indeed, she thought with a sigh. She shoved the heavy wooden crate back onto the lowest shelf and stretched her arms and neck, making her way topside for some fresh air.

It was a breezy evening, and the lingering light of sunset tinged the ivory sails pink. She glanced at the quarterdeck, then at the helm, but the captain was nowhere to be found. She had not seen him since they had quarreled that morning. Now she supposed he was probably somewhere below, preparing to take the night watch again.

Vicar was reading aloud from the Bible to half a dozen of the crewmen under the canvas shade on deck. She joined them and listened, smiling shyly at the men, who all made room for her, tripping over themselves to be polite.

While Vicar read about love from the Gospel of John, Allegra's mind drifted. She had a fair idea why the captain was no longer spending the nights in bed with her. While she appreciated his chivalry, she found that the vastness of the sea weighed heavily on her when he left her alone. Oddly enough, she missed the anchor of his warm body bowing the mattress, the comfort of his deep, steady breathing, for at night the solitude of the sea was enormous, and the ship's creaking sounded like the moaning of trapped ghosts.

At length, she bade Vicar and the others good night and made her way below, still troubled and deep in thought. Hungry, she stopped by the galley. Since Emilio wasn't cooking this evening, she rooted around for something light to eat and assembled a small bowl of fruit. She still didn't see Lazar, and she glanced into the sailors' gallery to see if he was in there, checking the cannons, but he wasn't. Mr. Harcourt had told her that they might run into enemies tonight as they passed the Strait of Gibraltar.

She entered the stateroom, devouring a juicy peach. When she knocked on the cabin door, there was no answer. She went in and promptly found the captain fast asleep, huddled in a great lump on the far edge of the bed.

She smiled in spite of herself and silently closed the door behind her. Her gaze fell upon the empty liquor bottle. Frowning in disapproval, she set her peach and her bowl of fruit on the desk and crossed to open the balcony door. She also pulled open a few window panels in the hope that a breeze might revive him. She glanced at him as she passed the berth where just the day before he had introduced her to what Mother Beatrice would have called the temptations of the flesh.

With one big arm, he hugged his pillow. His face was toward her, eyes closed, as he slept peacefully.

The sight of him wrung her heart somehow even as it enticed her senses. So much pure male beauty. So much weariness and hurting. How innocent he looked. This man would never intentionally hurt anyone, she thought. He was a good man, though hard, and if he struck out at the world, it was only because he was in pain.

Dear Jonah, she thought with a sad, fond smile, *wake up. Somewhere your destiny awaits you.*

He slept on.

She returned to her fruit bowl and ventured to the threshold of the balcony. Tossing the peach pit out into the waves, she began on the ripe red cherries. She was gazing out at the silvery streak of some flying fish over the water when Lazar made a strange sound from the bed behind her. Curious, Allegra turned around and gazed at him.

He was still sleeping, but fleeting expressions of anger or pain echoed from the realms of dream, playing over his tanned face, a dark flicker over his brow, a silent protest on his lips.

She watched in fascination for a moment, wondering if she should wake him.

He murmured, "No, no," then fell silent again, sleeping soundly.

Munching idly, she watched him sleep for perhaps a quarter hour.

If she were another woman, she thought, she'd have cast care to the wind and crept over to his bed. Caressed him. Awakened him. Lain with him—and not just for the sake of getting it over with.

Love me.

She was not blind to the fact that nothing pleased him more than when she initiated any physical contact between them, as if he were starved for it, which she knew full well he was not. Not he. But it was true—he loved to be touched, held, loved, as if this was his reassurance—and a part of herself she had never known existed was coming to light with an aching need to give this man whatever he required.

Oh, maybe he was right, she thought, licking off the cherry juice staining her fingertips. Maybe the simple comfort of touch *was* the answer to what ailed them both, for words caused as many problems as they solved.

Go to him.

She swallowed hard, set her bowl aside, and told herself he needed the rest before his shift.

Judging it a violation of his privacy to keep gawking at him this way, she began looking around the cabin for the copy of Mr. Thomas Paine's *Common Sense* that Vicar had lent her. She decided to read topside by the waning light of evening until the captain had readied himself and left the cabin.

She was hunting for the book on the cluttered desk when Lazar bolted upright in the bed and screamed.

He woke up midway through the scream and cut it off, gasping, wild-eyed with panic.

Allegra stared at him in astonishment. He stared back at her with terror in his eyes, looking suddenly very young and very lost, as if he wasn't sure where he was.

He jerked, startled, when a man pounded at the door, probably thinking she'd murdered him. "Everything all right in there, Cap?"

Lazar flinched, turning his head toward the door. "Aye . . . aye," he gasped out, raking a hand through his short hair as his chest heaved.

Heart pounding, Allegra came around the desk, staring at him. "Are you all right?"

"Oh. Ohhh, Christ," he groaned. He sank back on his pillow and threw a forearm over his eyes. He was rather mortified, she guessed.

"Are you all right?" she repeated.

He didn't answer.

She squared her shoulders, shaken to see fear in the eyes of her protector, a man who until this moment had seemed to her an invulnerable warrior. Hands trembling slightly, she poured water into the glass for him from the earthen jar, then went to his side and sat down on the edge of the bed.

He didn't move or respond or even take his arm from over his eyes. She could see the tension in every line of his body, all his self-control straining to hold his desperation in check.

She offered the glass.

"Don't touch me."

"I have water for you, Captain."

His voice was a low growl layered with years of anger. "My name is Lazar."

She let out a patient exhale and studied the bulkhead. "Will Your Royal Highness condescend to take some water?"

"Go to hell."

She grinned with relief to find he had his fight back.

"So," she drawled a moment later, "now I know what it takes to scare you. Domenic failed. My father failed. My father's soldiers failed. Goliath failed. I certainly failed. The

Genovese navy failed." She ticked them off on her fingers, then looked down at him. "I guess *you* are the only thing you are afraid of."

"Not the only thing."

"There, there, dear, we all have bad dreams. Drinking doesn't help matters," she added, poking him in the arm just to defy him and take his mind off the nightmare.

"Lecture me and I'll put a gag in your mouth."

"Ohhh, what's wrong?" she teased him, caressing his flat belly through his soft lawn shirt. "Are you embarrassed, my dear?" she asked in a parody of that bland, regal courtesy he used whenever he chose to be condescending.

"Wench."

"Pardon me?"

"Wench. Saucy, common little cock-tease wench."

She lifted the glass and poured the water on his head.

He sat up sputtering, water running down his face and chest. He stared at her in disbelief.

She smiled innocently.

"You like to live dangerously, don't you, Miss Monteverdi?"

He licked the water off his lips.

She wanted to lick it, too.

A gleam came into his dark eyes a second before he grabbed her and hurled her down onto the rumpled bed, romping atop her on all fours, tickling her until she shrieked for mercy. He bit her shoulder, then moved closer, nuzzling her neck. She pushed halfheartedly against his chest, delighted that she had succeeded in distracting him.

"You smell of sherry," she protested.

"I taste of it, too." He kissed her. "You taste of cherries. I like cherries," he murmured.

She slipped her arms around his neck and kissed him hungrily.

He started laughing drunkenly after a moment, breaking

their kiss. "The room is spinning. I'm still foxed." He collapsed on her, all fourteen-odd stone of him.

"Isn't that wonderful!" she exclaimed, shoving him back so she could breathe. "You're on duty in five minutes. Maybe you'll sink the ship."

"Who cares? I don't give a damn. I just want you," he said in a low, hearty voice, grinning with debauchery as he moved between her thighs and lifted her knee to hug his hip.

"I thought you were vexed with me," she confided with a bit of a sulk as she ran her fingers through his short, soft hair. "You avoided me the whole day."

"Nonsense. I never hold a grudge."

"No?" She cocked her head at him on the pillow, fighting laughter. "Aren't you the man with the terrible vendetta? The one who burned down the city?"

He narrowed his eyes and scowled down at her. "We can indulge your taste for argument later. For now, we're going to do what I like for a change." He lowered his head. "Wrap your legs around me," he whispered.

Instantly she turned red. "No!"

"Shh, come. Just for a moment. You'll like it. Since the first minute I saw you, I've dreamed of feeling these long, gorgeous legs around me."

"You're joking!"

"Oh, no, I'm not. You remember when I pulled you into the pond at the waterfall? I could see everything."

"No," she breathed, wide-eyed.

"Wet white silk," he whispered. "A sight I'll never forget."

She stared up at him, stared at the banked desire under his long-lashed eyes, the fullness of his lips, wet with her kiss. He was stroking her thigh, gently bringing her other knee up against his side. She reached up and kissed him again, doing as he asked, sliding her ankles behind his muscled thighs.

"Mmm, what a good little pupil you are, my virgin," he murmured, pressing against her in a way that made her shiver.

She drifted with a faint smile, shamelessly enjoying the feel of him between her legs. It seemed natural, effortless, to writhe slightly against that perfect fit. After all, Aunt Isabelle had said coyness was for provincials. Allegra was finally beginning to grasp what that meant.

"I had morals before I met you, you know," she told him dreamily as he nibbled her earlobe. "You could turn me into a wanton woman."

"I already have."

She made a sound of indignation and brought her legs down again from his body.

"Hey!" He scowled down at her.

She held him at bay with a speculative expression. "Tell me your dream."

His roguish expression darkened, and she saw that the darkness had been there all along, just beneath the surface. No, he was not ready to tell her yet, she saw. She lifted her fingertips and caressed his cheek.

"Was there a monster?" she asked softly, just a bit playfully, refusing to let that darkness take him away from her again.

He nodded.

"Did it try to eat you?"

When his earnest look of loss turned into a rueful half smile, she caught herself thinking, *I could fall in love with you so easily.*

"Talk to me," she murmured. "What ails you, Lazar? I want to help you. I won't judge you."

"I can't, Allegra," he said, gazing down at her with a silent plea of distress in his chocolate-brown eyes. The look could have conquered hearts of stone.

She stroked his cheek slowly, studying him.

"I can't," he said again.

"It's all right. It's all right, Lazar." She paused, running her hand back through his hair. "My Lazar."

He closed his eyes, holding perfectly still at her use of his name.

She leaned up and kissed his lips lingeringly. "Lazar," she whispered between kisses, "Lazar, my rescuer. My wild, lost, pirate-prince Lazar." She wrapped her legs around him as before.

Fiercely he kissed her, linking his fingers through hers on the mattress.

Well, she surely hoped he wasn't the prince, she thought, almost giddy as he moved downward over her body, kissing as he went. Allegra didn't think Princess Nicolette would much have appreciated what she was presently doing with *her* fiancé.

Lazar fixed her with a stormy gaze as he kissed her bared knee. She watched him inch her skirts upward; she was a bit nervous, but not nearly as nervous as perhaps she should have been.

Higher he went, grazing along the pale, tender skin on the inside of her thigh. Higher crept her hemline.

Lazar bent his head.

She let out a shocked, wide-eyed gasp, then her eyes drifted closed in astonished ecstasy.

Oh, she knew she should have stopped him—it was indecent, what he was doing—but it felt sinfully good. Soon she was too weak with longing to mind propriety as he drank of her, lapping intently, crouched between her thighs like a thirsty lion at the banks of a slow-moving river.

Moments passed. Only when she gasped for air did she realize she'd been holding her breath at the pleasure and decadence of his gift.

Someone pounded at the door to remind him of his watch, but he ignored it, holding her down with a gentle, insistent press of his left hand against her belly. At the interruption, she glanced down and became instantly fascinated, watching him. His expression of erotic devotion was almost too beautiful to gaze upon.

She closed her eyes and drifted back with a soft, soul-deep moan as she gave herself over to his will, accepting his hunger to assuage her body's need, this aching need he had found by patiently peeling away all her protests, refusals, denials, to the core of her—loneliness and longing for love.

God, he was a gentleman, she thought oddly, just before the mind-melting sweetness of sensation overcame her.

She arched endlessly for the stroke of his tongue, caressing his hair, grasping and twisting handfuls of the sheet as she writhed in bliss, her moans lifting toward the screams he liked.

Oh, she could love him. She was that great a fool. *And what of it?* she thought defiantly, then all thought dissolved.

There was anguish in her cry of reaching need. He had taught her only yesterday how to seek the climax, how to wait for it, lure it near and catch it, and when she did, she gasped his name again and again—if that was his name—clutching his muscled shoulders in ecstasy until her fingers' grip went limp.

Now it was she who lay there, half concealing her face with one arm thrown over her brow. He was a dark silhouette in the dim cabin as he rose over her. She was almost angry at him, now that she knew the sort of danger she was in.

"Why won't you let me hate you?" she asked wearily when she'd caught her breath.

"Because you are my lover."

"No, I'm not. I am your prisoner."

"You need me, Allegra. You know it, and I know it. And it's altogether possible that I need you, too."

"You are still foxed."

"No."

"Then it is some new scheme, some plot you've hatched for revenge—"

"No. I am done with that."

She crossed both forearms over her brow, feeling cornered. "Why are you doing this to me? Why don't you just rape me and get it over with?"

"I would never do that," he said as he took off his shirt and toweled his face with it.

"Why not?"

"Because." He paused in the dark, his back to her. "I know how it feels."

❧ CHAPTER ❧
THIRTEEN

"I beg your pardon," Allegra said, coming up onto her elbows.

Several minutes passed, and still the room was silent.

Lazar listened to the water's small splash in the basin as he rinsed her sweetness from his face, her elixir from his fingertips. He listened to the dark lullaby of the sea and the pounding of his own heart.

"Lazar?" she asked softly from the bed, brushing her skirts down as she sat up. "What does that mean?"

He put on a fresh shirt, then walked slowly to the lantern fixed to his desk and lit it. He stared at Allegra for a moment as the flame grew, musing, incredulous to think he had ever judged her less than stunning. She had the beauty of pure water, clean air, warm sun—essential things—and he knew now he needed her as much.

He also knew he was deceiving himself. The sooner Miss Monteverdi understood that her besotted captor was a suicide waiting to happen, the better.

Best to kill his futile hope now.

He walked over to the bed and sat down beside her. She stared at him wide-eyed, her irises the warm brown of cinnamon sticks.

She was incredible, he thought. How sweet she looked, with her lips swollen from his kisses, her chestnut hair pushed forward over one shoulder. He wanted to kiss every one of her buttery freckles.

He didn't. He lowered his head, pushed up his sleeves. Turning both loose fists palm upward on his lap, he showed her his wrists, and he waited.

Her long hair swung down in a silky curtain as she examined them. He watched her steadily, waiting for her to condemn him, reject him. She would have noticed the scars sooner or later, after all. He didn't expect her to accept him with these scars, after both her parents had taken their own lives. It was too much to ask of anyone.

She remained silent. He braced himself for the barrage. She gently pulled his right hand onto her lap. He didn't fight her. She laid her fingertips on his wrist, following the old white gash, the healed-over break in the thick blue vein he'd once slashed with the sharp edge of a broken plate in the bad place.

Moments passed, and he began wanting to believe she might not yell at him.

Still, he waited. Her fingers stroked his wrist slowly, tenderly, as if the old scar were mere chalk dust that could be brushed away, instead of the jagged mark of the thunderbolt branded on his soul.

He had been young and idealistic once, too, he wanted to tell her, an eternity ago. But the same storm that had saved him had also warped him, like a young tree struck by lightning, forced to grow into a distorted shape.

He wished she would say something.

Her head was still down when the first tear fell onto his wrist. They both stared down at it, and she began rubbing it into his skin there, as if it were some precious ointment that would take away the old, old hurt. At length she touched his left wrist in the same manner, then she took him into her arms without a word.

She held him tight, solid and still as a green island in all his tempestuous dark sea.

Neither of them moved for a long time. He closed his eyes, amazed at the sting of salt in them. He swallowed back a lump in his throat and stroked the curve of Allegra's back. He knew that he shuddered and that she held him more tightly when he did. She was whispering to him.

"What have they done to you, my darling? What have they done to you?"

He couldn't reply. He shuddered again, buried his face against her neck, inhaling her flowery scent, a healing balm so different in its effects than the opium that had brought about these scars, but equally intoxicating. She caressed the back of his head and his shoulders, his back. He wondered why he was not instantly aroused by these simple touches after having wanted her for so long, but all he could seem to fix upon was the acid stream of pain seeping out of his heart. She was mightier than it was.

He was amazed. He clung to her, his warm, ivory goddess, like the spirit of Ascencion embodied in a woman.

"What drove you to hurt yourself this way?"

"I should be dead," he whispered brokenly. "If I had any courage, I would be dead. I'm like an animal, just instinct. No pride. I left them to die. I should be dead, too."

"No, Lazar, no." She wept silently now as she had in bed those first few nights in grief for her father. Now her grief was for him, and somehow it made his own grief fractionally less.

She kissed the lone tear that trailed down his cheek, tasting it between her slightly parted lips. He was in too much pain to be properly humiliated by his own unmanly display. She gathered him closer still. He wanted to hide inside of her.

After a moment, she drew back and leaned her forehead gently against his. He kept his eyes closed, fearing to meet her even gaze. She caressed his chest with one hand, still holding him tightly around the neck with the other.

"I knew, oh, I knew who you were those first few moments in the tunnels, but I dared not believe."

"I didn't really expect you to."

"Lazar di Fiore, I will never deny you again," she vowed in a fierce whisper.

He let out an unsteady sigh and opened his eyes. There was pure determination in her dark eyes beneath the gold-tipped lashes, and what looked to him like love, or at least pity. He didn't want her pity. He looked away.

She captured his face softly between her hands and brought his gaze back to hers. He waited, watching her guardedly. She looked pensive, studying him. She traced his eyebrow softly with her fingertip, touched his lips with her thumb.

He sat there with a bleak expression, awaiting her verdict. Her full lips tilted down at the corners in a slight, motherly frown.

What an excellent mother she would be, he thought idly.

Futile. But he would have loved to make her big with his child. Life. Creation. These were the miracles with which she inspired him.

Pointless.

Of all the women he'd had, he'd never permitted any of them truly to know him, but Allegra had seen him in his blackest hour—indeed, had saved him from it. After that, there had been no point in attempting to hide from her. Thus she knew all too well the kind of thing he was. Of course she would not want him. He didn't blame her. Especially now that she knew he had half a mind on any given day to blow out his brains.

There were only two fit places for such a man, he mused in his misery. The cemetery or the sea.

She laid her palm against his cheek, and as she stared at him, he watched her eyes fill with tears. She forced herself to speak. "I was too frightened to believe you, and I pray you will forgive me for my cowardice."

"Of course, Allegra," he whispered. "Anything."

"You are so good," she said with a soft catch in her voice as she caressed his face.

"I am not good." He nestled his cheek wearily against her hand.

She leaned toward him and kissed him softly on the mouth as she cupped the back of his head. "I am here for you now, Lazar. I promise," she whispered. "I am ready to help you however I can. I will not fail you again."

"You believe me?"

She nodded fervently. "And I believe *in* you."

He stared at her, wondering if it was a good time to seduce her, but he felt too bruised inside to proceed. He just wanted to be near her, close enough to touch.

With one final kiss upon his brow, Allegra pulled back marginally from his embrace, and when she did, he saw there was a new, white-hot fire in her eyes. Her flawless face was serene, but her elegantly curved auburn brows were aligned in formidable determination.

He wondered if he should be worried, seeing that look. The blend of intensity and angelic calm in her expression awed him. He was not sure he was ready for this. She lifted each of his wrists to her lips—one, then the other—pressing a heartfelt kiss to each. Then she braced his shoulders in her hands, staring solemnly into his face.

"You are not alone in this anymore. Do you understand? My dear, long-lost friend, you must tell me everything, and somehow, together, I swear to you, we will put all these wrongs to right."

She understood now. This was not the life he had chosen; it was merely the one he'd fallen into, and it was not irresponsibility or hedonism that had made him cast off Ascencion. It was pain. Raw grief and loss. Every joke he made was his way of bearing those wounds. The poor, noble creature could not forgive himself for having survived when his beloved family had perished.

How could she have doubted for a second?

With every particle of her awareness focused on his soulful eyes, eyes as dark and full of mysteries as the night sea that surrounded them, Allegra held her breath, staring with barely restrained impatience at his satiny lips, as if she could will them to tell her everything she wanted to know, every detail of his existence.

Instead she heard only the great creaking of *The Whale*'s mighty timbers.

Her Prince looked worried. He was edging back from her earnest stare with a helpless but obstinate gaze. She was about to offer some coaxing words to help him along when one of his men came to his rescue, banging on the door.

"Gibraltar's four leagues off the bow, Cap! You comin' topside?"

"Aye!" he called with a quick jerk of his square chin over his shoulder. He turned back to her, unable to mask his fleeting look of relief, yet she sensed his inward conflict, as if half of him needed to unburden himself of his secrets, while the other half wanted to flee.

"I have to go," he said gingerly.

"May I come with you?"

He lifted her hand to his lips. "I'd like that."

He stood and offered his hand to help her climb out of his berth. She tried to put herself into some order so it would not be so obvious she had just been partially ravished. He scanned a navigational chart among the clutter on his desk, then he blew out the lantern, and they went to the cabin door. He paused there before opening it for her. His large, warm, callused hand sought hers in the dark, his fingers interlocking with hers.

"Wait," she whispered. "I've said a few things over the past few days that, well, I have to apologize—"

His forefinger descended gently upon her lips, hushing her.

"Things, perhaps, I needed to hear. Few people dare criticize me, Allegra, even when I'm in the wrong. You were honest, and you spoke your mind. I hope you will always do so." He traced his fingertip across her lips. "Every ship needs a compass."

Warmed all the way to her heart by his generous words, she kissed the finger he'd lightly pressed to her lips. He smiled in the dark.

"Duty calls," he said as he opened the door. "Let me show you how we pirates do business."

When they went topside, she followed Lazar around, feeling all the while that she was walking in the shadow of a legend.

How had he done it? How in God's name had he survived? When she looked back over all that had happened, she could scarcely believe he had been her beloved Prince all the while. No wonder he had found it in his noble heart to lift his vendetta, sparing her family. As she recalled those shattering moments on the eastern rampart, her expression sobered, and she lowered her head.

She believed in Lazar now, as Mama had believed in King Alphonse. Somehow she was going to have to come to terms with Papa's guilt.

She watched him efficiently dispensing orders at the helm of his warship, never showing any sign of his inward pain, and every idealistic, meticulously responsible atom of her being cried out to repair her father's sins.

It all made sense now—Lazar's unhappiness, his stagnating here in this outlaw life, Ascencion's unrest and anarchy. When the two were brought together once more, she knew there must be peace. Brokenhearted Ascencion and poor Captain Jonah would both be made whole again when Lazar was restored to his rightful throne.

She had no doubt that he was equal to the staggering task and deserving of the awesome privilege after all he'd suffered. The mercy he had shown toward her family proved he would be a just and righteous king. That he had survived horrors, yet retained the ability to be gentle, even to laugh at himself, proved his depth of character and his strength. He was everything Ascencion cried out for.

He will be even greater than Alphonse, she thought, infused with a brilliant, soaring sense of power as a night breeze lifted her hair back over her shoulders. She felt she could do anything for him, slay dragons, meet any challenge, however impossible.

But most of all she thanked God from the bottom of her heart that her tedious prudence had saved her in the nick of time. She lifted her gaze to the dark, starry sky, taking solace in the caress of the warm night breeze upon her cheek.

Thank God she had been careful. What a relief he didn't know she had allowed herself to become so foolishly infatuated with him. They could be friends now, she told herself. Dear friends. Allies.

Nothing more.

The knowledge left her with a hollow, rather sick feeling, but she knew it was for the best. Lazar belonged to Ascencion and the Austrian princess, not to her. If the Habsburgs were still willing, he would need that alliance to oust Genoa from Ascencion. For her part, if she allowed herself to love him, it would only lead to her own torment, and she had no intention of reliving her mother's tragedy, of loving a man she could not have. Better to be his friend—let Princess Nicolette break her heart trying to tame him.

For herself, better not to venture any closer to that all-consuming fire of his passion. Better not to know what heaven she'd be missing. She didn't need the heartbreak.

No wonder he had not forced himself on her, she thought almost woefully. No son of King Alphonse would ever do such a thing.

For a moment she puzzled over his statement that had opened tonight's entire discussion, that he knew how it felt to be raped. To the best of her knowledge—and it was by no means wide—only women could be raped. If she was mistaken in this, she rather did not wish to know it.

She concluded he must have been speaking metaphorically about his many tragic losses.

What a cruel loss of innocence, she thought.

As a youngster, she herself had barely survived the loss of her mother, but Lazar had lost his whole family, his home, his kingdom, his inheritance, his entire world. She was in awe of his strength; after all he had been through, she truly couldn't blame him for having attempted to end his life at some point in his past, but she thanked God with all her heart that he had failed.

As they approached Gibraltar, Lazar ordered all lanterns extinguished for they were about to pass within range of the British guns stationed there, on the southernmost tip of Spain. Allegra could make out the tiny lights of the garrison town on the distant peninsula.

The whole crew kept a tense silence. Even the sweeps had been swaddled in rags to muffle the slapping of the wooden oars against the waves.

When she asked in a whisper why such measures were necessary, Lazar explained that if they were delayed here by the British, the Genovese ships, less than a day's sail behind them, would catch up, and then they would have to do battle. If the Brethren lost, he said, every man captured would hang.

She shuddered and sent up a prayer at once for their protection. If her Prince thought she was going to permit anyone to hang him, he was a silly fool! she thought fiercely.

Every stroke of the sweeps inched them closer to the mouth of the Mediterranean.

Allegra turned her face to the east, in the direction where Ascencion lay somewhere miles and miles over the ship's stern. With a sense of promise, she offered her homeland a temporary farewell.

Then Lazar drew her into his arms at the helm. Standing

together, sharing their warmth, they waited in taut silence as *The Whale* led the other six ships through the narrow strait.

A patchy cloud covering further helped their cause by obscuring the waning gibbous moon, and within two hours the passage was safely made—Lazar's small fleet gained the Atlantic undetected. The crew relaxed with a collective sigh of relief. Flagons of rum were passed around. Here and there subdued shouts of laughter bubbled over the moonlit decks.

As the seven ships spread out again in loose formation, riding the rougher, colder swells of the Atlantic, Lazar turned her around to face him and caught her up in a long, hearty kiss. She threw her arms around his neck, forgetting for the moment her rededication to the cause of being careful, swept up in the joy of his triumph.

Someone lit a lantern again nearby, and when Lazar ended the kiss, gazing down at her, his bold, cocky grin was pure pirate.

"My little captive," he purred, sliding his arms tighter around her waist, "go to our bed, and get some rest. You're going to need it when I come down."

"Aren't you finishing the night watch?" she asked in sudden alarm.

He glanced over the decks with that hard, critical gaze of the weathered sea captain. "I'll mind the helm for another few hours, then I'll join you."

Oh, dear.

"Don't feel you must wait up for me. I'll wake you. Trust me."

"I couldn't possibly sleep," she said, choosing her words with care. "Perhaps I'll look through more of my father's files—"

"Now, why do you want to go filling your head with such matters tonight, of all nights?" He tenderly cupped her face. "We have both been waiting for this, Allegra. The time has come."

"But I don't think—"

"No, don't think, Allegra. Just feel," he whispered. "I can read your body's signals, you know. The darkening of your eyes when you gaze at me. Your nipples pressing through your dress, aching for my mouth. Give in to it, Allegra. Nothing stands between us now, no more pretenses."

"But—"

"Allegra," he said, "you're ready for me."

She stared up at him, wide-eyed. To deny it would have been a lie.

"You grow wet for me even now, don't you, my love?" he asked softly, seducing her with his deep, mesmerizing voice. "You thought you tasted pleasure when I made love to you with my touch and, this evening, when I drank of your beauty. But when we are one, Allegra, when I am deep inside you, you will see these things were but pale dreams."

Her eyes flickered. She leaned against the rail to bear her failing weight.

"Go below," he whispered. "Have a glass of wine. I shan't be long."

His heart was light when Lazar finally turned over the helm to Harcourt. With one final survey of the decks, he hitched his hands in the pockets of his well-worn black trousers and sauntered to the hatch, his face betraying no sign of the heady emotions churning within him.

The blissful sense of entwinement, his soul in hers, made his head reel a little. He could not stifle his sense of wonder. Never had he let anyone reach so deeply into him. Sea battles, raids, duels aside—this was somehow the most dangerous thing he had ever done. His relief was unbounded that at last Allegra knew a fair portion of the truth about him. Yet he worried about that determined look he'd seen in her eyes.

He walked slowly down the unlit passage, knowing that each step over the comfortably creaking planks took him closer to the cabin, where he would go about deflowering his virgin. Crossing the stateroom, he gave a soft knock on the cabin door, then went in. He stopped at what he saw.

"Ah, *chérie*," he said with a weary chuckle.

She was surrounded on the rug by a sea of files and documents, and she was fast asleep, half leaning against the armchair. The lantern was still burning near her, the small flame like the warmth that tightened in his chest at the sight of her.

She'll have a sore neck, he thought, seeing how her head rested at a skewed angle against the chair.

Lazar closed the door quietly behind him, locked it. He picked his way through the scattered papers and gathered her up in his arms, lifting her light weight easily. He carried her to the berth and gently set her down. She rustled in her skirts as she turned on her side in her usual sleeping position. He sat down beside her and just stared.

"Take the cakes to them," she ordered him in a queenly murmur.

He smiled in the shadows. "Yes, ma'am," he said softly.

"Josefina, put those . . . my *green* dress . . ." She drifted into silence.

"Ah, *chérie*," he whispered, "what am I going to do with you?"

He considered for a moment, then, with a huge yawn, Lazar admitted defeat. Her sleep was deep, and he was damned tired. It was near dawn, and this was not the way it should be for her. No deflowerings tonight.

To hell with these night watches, he thought wearily, rubbing the back of his neck for a moment.

He stripped down to his breeches and loosened Allegra's dress before climbing into the berth beside her and pulling her into his arms. She arranged herself fitfully, her face cradled on his bosom, her arm thrown across his stomach.

As he drifted to sleep, Lazar began imagining rows of orange trees in a sun-misty grove, as he sometimes did. He saw vines of shiny, ripe tomatoes and pale clusters of grapes dangling from a trellis. Then he saw Allegra, barefoot and laughing, holding her skirts above her ankles as she stomped the grapes in a great wooden tub for his homemade wine. When he thought of the old dappled gray plow horse that frequented such scenes in his fancy, this time he was leading the lazy animal, and perched atop its broad swayback were three perfect young children.

His eyes shot open with sudden awe in the dark. Yes. There was the answer, plain as day. The vine of his family had been hacked down, but he could grow it again. It need not die with him, as he had assumed all this time in his bitterness.

Children of the Fiori, he thought in wonder, living free and safe, far away from the endless burden of the crown, the endless jeopardy that leadership demanded. All he had to do was get his men situated back at Wolfe's Den, let them vote for another leader to head the Brethren, then he and Allegra could be on their way.

He could settle them on Martinique, or the Florida coast, or even somewhere in Naples or on Sicily, in sight of Ascencion.

He stared, unseeing, in the dark as his mind raced. When he realized he was in the midst of one of the happiest moments of his life, he was vaguely amused at himself, ever the cynic. But he had to admit that what Allegra said was true, in the end—
There is always hope.

Children, he thought, still awed.

He had been reasonably careful in his past amours. However much he had enjoyed the women he'd known, they weren't the sort he wanted raising his daughters and sons. Pride in his lineage had stayed with him. To the best of his knowledge, he had left no illegitimate babies in his wake.

For a while he caressed Allegra's arm while she slept. Here was a woman of beauty, grit, and moral fiber, he thought proudly. This was the one worthy to bear children from a royal line seven hundred years old.

He was mulling over how to phrase his offer of marriage to her without sounding like an utter idiot, when an insidious whisper in the back of his mind cast a shadow over the sunlit landscape of his imaginings. Perhaps it was years at sea that had made him superstitious, like all sailors, but, he thought, what if fate tried to strike down his happiness with its old trick of snuffing out those he cared about?

Don't be irrational, he scoffed at himself, taking Vicar as the example. The old frigate bird had been with him over ten years now and somehow managed to remain unscathed.

Still, the prospect of Allegra's coming to harm as a consequence of his past crimes or his dangerous career was almost enough to terrify him out of the idea. Surely she was better off with some tame Martinique planter. And babies?

Good God, what was more fragile than a baby?

His expression turned very grim in the dark. Numerous times now Allegra had called him selfish, and surely this was his most selfish move yet, even to risk it.

He argued with himself. The assassins, the old conspirators of the Council, now even Monteverdi, were dead, and by now Jeffers and his lads had probably shown Domenic Clemente to his Maker.

It was over. It had to be.

Surely now the curse that had seemed to cling to him was broken. He had already lost one family. Not even he could believe lightning would strike twice.

But when he felt Allegra's gentle, steady breathing against his neck, he knew he couldn't take that chance. No, he would trick fate, or at least try to compromise with it.

He would not marry her.

She would be his wife in every sense except the legal one. Then God might not strike her down to spite him. And on their farm, removed from the violence and chaos of the world, the Fiori could take new root. If danger ever came, he was certain he could protect his brood. That was the one regard in which he knew he was better than Father.

Yes, he told himself, it would be all right as long as he didn't marry her. He only hoped she'd understand.

With the matter thus uneasily settled, at length Lazar slept.

⚡ CHAPTER ⚡ FOURTEEN

In the white light of morning, Allegra woke her sleeping Prince with a kiss.

She had been up for some time, had washed, dressed, eaten, and prepared her notes from the final boxes of her father's files, which she had gone through last night while Lazar had finished his watch. Nearby she had breakfast for him from the galley to fortify him for what she had to say.

He was going to need it.

He shifted awake under the gentle brushing of her lips over his. She slid back before he beguiled her into more serious play, but he captured her wrist, still blinking against the morning light. He looked delicious, his short hair tousled, the sun-chiseled lines of his face softened by rest. All around him the sheets were still warm with his big body's heat.

Shooting her a sleepy smile, he sat up and reached for the glass of orange juice on the tray. Without pausing, he drank it all. She gazed at the lift and fall of his Adam's apple, thinking with an inward sigh that she had never known before how beautiful a man could look drinking a glass of juice. Lazar made a hearty sound of appreciation and set the glass back on the tray.

"Good morning, kitten," he growled playfully, pulling her down, sprawling, atop his bare chest when he flopped back onto the mattress. He kissed her in earnest.

She stopped him.

"What's wrong?" he asked.

"Your coffee will get cold."

"Not if it's anywhere near us two."

"What a rogue you are," she said in a scold that somehow came out tenderly.

"Somebody fell asleep on me last night." He kissed her on the tip of her nose.

She braced both hands on either side of him in an effort to push up from his warm, hard body and his bed before she was utterly beguiled. "Yes, I wanted to talk about that—"

"No talking." He held her down, both arms around her waist. "Kiss me."

She suddenly noticed the place against her body where he was very much a man, and very much awake.

"Lazar," she exclaimed, "we must discuss Ascencion!"

"Must we?"

It was difficult to think when he nibbled her earlobe like that. She used every ounce of her strength to pull back once more. She stared into his eyes. "Listen to me. There is so much to be done—"

"Mm-hmm," he purred, ignoring her every word as he led her hand to caress him down there.

She shivered at the feel of his titanic manhood but refused to cooperate, pointing a finger in his face. "Stop it! Now, behave yourself. Let me go, and get out of this bed. I've looked through the files, and we haven't a moment to lose."

"Agreed. I'm going out of my mind to have you."

"It is quite impossible!" She slipped free of him and fled across the cabin to a safe distance, panting in mixed lust and worry as she stared at him.

He sat up in bed and stared at her. Then his black brows knit in a thunderous line.

"Why," he asked forebodingly, "is it impossible?"

"You are already betrothed," she said in a small voice.

His stare turned incredulous.

She hurried over to a pile of her documents on the corner of his desk and picked them up, holding them toward him. "It's all here. Your engagement to Princess Nicolette of Austria. Her dowry is two million gold ducats, Lazar, enough to save Ascencion from collapse! The names and addresses of all King Alphonse's former cabinet members are here. Even my father thought these men were brilliant! They've been living in hiding throughout Europe since your father's death—Don Pasquale, the prime minister they used to call the Fox. General Enzo Calendri, the head of the armed forces. And the archbishop, Father Francisco—do you remember him?"

He didn't respond. He looked as though he were in shock.

"These men can help you. Lazar," she said, holding up the papers, "you can have your kingdom back. Everything you need to take back Ascencion is right here!"

He still stared at her, looked at the papers in her hand, then fell back onto the mattress and pulled the sheet up over his head with a vexed groan.

Oh, dear, she thought, frowning at the jut of his stubborn nose under the shroud.

"For what it's worth, I think you'll make a splendid king. Once we've smoothed out your edges just a bit," she added hesitantly.

A second muffled groan came from under the sheet. Lazar pressed his fingers to his forehead through the cloth.

"You have made it your life's purpose to drive me insane, is that it?"

She lifted her chin, taking exception. "My father might have been a traitor, but my loyalty to Ascencion is unquestioned. I intend to help you."

He pulled the sheet off his face, rolled onto his side, and propped his head on his fist to regard her with a flat gaze. "Help me *what*, dare I ask?"

"Regain your throne, of course."

He began to laugh.

She felt her cheeks warming. "What is so funny?"

He gazed toward the window and let out a long, tickled, heartbroken sigh. "You are, my little zealot. Don't think I failed to learn of your quest to save Ascencion single-handedly. I know all about your charitable projects, your meddling in politics, your democratic leanings. But trust me, stay out of this. You're in deeper waters than you can possibly navigate." He gave the mattress beside him a broad slap. "Now, come back to this bed and be deflowered."

Somehow she ignored his smoldering dark eyes, his lips made for kisses, and his golden hand now stroking the white sheets like an invitation to sin.

"There's so much I want to ask you. How did you survive the attack? How have you lived all these years? What were your parents really like? How did you come to be a pirate—"

"Don't," he said. "Just . . . don't."

"But I can help," she said softly, puzzled but determined. "I can find out who among the nobles are still faithful to the Fiori and whose sympathies lie with Genoa. I can help you handle the Councilmen, and I know dozens of important people in Paris whose support you could well use for the revolution—"

"Revolution?" he shouted. "There's not going to be any revolution! Bloody hell." He jumped out of the berth and angrily stalked to the washstand. "I'm not going back there, and neither are you, so forget it. Genoa can have it, for all I care."

She gave him a blank, disbelieving stare.

"I should have known you would do this," he growled. He splashed his face impatiently, getting water everywhere. He dried his hands and face on the shirt slung over the chair.

She was dumbstruck. She'd guessed from the many cynical things he'd said over the past few days that he was ambivalent about reclaiming Ascencion, but she had no inkling he would be dead set against it. He sat down heavily and thrust his foot into his left boot.

She seized upon her voice at last. "Lazar!"

"Yes, Allegra?" he asked wearily.

"You—you cannot be serious!" she sputtered.

"Why not?" He jerked the other boot onto his right foot.

"You cannot mean to tell me you sailed away when Ascencion was in your power, with no intention of formally overthrowing the Genovese. You cannot mean to tell me there was no *plan*."

He leaped to his feet, his eyes afire. "My mission, my plan, Allegra, was vendetta—a mission *two years* in the making, which you destroyed in a moment with your pretty tears!"

"Well, never mind that, then. We'll make a plan. At least we have the information in these files to help us." She held up the papers. "First we'll send word to your father's advisers—"

He marched toward her. She cried out when he grabbed the papers out of her hands and threw them, scattering them across the cabin.

"Worthless. Meaningless. Stupid words, words on paper! Nothing! I have no proof! No proof, Allegra. Do you understand? I can make no claim to the throne, for I have no proof of who I am!"

He trembled with rage as he glared down at her.

"But there are plenty of people still alive who knew you then and will know you now," she protested. "They'll all recognize you, if only you'll meet with them—"

"All those corrupt, smiling bastards with a vested interest in Genoa's continued reign, you mean? Ah, let's see. What am I to do? March into the Council's chambers and hand them my calling card? Of course! Then everyone could bow down and say 'God save the king,' and we'd all live happily ever after, I suppose."

"Why are you being sarcastic?"

"You are so naive," he said bitterly. "They'd butcher me, like my father, in a death even more pointless than this life of mine. It's too late, Allegra, thanks to your sweet papa.

Everyone thinks me dead, and—trust me—it's better for everyone if I stay that way."

"Even for those who are starving? And unjustly imprisoned? And whose lands have been confiscated—"

"We've all got our burdens to bear."

"Lazar!"

"Look at me, Allegra. Look at what I am. My presence on Ascencion would only tarnish my father's name."

"You are absolutely wrong. If I did not think you would be a just and kind ruler for Ascencion, I would not want you in power there, and I wouldn't help you."

"Obviously you don't know me at all."

"Lazar, how can you say that after last night?"

"Because you don't know what—" He suddenly cursed and turned away, and it was plain he wished he had not said it. "You don't know anything."

"Tell me," she said.

"Forget it."

"It has to do with those scars on your wrists, doesn't it?"

He said nothing.

She took a deep breath. "Lazar, were you raped?"

He turned white. "Jesus Christ, what a preposterous suggestion. I'm shocked you would say something so disgusting." Woodenly he strode to his locker.

She stared at him. He was lying.

His whole big body was rigid as he scrambled to put on his clothes. She read the panic in every hard line of him. She lowered her gaze, heart pounding.

She found she was suddenly enraged.

Papa, she thought, I hope you are in hell.

She could not think of one single thing to say in the agonized silence while he hunted desperately for a waistcoat in his locker, as if he could not see the one hanging right in front of him. *Who was it? Who had dared do such a thing to him?* It must have been long ago. His powerful body and deadly skills had indeed been developed to a purpose, but, once, he had been a lost, bewildered boy. *How unprepared he must have been for the horrors he's endured.*

She swallowed a lump of emotion in her throat as she gazed at him, unable to bear the fear making his movements jerky, almost wild.

She had never once seen him move awkwardly. Now his hands fumbled merely to tie his shirt's neck strings. The only thing she could think of to do at the moment was to save his pride, even if it meant pretending she believed his lie, at least for now. Something told her if she spoke kindly to him now, it would destroy him. She lifted her chin.

"Lazar di Fiore, you have a duty," she said in the coldest possible tone.

He turned on her with a strange expression of mixed anger and relief. "Don't you dare presume. My only duty is to myself."

"How can you say such a thing after all your father sacrificed?"

"Postscript: my father is dead. I am alive. And if you don't mind, I intend to stay that way. Now, would you please do me the honor of leaving me the hell alone."

"No."

He stared at her for a moment, then scowled at the floor-boards, hands on hips. "No. Of course you wouldn't." Finally he heaved a great sigh and came toward her. "I know I am a disappointment to you, Allegra—"

"No, you are not," she said savagely.

"—and I am sorry. I admire—perhaps even envy—your ide-alism, but I cannot—I will not go back to Ascencion. I'm no hero, and certainly no martyr. Were I to go back at this point, they'd hang me for piracy. As I've taken great pains to avoid hanging thus far, you'll pardon me if I prefer to prolong my short, unhappy life. Though God knows why I bother," he added under his breath.

"You forget that I've seen you in action, Your Majesty. Somehow I have trouble believing you fear anyone, least of all the Genovese courts-martial."

With a melancholy laugh, Lazar shook his head, resting his hands on her shoulders. He grazed her cheek lightly with his knuckle. "How now, is that a compliment I hear among all your disparaging remarks? I could sorely use one at the moment."

She gave a sad smile at his limping attempt at humor. The naked despair she saw in his eyes doubled her resolve to get him back his rightful heritage.

She took his hand and gave it an encouraging squeeze. "Think of it, Lazar! Such changes you could make. Such cities you could build. At last, here is a task worthy of you! You could carry out the reforms your father only dreamed about."

"I'm shocked you think me capable of it," he muttered.

"Impossible man, of course you are." She reached up and caressed his scratchy cheek. "People would follow you, you know. I've seen how people respond to you. Governing Ascencion could not possibly be harder than commanding men like this crew of yours. If you will have a little faith, I know we can do it. How your people would love you—"

"Allegra, you're killing me. No more," he whispered, closing his eyes.

"But I cannot bear the injustice of it! It's so unfair! And to know my own father was the one responsible—"

He shook his head. "What's done is done." He pulled her close and stroked her hair, his chin resting atop her head. "All I really want is peace and quiet. I'd like to grow some grapes, I think, and to be able to sleep at night without the worry of someone cutting my throat."

"Oh, God, do not say such a thing." She shut her eyes against the image. "I will help you," she whispered fiercely. "Somehow I will help you."

"Then help me this way," he murmured, lowering his lips to hers. "Make me forget."

He kissed her slowly. "I have a plan, too, *chérie*. Do you want to hear it?"

She nodded, eyes closed, while his caresses soothed the tension from her.

"My plan is to lead you over to that bed and make love to you, make a child with you. Our child. I want to put the past behind me, Allegra," he whispered. "I want the future with you."

She clung to him, staggered by his words. She accepted his drowning kiss so full of grief, until she felt his heart pounding under her palm as she caressed his chest. She had no idea how she was going to resist him, or even if she should.

"Live with me," he said. "I have gold. I can take care of you and our children. I want to buy a plantation or a farm—"

She tore herself out of his arms and walked stiffly to the other end of the cabin, her back to him. She hugged one arm about her body and covered her mouth with the other to keep from sobbing aloud.

Behind her, Lazar was silent.

The man was mad. How could he choose her over his kingdom? How on earth could she be so insane as to refuse? She pressed her eyes shut, fighting for self-possession. She had to think of what was best for him. Best for Ascencion.

"I can't offer marriage—"

"No."

Silence.

"You do not want me," he said in amazement at last.

Her hand over her mouth stifled the bleak truth she might have sobbed out, if not for the imperative to maintain her composure, *I am not recompense enough for all you've lost.*

"She does not want me." The note of astonishment in his deep, soft voice turned to something harder, colder. "Well, then. Fine. If that's the way you want it."

She could not speak, did not turn around. Her whole body trembled. Lazar spoke, his voice low, rough.

"Tonight, Allegra, you'll pay your debt. I just ran out of patience."

The door slammed.

"Pumpkin honey-bunch!" Maria called down to the dim wine cellar beneath the country house. "My sweet boy, your luncheon is ready!"

"In a minute!" he shouted harshly up at her.

God, Maria annoyed him. And poor, innocent little Allegra, he thought. Domenic paced back and forth slowly before the three big, variously bleeding men the black-eyed savage had left behind to kill him.

The first he had used as an example to show the other two what would happen if they didn't cooperate. What was left of that poor creature slumped against his bonds in the chair, wimpering now and then. He was close to death.

The second had merely had a good beating from Domenic's assistants, a little of the old-time Inquisition treatment, good for the soul. Alas, the second fellow wouldn't last much longer unless he started giving up some interesting information very soon.

The third, a cutthroat by the name of Jeffers, was the one Domenic expected to talk. So far Mr. Jeffers was unscathed. It pleased Domenic to let Jeffers wait and agonize, wondering when it would be his turn for torture.

"Pirates, eh? We're still sticking with this story, then, are we, gentlemen? Unfortunately, I still don't believe you. Quit your crying," Domenic snarled at the second man. "Now, for the last time, I'm going to ask you nicely. Tell me. Who. He is."

Jeffers tremblingly spoke up to repeat the same story they'd told him a hundred times.

"He's called the Devil of Antigua, Yer Worship, and his name is Lazar."

"Lazar who? What is his family name?" he growled expectantly.

"I never heard it, sir."

"We *are* pirates, it's true!" the second man screamed out all of a sudden. "The Brethren! Tell 'im the coordinates of Wolfe's Den, Jeff! Go on—tell 'im! I don't give a damn anymore—let 'em all hang!"

Jeffers was silent.

The dying man made a garbled moan.

Domenic considered his one unscathed prisoner's veracity while the man watched him like an abused dog.

Between the rebels he'd captured and these men, Domenic was left with two opposing stories from which to choose. First there was the tale according to these crumpled, cowering men that the black-eyed savage was truly a pirate called the Devil of Antigua. Originally an Ascencioner, he had sailed all this way for a vendetta against the dimwit Monteverdi, then decided at the last minute not to carry out his revenge.

It didn't add up.

The only other option was that the myth that had whipped the general populace into such a frenzy was coming to fruition—that he was none other than King Alphonse's elder son, Lazar, come back from the dead somehow to restore Fiori rule.

"Sweeting! Your luncheon's getting cold, my love!" Maria called gaily from the top of the stairs.

"Shut *up*!" he screamed at her. God, the woman acted as though she were his wife rather than a servant—albeit a special kind of servant.

Maria's mouth was quite clever so long as she wasn't using it to speak.

"Pirate, pirate, pirate," he mused, pacing back and forth before the men, tapping the flat of his dagger against his lips.

Or prince—Nay, king?

It was reasonable to assume that if their captain was indeed

Lazar di Fiore, he might not have admitted his true identity to these common rude men. Royalty, after all, was not given to explaining itself to anyone.

For his part, Domenic found it easier on his vanity to think that if he had been bested that night, at least it had been by a king and no common Ascencion dog.

He sighed at his prisoners. "Perhaps you truly don't know anything. Perhaps I tortured you poor souls all for naught. What a waste of my time." He pivoted at the end of the cellar, then strolled back.

Objectives, he said firmly to himself.

One: Get Allegra back from that savage; otherwise, people would think he simply didn't care what happened to her, and that wouldn't look very good, would it?

Two: If that scoundrel was Lazar di Fiore, block him before he came back to take power. Because if he *was* Lazar di Fiore, Domenic had no doubt that he would be back.

Yes, he thought, he had to proceed assuming the worst. No one was going to take his power away from him after he had worked so hard and groveled so many times before men who were not worthy to wipe the mud off his boots.

But then *why* had Fiore sailed away?

Domenic sensed a design in it as devious as his own mind. He had to admit that the black-eyed savage was his equal in strength. He had to assume, then, that his opponent might also be his equal in wit. Though he doubted it. He could not guess at the other man's strategy yet; he knew only that if Lazar di Fiore returned, there was no way he, Domenic, could remain in power.

Unless . . .

Unless he waged a full-scale crusade to bring the Devil of Antigua to justice as a pirate before he could declare himself as the Fiore heir. Domenic smiled as he sorted out his next move.

You want to play games with me, you black-eyed bastard?

He would set a huge price on the pirate's head, and Domenic

would make the people love him as they loved Allegra. He would take advantage of their love for her by declaring publicly that he would get her back safely and uphold their betrothal, even though the whole world would privately concur that she was ruined beyond repair.

He would show them he had that great a heart.

He was even willing to overlook the fact that the black-eyed rogue had probably forced his way between her long, slender legs. There was something vaguely arousing to him about the thought of that big, hard body riding her as she fought and bucked and wept.

Well, at least he could take consolation in the certainty that his frigid girl was not enjoying it. She'd better not be enjoying it.

Because that, he thought darkly, would really make him angry.

Issuing ultimatums was the mark of an amateur, Lazar knew, but hurt pride had made him strike out at Allegra. He'd regretted the arrogant threat the moment it had left his lips, because he did not want it to happen that way for her, not in anger. There was something so fragile about her, and now he must break it. He had staked his dignity upon having her tonight, and if he did not carry out his threat, she would think him weak-willed as well as a selfish, pleasure-seeking, suicidal coward.

He told himself he didn't give a damn what she thought of him. All he wanted was relief for his suffering flesh.

He went about his tasks for the day, distracted and brooding. Not even Vicar dared approach him. Wherever he turned, his men annoyed him, this one dawdling, missing his order to turn the mizzen topsail to starboard, that one clumsily spilling a bucket of the hot tar for the deck, another pair on the fo'c'sle, laughing like imbeciles over some lewd joke.

He knew it was his black mood making them so nervous that

they fumbled, so he climbed up to the crow's nest just to get away from them, ignoring his own observation that the tiny perch was not as much fun without Allegra and her fear of falling.

Surveying the horizon through his folding telescope, he found there was nothing to see but giant cumulus clouds and the other six ships bearing the Brethren home to the West Indies.

He lowered the glass from his eye with a heavy sigh.

"Damn you, Allegra," he murmured to the air.

How had they come to this impasse? Just when he'd allowed her closer to him than he'd ever let anyone—stalemate. He did not like how much he cared about her feelings, her viewpoint. His own preoccupation with her was all out of proportion, and obviously she did not return his sentiments.

But I opened myself for her, he thought, a strange ache in his chest. *What the hell else does she want of me? Is it because I didn't offer marriage?*

Maybe it wasn't marriage, but it was still the finest offer he'd ever made a woman, and she had not even considered it. Flatly refused. He could think of fifty women who'd have kissed the ground at his feet if he'd asked them to bear his children.

Not the headache. Not Allegra, damnable woman, his noble, high-minded little martyr.

From now on, he vowed, he would stick with nonvirgins who were just as selfish and shallow as he. But surely he had not read her so wrong. She wanted him. He could feel it.

Ach, the girl was daft. She was so damned driven to save the world, and him with it, that she gave no thought to her own happiness. It was enough to make him puke.

Not only had she cast away her life to save her miserable family from his butchery, oh, no. Now Saint Allegra would give up what he suspected she very much wanted as well, for Ascencion's sake.

For *his* sake. His happiness, whatever that was.

Didn't this girl have any sense of self-interest, even practicality? he wondered. Didn't she see she was ruined? Well, he would not bloody *permit* her to sacrifice herself for him.

He was particularly capable of ruthlessness when the occasion called for it, and where she was concerned, he fully intended to get his way. With a narrow, crafty smile, he decided he was not merely going to seduce her; he was going to get her pregnant tonight. He would trap her with a child, force her to be happy, damn it.

God, what a stupid idea. That's just what he needed. What would he do with a squalling brat? What had he been thinking, with all his mawkish dreams? How Captain Wolfe would have laughed at him, taking this starry-eyed girl so seriously. Bedding her was the only reason he'd brought her aboard in the first place. The sooner he'd had his fill of her, the sooner life could return to the empty joke it was. Then maybe he might start thinking clearly again.

He left the lofty crow's nest and stalked to his cabin, throwing the door back. The lady was not in, thank God.

He shut the door and locked it. Scoffing at his own soft-headedness, he poured himself a large glass of his finest rum, warily approaching the files the virgin martyr had optimistically left on his desk.

Each of the various account books and official logs and ledgers that he'd taken from Monteverdi's offices dealt with different facets of the state of affairs on Ascencion. He only meant to take a brief glance when Allegra wasn't there looking over his shoulder to wheedle and gloat. A simple means of distracting his body's agitation. He had not intended to get absorbed for almost three hours—or infuriated.

Afternoon turned to evening, and still Lazar sat at his desk, his left eye twitching in rage as he carefully examined the documents. Ascencion's impending financial ruin was neatly spelled out right there in the report before him. For the life of him, he could find no evidence of any sort of plan under way for averting the disaster.

It was enough to sober any half-cocked hedonist.

Instead, the records showed exactly how Genoa had been bilking Ascencion for all she was worth for the past fifteen years. Now that fortunes had been made and collapse was imminent, the Genovese were quietly pulling out, and hostilities were running hot as the coffers ran dry.

One report after another detailed the revolt of the peasants against the rich, the inhumane crimes by the rich against the native poor. He studied the census, with its appalling vagrancy and infant-mortality rates, pored over reports on everything from crops to crime. He found out about the critical shortage of doctors, the system of graft, the growing influence of the crime families.

No practical solutions had been offered.

On the economic front, even the widest-known, most proven new theories of modernization had been ignored. There was not a word about building a modern canal or turnpike system, nor the creation of decent roads, though this would have been an obvious way to put some of the miscreants to work and to harvest the highland timber forests of Ascencion where he had played Robin Hood with his friends when he was a boy.

Presently he let out a disgusted sigh and pushed the papers aside. He felt a headache coming on to add to his misery, along with his need for a woman.

He got up and poured himself a brandy this time, stretching a bit from the long hours spent at the desk. For perhaps half an hour, he brooded in spite of himself on the various strategies he'd have employed to solve Ascencion's ills—hypothetically speaking, of course.

And when he began to feel a brilliant eagerness coming over him for the huge project, with all its challenges and intricacies, he shut the document boxes and had another drink.

He refused, *refused,* to get caught up in Allegra's fantasy. He was not that man. He was not her Prince. Well, he was, but in name only. He had not one noble, self-sacrificing bone in his body, and he was damned glad of it. With his left eye ticking with foul temper, he told himself there were better things to think about.

Allegra's breasts, for instance, and the joy it would bring him tonight to steal her chastity.

She would be easy. He would make her burn and buck and scream for him, show her what he thought of her morals and all her haughty disdain. Yes, he thought, a little wild sex would put her in her place.

He dropped his gaze to the cruel green sea. The sun was going down.

In bed, he thought dismally as he raised the brandy to his lips. At least there was one place he wouldn't disappoint her.

Already the sun was setting, and Allegra still did not know how she should answer her captor's ultimatum.

She spent the day at various tasks, keeping her hands busy with organizing her father's papers, mending one of her gowns, and staring mournfully at her mother's miniature, all the while trying to come to terms with Lazar's dark promise.

She tried to take a nap in the storeroom, using her half-mended gown as a pillow, because she didn't dare lie down in the cabin, where he could come along at any time. The floor was uncomfortable, and the ghosts wailed around her in the creaking, squeaking timbers of the ship. She closed her eyes.

He wanted to leave the past behind him. He wanted the future with her.

This man—the bravest, most incredible, lovable, heart-broken man she had ever laid eyes on—wanted her to live with him. She still could not absorb it. He had said she was his compass—*every ship needs a compass,* he'd said—and he had said, *Love me.* He had told her beautiful things, told her she was beautiful. He wanted to make a family with her—Lazar di Fiore—her Prince.

And she had said no.

She was too sick to her stomach with the knowledge to cry. He had offered her a fantasy on a silver platter, but it was all wrong. Ascencion needed Lazar far more than she did. Oh, she needed him, to be sure, but she needed her sanity more, and what Lazar truly needed was his kingdom, his home. In his rightful place, he would find healing for those wounds of shame that had struck all the faith from his soul.

"You do not want me." How could he think that? Foolish man! Why must he torment her so? she thought, squirming peevishly on her hard bed. Why couldn't he leave her alone? And as for tonight, should she fight him? Resist?

Could she?

All he had to do was kiss her once—nay, he need not even touch her—he need only stare at her the way he did, and she would be helpless to resist him. That was the bitterest part of it. Tonight he would come to her as Lucifer, testing her moral strength, probing her for weakness with his many arts of temptation. How could she cling to safety when her body cried out for him, when every look he threw her burned with need? What choice would her heart give her but to bestow on him whatever he asked, everything she had to give?

No, she must give him no encouragement. She must stand firm.

She was willing to do anything to help him regain Ascencion, but she would not cast her heart away on a man she could not have, as Mama had. She would not sentence herself to a lifetime of loneliness, and if she gave herself to him tonight, there would be no way to withhold her complete devotion.

She could deny herself for his higher good tonight, she told herself, just as she had denied his shimmering offer today. Hiding from his destiny on some idyllic farm with happy children underfoot, why, it all sounded lovely. But on Ascencion, their people were being persecuted. For their sake, she could not afford to become his plaything. Only, she did not think he would have it any other way.

She'd seen the hurt in his eyes when she had rejected him. The fool. For wounding his pride, tonight he would take slow, delicious revenge on her, and the truth of it was, she longed for it.

Truly, wasn't there a simple means for letting them both have their way? He could become the king, and she could be his mistress. Men in power kept mistresses openly, whispered the voice of the tempter in her ear, for these men married strangers for reasons of gain.

Sometimes they loved their mistresses more than their wives. Why could she not be his mistress and see to it that he married Princess Nicolette Habsburg?

Oh, because it's against the Sixth Commandment, for one thing, she scoffed at herself.

'Twas out of the question. If she did not remain firmly grounded in integrity, what use could she be to him or herself or Ascencion or anyone else, for that matter?

Perhaps she should do it anyway. Toss sanity into his sea like a halfpenny into a wishing well. Take the torment. Break her morals for him.

Maybe then he would be satisfied, she thought in misery, when he'd taken her pride in exchange for his own, when there was nothing left of her to plague him. He'd stripped her of everything else, her demon-prince. Why should she hope he would leave her her soul?

Finally, she rose, putting away the files she had been unable to concentrate upon. She squared her shoulders, smoothed her hair, and walked aft through the dark passageway, listening to Lazar's ghosts.

She would be truthful. She would be steadfast. She would be proud.

The stateroom was empty, dim. Emilio had cooked no special dinner for them tonight. Vicar was nowhere in sight.

Allegra stilled the trembling of her hand and reached for the knob to the cabin door. The room was dark, the curtains billowing eerily over the door to the sea balcony. She could not see him in the dark, but she could feel him there. Then he spoke, his voice like black satin.

"Lock the door."

❧ CHAPTER ❧
FIFTEEN

Heart pounding, Allegra obeyed his low command, then turned back to face the dark room, discerning Lazar's broad-shouldered silhouette in the armchair. She could just make out his pose there in the shadows. He was fully dressed, she noted with some relief. Quite elegantly dressed, no pirate, he. He sat with one ankle crossed over the opposite knee, elbows braced on the arms of the chair. He was sipping wine, trailing the rim of the glass back and forth against his lips thoughtfully.

"Come here."

Hesitating, she went and stood before him, though she kept a safe distance, some five feet away. She did not need to go any nearer to sense his dangerous mood. This was the side of Lazar she had encountered only once before, the dark creature of brooding storm to whom she'd pledged herself when she had made her reckless oath.

"Closer."

She took a step. He was silent. She could feel his gaze traveling over her, and to her shame, her body responded at once.

"Take down your hair."

With trembling hands, she obeyed, as if in a trance.

"I will be gentle, you know," he murmured. "I won't use force. I won't need to."

There was a charged silence as they stared at each other with equal hostility and attraction. She strove for clarity against the drug of want.

"Why are you playing this game with me?" she asked quietly. "I only want what is best for you, as you well know."

"We hedonists are fond of games."

"Have you been drinking your poison again? You will have nightmares."

"And I will lead you into them with me. Take off your gown, *chérie*."

She swallowed hard, not knowing what to say to him.

"Must it be this way?" she asked, hearing the wistful note in her own voice, the longing barely denied.

"Oh, yes," he whispered. "Take off your dress for me."

She couldn't.

She stared at him, trapped, awed by him. His eyes were black and feverish, bright with pain from those wounds he hid. He took a drink. She caught a glimpse of his white teeth in the moonlight when he licked his lips.

When she did not begin undressing, Lazar shoved himself up out of the chair and drifted toward her, predatorlike. Her breath came faster as she watched him approach. He towered over her. His shoulders seemed to her two massive cliffs, and every weathered line of his face was rugged. There was no sparkle in his eyes tonight, no smile on his narrowed lips.

"Please, I cannot fight you," she whispered. "You will destroy me."

"My, my, so dramatic. It is only sex," he said, circling behind her.

She pressed her eyes closed dizzily when he began deftly unbuttoning her dress.

"Lazar, I didn't mean to hurt you. I would have liked so very much to live with you on your farm—"

"That offer no longer exists."

She stiffened. "I did not presume that it did."

His fingers paused midway down her back. "Yet here you stand."

"Yes."

"Waiting for a good fuck, eh, my little saint?"

She flinched at his words, deliberately intended to abase the beauty of what they had shared.

"No. I do not want to be here. You know as well as I do that it's wrong. I'm here because I gave you my word of honor and because I am not a coward. Besides, there is nowhere on this ship to hide."

"Right you are." She could feel his hot breath on her neck as he ran his hands down her sides, grasping her by the hips from behind to pull her backside against his loins. "You are mine. There is nowhere you could hide from me. If you ran from me, I would tear the world apart to find you, and until I did, I would come to you and take you in your very dreams."

She closed her eyes with want, every muscle straining, every inch of her skin alive with her awareness of him. He finished unfastening her dress with astonishing speed, then parted it from behind and slipped his hands under the material, reaching around to take her breasts in both his hands, caressing each nipple slowly with his thumbs, not gently. She bit back a gasp of desire.

She could not believe herself. She had been in the room with him for only minutes, and already she was teetering on defeat, playing right into his hands.

"Please, let me go," she choked out.

"You don't seem to know how much I need this," came his dark whisper at her ear. "I am not a fantasy, Allegra. I am a man, of flesh and blood, and I have needs."

She closed her eyes in desperation. "If you make love to me, I will never get over you, Lazar. I will hurt for you always."

"But that's what I want, *chérie*. Burn here with me in my hell."

Weakened, she leaned against him, consumed by his passion, almost helpless with desire. He pushed her dress down on one side and began kissing her shoulder, teething it gently. Her body throbbed, pulled deep inside, craving him.

She had to rally her senses. When he slid his hands inside the front of her dress again, inching down her belly to slip his fingers between her legs, she nearly sobbed with need, dropping her head back against his broad shoulder.

"Mmm," he breathed. "Wet, wet silk."

"Lazar di Fiore," she whispered, "you break my heart."

He paused.

Withdrawing his hands from inside her dress, he turned her in his arms. She was shaking. Holding her by the shoulders, he searched her face almost tenderly.

"Why, *chérie*? Why do you say such a thing?"

She did not lift her head until he pressed under her chin with his fingertips. She looked up into his eyes.

"Because I understand now. You have survived at the cost of your honor."

His dark eyes registered shock; then fury leaped into them. "What did you say?"

She stepped back in fear, yanking her dress up over her shoulder, heart pounding as she fought for her survival. "You would paint yourself the victim, justify taking whatever you want from anyone who stands in your path because you have been wronged. But it's the people of Ascencion who are the real victims in all this. You say my father betrayed King Alphonse," she wrenched out, "but you're the one who's betraying him now."

He turned pale as he stared down at her, stock-still. "Don't you dare say that to me."

"It's true. Look how your pain drives you to behave. Can't you see you will go on suffering until you do what you know to be right?"

He stared at her in utter silence.

"I am here tonight because I care about you, and it is because I care that I must say this." She drew a breath. "Your Highness, you have betrayed your people, your father, and yourself. I cannot give myself to such a man."

Staring down at her in stunned silence, he opened his mouth, but he did not say a word. He shut it again, his square jaw tightly clenched.

Abruptly he pivoted on his heel, stalked to the door, and left the cabin, slamming the door thunderously behind him.

Allegra stood there shaking in the darkness. "Oh, God," she whispered, "what have I done? Now he will kill me."

She heard his footfalls march angrily across the stateroom and out into the passageway.

Swiftly she crossed the cabin and locked the door behind him, then braced the desk chair under the handle, her hands shaking violently all the while, for this time she knew she had pushed him too far.

She sat huddled in the darkness at the threshold to the sea balcony, trying to discern what the men's voices were saying above. She thought she heard Lazar's voice among them.

She had just closed her eyes in a futile effort to calm her scattered, panicked nerves with a prayer, but she gasped and jerked in place when the first cannon boomed.

Bitch.

Lazar stalked to the stern, the blood thundering in his ears. There he ordered the drop of the anchor, baffling the helmsman and the night watch. Next he marched to the small cannon on the forecastle and personally sent off the triple boom, signaling to the other vessels for a full stop.

He paused to light a cigar from the sulfur match he had used to spark the cannon fuse, then waited, carefully restraining his fury as he smoked and willed his mind to calm, gazing broodingly at the waves.

Soon the six other ships signaled back that they, too, would cast anchor, but he knew it would be some time before his undercaptains arrived in their longboats.

"Cap, what's amiss?" Harcourt asked worriedly.

"Look lively," he growled at his faithful boatswain.

The man cringed and slunk away. Lazar prowled to the fore, one fist on his hip. Cigar clamped between his teeth, he climbed up onto the bowsprit and clung by one hand to the jib lines, staring up at the silent, steadfast stars beyond the spectral drapery of the sails.

Engulfing those tiny lights, dark heaven, he supposed, laughed in mockery at him, its whipping boy. All around him, the sea was black as an Arab's eyes, and in it glided many silent sharks.

Now might his own soul be tried, he thought grimly, and he would learn if there was any of his father's courage in him.

"So be it," he said in soft menace to the skies.

As for you, my fair Allegra, you will eat your words, and God help us both.

"It's suicide!" scoffed Bickerson, captain of *The Tempest*.

Lazar cast him a simmering look. The lantern swung gently above the table in the stateroom, where he, Vicar, and the six pirate captains gathered.

"No reward?" Fitzhugh asked.

"None," Lazar replied.

Captain of *The Hound*, Fitzhugh was a taciturn Scot with long gray sideburns and bushy eyebrows to match. He was about Vicar's age, one of Wolfe's first recruits from the earliest days of the Brethren. Fitzhugh was more cautious than most of their breed, and piracy, to him, was a business. However, his galleass, though antique in design, was the most heavily armed ship of their small fleet.

"You know I'm with you, Cap," Sullivan muttered, "no matter what these quake-buttocks do." The usually jovial Irishman paced the room restlessly, arms crossed.

Clearly, Sully had something on his mind, Lazar thought.

"Captain Morris?" Vicar asked the foppish young American, a self-styled buccaneer with no qualms about cutting throats.

"I'm thinkin' it over," the boy captain answered, toying with the dirty lace flounces of his sleeve.

Russo, the fiery Portuguese captain of the brig *Sultana*, slammed both hands down on the table, glaring at the company. He pointed at Lazar. "This man has made you rich and once took Wolfe's beatings for you all!" he cried passionately. "One favor he asks—do it, I say!"

"We got to get our goods to market in Cuba," insisted Bickerson, the giant towheaded Dutchman. "You know our buyers don't like to be kept waiting."

"Ain't them I'm worried about, personally," young Morris drawled. "It's them damned Genoveesies behind us."

Lazar steepled his fingers. He could still taste his anger. "Landau, you have been silent."

The tall, wily Frenchman, the disowned son of a gentleman, was captain of the swift and beautiful brigantine *Dragonfly*.

"My objection is that you will tell us nothing," Landau replied. "You ask us to turn back, perhaps engage once more the ships that follow us, pass Gibraltar again, and skim the Barbary Coast, where there are treacherous shoals—all this for no recompense. We are your friends, Lazar, but you must at least tell us why it is so important that you go to the fortress of this opium trader."

"You're either with me, or you're not," Lazar answered with a shrug. "The particulars of this affair shall remain my own."

"This man's got pure lead eighteen-pounders for balls!" Morris said in delight at his reply. The boy captain took a swig from his flask. "What the hell," he declared as he wiped his mouth on his dirty lace sleeve. "I'll do it."

"That's three," Vicar said, glancing at him.

"Fitzhugh?"

" 'Tis madness," the old Scot grumbled. "Sounds to me like a young man's pursuit o' glory, and I suspect the end and purpose of it all is to impress a woman. I'll not be riskin' my crew for the pleasure o' your glands!"

Lazar was contemplating how he could possibly answer that when Allegra came into the stateroom from the cabin, as if on cue. He noticed she looked pale and frightened, but he refused to acknowledge her while the other men scraped their chairs, following Vicar's example to rise.

"Is there a battle? Have we been fired upon?" she asked, glancing toward him.

Six men leaped to assure her all was well—it had just been the signal cannons. Lazar stared at his hands on the table while Vicar undertook to present each of the captains to the indomitable Miss Monteverdi.

Lazar was wholly aware of her, though he did not so much as glance her way. He could smell her, feel her, from three feet away. Fresh-scrubbed and radiant, her ivory skin had never looked more tempting. Her peach-colored dress was demure, safely buttoned again. Her gold-streaked hair was pinned up neatly, and she was every inch the convent-school miss.

Who would ever suspect such a delicate-looking creature had a tongue like a scorpion's tail? he mused.

While the flamboyant young Morris tried to strike up a conversation with her, the Frenchman shot Lazar a look of understanding. He had been there on the wall when Allegra had defied him, and Lazar could see in Landau's admiring gaze at her that the Frenchman applauded her courage.

When Landau introduced himself to her, gallantly kissing her hand, Lazar noted with some dry amusement a pulse of genuine jealousy in his own breast. Another novel experience. But Landau turned back to him with a smile when Allegra went on to greet the next man.

"Very well," Landau murmured. "I will play along with this game of yours, and perhaps someday, my friend, you will tell me what it all meant. But I'm warning you, if my ship takes so much as a scratch . . ."

Lazar gave a shadow of a smile at his idle threat, then they both watched Allegra cast a spell on old Fitzhugh. Vicar cast him an amused glance when the old sea captain took her hand as though it were made of china, clutching his cap over his heart.

After Russo's warm welcome and Sullivan's courteous but uncertain one, Lazar was amazed—but showed no expression whatsoever—when Allegra came around the table and stood meekly behind and to the right side of his chair in what appeared to be a gesture of obedience. Then he realized why.

She was merely pointing out to those whose eyes gleamed with interest that she already had a protector.

She laid her hand on his shoulder.

The nerve of this girl, he thought. Laying claim to his protection moments after denying him his rights to her body and insulting him as he had never been insulted in his life.

Nevertheless, he lifted his left hand across his chest to his right shoulder, where she linked her fingers through his. He said not a word, watching the company without expression.

As she stepped up closer behind him, he felt her fear of him, and perversely it pleased him. It was the only satisfaction, it seemed, he would have of her. A vague sense of guilt gnawed at him for how he had talked to her and treated her, *but damn it,* he thought, *I am not apologizing. She's getting what she bloody wants.*

Fitzhugh stared at Allegra, then looked up imploringly at him. "Take these glory chasers to the River Styx itself if ye will, Cap, but dunna bring this child into danger with you!" he said angrily. "Bickerson or I will see her to safety."

"Oh, I am staying with Lazar, sir," she said quietly and very fiercely as she placed her other hand atop his.

"Miss, 'tis very dangerous."

"Is this true?" she asked Lazar.

"Fitzhugh is an honest man."

She regarded the Scotsman evenly. "All the more reason for me to stay by his side."

Something sparked painfully in Lazar's chest at her

words. He could not comprehend the creature. One minute she cut him to ribbons with her sharp tongue, then she came and stood by him as if she were his obedient wife—*whither thou goest, there go I.*

She might speak differently if she knew where he was taking them.

"Brava, bella," Russo said with a broad grin.

"Quelle femme," murmured Landau.

When Bickerson saw he would have to go on alone, his protests collapsed, and the thing was unanimous.

Within the hour, Lazar would turn the fleet around, taking them back east and south to the Barbary Coast.

Though at the moment he would not have deflowered the sharp-tongued little shrew if she begged him to on her knees, he had to admit she was right once more—tediously, stingingly right.

She could not respect him, and he could not respect himself, if he did not do this thing, and he was sick of fighting the inevitable.

If he wanted Allegra, he had to help Ascencion. To prove that Ascencion was rightfully his, he would have to be able to produce the signet ring, and that meant facing his worst nightmares.

By God, if it took him all the powder in his hold, he would blow Malik's lovely hell sky-high, and he would get that thrice-damned bloody ring.

Or, more likely, die trying.

For the next half hour, he and his men discussed their course, the winds, and battle formations in case of a confrontation with the Genovese ships, though in truth Lazar did not believe the enemy vessels had followed them into the Atlantic.

At length, all the captains except Sullivan returned to their vessels.

"I got a matter to discuss with ye, Cap," he said, eyeing

Allegra warily. She had been silent behind his chair all the while.

"Speak freely, mate."

"Found a stowaway when we left Ascencion," he said. "I brought him aboard so you could question him if you want. He's in your brig."

"Bring him in."

While Sully leaned out the stateroom door and ordered one of the crewmen to fetch the prisoner, Lazar turned to Vicar, aware of Allegra nervously watching him all the while.

"I want you to clear your cabin."

Vicar stared at him for a moment. "Aha, I see."

Warily, the older man rose, clapped him on the back in sympathy as he passed, bowed to Miss Monteverdi, and left the stateroom. At the door, Sully bade him good night. The Irishman then closed the door and turned to Lazar with a frown.

"This stowaway, Cap," he said. "The man tells wild tales. He says"—he hesitated—"he says you're the rightful king o' that island. King, he says! Says they killed your family, and everyone's been waiting there for you to go back and take over."

"Is that so?" Lazar asked lightly.

Sully looked utterly puzzled, watching him suspiciously. "I kept him locked in me brig, but aboard ship his tales have been spreadin'. All me men are asking questions, and I want to know what I'm to tell 'em. Well, hell, is it—true?"

Lazar gazed at his trusting old friend for a long moment.

"Yes," he said. "It's true."

Lazar could feel Allegra's gaze dart to his face. Before Sully found his tongue to reply, the prisoner was brought in. Lazar flattened his gaze in displeasure at the sight of the same fat, ill-kempt little guitar player, Bernardo, who had accosted him in the square after the raid.

"Sire! Oh, my liege, I have risked my life to follow you—"

Abruptly he stopped, his beady-eyed gaze clamping on the late Governor's daughter with recognition and instant malice. For her part, Allegra returned his hostile appraisal with a matter-of-fact glare, folding her arms over her chest.

"Miss Monteverdi is under my protection," Lazar said icily. "You may remain aboard *The Whale*, for you may prove useful in some small way, but if you give the lady the slightest insult—if the mere stench of you should offend her nostrils, my friend, you're shark bait."

As soon as Sully and Bernardo had gone, Lazar swept to his feet and went into the cabin.

Allegra followed her towering captor at a wary distance, daring to go only as far as the threshold of the room where she had so narrowly escaped the loss of her virginity . . . *for now*, a voice whispered in her head.

Careful to stay clear of him, she stared at the broad outline of his massive shoulders and muscled back against the night's blue glow. He moved about the cabin with restless grace, his profile hard and introspective as the orange flame rose from the lantern he now lit.

"Lazar, what on earth is going on?" she asked timidly.

"Collect your belongings from this room, Miss Monteverdi." His voice was hard and flat.

"I—I have nothing here," she stammered. "My trunks are in the storeroom below."

He strode over to the washstand and picked up her silver-handled comb. He brought it to her and held it out at arm's length with a look of sharp reproach. She took it and held it close to her bosom, frightened by his remote demeanor.

"Come." He brushed by her as he went into the stateroom. "Follow me, please."

She did, heart pounding. They went to the second cabin, which was tucked under the companionway. It was the only other cabin on the ship, and it was shared by Vicar; Doctor

Raleigh, the ship's surgeon; Mr. Harcourt, the boatswain; Mr. Donaldson, the purser; and Mutt, the head carpenter—all of whom were presently carrying out their bedrolls and their few belongings.

She lowered her head, ashamed that these men were being removed from their quarters all because she did not wish to let the captain have his way with her, but Mr. Harcourt offered her a rueful grin as he passed, as if to say, *Don't worry, miss.*

Vicar gave her a bolstering wink and chuckled to himself as he went off down the passageway to sling a hammock with the others in the common sailors' gallery.

When they had gone, Lazar cast a critical eye over the cabin, which was only about half the size of his. Then he gave a curt nod.

"Good night, Miss Monteverdi."

"Lazar, please. Why are we turning around? Where are you taking us? What is the danger Captain Fitzhugh spoke of? Tell me what is going on."

He paused, half turning toward her. He pierced her with his most severe, sea-captainly stare, the one that made the crewmen quake.

"I'll tell you exactly what's going on, *chérie*. Once more you've turned me to your will. Go on—congratulate yourself. Only this time it may well cost me my life. But never fear—when I am dead, you'll still have your virtue to comfort you," he fairly spat.

"Are we going back to Ascencion?" she whispered, holding her breath.

He stared down at her for a moment, his eyes fiery black, yet cold. "First I need proof of my identity."

She sucked in her breath. He was truly going to do it! "What is this proof? Where must you go to get it?"

"You're pushing your luck, my girl," he warned.

"Please tell me," she asked meekly.

Slowly he stalked toward her. She shrank from him, backing

away until she found he had driven her up against the bulk-head. He loomed over her, breathing harshly.

"I've set a course for the Barbary Coast, madam. Otherwise known as hell." He reached down and slid his fingers between her legs, cupping her woman's mound with an intense caress as he lowered his head, skimming the line of her cheek with his lips. "You'd better be worth it," he murmured.

He withdrew before she had time to protest, going back to the door.

"This door has a good lock," he said, pausing. "I suggest you use it."

Then he left her standing alone in the bare little room, wide-eyed, holding her comb to her chest.

Shaken by his touch, she sat down weakly, then began to wonder what on earth proof of his true identity was doing on the Barbary Coast.

❧ CHAPTER ❧ SIXTEEN

After two days of receiving from Lazar what she believed was called the cold shoulder, Allegra was chastened but in no wise prepared to apologize for her pitiless honesty.

She spent the first day rather pleased with herself. She had preserved her chastity, which had been her chief aim, as well as gotten the obtuse, stubborn, bullheaded Lazar di Fiore to take the first steps toward reclaiming his throne. As for the way he was ignoring her, she could only scoff at him behind his back.

Poor, spoiled prince, sulking because he hadn't gotten his way! She had stopped him from playing with his new toy. *Well, let him sulk!* Every ship needs a compass, he'd said. He had asked her to always tell him the truth, but obviously he couldn't take it, she thought righteously.

Then she spent another night alone.

By the second day, his cool, relentless courtesy had her a little panicky. She missed his roguish grin like the loss of a friend, and she began to brood on the danger he said he must face.

Surely he did not expect to die. He was only being dramatic when he said that so she would feel guilty for not having given in to his carnal wishes.

The most vexing part was that he would not let her into the cabin to help him work on his plans for Ascencion, the one thing she longed to do. She knew he was denying her involvement in his enterprise just to be spiteful, but she was sure that sooner or later the great blockhead would realize he needed her counsel at least on some matters.

That afternoon, she dressed in her most charming muslin day dress, tied her bonnet ribbons under her chin, and marched herself topside, intent on finding something useful to do.

Mounting the hatch, she took in the azure sky and lively indigo sea, and spied Lazar under the clouds of snapping canvas, surveying his decks from his post on the quarterdeck. Hands clasped behind his back, tricorne shading his head, he looked every inch the grand sea captain. She tried to read him but could not, for his countenance was as smooth, serene, and hard as golden marble.

She gazed across the decks at him, hanging back uncertainly as she wondered if she should go try to talk to him, but when he saw her, he turned away, pacing abeam on his quarterdeck.

She narrowed her eyes in resentment and walked instead to the ship's waist, where she offered to help the sailmakers mend canvas. The two sailmakers working this afternoon were garrulous, good-natured men, both from French islands in the West Indies. When she said she was willing to assist them, they were happy to tell her anything.

"Why is your captain called the Devil of Antigua?" she asked, sitting with them on mounds of netting in the shade.

Pierre laughed. "Now, that is a story! Up until four years ago, the Brethren had a different leader—"

"Captain Wolfe?" she asked.

The men nodded.

"What was he like?"

They grinned, and Jacques shook his head. "Put it this way, miss. You ever seen in a church how the artists paint the Creator? Aye, Jehovah, miss. Long white beard, fierce gray eyes . . ."

"He looked like God?" she cried.

"Aye, but missing a leg. They say he got it bit off by a shark, fishing one day. Hunted the thing, killed it, and spat in its eye. Then fed it to his men."

"My word," she said, blanching as they laughed.

"Aye, he had the instincts of an old-time sea dog, but if you crossed him . . ."

He shook his head ominously.

"He was a madman. A cruel—excuse me, ma'am—son of a bitch," Pierre declared, laughing. "But you had to love him. Of course, he was known to get a bit carried away with the cat-o'-nine, and that was his downfall."

"Did Lazar kill him?" she asked, wide-eyed, remembering the mesh of scars across his poor back.

"Oh, no, miss! Cap loved that old man."

"Loved him? Surely not." She furrowed her brow. "Wolfe flogged him."

"Aye, there was a match of wills." Pierre chuckled. "Wolfe couldn't break him, so in the end, he adopted him for his own son."

"What?"

"Aye, Wolfe never had any children of his own, so he made Lazar his son. Cap joined the Brethren, see, when he was just a boy."

"How old?" she asked, keenly recalling that Lazar would have been thirteen at the time of the Fiori murders.

Pierre and he consulted. "Maybe fifteen, sixteen? Seventeen at the most."

Jacques laughed. "Would've cut your throat if you laid a hand on his supper. He's tamed himself down a lot since then," he added.

She immediately wondered where he had been during the ensuing years between his disappearance from Ascencion and the time he had joined Captain Wolfe.

"Are you sure you want to hear this, *mademoiselle*?"

She nodded eagerly, then the men were interrupted by a question from one of the other crewmen, concerning a torn mainsail. Furtively watching the broad-shouldered man on the quarterdeck, she only half listened to their shouted conversation.

Most of the time, Lazar stood with one fist propped on his hip, she saw, a cheroot stuffed between his fingers, while the other hand held a voice trumpet to his lips as he sang out orders to the crew in his deep, commanding voice.

He loves this, she thought.

Occasionally he sauntered to the rails and peered out over the sea with a folding telescope, picking out some road for his fleet invisible to her eyes through the glassy main.

The sailmakers turned back to her.

"Anyway, we made a raid on Antigua four years ago," Pierre said, then the two men exchanged a grim look. "The men became crazed with blood and gold and rum. It was a bad raid. Twenty men or so started a mutiny right in the middle of it. They killed old Wolfe."

"Cap brought the men under control and got us out of there before the navy came. Then, back at the Den, he executed those that mutinied. The men took a vote, chose him. He's been the leader of the Brethren ever since."

"Took a vote?" she cried in astonishment. "He was *voted* captain?"

"Oh, aye, we always vote. That's our way," Pierre said mildly.

She stared at him. "You mean he governs the lot of you by a democracy?"

The two men looked at each other. "Guess that's the word for it, miss."

She shook her head as if to clear it. "What do you think of Lazar as a leader?"

"Never was a better," Jacques declared.

"He's a hard one, but he's fair," said Pierre.

"Is he ever cruel, like Wolfe? Does he give out floggings?"

"He'd never flog a man," Jacques said at once. "No, Cap's

got only a few rules, but if you break one, you get only one more chance, then—" He made a gun out of his hand and, smiling, pretended to shoot her in the head. "Boom."

The silly man could not know how his gesture chilled her. Gooseflesh ran down her arm as she recalled Lazar's firing squad and his earlier stated intention of shooting her while Papa watched.

"I wonder how many people he has killed," she murmured.

"I don't rightly know."

"Ask him." Jacques chuckled as he threaded his needle.

"Don't you dare, miss. He's funning with you. Cap's a private man."

"Ask me what?" a deep voice suddenly asked, its tone ominously polite.

All three of them blanched as they looked up to find Lazar standing on the platform above them. His smug expression told her he had overheard her prodding the men for information about him. She narrowed her eyes at his gloating look, her courage instantly rallied.

"How many people you've murdered, Captain, sir," she said boldly.

"Why, Miss Monteverdi, I never bothered to keep count," he sweetly replied. He shot his men a thunderous warning look, then wished her a polite "Good day," and sauntered away.

Oh, I detest that man, she thought.

That night, they passed a tense, silent dinner in the stateroom. Stealing covert glances, Allegra noticed that Lazar barely touched his plate. He drank water instead of wine and seemed completely absorbed in his thoughts.

Though this might have been due to the danger ahead, she had a sinking feeling it was her unwelcome presence that made him so quiet. After all, whatever he had to face, she couldn't imagine anything that would truly scare Lazar except for his own nightmares.

No, he was probably regretting that he had ever taken her

captive, she thought, almost sulking. No doubt by now he was utterly relieved he had not made her pregnant as he'd suggested, for then he'd have been shackled to her indefinitely, tied to her and her child because of his sense of . . . honor, she thought in dismay.

Why had she accused him of having no honor? Wasn't that a bit extreme?

She stared down at her plate, aching with wonder at how it could be that they sat here like two strangers after the intimacies they had shared. He'd had his fingers inside her, for God's sake, her breasts in his mouth. Now he wouldn't even meet her gaze. Allegra wanted to crawl into her bunk, pull the covers over her head, and stay there for the rest of the voyage, only her bed was too lonely without him to spend any more time there than absolutely necessary.

She could not comprehend why she should be the one to feel so miserable when *he* was the one in the wrong. Nor could she fathom why she was hurt by having been cast aside when her sole aim had been to preserve her virginity.

Well, she had certainly succeeded.

Soon, she thought, when it came time for him to take back Ascencion, he would almost certainly uphold his old betrothal and marry Princess Nicolette, just as Allegra had wanted him to.

The thought made her feel considerably more awful.

She took a drink of wine, then looked up when Lazar stood, set down his dinner napkin, and excused himself from the table in a mumble. Vicar and she sat looking at each other. Abruptly Allegra threw down her napkin, braced both elbows on the table, and held her head in both hands.

"He is troubled, dear. It's not your fault," the old Englishman consoled her.

"I can't take this," she heard herself say in a taut voice. "My fate is in the hands of a man who hates me."

"I'd hardly say he hates you." He chuckled.

She lifted her gaze to his beseechingly.

Vicar reached over and pinched her cheek. "Ah, my dear. Don't let him get away with anything. You stick to your guns. You'll be all right."

She forced herself to smile at him. "You are a kind man, John Southwell."

"Bosh," Vicar mumbled. Coloring a little, he took a sip of wine.

"Vicar? Have there been many young ladies he's kidnapped?"

He almost choked on his wine for laughing. Blotting his mouth with his napkin, silvery eyes dancing, he shook his head. "Miss Monteverdi, you are the first. You are also the first female I have ever seen cause the lad to lose his temper."

Her shoulders dropped. "That just proves all the more he despises me."

"Is that what it proves?" he asked with a twinkle in his eye. "Don't be too sure."

Later she lay in bed, arms folded under her head, staring up at the shadowy planks of the deckhead. No longer could she deny the truth. She had hurt Lazar. Badly.

He was *not* a fantasy. He was a man of flesh and blood, and he had needs.

He had taught her that she, too, had needs. She missed the feel of his rough, callused hands, so sure, so gentle.

Why did I have to hurt him?

Oh, what is wrong with you? she snapped at herself. Impatiently she shifted onto her stomach and listened to the creaking of the ship's oaken timbers and the dull boom of the sea against the hull.

She didn't know how many minutes passed, possibly an hour. Every time she closed her eyes, she saw only his face, the look of full absorption in his task as he kissed her in that place she had never known a person could be kissed. Just thinking of it was almost enough to make her moan aloud.

What was the sense of denying him her virginity after she had allowed him to do *that*?

In her mind's eye she could almost feel his hands on her skin, see her own hands on his broad shoulders, tracing the sculpted grandeur of his golden chest, pulling restlessly at his lean hips, holding his hardness against her.

When she closed her eyes, distraught with longing for him, it occurred to her that there had to be some way to give him such pleasure as he had given her. How wonderful it would be to make him submit to her in pleasure for once! As a lover, Lazar had given of himself so completely, but he had never shown her how to give to him, how to pleasure that magnificent, warrior's body.

All of a sudden she gave up trying to fall asleep. She got up from her bunk. Trembling, she quickly pulled her rose-printed muslin day dress on over her chemise, tied it behind her, and went in search of her captor who had called himself her lover. She was going to apologize before her better sense could stop her.

It was the only sensible thing to do, she told herself defensively. The man held her fate in his hands. Only a fool would vex and insult him.

She glanced in the stateroom, but it was dark and empty, and no light shone from the crack under the cabin door. Resolute, she made her way down the dark, narrow passageway and to the aft hatch. She was halfway up the ladder's rungs when she stopped, hearing his deep, jolly laughter and herself being discussed.

"So, what happened, Cap? We all want to know."

"Laying bets on my love life again, eh?" Lazar drawled.

"Bored already?" one asked.

"Wouldn't give in, eh, Cap?"

"Leave 'im alone. A man's got to be a gentleman," she heard another protest. She believed it was Mr. Donaldson.

Lazar laughed idly. "She's not my type, is all."

Allegra sucked in her breath as she stood there on the companionway, listening to the exclamations and scoffs.

"If she's not to your fancy, why, pass her along!"

"Now, now. Miss Monteverdi is still my ward," he chided them.

"Ain't you gonna bed her, Cap?"

"Not if she were the last woman on the earth," he replied amiably.

Allegra's jaw dropped.

"Why not, Cap? She's a fine-lookin' girl."

Why indeed?

"Aye, she's pretty enough," he said in an easy tone.

"Seems right clever, for a woman."

"Oh, she has been blessed with wit, to be sure, and virtue," Lazar said casually, without malice. "Virtue piled upon virtue so that she stands on a veritable mountain of holiness so high she has the very ear of God. Believe me, lads, none of us lowly salts are worthy to touch the hem of her gown."

They laughed. Allegra stood in the dark, openmouthed, but he was not done.

"No, gentlemen, for all her charms, I'm afraid Miss Monteverdi is a harpy, a prude, a sharp-tongued little shrew. Whatever man has the ill fortune to wed her will surely go to an early grave, fatally henpecked."

Allegra's eyes filled with tears of horror. One hand over her lips, she climbed back down the companionway and fled back to her cabin, where she locked the door and cried and cried.

Because she knew every word of it was true.

Late that night, Lazar stood alone in the passageway, fighting with himself before the door to the second cabin. The blackness was closing in on him. He had worked for hours on the letters he would soon dispatch to his father's former advisers when they reached Al Khuum. Now he was raw with fatigue, but every time he tried to sleep, he was instantly plunged into nightmare. Merely standing here, he trembled a little.

Chérie.

If only he could go to her and lie in her arms.

The nights he'd spent holding her were some of the sweetest and most peaceful he had ever known. He would have given his ship and every gold coin he'd ever stolen to take back that arrogant, idiotic ultimatum that had led to this.

He braced both hands on the lintel of her cabin and leaned his forehead against the door, eyes closed.

Help me, chérie. *I am afraid.*

He shuddered, letting out a long, slow breath. But he did not knock. He would not, could not, give her another reason to scorn him. Her words still clung like poisoned quills in his hide. By God, he would win her respect.

He was not her Prince, not that perfect man she deserved, but he wanted to be.

If I survive this, he thought, *perhaps then I will be worthy of you.*

When the captain summoned her the next evening, Allegra was forced to leave the shelter of her musty little cabin. She had hidden there all day, nursing her hurt feelings, too ashamed to show her face on deck.

As she made her way to the cabin in answer to his order that she attend him, she was resolved to keep a dignified silence. At least she did not have to fear that he had called her to seduce her. No, he did not want her even if she were the last woman on the earth. Knees knocking at the prospect of facing him again, she rapped on the cabin door.

"Come," answered the forceful command.

She took a deep breath, lifted her chin, and entered. Lazar was standing behind his desk, dressed as he had been the first night she saw him, the marauding barbarian in black.

That did not bode well, she thought.

"Good, you're here," he said briskly.

Allegra pulled the door closed, then folded her hands behind her back, her face an expressionless mask. "What is your will?"

"Have a seat."

Without looking at her, he took his two elegant dueling pistols out of the drawer, then set a pouch of gunpowder next to them. She obeyed, going stiffly to the armchair. She sat up straight, folding her hands primly in her lap just like the prude she was.

Calmly, he loaded his weapons, never looking at her. "Within half an hour, I shall disembark. There are a few details of which I must advise you. First, you are to stay belowdecks until we are done here."

She itched to ask why, but she refused to, commanding herself to be silent. She would show him! For once she would take his word at face value and not question his every move. Obviously the man knew what he was doing.

Lazar rubbed the heel of his hand against his forehead in a weary, careworn gesture.

"Second, there are a few things I have to say to you." He moved around the desk and braced his hips against it, folding his massive arms over his chest as he studied her. Seeing that penetrating stare, she braced herself for a scathing dressing-down along the lines of what she'd overheard last night.

"I behaved abominably the other night, and I am heartily sorry, Miss Monteverdi."

She lifted her gaze to his in astonishment.

"May I have your pardon?" he asked soberly.

Dazed, she stared up at him. "Of course."

"Thank you." He turned his back. "The truth is, I am sorry for all of it," he mumbled. "I destroyed your life, as you've pointed out on numerous occasions, but in return, Miss Monteverdi, you have given me more than I can repay you for."

She stared, flabbergasted, at his broad back. *What on earth?*

"For that reason, I have made you sole beneficiary of my will. Give me your hand."

"Your *will*?" As he stalked toward her, she obediently held out her hand. He pressed a small key into it, though he never looked at her.

"This is the key to the safe. If I don't come back, I want you to have the Fiori heirlooms. I know you won't sell them," he mumbled. "I have named old Fitzhugh as your guardian to conduct you to some suitable acquaintances of mine on Martinique, a few elder ladies who will act as your chaperons until you acquire a husband there among the gentlemen planters. I'm sure you'll find someone there you can tolerate at least as well as that ex-fiancé of yours, and because you are still a—well, there are no difficult matters to explain to a future husband."

Pale with dread, she stared at him. "My God, Lazar, you are in real danger, aren't you?"

He cast her a cynical look. "Are you concerned for me at last, hmm, *chérie*?"

"Why have we come here?"

"Oh, pirate business," he said with idle insolence as he sauntered back to his desk.

Her heart was pounding. The key grew sticky in her suddenly sweating palms. "Please don't be impossible now. What place is this?"

"A kind of hell," he admitted with a slight, bittersweet smile, then he lowered his head. "I lived here for a while when I was a boy. When I left Ascencion, I was wearing my royal signet ring. The master of this place stole it from me. I've come to get it back."

"Who is he?"

He stared at her, as if weighing whether or not to tell her. "He is called Sayf-del-Malik," he said. "The Sword of Honor."

"Can you make him give it back?"

"When he learns all my ships' guns are pointed at Al

Khuum, that should give His Excellency sufficient motive to obey me."

"What if he still refuses?" she whispered.

He was silent for a long moment. "I'll do my best, Allegra, but if he tries to humiliate me, I will fight to the death. He will not shame me again. He may take my life, but he will not have my pride."

"He won't dare," she forced out, understanding more than Lazar realized about the kind of shame he meant. "You're not a boy anymore. Besides, your men will be there to stand with you and protect you—"

"No," he said. "I'm going alone."

Allegra felt exactly as if Goliath's mighty fist had just knocked the wind out of her once more. "Alone?"

"It's the only way." He cast her a grim smile. "Take heart, Miss Monteverdi. If I have not returned in two hours' time, the Brethren will open fire on Al Khuum with full broadsides. You may soon be rid of me for good."

Lazar crossed the cabin to his sea chest and took out a honing stone. Sitting down at his desk, he commenced sharpening the blade of his Moorish knife.

He looked over curiously at her when she shot to her feet, distraught, hands bunched into fists at her sides. She stared at him in stunned dread, her heart pounding, her hands icy, her cheeks growing hotter and hotter.

"I knew it. This is all my fault," she said in a voice that shook. "You mustn't risk your life over what I said. I take it back. I take it all back, everything I said. You mustn't go."

"Indeed I must, if I am to take back Ascencion. That is what you wanted, isn't it, Allegra?" he asked with a penetrating midnight gaze.

Helplessly, she stared at him. "Yes, but—send someone else. If you're going to take back your throne—innumerable lives depend on you, Lazar—there is too much at stake to make a show of pride—"

"It's not pride, Allegra. It's honor, as you pointed out. Besides, I can fight my own battles."

She fell silent for a moment while the blade rang against the stone, spraying sparks.

"Please don't do this," she heard herself whisper. "There's got to be some other way. Maybe you don't need the signet ring. If you contact your father's advisers, no one will deny you. . . ."

Her voice trailed off, for she saw she was having no effect on him.

As he tested the knife's deadly sharpness between thumb and forefinger, his booted heels propped up on his desk, his thoughts seemed a million miles away.

"Lazar, listen to me—"

He swung his legs down off the desk. "It's the point of the thing, Allegra. Quit arguing."

"You don't have to do this!"

"Yes, I do," he said with quiet, contained ferocity. When he looked up at her, his stare was like a lightning bolt.

She drew back.

"No fear, Allegra. Do not waver. I need your strength now."

Chastened, she clasped her hands together and brought them up under her chin. She closed her eyes and lowered her head. "Take men with you, Lazar, for the love of God," she said, emphasizing every word. "Surely there are some of them you can trust to keep whatever secrets you wish to hide."

"Vicar's coming with me." He smirked and glanced at the ceiling. "I was unable to dissuade him."

"Vicar!" she burst out. "What's he going to do? He's no fighter! Take Sully and Captain Russo, or that savage young American—"

"It's not that kind of fight."

"What do you mean?"

"You would have to know Malik to understand." Inner

shadows flitted over his countenance, darkening his eyes. Then he tossed the knife and honing stone onto the desk.

"Let *me* go with you. If it is a battle of wits rather than force, I see no reason why I shouldn't accompany you myself."

"You really are adorable." He chuckled. "What are you going to do, my fierce kitten? Hiss at the bad man?"

"I resent that!" She lifted her chin, eyes ablaze. "I told you I would help you however I can!"

"Out of the question." He stood and continued girding himself for his battle. He fastened the pistol holster around his waist, then lifted the leather shoulder strap of his sword's sheath over his head so it lay across his chest.

Heart pounding with dread, more desperate by the second, Allegra suddenly wished she had never brought the quest for Ascencion before him at all.

Tentatively, she rounded the desk and went to him, reaching up to slip her arms around his neck, ignoring the arsenal of weapons he wore.

"Stay. Please. You have nothing to prove." She held her breath at her own recklessness, gazing up into his midnight eyes. "Lie with me. Teach me how to pleasure you," she whispered. "Don't go."

He stood tall, but looking down at her, his eyes flickered. Then he shook his head, removing her arms from around his neck.

"I cannot risk leaving you to raise a fatherless child."

She punched his chest. "Stop it! You're not going to die! I forbid it!"

He stared down at her, his expression increasingly stark. "I've been wanting to tell you, Allegra, how beautiful you are." He swallowed hard and looked away. "So very beautiful."

She clutched his open vest in both her hands, pleading with him. "Please don't leave me. I cannot bear to lose you." She threw her arms around his neck and held him tight, clinging to him with all her strength as tears flooded her eyes.

He wrapped his arms around her waist and lowered his head, kissing her with savage hunger. She devoured his kiss as two tears coursed down her face, for she knew now that the real reason he had summoned her was to say good-bye.

Too soon, Lazar ended their kiss, panting.

Wiping the tears from her cheeks with his thumbs, he took her face between his hands and stared fiercely into her eyes. "I will come back to you."

As she met his feverish stare, she could see him struggling with himself and knew she was only making the whole thing harder on him. Somehow she bit back her pleas.

"Allegra, I would have your blessing," he whispered.

"Oh, very well, just go," she cried, whirling away from him before she broke down in sobs, for that would only further erode his confidence. "Do what you want! I don't care! Just go!"

"Allegra, I—" He stopped himself. "Good-bye, *chérie.*"

Behind her, the door closed.

She whispered, "Good-bye, my Prince."

⊰ CHAPTER ⊱
SEVENTEEN

Lazar stomped down the gangplank with Vicar a step behind him, holding a torch that cast a circle of light in the blackness. They had taken only a few steps when Lazar felt the rickety dock begin to shake. Footsteps pounded toward them. Suddenly two dozen Moorish cutthroats came rushing out of the hot, dry African night.

Vicar breathed an expletive.

"*Marhaba,* my brothers," Lazar barked, blade drawn. "*Assalamu 'alaykum.*"

This drew them up short. The first of their number approached slowly, his dirk pirouetting in little deadly circles at the level of Lazar's heart. Lazar watched the man warily, appreciating the finesse even the lowliest of them possessed when it came to weapons.

"It is *The Whale!*" one of their company cried in excitement from the back. A few of the others went to the bow to squint at his ship's figurehead.

"It is so," they called to the ones making a thorny hedgerow of weapons around him.

"*Shaytan* pasha? Is it truly you?" the first one, with the dirk, said, frozen, suspicious under his grimy turban. His black eyes were wary.

Lazar gave a wan smile. "Seven trades and no luck," he replied.

The man cried out and whirled around to the others, ragged robes spinning, then turned back to him.

"Peace of God be with you, my brother! My brothers," he cried, "it is the mighty Devil of the West! He has returned! *Ahlan wa sahlan, Shaytan.* Welcome back! His Lordship will be overjoyed."

"Ahlan beek. I'm sure he will," he murmured, and shook the man's outstretched weapon hand. He followed the handshake by touching his hand over his heart as the Moor had. It showed sincerity. "Blessings upon you, brother. Have I had the honor of meeting you before?" he asked mildly.

The swarthy man stepped too close to him with a broad, white-toothed grin. Lazar grimaced inwardly. He'd forgotten about that. They always had to stand nigh bloody on your toes when they talked to you. He forced himself not to back away in spite of the disdain rising in his throat.

"You know me not, Shaytan pasha," he explained, "but I, of course, have heard the legends of your great deeds so that, forgive me, I feel I already know you well. I am Hamdy, son of Ibrihim the Ugly. Let us take you and your men to His Excellency."

"Shukran," Lazar said with a nod of thanks. Then he followed the Barbary corsairs over the dead, dry ground to the palace of their sheik.

"It is a miracle," Hamdy was saying, shaking his head. "His Lordship in his wisdom predicted you would come the very day we heard of your mighty battle at Ascencion!"

"Did he?" Lazar said lightly.

He watched the glittering sand give way softly under his boots. He remembered scorpions. The road to Malik's fortress was lined with desert rocks, here and there a few scrubby palms. The terrain was dead and bleak on all sides. The sea below seemed dead, too, as it washed the bone-white shore.

He looked up and saw the outline of the building under the moon, poised on a field of blue like one of Judas's silver coins.

Memories crashed back. He tried to stop them. He reached for his flask and drank it dry, knowing he'd need its liquid courage. There was a bitterness in his mouth that all the rum in the world could not wash out. God knows he'd tried.

He was thirteen. . . .

He walked up the road behind the Moors, mesmerized by the regular, easy swing of their dirty, flowing robes. He gripped the hilt of his sword, knowing it could not save him.

"Are you all right?" Vicar murmured beside him.

Lazar realized he was shivering. He was thinking of the time, four years ago, when he had returned to Al Khuum for vengeance on Malik. Molded by Wolfe and the wreaking of death, newly made captain of his first ship, puffed up with pride by the way he'd snuffed out every man who'd been part of the mutiny at Antigua, he thought himself quite fearless and hoped to exorcise once and for all the demons that still screeched in his head.

He had failed.

His old friends among the Janissaries, Malik's creatures now body and soul, had beaten the devil out of him with their usual, good-natured brutality, leaving him to come to his senses on his ship, bruised and humiliated. They had expected just such an attempt from him for a long time, it turned out. They knew him better than he liked. No one was surprised, and Malik was not even frightened. Everyone laughed at him.

Ma'alish, they had said. Never mind. It's in the past. It's not that serious.

On that day four years ago, he'd realized, to his astonishment, that they had not all been affected the same way he had by Malik's torments. They had no idea what it had done to his spirit, how the hatred and the evil of Al Khuum had warped him—and he was too proud to let them know.

He looked up, startled, to find himself in the gold and marble salon he knew so well, with its crimson, pillow-strewn divans and silk-hung walls and marvelous tiles. And there, on the magnificent golden throne, was Sayf-del-Malik: black-eyed, unmoving, beautiful, and deadly as a shark. The Sword of Honor.

Two fingers obscured his mouth as he gazed at Lazar in thought.

Every muscle in Lazar's body went taut. That slow, razor scrutiny was something he would never forget. Eons could not erase it.

"So," Malik said, dropping a hand languidly to the arm of the gilded throne. His eyes flickered with desert heat. "My young falcon has returned to my gauntlet. He soars in the heavens, but still he knows his true master. Malik will always be your master," he murmured, the heat of his black stare sharpening to unbearable intensity. "Won't I, Lazzo?"

Allegra was frantic, pacing the deck as she watched Lazar and Vicar go off down the dock, surrounded by heathen cut-throats who jabbered in a tongue she could not begin to comprehend. The group went up the road that ran parallel to the white, moonlit beach until they disappeared over a ridge at the cluster of distant ragged palm trees.

She whirled around to face the somber, silent crew, but the men turned away from her pleading gaze. She knew they had to sense the danger, but she saw they would not disobey their orders. She had never felt so helpless in her life.

Farther out in the bay, the six other ships rode at anchor, waiting. In two hours they would open fire on the fortress and the desert town if Lazar was not back with the signet ring in his possession. She wanted to kill him for not taking anyone with him except Vicar. Proud, obstinate man!

"I can't take this," she said to the air. She tried to pray as she stood there but had no patience for it. *I have to do something.*

She smelled Bernardo before he came to stand at the rails next to her. The hostility between them remained as strong as before, but she had grudgingly admitted that the Ascencioner's devotion to Lazar was unshakable.

"Are you thinking what I'm thinking?" he growled.

She turned to him. "I've got to help him. I'm going mad."

"Can you use a weapon?"

"I can try," she vowed.

"Come on."

Lazar looked his old tormentor in the eye, aware of nothing else around him. "I've come for what you stole from me."

"Stole—what's this? Am I a thief, Lazzo? Surely I never took anything that you were not eager to give," he murmured, touching his tongue to his dry lips.

Lazar reached for his pistol at the insult, but six sword points surrounded his throat before he could pull it out of the holster.

"Diir baalak." Malik laughed, chiding him softly. "Be careful of the devils you wrestle, my rash young friend, lest they overpower you. But look at you! A devil in your own right already, and you, not yet a man of thirty summers. My, my, so young, and already your powers of destruction exceed my most hopeful calculations. You might be interested to know," He said over steepled fingers, "Genoa has thirty ships out looking for you. And the new governor of Ascencion has put a price on your head—a Viscount Domenic Clemente, I believe. A thousand louis d'or. Yes, my friend. These are dangerous times."

Lazar glanced behind him, unsurprised to find the corsairs blocking his way out.

"Come, come, you're worth much more to me than that, Lazzo. Why the worried looks? I have not betrayed you." Malik accepted a cup of coffee from a servant and sipped it. "After all, were I to hand you over to them, I should never have the pleasure of your company again."

"Nor shall you."

Malik's smile was a mocking curved blade. "No? I do wish

to protect you and your men, of course, but these ruffians of mine, they are creatures of such avarice, and this prize for them seems effortless. Such a swift ship . . . such a fine crew. Genoa would pay handsomely, I think, for the pleasure of seeing them hanged. But you, my wicked boy, you I should keep for myself at all costs."

"There are six ships in your harbor that will open fire on Al Khuum if I have not returned in two hours' time."

Malik laughed. "Of course there are."

Lazar stared at him. "I am not bluffing. Give me back the signet ring. That's all I want. It is rightfully mine."

The bey's black eyes glittered as he gestured a man toward the door to investigate his claim. "Even if you are telling the truth, we both know your men are too devoted to open fire while you're here."

Lazar shrugged, but his bravado was wearing thin. "Give me back the ring, or we'll find out."

"I daresay I shouldn't require even one hour of your time, Lazzo," he said with an intimate smile. "Do you remember the games we used to play?"

Oh, he remembered. That simple, soft-spoken question did more to shake loose his careful self-control than the legion of corsairs blocking his exit, and Malik knew it.

Suddenly the curse of this place was becoming too much for him. The very smell of it was beginning to overpower him.

Vicar broke in smoothly, his voice like a razor's edge. "Why, Your Radiance, what pious man would so threaten his brother's son? Allah be praised."

Malik sat back in the golden chair and joined his hands lightly, a smile on his lips, fury in his eyes. "How noble you are to protect your young friend, Doctor Southwell, but Captain Wolfe is long dead, and I daresay the slave can speak for himself. He learned to fight among my Janissaries, you know, my jackals of the desert, so surely he need not cling to your coattails, if he is a man. Are you a man, Lazzo?"

Lazar's head was down. He was frozen with shame, couldn't move, couldn't speak.

Malik laughed at his helplessness, as he had when he was a boy in chains, unable to defend himself.

"Is this, then, the great Sword's hospitality?" Vicar replied icily.

Lazar only half heard them arguing. His gaze traveled, panicked, over the marble floor.

Why had he come here? Why had he thought himself invincible? What illusion of wishful thinking had made him think this scheme would work? He hated the desert. He didn't have to be here. He wanted to scream, to disappear. He wanted to gouge out those insidious black eyes, but he couldn't move.

When he looked up, he saw that one of the Moors had a knife pressed to Vicar's throat.

In a rage beyond thought, he spun past the sword points around him and, pulling out his pistol in fluid motion, fixed the steel barrel on the back of the man's skull.

He ordered him in Arabic to drop his weapon and was obeyed.

Malik laughed softly.

Lazar whirled on him, and his voice shook with the wrath of seven hundred years of royal command. "Return what you stole from me!"

"Well, well." Malik chuckled, obscuring his mouth again with two fingers, caressing him with his gaze. He considered for a long moment, then handed the coffee back to the fair-skinned slave. He flicked his wrist and produced, like a magician from his sleeve, the signet ring.

"Could it be this trifle you seek?" The sheik held up the ring between his thumb and forefinger, a weighted O of gold and onyx, with a ruby that sparked like fire in the lion's eye. "Perhaps if you provide me with the proper amusement, you may have it back."

Heart pounding, Lazar flicked his fingers around his pistol, and he swallowed hard while the edges of his control began to fray with insane rage. He was fairly certain at that moment he would not leave alive this time, and he was beginning not to care. He could not submit to the unclean ordeals Malik would put him through. This time he would fight to the death, and so be it.

"We have much to discuss, you and I," Malik told him softly.

"No. Forget it," he ground out.

With an impatient snap of his fingers, Malik caused the Moors to take hold of Lazar by the arms.

"Let him go, you heathen bastards!" Vicar cried savagely, struggling against the turbaned man who held him. Another man lifted the butt of his gun and struck Vicar out cold.

Lazar shouted as Vicar went down, shaking off the clinging Moors like a bull routing a pair of dogs.

Seeing this, Malik clapped his hands twice to summon the Janissaries. "Now then," the sheik said, eyes aglow. "To the games."

The corsairs nervously moved to the edges of the salon to make room for Malik's huge bodyguards.

Just then the man Malik had sent returned to inform His Excellency that his threat was true; six ships in addition to *The Whale* waited in the harbor.

"Well then," he said in amusement, "we'll have to hurry, but never fear, my boy. We'll have you back in time." He beckoned in some men behind Lazar.

Lazar turned to face the two Janissary warriors who appeared in the doorway. The first was his old friend Gordon, a gold-haired English giant who'd been known in his youth for his practical jokes—but there was nothing left of his friend in that dead, metallic-gray stare. If Gordon even recognized him, he showed no sign. The second was a dark-skinned young African—a more recent recruit—built like a mountain. His brown eyes wore the same dead, murderous expression as Gordon's.

Malik's eyes shone with red demon glee. He rose from his golden throne and minced down the platform steps. Lazar watched him warily. Circling behind him, Malik slipped his hands into Lazar's holsters, carefully dragging his pistols out of them.

"You won't be needing these."

With a snarl Lazar jerked away from him, removing his knife, his sword, and his vest for combat. He knew the rules of Malik's deadly game from long experience.

"If you win, you get this," Malik said, rolling the signet ring between his fingers.

"And if I lose?"

Malik gave him a dark smile. "Then you come home forever, Lazzo. To Master."

Lazar was going to be furious at her for leaving the ship, but it didn't matter. Allegra had no idea how or even *if* there was anything she and Bernardo could do to help him, but within a quarter hour, they were hurrying down the sandy road in the direction the Moors had led him and Vicar.

When one of those mysterious wild animals of the desert howled again, she tilted her head down to smell the reassuring scent of Lazar, which permeated the soft fabric of the gigantic shirt she wore, tucked into a pair of his black trousers, his belt wrapped nearly twice around her. She had hidden the long plait of her hair with a dark silk scarf tied into a skullcap like Lazar's, and all she could think of was how he was going to laugh when he saw her.

It had been Bernardo's idea that she don masculine garb, to draw less attention to herself.

In addition to being terrified, she felt utterly ridiculous. Her costume was so hastily thrown together she did not think she was going to fool anyone. The fact that she was armed with a knife only made her more nervous. Perhaps it should have made her feel secure, but it only reminded her to hope she wouldn't need it. She clung to Lazar's statement that his meeting with this Malik creature would be more a battle of wills or wits, rather than outright violence. In all but the third, she felt she could hold her own.

Another howl sounded, closer this time, filling the night. It trailed off, dwindling to a ponderous stillness broken only by the murmur of the sea laving the desert beach.

"Whatever that thing is," Bernardo muttered, "it's hungry."

She murmured agreement and glanced over her shoulder to make sure the animals weren't stalking them. Behind them, *The Whale* was still plainly visible as it waited in the berth, its white sails drooping on the spars.

"Remember," she told Bernardo, "these people call him Shaytan of the West. I hope we can communicate with them a little."

Ahead, over the sandy hill, rose an ancient-looking fortress, squat and square, made of light-colored stone block that gleamed in the moonlight. As they drew closer, she saw that darkness and distance had masked the true condition of the structure, for in fact at closer range it looked a thousand years old, preserved by the dry heat, but nevertheless slowly crumbling. Many robed men lounged on the steps and under the portico before the entrance.

She and Bernardo stopped, still a couple hundred yards away. It was dark, so no one noticed them yet.

"That's where they took him," she murmured. "Let's go."

She walked on.

When a small band of the Moors saw them coming, she turned to wait for Bernardo to catch up to her, only to find he was running away, bolting back down the road without a word. Her eyes widened.

"Bernardo!"

He kept running. She turned back furiously to study the

foreign, swarthy faces of the men coming toward her. They had Lazar. She couldn't do him any good out here. She raised her hands slightly to show she would not fight, walking slowly toward them.

"Where have you taken the man called Shaytan? I want to see him," she said in a steely voice, though she doubted they could understand her any more than she could them.

Two of them grabbed her arms and, after removing her knife from her belt, they took her to the fortress.

Other Moors were standing around, conversing in agitation and smoking long pipes under the stars, their eyes red from the pungent spice. One man sat on the bottom step, playing a rectangular stringed instrument in a seemingly random series of long notes that slid high and low with silvery fluidity. Here and there men called out to her captors in their strange tongue.

"Where is he? Where have you taken *Shaytan*?" she shouted.

One gave an incomprehensible answer, nodding.

"Take me to him," she persisted. "Now!"

They babbled and pulled her along.

She tried another tack. "Let me see Malik."

They laughed and gave one another knowing looks. *Malik* was the only word she could understand as they talked.

Inside the fortress, she marveled at the exotic, columned halls of gilt and alabaster. Clearly the dilapidated condition of the fort's exterior was a ruse to ward off unwanted attention. Inside, it was sumptuous. The floor was of purest white marble, and the walls were decorated with colorful, intricate tilework. She struggled against the Moors' grasp, trying to look into every room they passed, hoping to see Lazar. Meanwhile, the halls echoed with the sounds of a roaring crowd, as if some sporting contest was in progress somewhere in the huge maze of halls.

The sound grew fainter as she was taken through a wide doorway guarded by two giant, obese, and unmoving Ethiope eunuchs standing on either side of the hall. The doorway was hung with silky veils, softly obscuring from full view the chamber beyond.

Her captors prodded her and gestured that she should go in. She glanced warily at the two motionless, ebony-skinned sentinels as she parted the gauzy veils overhanging the doorway.

She found herself alone in a large, airy chamber dimly lit by thuribles full of low fire on tall, twisted iron stands. Incense burned in their basins along with the coals, making the air thick and soft with heady fragrance. The room was lined with graceful white columns, and in the center was a lovely tiled bath with a lilting fountain. Everywhere woven carpets were strewn over the cool marble floor, and colorful silks hung from the walls.

As she glanced about, trying to find an exit so she could search the fortress for Lazar, she heard a soft, scuffling sound behind her, and she turned around to find a lad of about fourteen standing between two of the columns. He glanced to the right and left, then beckoned her over.

He was an exceedingly beautiful youth, compact and well proportioned of form, with none of the gangling awkwardness of his age. He had jet-black hair, brooding dark eyes under long, thick lashes, and full lips that gave him a sullen, sensual pout that was a bit unnerving, considering his tender years. He was dressed in flowing white robes like the men outside, but his were made of finest lawn. When she approached, he nodded to her and asked a question in what she supposed was Arabic.

She shrugged and shook her head. "I don't understand. Do you speak Italian?"

They settled on Spanish.

"I come from Andalusia," he said with a quick smile that never reached his eyes. "My name is Darius Santiago."

"You have to help me!" she said. "Then maybe we can both get out of here. How do I make them let me see Malik?"

"Don't worry. He'll come looking for you soon enough," he said with a short, cold laugh. "He takes the greatest interest in all his newest slaves."

She stared at him without comprehension for a moment. "Slaves?"

He looked at her quizzically. "Don't you know?"

Oh, my God. Staring at him, she knew now. Lazar had been a slave here.

She stood there, motionless, barely able to breathe in her shocked horror. She felt as if her world were crashing down around her, but there wasn't a moment to lose.

Quickly she introduced herself, and though Darius did not seem to believe she was in fact a female under her masculine disguise, he listened intently as she explained that in less than an hour the city would be shelled. When she told him Lazar was somewhere in the fortress, Darius's onyx eyes lit up with awe.

"So that's what all the commotion is tonight! To think of it! He is here, the great *Shaytan* pasha! By all that is holy, what I would not give to serve such a warrior!"

"You've heard of him?"

"Of course." He snorted, tossing his black forelock out of his eyes. "Everyone here knows of him. Many times I've heard tales of him—tales that give me courage when I long to die. He survived this place, and so will I. Sword will not break my spirit! I will escape, like *Shaytan*, and be mighty and powerful, like him! But when I come back to kill Malik," he added, a savage gleam in his black eyes, "I will not fail."

"Can you help us?"

"Perhaps. I will go spy out the situation. Wait here."

"I'll come with you—"

"They won't let you," he said, "but they're used to me. I'm allowed free movement throughout the fortress."

"Please hurry," she implored him.

He nodded and prowled off silently, but before he reached

the doors, he turned and gave her a hard look. "In case Malik comes for you in the meantime, take my advice. Don't ask him for pity, and try not to scream. He feeds off fear and the pleasure of causing pain."

With that, Darius pivoted amid swirling white robes and slipped out the door, allowed past by the two giant sentinels. Allegra closed her eyes for a second, striving for calm.

She was entrusting Lazar's fate, her own, and Ascencion's to a child. But for the moment she had no choice.

She would have rather done anything at all but stand still and wait in this place, where the echoes of pain and innocence violated filled the serene, vaulted spaces. Every lovely inch of it made her blood boil. Here and there grew miniature fruit trees in clay pots, but underlying the salon's mood of earthly delight was her knowledge that Lazar had been terrorized here, an orphaned innocent. She had never seen an uglier place in her life.

Her gaze wandered to the corner, where she spied a lovely wrought-iron cage. Inside it was a great, gorgeous cockatoo with a short, curved beak and long white plumage with the luminescence of pearls. The unearthly creature seemed to study her from across the exotic salon.

Just to give her hands something to do, she marched over to the cockatoo's cage and opened the little door. When the bird did not fly out at once, she reached into the cage for it. To her relief, it did not bite her but endured her touch wearily, used to being handled.

But when she carried it to the window, an excitement came over the bird as it smelled the night air. Its wings began to beat; its clawed feet scratched her hand. The beautiful thing didn't know its own strength. At the window she raised her hands, releasing her protective grasp on the soft body.

The white-plumed bird spread its wings and climbed free into the black night.

* * *

Lazar was tiring.

He could feel the burning, molten rock in all his muscles; he tasted the blood from his battered lip. It felt as though he had been fighting forever. Gordon, mute and mechanical, his gold hair plastered by sweat to his forehead, kept coming.

After a wild battle, Lazar had dislocated the African's right shoulder. Now it was down to Gordon and him—a fair fight, only now he was already tired from when the two of them had been pounding on him together.

He was astounded at the savagery with which his old friend rushed him. He kept leaving himself open unintentionally, because each time he peered into his friend's eyes and saw the malicious automaton there, it distracted his concentration. Gordon was too well trained to spare these opportunities.

Earlier Lazar had made a few choice remarks to try to jeer his old friend into some more human sort of reaction, but it was no good. Now grimly, silently, and with the beginnings of real despair, he labored on, pressing his body and skills to the limit against his inscrutable opponent.

They barreled across the marble floor like embattled titans, heedless of the thundering mob that looked on. They beat each other brutally, then parted and circled for a moment, panting hard, blood dripping from noses and various cuts onto the white marble floor. When they engaged again, Lazar slammed Gordon in the jaw with a powerful left jab.

Gordon stepped back to catch himself from the impact, then stepped forward and rammed him in the forehead with his own skull. Lazar saw stars.

While his head was still reeling from the brunt of the Englishman's rocklike pate, Gordon decided to strangle him. He drove Lazar back against the cool tiled wall with Moors scrambling everywhere to get out of the way.

Lazar clawed against the iron grip around his throat. His lungs began to scream for air. He pummeled the lummox in the gut, but Gordon brought his knee up into Lazar's belly in reply.

As the airless minutes passed, the great hall began to get dark . . . speckled . . . distant . . . and then Gordon dropped him onto the floor, and it felt as though he cracked his head on the marble.

As he lay on the cool floor, gasping for breath, his eyes full of black clouds and double vision, Lazar heard Malik announce Gordon the winner, heard the pitch of eager heat in the sheik's raised voice.

Lazar groaned in defeat, a low, animal sound.

By the time he opened his eyes again to face the Moors who would come to collect him, they already had his hands tied with rough ropes. Everything was very slow, like a dream. They dragged him to his feet and prodded him toward the dark, unspeakable chamber.

Fifteen minutes later, Darius came tearing back into the dim salon. Allegra ran to him, her heart in her throat when she saw his stricken gaze.

"They've got him. They're headed this way."

"What's happened? Is he hurt?"

"Here." He reached under the drapery of his robe and produced two pistols, one of which he tossed to her. She gasped when it almost slipped through her hands. When the boy presented Lazar's all-too-familiar Moorish knife and pressed the leather-wrapped hilt into her hands, Allegra stared at the weapon in dread.

"Where did you get these?"

"Stole them from under Malik's throne. I can steal anything. Come. We must hide."

Her heart was pounding wildly. The blood roared in her ears as they crouched down beside a divan behind a wall of shimmering veils. A second later came the sound of voices and footfalls approaching the doorway where the Ethiopian guards stood.

"They put the old Englishman in the dungeon," Darius whispered quickly.

The white-robed man who stepped into view under the arch between the slender columns was lean and swarthy and plainly in a state of agitation. He glided ahead, then doubled back impatiently, waiting for the others. There was a sinister grace about him, and she knew from the way Darius's whole body tensed beside her that it had to be Sayf-del-Malik.

When Lazar came through the doorway, she felt as if her heart simply ripped in two at the sight of him.

His wrists were bound before him, his head bowed in defeat. His posture was one of exhaustion and pain, and by the dim light of the thuribles, she could see the sheen of sweat coating his arms and, here and there, trickles of blood on him. He looked ruined, brutalized. She could not take her eyes off him.

Deep in her veins she felt the first whisperings of a divine rage like nothing she had ever felt.

Meanwhile, Malik hurried the guards along as they shepherded her dazed champion. The party passed, slowed by the prisoner's labored pace. At the end of the hallway, Malik opened a door on the left and ushered Lazar inside, then dismissed the other men.

Beside her, Darius was trembling. She thought this was due to fear until he spoke, and she realized it was hatred.

"Let's go," he said in a voice that made her blood run cold.

As she followed the Andalusian youth down the dark, wide hallway, she began to feel strangely collected. When they came to the closed door where the sheik had taken Lazar, Darius paused to put his ear to the door. Silently the boy set down Lazar's pistols by the wall.

"They're talking," he whispered. "I'll distract Malik. When he turns his back to you, kill him."

She nodded. *Yes. Kill him.* For Lazar she would kill this Caligula without a qualm.

She suddenly understood Lazar more intimately than she

ever dreamed she would, his rage of vengeance that had made him want to blot out her whole family and burn Little Genoa to the ground.

Darius waved her a step back from the door, then he knocked. At Malik's bark, he announced himself. Darius stared straight ahead, his cheeks turning scarlet when Malik's tone changed from rudeness to welcome, fraught with husky invitation.

Allegra shuddered, glad she could not understand the words.

The boy visibly steeled himself, then went in. Opium smoke wafted into the hall when the door opened. Darius left the door slightly ajar behind him, and Allegra waited.

"Come in, boy. I find my mind fired with interesting possibilities," said Malik, in Spanish this time. "There now, go to poor Lazzo. Wipe off his wounds. Don't be afraid of him. He is quite restrained. Is he not like a lion in a cage?"

Allegra clenched her teeth. Her heart was pounding. Her sweating palm slicked the handle of the great Moorish knife. When she realized how close she'd have to get to Malik to kill him, she silently picked up one of the pistols, but on second thought, she tucked the gun into her belt, for she dared not use it. Her aim was unpracticed, and Lazar too near.

"Don't touch me," she heard Lazar warn in a low, deadly growl, then Darius yelped from within the room.

She heard Malik laugh. His evil was palpable in the air.

She edged toward the door. Holding her breath, she peered around the corner. Lazar had knocked Darius halfway across the room to ward him off, and Malik stood perhaps five paces from her, his back to her, looking down at Darius on the stone floor.

"Boys, boys, I want you to be friends. Is the Andalusian not a rare youth, Lazzo? He has the heart of a wolf, but his face is fresh as dew."

Her mind was calm and extraordinarily clear.

Allegra closed her eyes, wiped a bead of sweat off her

cheek, blessed herself with the sign of the cross, then, with a heart full of thunder, walked into the chamber and, without a moment's hesitation, sank the knife with all her strength squarely between Malik's shoulders.

Flesh yielded to metal with sickening give, then the impact as the blade glanced off the spine jarred her wrist, and she shrieked in spite of herself.

Malik howled, and Allegra jumped back when he whipped around, his face feral.

Darius ran to shut the door as Malik bellowed with disbelief. Allegra stood frozen in place, hands clapped over her mouth at seeing the knife hilt jutting from the man's back. Malik twisted in a circle, thrashing, screaming. He dropped to his knees.

"Shut him up," Lazar grunted.

Darius brushed by her, pulled out the knife, and, reaching over the Arab's shoulder, calmly slit his throat. The cut complete, Darius dropped him, facedown.

Suddenly blood was everywhere.

For a second the boy merely stared down at Malik as if he could not believe he had done it. Knife in hand, his chest heaved. Blood streaked the white lawn of his robe. Then Allegra's own blood turned to ice, for Darius laughed.

The laugh turned to a vicious, sudden snarl, and he swooped down on one knee over Malik's body, stabbing the dying man numerous times with dark and unrepentant zest.

"Darius!" she said, drawing back from the child, wide-eyed.

The boy stood, still staring down at the dead man in black satisfaction. "He deserves it."

Back to cool efficiency, Darius wiped off the crimson blade on the white linen over Malik's shoulder while the blood flowed and pooled. Lazar lifted his hands and Darius cut the ropes from his wrists. Then the boy bowed his head and offered Lazar his Moorish knife, hilt first.

"Prince of Ascencion," he said, his voice hushed and rapid, "please accept the help of one who has suffered as you have.

We must flee while there is time. Come. Your friend the Englishman is in the dungeon. I'll show you where."

But Lazar was staring only at her.

Her eyes welled up with tears at his mute and fractured gaze. She searched his poor, half-swollen face, at a loss for words. She moved toward him, but he warded her off.

"Don't touch me," he whispered.

And then, without another word, he snapped out of his ghastly stupor and was out the door. Darius did not miss his cue, following half a step behind. For a moment, Allegra was alone with the corpse. She glanced down, tempted to kick the dead man on the floor, his waxy brown face frozen in a rictus of rage. She looked away in revulsion, and it was then that she noticed a spark of gold on the chamber floor.

She picked her way around the viscid lake of blood spreading around Malik and picked up what proved to be the item they had come for. One glance at the image on the ring showed her the lion of the Fiori coat of arms. Lazar's signet ring, made to fit a boy's finger.

Proof.

Happy now? She closed her eyes, sick with remorse that she had driven him to come here, to face this. *Has he suffered enough yet for the accident of his royal blood?*

Love me. That was all he'd asked. She dropped her chin almost to her chest as she clutched the ring tightly. How was he ever going to recover from this?

Distantly she heard the alien shouting of the guards. The far-off alarm roused her to action. Allegra ran out of the room and turned down the hall after Lazar and Darius. She caught a glimpse of them just as they turned the corner ahead. She pounded down the stone corridor after them, not daring to call out for them to wait.

"We can get out through the dungeon," Darius panted, running beside him down the torch-lit corridor.

Only years of obeying honed instincts enabled Lazar to move at all. His mind was blank with shock, as though a mortar had just exploded in front of him. None of it felt real. His soul was cleaved in two like an earthworm by the plow, but his body fought on, mindless and precise, refusing as usual to die even when death was the only decent thing to do. He felt as if he were watching himself in action from somewhere outside his own skin, displaced as a ghost hovering over its own corpse.

They skidded to a stop before a forbidding wood-and-iron door. He knew Allegra wasn't far behind. She was going to have to look out for herself at the moment, because he simply could not face her.

Automatically Lazar drew his pistol, shot the lock asunder, and hauled the great door open. With the grace of a small jungle cat, Darius darted down the dozen steps ahead of him into the dungeon's echoing blackness. The great vault smelled like human dung and musty hay. Torture devices crouched in the shadows, lurking monsters. The cells were constructed of rotting wood and rusted iron bars. Warily, Lazar descended the dozen steps to the packed-earth floor.

He quickly dispatched the warden who accosted them, while Darius trotted down the row of cells in search of Vicar. As Lazar joined him to shoot the lock open, he heard another prisoner down the row, shouting and banging on the bars, pleading with him to be released.

Lazar asked Vicar if he was all right. Vicar nodded grimly, though he looked like hell, then Lazar gestured to the boy to lead the way. Darius scampered to the other end of the sprawling dungeon and up another pair of dusty steps to yet another massive door.

"It leads to the amphitheater," he said. "No one will be out there now, but we'll have to make a run for it."

Lazar nodded, but he had his doubts about their making it out of this place alive. As he reached for the lock, Darius cried out, pointing behind them.

"Someone's coming!"

Lazar turned and saw a slim silhouette in the doorway at the other end of the dungeon. He knew that slender outline at once. He clamped his jaw against an agonized animal moan.

"What the bloody hell is she doing here?" Vicar groaned.

"She?" Darius exclaimed.

"Never mind. I'll go get her," Vicar muttered.

Lazar let him go, using the precious extra moments to reload his pistols. Vicar hurried back down the steps, walked briskly down the row of cells, and stepped over the warden's corpse.

"Miss Monteverdi, over here!"

"Vicar?" she called in a tremulous voice that filled the black dungeon.

The sweet echo made Lazar flinch.

How could he ever look her in the eye again? He could not. He'd come here to win her respect and had instead been utterly shamed in front of her.

It was time. Time for what he should have done long ago. *Just an hour longer. Just see her and Vicar and this ferocious child back safely to the ship. Then no more pain.*

He thrust his pistols back into the holsters and folded his arms, facing the door as he waited. The boy looked up at him in question. Lazar ignored him. A moment later, Vicar returned, tugging Allegra along by the hand. Her face was a pale oval in the darkness. With a glance Lazar noticed she was wearing his shirt and trying desperately to look brave.

He turned away from her quickly, because he could not bear to see the revulsion he knew would be there in her eyes.

Without further ceremony, he yanked the lock back and shoved the thick door open, both guns primed. But he met with only the empty, dusty ring of the amphitheater, where his friends and he used to train and had bled so many times for Malik's entertainment. Above, the brilliant desert night was gaudy with stars.

The main block of the fort was nearby. Judging from the

chaotic sounds coming out of it, Lazar realized Malik's body must have been discovered. Maybe he should have been glad the fiend was dead, but he felt nothing, nothing at all.

Just as he started for the exit of the amphitheater with his small band following him, the shelling began. He had ordered his captains to pound the place to dust.

"Run!" Vicar yelled.

With the sand flying up in geysers before them, they fled all the way back to the waiting ship, leaving Al Khuum to its destruction.

⊰ CHAPTER ⊱
EIGHTEEN

When they gained the ship, Allegra watched Lazar closely, trying to read him. A terrible feeling of foreboding was taking shape inside her. Aside from the fact that he would not look at her—indeed, he seemed to be pretending she didn't exist—he seemed perfectly fine.

He was shattered, and she knew it, but not so much as a single small crack showed in the walls he'd thrown up so fast and so well around him.

He stood on the quarterdeck, dispensing a stream of orders to his crew, the men feverishly working the capstan to lift the anchor, hauling up the gangplank, and scrambling up the ropes as the sweeps maneuvered the ship out of berth. Patiently he heard out Bernardo's groveling apologies and granted forgiveness, then half carried Vicar to the sick bay to be treated for a nasty blow to the head he'd taken.

Returning topside a few moments later, he made certain that the ship passed the shoals safely and was under way in the warm current of the Mediterranean.

He gave Darius some of his clothes to wear, instead of the hated Arab robes of the slave, though she doubted they would fit the boy any better than they had fit her. Lazar sent him to the galley to be fed but, as an afterthought, stopped him before he descended the hatch. By the lantern's light, she saw him give the boy his curved Moorish knife. The boy took the gift with an awed, upward gaze of instant devotion to the man. To be sure,

Darius had used the knife well, but Allegra found it ominous indeed to see Lazar giving away his favorite weapon.

She watched him return to the helm, where he went over their exact course for the full voyage one more time with Mr. Harcourt. Still ignoring her, Lazar then left the helm and went to the bow of the ship. She stood watching him while he looked out at the sea, and she saw that he was lost in himself despite the facade.

She hesitated, not knowing how to go to him after those moments in Malik's chamber.

Before she could approach him, he left the bow, the moon glinting on his pistols, and when he passed the mast, he paused, tilting his head back to gaze up at the sails. For a long moment, he ran his hand lovingly over the smooth wood of the mast, and it was then she knew.

He had made his final preparations. He had taken care of everyone. She had just watched him say his final good-bye to his beloved ship.

"Oh, God, no," she said under her breath as her knees began to shake. Dread took her like a shark, in one bite.

At the base of the pine mast, Lazar lowered his head, turned away, and walked slowly toward the hatch. She stood there, frozen, trying to believe she was wrong—surely her own worst nightmare would not rise to engulf her now. Surely her own brave Lazar would never give up. Victory was within his grasp.

The moment he was out of sight, she tore after him.

Lazar locked the cabin door and went to his desk, where he sat down heavily in the chair, pride crushed, soul battered, whole body aching. He opened the top drawer and began searching for the silver bullet he had saved for this occasion.

He couldn't find it. When he realized Allegra was banging on the door, he looked up. His lost gaze fell upon the pile of files and documents about Ascencion. With a savage pass, he swiped them all to the floor, scattering them. He yanked the drawer right out of the desk and overturned it.

"Damn it, where is it?" he muttered aloud.

"Please, Lazar, please let me in."

He didn't answer. He heard her run away, screaming, for men to come and break down the door. He crouched down and rooted through the spilled contents of the drawer, but by the time he held the little silver bullet between his thumb and forefinger, he knew he couldn't do it.

He could not do this to Allegra.

How he was going to live, he did not know, but life held him, thrashed him in its jaws like a lion and would not let him go.

Suddenly he couldn't breathe. He stood up quickly, dizzy. He removed his pistol holster and threw the whole thing across the room before it ever tempted him again. He tore himself free of his sword's shoulder strap, cast it off, and stalked to the balcony for air, panting, clutching the silver bullet. At the rails, he threw the bullet as far out into the ocean as he could, then he braced both hands on the wood and hung his head in utter despair.

Vicar had a key to the cabin, but with a crowd of men standing behind her, Allegra fumbled with the lock in her terror and haste. At last it sprang free.

Then came the hardest moment of her life.

Steeling herself, she laid hold of the doorknob. But before she could turn it, it turned itself. The door opened, and Lazar stood there, looming in the dimness.

"It's all right," he muttered to the men. "Go back to work."

With a cry, Allegra threw herself against him, wrapping her arms tightly around his waist. She ran her gaze over the length of him, trying to discern any evidence to show he was a threat to himself. Except for how battered he was by his fight, he was safe.

Thank you, God. She pressed her cheek against his chest

and listened to his pounding heart, her entire body weak with relief as she realized she must have overreacted. Turning to the men, though she did not let go of Lazar, she murmured an embarrassed apology for having upset them. They cast wary glances from her to Lazar, then nodded and went back to their work. Vicar sent him a piercing look and said not a word, turning away.

Standing with her arms around Lazar in the open doorway of the cabin, Allegra called to the last man leaving the stateroom.

"Have the galley heat water for him. Your captain will have a bath," she said without so much as a blush. "Tell Emilio to make him something to eat—something soft to chew," she added, glancing up at his poor, bruised jaw. "Then tell the ship's surgeon to bring me poultices and cloths for his wounds."

The crewman nodded and hurried off to do her bidding.

Lazar was silent, his expression remote, as if his face had been chiseled from granite. He still made no move to return her embrace. She figured he was probably furious with her for leaving the ship, in addition to being humiliated. On the other hand, he didn't object or push her away either.

She took him by the hand and stepped into the cabin. She closed and locked the door, then paused, looking up to search his face. A moment later, she led him to the big, comfortable armchair and bade him sit.

He did. He watched her warily as she slid off the dark scarf she had tied over her plaited hair. Holding it in her hand, she folded her arms over her chest as she stood across from him, critically eyeing every visible cut and scratch and bruise on his powerful body.

When she noticed the stark, fractured plea in his midnight eyes as he gazed at her, her eyes flooded quickly with tears. She stepped closer and laid her hand against his cheek. He pressed his cheek against her palm, closing his eyes with a look of exhaustion.

"Why did you come? You shouldn't have come," he whispered brokenly.

She stared at the beauty of him, his long, black, feathery lashes closed. Her bold, proud pirate captain, her Prince, was not simply hurt; he was shamed down to the core of his soul. She felt that wound as though it were her own.

"Lazar di Fiore," she whispered, "I love you more than life itself."

His eyes flicked open suddenly. His brow furrowed a little as he looked up at her suspiciously.

There was a long silence. He pulled away from her hand and looked away.

"I don't want your pity," he forced out in a stony voice. "Just leave me alone. I know the sight of me repulses you. You don't have to keep up this charade—"

"Sweetheart," she interrupted him softly, "look at me."

Jaw clenched tight, he looked up insolently. "What?"

"Do I look repulsed?" She gazed at him with her heart in her eyes. "You arc the bravest, greatest-hearted man I have ever known, and your strength to have survived such a place awes me."

As he stared up at her, the fractured look returned. "Don't torment me," he whispered, dropping his gaze suddenly. "It's bad enough that I failed—"

"You didn't fail. You just needed a little help." She reached into the pocket of the trousers she wore and pulled out the signet ring, offering it to him. "You did it, Lazar. You kept your word to your father."

He took it slowly, and now his eyes filled with tears that quickly vanished.

"Now Ascencion will be yours, as it should be."

He lowered his head and was quiet for a long moment. "I only wanted it so you would not think ill of me, but I know you cannot love me now."

At his confession, her throat closed with emotion. She could not speak. She nudged his knees apart with her own to stand between them and pulled him into a sheltering embrace about his wide shoulders and his head. He rested his cheek against her bosom. She held him close.

"I do love you," she whispered. "That's why I followed. I knew you were in danger."

"You walked into Al Khuum for me," he said, dazed.

"I would follow you into hell itself, Lazar."

"Aye, you just did."

"And we made it out because we are stronger together than either of us is alone, my love," she whispered. "You're safe now." She pulled his skullcap off and ran her fingers tenderly through his velvety jet-black hair, vaguely noting that it had grown fast. She leaned down and kissed his head.

"But . . . Allegra."

"I love you, Lazar. Nothing is going to change that. There is no reason for you to feel you need hide anything from me."

His right hand cupped her arm, and he pulled her down onto his lap. He stared down into her eyes, searching them as if he sought to see into her very soul.

"What is it?" she whispered.

His dark eyes flickered.

"You love me?" he asked barely audibly. There was so much wistfulness in those three tiny words it brought fresh tears to her eyes.

"Yes, I do. With all my heart."

"I lost everything, everyone I ever cared for," he whispered, head down. "How shall I ever bear it if I lose you?"

She went down on her knees before him, her hands on his shoulders. She stared up fiercely into his eyes. "You will never lose me. Never. I will be with you always."

"I can't marry you," he said heavily.

"Shh, sweetheart. I know that," she whispered as she stroked the broad muscle of his arm. "I understand about your old betrothal—it's best for Ascencion. Just give me some place in your life. I will be your mistress, your friend, whatever you want, Lazar. Just let me be near you."

With a pained expression, he captured her hand and held it to his lips for a long time, his head down, eyes closed in distress. "You deserve more than to be anybody's mistress. I want you for my wife, but I cannot have you."

She smiled gently as she smoothed his hair back. "In my heart, I am your wife. That is enough for me."

"Chérie." He pulled her back onto his lap and held her so that she faced him, her legs around his hips, her head on his shoulder. "Never let me go."

"Never," she whispered, hugging him more tightly to herself.

They clung to each other, huddling together for comfort like two orphaned children, as if the other were all they each had left in the world. They were silent for some time, both dazed by the night's events. Now they sat there, simply stroking each other's hair, arms, and back, learning the feel of each other all over again, basking in the reassurance. She caressed his neck several times, just to feel with her fingertips the blessed pulse of his heartbeat.

"I can't bear to think how close I came to losing you," she told him, kissing his cheek. "But you told me you would come back to me, and you did."

"I would do anything for you," Lazar whispered with strangled savagery. "Allegra, I just want you to know—all that hell—I would go through it all again to arrive at this moment—to have this with you. Allegra, I've never said this to anyone before. I love you."

She stared at him in anguished joy.

"You are the dearest man," she choked out, pulling him close, eyes shut tight. "I love you, too."

"Kiss me, *chérie.*"

She did, very gently. When he deepened the kiss, he flinched, pulling back.

"Ow," he said ruefully, touching his jaw, swollen on one side from his fight.

She smiled, shaking her head at his bruises. "What a sight you are, Fiore," she said, smiling very slightly in spite of herself.

"Fine words from a woman wearing men's clothes."

With a gentle touch, she examined a cut above his right eyebrow. "Poor thing, look at you," she murmured. "I don't think there'll be any more kissing for you tonight."

"It's worth the pain," he growled with a faint shadow of his old, playful smile. He leaned toward her again.

She stopped him with a soft gaze. "My love, if we begin, I don't think either of us will be content to stop at kissing. After seeing him tonight—are you sure you're ready?"

He was quiet, somber for a moment, and then he looked shrewdly into her eyes.

"You must not blame yourself—ever," she said. "I saw how he was. The man was filth, and I'm glad I stabbed him."

His eyes widened. To her surprise, he laughed softly. "What's this? My kitten has turned lioness?"

Her answer was a slight, lazy grin. "That's right, Leo."

Smiling vaguely, he touched her cheek, though he didn't meet her eyes. "If you can still bear the sight of me, then I guess it truly *is* in the past." He ventured to look into her eyes again.

"Well, let me tell you, my friend," she purred as she placed a kiss on his neck, "I would like to bear more than the sight of you tonight."

He shivered a little. "Is that so?"

Their caresses filled with a different intention, from shared consolation to silken enticement. Lazar leaned back in the chair, staring at her as she parted his vest with both hands and ran her nails lightly down his chest.

"Tonight, my warrior, you will show me all the places you're hurting, and I shall kiss them all."

"That could take a while," he whispered with a brief, devilish lift of one flared brow.

"I hope so." She leaned down and kissed his chest once.

Their slow, languid play was interrupted when the crewmen banged on the door, bringing the tub and first buckets of water for his bath. Allegra moved back a few inches from him and smiled tenderly as she caressed his face.

"You let me take care of you tonight, *capisce?*" she said softly.

He reached out and tapped her nose gently with one fingertip. "I am yours to command," he whispered.

She smiled again, sighing with love as she slid off his lap and let the two crewmen into the cabin to complete their work. Lazar slouched wearily in the armchair, long legs sprawled out before him, his dark eyes watching her every move.

Working in silence, the two crewmen hastily filled the great wooden tub near the stern wall. Allegra lit three candles to pierce the dark of night, then poured glasses of wine for herself and Lazar.

When the mates had gone, she locked the door behind them once more and scattered dried flower petals across the surface of the bath, then she turned to the chair where Lazar rested, eyes closed, his face turned away from her. She went over to him and gave his flat stomach a fond caress.

"My dear," she called, gazing softly down at him.

He turned his face to her and covered her hand with his where it lay on his stomach. He captured her hand, kissed it, then placed it over his heart.

Mystified, they stared at each other for a timeless spell.

She leaned down and kissed him on the forehead, then began, gingerly, to undress him. He lay back, watching her in weary, wry amusement while she slid the vest lower and reached boldly for his belt. His frank stare made her skin warm as she unbuttoned the fall of his breeches.

"You're doing a good job," he remarked, his eyes dancing, his expression subdued.

When all the golden, gleaming sculpture of his naked body was before her, her gaze swept over him in pure worship, the hard swells of muscled breast, the intricate ridges of his chiseled abdomen, and all the smooth expanse of taut, fine skin, like rose-copper satin in the warm candlelight. She stared at his strong legs and his feet, and then she stared at his most masculine part in wonder. It was relaxed, and already it was huge. It would kill her, she thought.

He laughed as if he could read her mind, then turned away, going to the tub.

"Are you going to scrub me now, Miss Monteverdi?" he asked.

"Thoroughly," she replied, blushing already.

A moment later, he descended into the tub with a luxurious sigh.

"I'm all yours, *chérie*. Do with me what you will."

She stood, and as she approached, she clasped her hands lightly behind her back. "You are comfortable?" she asked, pausing several feet away.

"Mmm," he purred. His inky lashes drooped with pleasure as he sank back against the rim of the tub.

"Very good," she said. Then she walked around to stand fully in his view, where she took off her clothes for him, just as he had asked her to the night she had denied him.

Lazar hooked his arms over the rim of the tub and watched her every move with fire in his eyes.

When all her clothes were removed, she loosed her braids and fluffed her hair free over her shoulders.

He tore his heated stare from her body and looked up into her eyes. She quivered as she stood there, naked, before him. She gazed into his eyes with an incredible sense of aching sweetness, and he barely breathed, he was so still. But for the deep, soughing murmur of the sea on the hull and the slight creaking of the great ship as it rocked on the water, a reverent silence filled the cabin—their reverence for each other. A moment passed. Each delicate current of air crept across her skin like cool ribbons, and behind her the long, translucent curtains blew slowly on the evening wind from the sea balcony. She became acutely aware of shy little territories across her body she had never noticed she possessed—all because his stunned and poignant gaze was as eloquent as touch: for the first time in her life that she could remember, she could actually feel the oval turn of her navel, the outward curve of her knee; it was, all of it, for him.

"Come to me, my Allegra," he breathed at last.

She walked toward him, took his outstretched hand, and joined him in the bath. He put his arms around her as she lowered herself into the hot, scented water. He pulled her to him, pressed her to him, showed her for the first time the texture of his bare skin all against hers. She closed her eyes in rapture. He lifted her hand and kissed her pale wrist. He kissed her palm, the juncture of her thumb and fingers. He licked vaguely at the tip of her thumb, nuzzled her fingertips, caught her pinkie gently between his teeth. Then he placed her hand over his shoulder and pulled her more tightly into his arms.

The warmth and beauty of him all along the front of her body mesmerized her, the powerful thighs under her buttocks, the expanse of his broad shoulders looming before her for all the world like some dear, solid fortress. She embraced him, ran her open hands slowly up his back over the tough, gnarled skin there. She threaded a trail of kisses from his earlobe down his neck, drunk with the feel and salt and musk of him.

His hands moved down over her hips, limning the shape of her silhouette in the water while he buried his face in her hair.

"I've waited for this for so long," he whispered, trembling.

"I know you have, sweetheart. So have I."

Her hands slid over the supple mounds of his shoulders to glide together behind his neck. She could hear her own deep, rapid breath against his skin.

He gripped her buttocks in both of his hands while his breath came faster at her neck. She ran her fingers up the back of his neck, through the short, glossy black of his hair, eliciting from him an almost inaudible moan. When she looked down at him, his sea-black eyes were liquid pools of longing.

"I love you," he whispered. He began to kiss her. He kissed her eyelids, her cheekbones, the corners of her lips, and when she sought his deepest kiss, he ravished her mouth.

Kneeling, she settled astride him in the tub, and as they moved together, some of the water overflowed the side. The rising steam from the bath soon covered them in sweat, and the flower petals clung to their skin.

She strained against him, intensely aware of his swollen member resting upright against her belly. It bumped the lower arcs of her breasts as she chafed restlessly against him. She ran her open hand down his stomach, felt his hot quiver of antici-pation as the muscles leaped beneath her palm. He drew in his breath and tilted his head back, eyes closed, when her fingers grazed his rigid shaft.

"You like that," she said, watching his face.

He nodded dreamily.

She drew out her touch, tracing the mysterious length of the organ to the curious rim near the end. She could tell it pleased him when she cupped the thick, round tip, but after a while, he captured her hand and guided her, wordlessly teaching her his secret wishes until she understood just what to do.

Then she was ruthless, serving his wondrous body with dili-gent ardor until he shoved wildly against her grasp. He clung to her with one hand, his grip white-knuckled on the edge of the tub. His groans fascinated her, plucked barbaric notes deep in her blood. His face, rapt with the pleasure she was giving him, was more beautiful than ever. He stopped her suddenly, clamping his hand around her wrist.

"No more," he gasped as his chest heaved. Trembling, he raked his hand through his hair.

"Then I shall bathe you now, my Lazar," she told him indulgently, smiling with a very feminine sense of satisfaction as she kissed his ear. "And when I am through, you will be clean of all the dust from that place forever."

She proceeded to give him a slow and thorough bathing, discarding the sponge to clean his face with her fingers in a tender, stroking massage. She leaned down and kissed him, and he bit at her lower lip with a playful growl. This time it was she who deepened their kiss, wrapping her arms around him, parting his lips to fill his mouth with the vigor and taste of her. Her eagerness fired his passion, and she reveled in his exquisite devouring. He melted on her tongue like warm, heavy rain.

He moved on, kissing her neck, her shoulder, her chest. She sighed anxiously as he took her breast in his mouth. He teased and tantalized each nipple in turn until she thought she would swoon, breathless with delight. She ran her hands over the thick bulges of his biceps as he sucked and swirled his tongue around her erect crests. She gloried in the softness of his mouth and the hardness of his strength with sweet, rising lust.

Reaching down between her legs, his fingertip found the center of her pleasure, hard and smooth as a polished opal, but she stopped him with a whisper, determined that he should receive pleasure from her more than give it tonight. "Patience, my love. I'm not done washing you yet."

He gave her a heartbreaking smile as he lay back again against the rim of the tub. "You may make a saint of me yet, Miss Monteverdi."

She smiled, pulled him forward, and reached over his shoulders to wash his scarred back lovingly. Finally, she ordered him to close his eyes, and she dunked him under the water. He brushed the water from his eyes with a hearty sigh. He gazed into her eyes for a moment tenderly.

"There's something I want to tell you," he said. "Now that you know the worst of it, you might as well know the rest."

She stared at him evenly. "Go on."

He gathered her into his arms, and it was several minutes before he spoke. "That night—the night of the storm—my father told me to run. So, I did. The assassins chased me to the brink of the sea cliffs, where the only choice I had was to die at their hands or jump, just like your legend says. As they closed in on me, I turned around and jumped off the rock face. They weren't expecting that. But my father had told me to survive at any cost for Ascencion's sake, and I never dared disobey him."

He took a drink of wine.

"Somehow I managed to miss the rocks below. The storm washed me out far from land," he went on. "I was in the water for probably twenty hours, well into the next day."

"How awful," she murmured.

"My mind was a blank after what happened to my family." He was quiet for a while, then he kissed her forehead and continued. "It was not so much the thirst and fatigue that bothered me as this one big, ugly, *ugly* hammerhead shark that kept swimming by me. I thought for sure I was dead. I hate sharks." He gave her a rueful half smile. "How I kept still until that thing lost interest in me, I have no idea. I only thank God I had no cuts or abrasions from my fall to entice it with the scent of blood."

She stared at him, wide-eyed.

"Blazing sun above frying me, damned ugly shark below. Then a ship finally came. A felucca. I didn't know what it was, it looked so strange, but I didn't care."

She gave him a puzzled look, and he explained, "Felucca. That's the name of the narrow, lateen-rigged ships the Barbary corsairs prefer."

"Oh," she said in awe. "Malik's men rescued you?"

"I don't know if I'd call it rescue." He gave her a grim smile. "But they did get me away from that shark, and they gave me water. I was barely conscious enough to drink it."

"How frightened you must have been to have found yourself among those heathens."

"Don't recall. I imagine I was, but after what I had seen happen to my family, I didn't really care what became of me."

She winced and reached out to caress him. He took her hand and played idly with her fingers as he continued. "I was taken to Al Khuum and held there for two years until Captain Wolfe came to discuss the opium traffic with Malik. Wolfe took pity on me—or, rather, saw a use for me—and aided my escape."

"Two years?" she whispered. "Oh, my love, how ever did you endure it?"

He shrugged. "The second year wasn't so bad," he said, glancing up at the deckhead as if to avoid her sympathetic gaze. "That's when Malik sent me to train with his Janissaries— bodyguards, all slaves taken in childhood, trained for the express purpose of defending the sheik. Deadly warriors. I had to convert to Islam and take a vow of chastity," he said with a shallow laugh. He shook his head, mulling over his own thoughts. "I threw myself into my training and learned all I could, living off my fantasies of vengeance."

"What about the first year?"

He glanced uneasily at her. "I was like that boy Darius, a servant. But I kept trying to run away, causing problems. I even set the grand salon on fire. Malik almost killed me for that, which would have been fine with me. But instead he . . . found a way to keep me docile." He narrowed his eyes, then looked up at the ceiling again. "Opium. I would have done anything for it. I lived for it. It was extraordinarily degrading, a slavery within slavery."

She reached to hold him, but he held her off with a gesture.

"When I realized that he could control me for the rest of my life with that drug, I forced myself to refuse it. I went rather mad, hallucinating. That's when I cut my wrists. I was thirteen."

Tears flooded her eyes. "Sweetheart," she whispered. She leaned forward and kissed his cheek gently. "It's all behind you now. I promise."

"No, Allegra, I don't think it ever will be." He looked up into her eyes with a lost, tortured stare.

"Why do you say that?"

He shrugged slightly, looking very young. "Nightmares," he whispered.

"Lazar." She took his face between her hands and kissed him gently on the mouth.

"I don't have nightmares when you sleep with me," he told her in a choked whisper. "I have never needed any living thing as I need you."

She was very still in his arms. She laid her head on his broad shoulder. "Lazar," she said softly, "they say when a man and woman become one, each bears half the other's pain. Show me how to give myself to you."

He paused and hugged her close, all his muscles taut. He stroked her hair to the ends of her tresses. Reverently he traced the curve of her lower back.

"I cannot let you give this gift to me."

"Why? It is mine to give to whomever I choose."

He found her heels and cupped them in his palms, then he rested his forehead on her shoulder for a long moment.

"I am so unworthy of you," he whispered, looking up into her eyes, distraught. "Before I ever met you, I planned to kill you, Allegra. I was going to shoot you, take your beautiful life—"

"That is long past," she told him gently.

"Allegra—"

"Lazar." She silenced him with a soft kiss, gazing into his stormy eyes. "You asked me to love you. You had to know I would. Make me one with you."

As he searched her gaze almost helplessly, she caressed him lovingly, wringing a moan from him as he closed his eyes. He gripped her shoulders, head back against the rim of the tub, as she pleasured him, aware only of him, his wishes, his needs.

He opened his eyes and pulled her close by the back of the neck to kiss her, plunging deeply, wildly into her mouth as he reached under the water and began stroking her in turn.

When they were both quivering with desire, he lifted her in his arms in one smooth motion, and they left the tub. Kissing her all the while, he set her down on his berth. Her warm, damp body made the sheets cool and wet around her. She laced her fingers through his, then slowly she lay back, drawing him down atop her.

Endlessly he kissed her. Willingly she gave him her soul in every breath. With smooth, bridled power, Lazar slid her farther back onto the bed and covered her with his hard, muscled body. She held him, kissing and yielding completely. He spread her thighs wider with the softest possible caress, pausing to stroke her wetness.

Guiding himself against her, he entered her.

He moved as a man on holy ground, conquered by her surrender. With the grace of a goddess, she gave herself to him, flawed, fallen man, without promises of any kind in exchange, simply because he had needed her more than he could bear.

Lazar vowed to himself he would take it slowly, though his arms, his whole body, shook with his desire for her. He nuzzled her mouth very tenderly, feeling intensely protective toward her all in a surge, his brave kitten, whose need to give to him had overthrown her own need for safety, freely giving him her gift beyond price.

"So innocent," he whispered, taking her slowly, inching deeper and deeper into the hot bliss of her mysterious passage until he came up against her maidenhead.

Her breath was wild at his ear, her lithe body trembling like his own.

"It will hurt," he told her.

Her arms were tight around him. "Yes, I know. Oh, yes, Lazar."

He shut his eyes and claimed her, rending her maiden shield with a shock that went down to the center of his being as Allegra cried out. He tried to pull away, but she embraced him tightly, fighting back her tears. He remained inside her, perfectly still, as her body gradually accepted him.

While he waited, he sought and found her sweet, soft hand, kissing her palm and delicate fingers until her pain became her pleasure, and she sought it.

After several moments, he closed his eyes in ecstasy to feel her hips rise, inviting his rhythm.

It was relief, reprieve, redemption.

She was covered in an Edenic dew beneath him, petting his sides and his waist, bringing every inch of his skin to life. He had not known what sex was until now, he thought, his mind dreamlike with it. He was unbearably alive, new-fashioned from the hand of God. He was Adam discovering paradise.

"I love you," he whispered, still amazed to form the words on his tongue.

When her gold-tipped lashes swept open, she gazed up at him with a stare of mixed passion and alarm. He traced the curve of her face, smiling softly.

"Don't be afraid. Just let it happen."

He smiled vaguely at her again when she nodded, thinking he could drown in her eyes so full of trust in him.

"Lazar?" she whispered.

"Yes, *chérie?*"

Her eyes misted. "It hurts, but it is so beautiful."

"Sweetheart." Too moved to say more, he lowered his head and kissed her deeply as he loved her with more tenderness than he knew he possessed. He bent to reverence her breast, and he caressed her creamy skin with its dusting of freckles, her arms and chest, her lovely hips.

After a few moments of these attentions, she gave a drowsy moan and grasped his waist, asking him with her insistent touch for more. He thrust deeper, still moving carefully because of his size and her inexperience. He drew back and gave it to her again, again. A few more deep strokes, and he pulsed still bigger inside her, his heart beginning to pound. He felt his control dissolving.

How will I ever get enough of her? he wondered at the back of his mind.

She whispered his name, calling forth the storm he'd held back so long, a fury of passion he had never unleashed with any woman. He became aware that he was speaking to her, growling at her through his breathlessness, making fierce demands that she never lie with another, never dare leave him, let him take her every night, and every breath she breathed against his mouth was yes. The tide carried him closer.

"Allegra."

When he gasped her name, she thrust her tongue into his mouth, seizing her opportunity like a pirate. Holding his face between her palms, she ravished his senses with her wild, virgin kiss, shattering the remnants of his control.

He took her like a hurricane, as if she were the last woman on the earth, the only woman.

He was too rough, too fast, he knew, but he couldn't stop. It was not seduction, no; he was mating with her, with this woman and no other, driven to blinding need by the animal imperative of instinct, survival. He braced himself on his hands above her, arching his head back, consumed by her body's writhe and pull, pumping gigantically into her. Her breasts shook with his rhythm—he thought the whole ship rocked. Her nails raked him, and her groans twined with his, one louder than the next.

She hit her climax, hard and suddenly, convulsing under him with a series of high-pitched, frenzied little screams of wild delight. Her body gripped him tight in its wet, silken glove, unbearable pleasure as she baptized him in her liquid surge.

The intensity of her orgasm drove him over the edge. Every muscle in him went rigid, and he clasped her under him, roaring out as he shot forth, filling her with his essence. Eternity shattered around him as if he'd struck his head on one of the star's crystal spheres and broke it.

The vision of heaven left him covered in sweat.

"Oh, my God," he said at last as he fell upon her soft body in a jellied heap of shaking limbs and sweat.

"Ohh, Lazar," she murmured.

Unseen by her, he grinned with weary arrogance against the pillow as he caught his breath.

Moving languidly a few moments later, she drew her knees up against his sweat-slicked hips, arching her back with a cat-like stretch beneath him. The movement wrung from him a soul-deep groan that turned to a laugh when she idly raked her nails down his arms. She answered his nibbling kiss with a throaty purr of satisfaction that sent his pride soaring.

He felt himself throb within her, and somehow he found the strength to lift his head and look down at her. Her eyes were closed, and the beatific look on her face made him smile. She was Venus in his arms, positively decadent, the goddess of sensuality he had intended to turn her into from the start.

"Liked that, did you?" he growled softly.

She nodded, never opening her eyes.

She winced when he eased himself out of her body. He moved to her side, still lying partly atop her, his arm thrown across her flat stomach. She was very still, one arm sprawled carelessly above her on the mattress, her chestnut hair cascading all over his pillow.

He rested his head beside hers, brushing the tip of his nose back and forth against the elegant line of her cheekbone. In the warm silence, Lazar thought he could be content to lie there for the rest of his life, just smelling her skin, and if he ever got bored with that, he would take up counting her freckles.

She linked her fingers through his, then closed her eyes with a sigh.

They lay together in motionless union, only breathing, deep and spent, drifting as one upon a timeless current of peace. Soon they slept, their bodies still entwined.

❧ CHAPTER ❧
NINETEEN

The three weeks that passed as the fleet crossed the Atlantic were the most exhausting, exhilarating days of Allegra's life. Lazar and she forgot meals and barely slept, caught up in the whirlwind of designing Ascencion's future and, she very well supposed, shaping their country's history.

They argued over which coast should get the shipyards and how exactly the penal code should be reformed, but the one thing they agreed upon was that he should marry Princess Nicolette Habsburg and her two million gold ducats. They discussed it only once, then mutually avoided the topic.

Allegra knew full well Ascencion needed the money because her father had robbed the place blind. Princess Nicolette, like her older sister, Marie Antoinette, who had married the Dauphin of France, had been born and bred to fulfill the position of queen.

She contented herself as best she could with her role as the mistress he loved and whose opinion he valued when it came to making decisions for the good of Ascencion. It was a fall from grace for a woman who had once tried so hard to be a good little girl, but she loved him unto distraction and would not have missed the restoration of Fiori rule for the world. Everything she had to give was his for the asking.

Still, every time he came to her and made the world dissolve behind the blue velvet curtains of his bed, she fell a little more deeply in love with him, until she wondered how she would ever stand it when the day of his royal wedding came.

As the days passed, they were aided in their quest by Vicar's wisdom and Bernardo's knowledge of the people's wishes. Bernardo, incidentally, had approached her to offer his deepest apologies for having deserted her on the coast of Al Khuum. Gazing at her almost in awe, to her amusement, the fat little bard of the people swore that if there was anything he could ever do for her, she had but to ask. She only chuckled at him. There was too much work to do to hold on to petty grudges.

From the moment Lazar pulled her father's boxes out into the cabin and opened them, Allegra learned that even as highly as she'd admired her captor before, she had still completely underestimated him.

The enormity of the task galvanized him, as if he thrived on the very challenge of it. The fact that it seemed impossible marshaled up resources of strength, imagination, and ingenuity within him that took her breath away and that he clearly never realized he possessed.

Lazar was tireless. His ability to concentrate on a dozen different problems at the same time astounded her. Sure enough, when he grasped the answer to any one question, he found a way to tie the solution in to several others in unexpected ways, his mind as nimble as the deft, browned fingers with which he tied his intricate sailors' knots. In awe, she watched him forge a kingdom out of thin air.

She could arrive at no other explanation than that he had been born for it and that he was the most brilliant man she'd ever met.

She made contributions of her own to his enterprise, such as her plan for a system of schools for the peasant children of Ascencion and her ideas for how housing could be improved for the pensioners. She also suggested that a memorial grove be planted at the site of the royal attack, with a tree to commemorate each person slain that night.

Every time her energy flagged, he would fire her excitement anew, presenting with a mischievous sparkle in his eyes some brilliant new idea based on this or that concept he'd encountered in his travels around the globe. A solution to the problem of transportation on Ascencion could come from the Netherlands, while a broad point of law could be inspired by anything from ancient Rome to the wild savages of the New World, to the Brethren's creed of one vote per man.

In one night—with a little help from Vicar—he sketched out a constitution and a parliament based on the British model, two things Ascencion had never had. The next day he blocked out a new Belfort, a modern city inspired by Paris, with broad thoroughfares and grand public buildings. It was to stand on the grounds of the medieval Belfort Castle, high in the cool, forested central highlands of Ascencion.

That evening, he tackled the problem of insufficient ports to maximize Ascencion's excellent natural harbors, with docks and warehouses to better accommodate the fishing industry, one of the country's staple resources he meant to revitalize. He decided Ascencion should have a university, at least a military and naval academy, so that the next time invaders came— and they always did, he said—the standing forces would be well trained.

When she finally coerced him into taking a short nap, he woke up with a font of ideas about reforming the tax structure. His fingers were stained with ink, his clothes a rumpled mess, but when he cast her a weary smile from across the stateroom where they worked, surrounded by a sea of scribbled papers, she imagined he was happier than he'd ever been since the loss of his family.

Yet he was changing, being transformed by his task. With every passing hour, he seemed a little less pirate and a little more prince—or, more specifically, young king preparing to return from a long and unjust exile.

With his lack of sleep and food, he even began to look

slightly different. Perhaps he had lost three or four pounds, but his face took on a look of lean intensity. A leonine calm tempered the fierce expression of his fiery eyes. His roguish swagger became a clean, collected stride. It was as if everything extraneous in him were being burned away, like the impurities from a fine sword in the smith's furnace.

She could see that the men, too, felt the changes in him, though he still did not permit them to know his true identity. They began reacting to him differently, obeying their orders with a bit more snap in their step. Where he had captained them before with a mix of raw charisma and force, now his command deepened to true authority, mastery.

Though he now had his signet ring, unassailable proof of his identity, and would soon be joined, he hoped, by his father's powerful and well-connected advisers when they reached the West Indies, he realized a show of muscle might still be necessary to induce Genoa to pull out of Ascencion. For that reason, he decided to include the Brethren in their enterprise, if the men were willing. He thought it not impossible to turn his pirates into Ascencion's first royal navy.

He refused to see that there was something hilarious in the notion, though Allegra nearly fell down laughing.

Among the Brethren were seasoned captains, he retorted, shipbuilders, fearless and disciplined crews. He believed that if they joined him and took an oath to leave the life of crime, Ascencion could soon possess one of the finest navies on the seas. With the timber forests in Ascencion's highlands, he told her, a highly profitable shipbuilding industry could also be started.

The evening they sailed into the Carribbean, she found the young king on the sea balcony, staring down into the foamy waves. He did not look up when she joined him at the rail—she had long ceased fearing that she might fall in. How much deeper could she fall?

She gathered by his brooding expression that his mind was heavily weighted.

Coming up behind him, she rubbed the broad curve of his back with a comforting caress, wishing there were something she could do to soothe the troubled look from his brow.

"Have you eaten?" she murmured.

He mumbled a vague answer. They were both silent for a moment. She ran her hand down his arm, then leaned against him, sighing when she thought of the plan he had proposed weeks ago, that they live out the rest of their lives together on some idyllic farm. Sometimes she wished, oh, she wished she had cast responsibility to the wind and said yes.

She caressed his hand on the rail, and he turned it palm upward, linking his fingers through hers.

I love you, she thought. I love you so much.

"What if they think it's a hoax?" he said. "What if they don't come?"

"Your father's old advisers?" She smiled up at him with pride in her eyes. "They'll come."

"All the way to the West Indies? I don't know. General Enzo will come. That I know," he said, nodding to himself. "That old bear's not afraid of anything. But I need Pasquale."

"They'll all come," she assured him.

He stared down at the waves for a while, deep in thought, but when he turned to her, there was that lustrous, golden fire in his eyes she had come to know well.

"Why don't you help me take a break from all this work?" he murmured, trapping her against the rail, an arm on either side of her. He lowered his head and kissed her hungrily, then captured her hand and pressed it to him, caressing the back of her hand insistently over his manhood as he asked for her without a word.

One couldn't ignore a royal command.

She was becoming rather adept at unbuttoning his clothes, but he was fully aroused even before she grasped him.

"Naughty girl," he breathed. "Take me into your mouth."

She went down on her knees as he tilted his head back in pleasure, leaning in the doorway of the balcony.

They never even made it to the bed. He lifted her skirts, and he took her on the floor, both of them still almost fully dressed. On his knees, he entered from behind her, and she was ready for him. Grasping her hips, he plied her body with slow, tantalizing strokes. Again and again, he thrust smoothly, all the way in and out to his magic tip as he caressed her backside with his warm, callused hands.

She moaned for more when he paused to collect his control, for in the doorway she had aroused him to fever pitch, pleasuring him with her mouth and hands. He coiled her hair around his hand and gave it to her, relentlessly driving her to the edge of rapture.

Then he hunched down over her back, gripping her in place, possessing her there on the floor like a wild animal, and she was his mate.

His breath was harsh and fast at her ear. "Who do you need, *chérie*?"

She gasped his name again and again, arching on her hands and knees before him, ignoring the vague, separate sense of hurt that had begun to form deep in her heart, underneath the pleasure.

"Is that deep enough for you?" he asked in a hot, arrogant whisper at her ear.

She groaned, a breathless whimper, for with every stroke the tip of him kissed a spot deep in the core of her body. He squeezed her nipple hard through her dress, but when he reached down between her thighs, she lost her mind. While she was still writhing in the throes of release, he came hard and fast, ravishing her until he was spent.

Moments later, behind closed eyes, Allegra tried to absorb the rage of love that had swept her away so completely. She was scandalized by her abandoned response to him and uneasy about how completely she surrendered to him, holding nothing back. The man was not her husband, after all.

Lazar lay atop her, catching his breath.

"That was incredible," he panted.

She lay still until he got off her. Puzzled by the dull misery that had seeped down into her limbs, she dragged herself wearily from the floor. Moving dazedly, she knelt and stared blankly at the rug.

"Allegra, what's wrong?"

She looked up at Lazar, who was standing, tucking in his shirt as if nothing had happened.

She lowered her gaze, unwilling to complain, for she had chosen her fall of her own free will. She refused to regret.

"Nothing," she mumbled.

"You sure?" he asked brightly.

She nodded.

He grinned. "Good."

He leaned down and gave her a quick kiss on the cheek.

"Thanks," he whispered, then he strode jauntily toward the door, revitalized.

Thanks? *Thanks?* she thought in disbelief.

She stared straight ahead. She would not cry. She loved Lazar, her Prince. He could use her if he wanted to.

"Hey, old man."

Vicar peered over his spectacles in query as Lazar came sauntering over to the shade where the Englishman was stationed, as usual, with his nose in a book.

"Well, haven't seen much of you lately," Vicar said, his lined face a wreath of smiles—until he saw the boy, Darius, following in Lazar's footsteps.

It seemed the boy had appointed himself Lazar's keeper, for Darius shadowed him everywhere, serious and silent, a grim wisdom in his face incongruous with his fourteen summers.

Regarding the youth, Vicar's face took on that frown of

scholarly disapproval Lazar had learned to avoid whenever possible in his earlier years. He had the feeling Vicar was preparing to make a new project of the fierce young Darius Santiago.

Lazar privately chuckled over it, for he was quite sure this time Vicar had met his match.

"I see you brought your first royal knight with you," Vicar remarked, looking the boy over with a critical eye, ever the schoolmaster.

Darius shot him a scowl, not realizing yet that Vicar was only teasing him.

"Ach, lighten up on the lad. He's not used to your British humor."

"Hmm," Vicar replied in his most professorial tone, tapping one arm of his spectacles against his lips. "And how did the shooting lesson go?"

Lazar grinned and looked at Darius as the boy tossed his black forelock out of his eyes. He didn't dare tousle this lad's hair, for fear of getting his arm sliced off.

"He's not much with a rifle, but actually he's pretty good with a knife. Aren't you?"

"I'll learn," Darius assured him, following along as Lazar helped himself to one of Vicar's cheroots and lit it from the table lantern, as was his habit.

Vicar smacked Darius's hand away from the box of cheroots when he reached for one in turn. Darius stared at him half in defiance, half in disappointment, until Lazar gave him his own cheroot and took another one for himself, casting Vicar an insolent smile.

Promptly, the boy burst out choking on the smoke, though he fought to hold his coughs back.

"You see?" Vicar chided him, eyeing the cheroot.

Darius swallowed his coughs with a look of pure determination.

"Perhaps instead of weapons, your teacher might next

attempt a lesson in history, or literature, or mathematics," Vicar suggested with a dour look at Lazar.

"I am already smart," Darius informed him gravely.

"Young man, that is a very stupid attitude. Ask the captain," Vicar said. "The captain enjoys all the arts and humanities. He can even recite poetry—or could, anyway, before those last few blows to the head."

"There is nothing wrong with my head."

Darius looked up at Lazar skeptically. "Poetry?" he repeated. "No."

"I'm afraid it's true." Lazar clapped the boy on the shoulder. "What do you say, greenling? You saved my life—I owe you. Where do you want to go to school?"

Darius started laughing and looked at Vicar. *Now* he thought he was being teased.

"I'm serious," Lazar told him. "I'll pay for it."

His laughter stopped. Instantly the boy was uneasy. He looked from one face to the other, suddenly on his guard. His fear pained Lazar.

How Malik could warp a life, he thought.

Vicar briskly tried changing the subject. "There's no need for formal schooling to begin one's education. Young man, I want you to read the first chapter of this book tonight. Tomorrow we will discuss it, and I expect you to be prepared to answer questions. I shall give you a quiz, and if you fail, you shall have to help tar the deck."

Darius drew himself up, lifting his chin with a prickly Spanish grandeur and an arrogance that was almost breathtaking. Lazar shook his head to himself, unable to fathom how such pride had survived Malik, but perhaps the boy's bloodthirsty vengeance on the sheik had cleansed him of the shame.

The boy glanced in disdain at the book, making no move to take it from Vicar's hand. "I have no need for book lessons, *señor,* for *I* have the sixth sense."

"Do you, now?" Lazar said easily as he puffed on the cheroot. Somehow he could believe it. He had not heard the boy make a boast yet that he could not carry out.

Vicar was not impressed, returning the boy's masterful stare with a smile of amusement.

"I think what our little *hidalgo* here is trying to say is that he can't read."

"I'll tar the deck," Darius said insolently. "I am not afraid of hard work."

Lazar scratched his jaw, amused by their battle of wills—it reminded him of the old days, when Vicar first decided to join him —but he still rather thought the boy might be dangerous if crossed, and he didn't want him cutting the old man's throat next.

"Greenling, do me a favor," he said as if he had just thought of it. "Go down to the galley, and find out what Emilio is making for my supper. Then go tell Miss Monteverdi, too, *capisce*?"

"Aye, *Cupitán*," he said solemnly, tossing the forelock out of his eyes again. Darius glided off, silent and mysterious as a cat.

When he was gone, Lazar looked at Vicar and could only shake his head.

"Where on earth did you find that creature?" said Vicar.

Lazar chuckled. "No, sir. He found me," he declared.

"And won't be letting you go anytime soon, I daresay."

"Puzzling little fellow, isn't he? He seems to feel at ease only when you ignore him or give him some job to do. Move too quickly around him, and he jumps away as if you're going to hit him." Lazar shrugged. "Well, I gave Emilio strict orders to fatten the kid up, anyway. He'll probably sprout up half a foot once he starts eating properly."

"Then you'd best try to civilize him quickly." Vicar chuckled.

"I'm not sure it's possible."

"How's the missus?"

Lazar's lips pursed into a thin line of thought as he took his usual place, leaning against the capstan. For a moment he tapped the ashes from his cheroot, then crushed them out under his boot heel.

"She's not well," he answered at length. "Not well at all."

"Is she feeling under the weather?" he asked hopefully. "Perhaps I shall soon be a granduncle."

"It's not that. She's unhappy. I am making her unhappy. This whole arrangement is hurting her." He touched his heart vaguely. "And it kills me."

"You know my feelings on the matter," Vicar disapprovingly replied as he perused his page.

"I know." Lazar let out a slow exhale of smoke and watched it vanish, mulling over his worry about his little captive. "But I still can't marry her."

Vicar shot him a severe look, as if Lazar did not already feel guilty enough. "You and your curse. The only curse that plagues you, boy, is obstinacy."

"I cannot take the slightest chance that any harm could come to her. It's *because* I love her that I can't marry her."

"Have you told Allegra about your so-called curse?"

"No," he admitted.

"Because she would laugh in your face—as well she should."

Lazar looked over at him a trifle indignantly. "Don't you think you're being a little harsh on me? I'm trying to do what's best for Allegra."

"Lie to yourself and to her, if you like, but do not attempt to lie to me."

Lazar heaved a sigh and turned away. "You know what will happen. She'll be snuffed out." He snapped his fingers. "Just like that."

"Bosh! Stuff and nonsense. How can a grown man, an educated man, cling to such an absurd superstition?"

Lazar folded his arms over his chest and stroked his jaw

with his thumb, staring down at the planks. "She is losing respect for herself because of me."

"You sound surprised. What did you expect? You have asked her to throw away her integrity, the thing for which she values herself most."

"I have not—"

But Vicar interrupted him almost angrily. "That woman is no vapid, idle, twittering fool like your past mistresses."

Lazar arched a brow, turning to him. "I didn't know you felt so strongly about them."

Vicar snorted. "What a mule-headed dimwit you are. Do you know how rare this is, what you've found? Do you know that *I* have never loved as you now love—that no man on this ship has ever been loved as she loves you? Yet there you stand, throwing it away. Typical—typical! I am only surprised Allegra herself did not see the folly of making you so comfortable. She is too sensible for this." Vicar shut his book and climbed stiffly to his feet. "I don't want your company tonight, Fiore. You are too vexing."

"What the hell am I supposed to do?"

"Marry her," he said. "For once in your life, have a little bloody faith in something other than your pistols and your sword."

Lazar stared after him.

"Bloody hell," he said to himself, resting both hands on his hips.

Maybe the curse *was* nonsense.

God's truth, as wives went, he was beginning to despise Nicolette Habsburg already for the simple fact that she wasn't Allegra. He would sire children upon this unknown woman, who would inherit all he had, while any children he had with the woman he loved would be treated as bastards in the world, albeit royal ones. And how would Allegra be treated?

He knew the answer to that. Her heart was so tender. The slights she would receive would hurt her, scar her starry-eyed faith in people and the world, one of the things he loved best about her.

The part that made him feel most guilty, however, was the fact that he had preyed upon her inherent sense of responsibility and selflessness to get his way, lied to her about the reasons he wouldn't marry her. Not lied outright, but let her assume his refusal to marry her was based first on the fear that the people would never accept a Monteverdi as queen and second on the need for the princess's imperial dowry to help stabilize the economy.

In truth, he knew he could surely overcome both obstacles with a little time, the people's grudge against Monteverdi, as well as Ascencion's looming bankruptcy. The real reason he would not marry her was because of his curse—and what if it was all in his head?

It amazed him that she had never even asked him to do the honorable thing by her, only for Ascencion. For herself, she had never asked for anything but to be near him. Yet for all he knew, even this sacrifice was not enough, his attempt to trick fate by keeping her his mistress only, not his wife.

But damn it, it wasn't fair. She deserved to be the queen. Ascencion needed her. He needed her. With her vision and high-minded ideals, she was good for Ascencion, and she was certainly good for him. How was he going to be at his best for his people without her?

But what if—?

What if.

The whole damned thing is irrational, he said to himself. *What if you waste your whole damned life believing in something that doesn't exist?*

But the evidence remained: every member of his family was dead but him; Wolfe was dead, yet he lived on. Even the dog he'd once kept aboard was dead, swept overboard in a storm.

No, the risk was great enough leaving her merely his mistress. He could not take the chance of harm's coming to her because of the curse on him. Fate had it in for him, as he well knew. For once in his life, he would try to do something unselfish.

The deep blue of the Atlantic had given way to the warm, glassy turquoise of the Caribbean. For the past two days, the weather had been stifling hot and overcast, and Lazar had told her he expected a storm.

Presently they were playing catch, tossing a crumpled piece of paper back and forth as they argued good-naturedly about where the university they were planning should be located, and wondered aloud what Emilio was cooking for dinner, for they were both hungry.

All of a sudden there was a terrific crash.

"Well, there's your thunderstorm," Allegra said in surprise. She glanced toward the balcony, and, though the day was dark, there was no rain yet.

Lazar was staring at her and slowly turning white.

"No," he said, his voice oddly strangled. "That was cannon. We've just been fired upon."

The instant, frantic shout of a crewman at the cabin door confirmed it. "Cap, it's that damned new British admiral, out for our blood again!"

Lazar closed the distance between them with three swift strides. He took her by the shoulders.

"Gather water, some food, bandages, and a few candles. Take the blankets and pillows from the bed, and set yourself up in the center cargo hold in the mid-deck. Take the Fiore heirlooms with you—"

"Our notes, too?"

"Yes, sweetheart. Take my pistol. You never know." He hushed her protest before she could utter it. "Vicar will load it for you. Be quick. Don't stay here in the stern. It'll be one of the main targets, along with the bow."

She nodded, wide-eyed. "Be careful, my love."

He grinned.

"Don't worry, *chérie*. There's still plenty of pirate left in me. I love you," he whispered.

He stole a kiss, then dashed out the door before she could tell him she loved him, too.

Outwardly he was cool and nonchalant, but inwardly Lazar could not remember wanting to avoid a fight as much as he did now. Harcourt relayed his orders, rapping on the scuttle while the barefoot men pounded a tattoo across the planks.

"Tumble up, men! Ship ahoy! All hands, lay aloft! Full sail, lads! Lay aloft!"

They weren't much for looks, but the crew of *The Whale* was as stouthearted as a pack of wolves and trained for deadly efficiency. Lazar paced the quarterdeck, jittery.

Sailors shimmied up the standing rigging to the yards, and gun crews stacked piles of artillery around the pieces, while in the waist, the carpenters gathered all the supplies they'd need to plug holes or douse any fires the vessel sustained. Lazar turned to the starboard horizon and peered through the folding telescope, then lowered it from his eye.

There was no need for worry, he told himself. He meant to run, but even if it came to a fight, 'twas an easy win. There were only ten ships to their seven—so far.

That ambitious new British admiral must have found out somehow that most of the Brethren had left, he thought. Must have planned this ambush for them on their way back to Wolfe's Den. The exact location of the pirate island amid the dozens of little nameless islands remained a secret the British had failed—so far—to learn.

Lazar eyed the enemy through his folding telescope. The hundred-gun butter boxes on the horizon might never catch them, and though the frigates were swift, escorting the men-of-war, they carried no payload to match *The Whale*'s seventy-four guns. He looked through his glass at the decks of his sister ships. Everyone seemed prepared. He hoped Morris, the boy captain, didn't try anything foolish.

With evening upon them and a good blow rising up over the taffrail, he could almost hope they'd exchange a few preliminary shots to explore each other's capabilities, then retire like dueling gentlemen for the night, for it was going to be a rough one. The lowering sky promised a hard summer storm.

If the weather granted him an overnight reprieve, he would do aught in his power to slip away without a fight. The stakes were too high now. Every battle brought its risk, but he was not prepared to take leave of the world just now. For once in his life, he had too much to live for.

His woman was below, and for all he knew, she could be carrying his child even now.

Aye, he thought, better a good run than a bad stand.

His mind made up to run rather than fight, he ordered the foresail and trysail set, the topgallants only slightly reefed, the royals trimmed. He could see his men were glad of his decision.

In the next hour, the sun slipped over the horizon ahead of them, and the black clouds in the southeast behind them gathered and grew, unleashing cool gales that notched the ship up to a speed of twelve knots, near hull speed. The carpenters began handing out oilskins to the gunners, who spread out the water-resistant tarpaulins over their powder stores. There were a few sou'easters for those on deck manning the lines. Lazar turned his back to the wind, lit a cheroot, and muttered orders to Harcourt, who sang them out.

"Loose the topsails, double-reef 'em, lads! Hoist the foretop stay! Square the yards, men! Get those head yards braced aback!"

The evening sky purpled to the color of a blackened eye.

Lazar denied Harcourt's suggestion of loosing a drogue anchor in case the wind grew too wild, replying that he would reconsider once they had gained more distance on the enemy.

For now, speed was of the essence. Admiral and company had the wind square behind them, allowing the British a swift run, gaining on them, while the Brethren, heading due west, had to broad-reach with the wind from the port quarter.

Faster, he thought urgently.

Under the cover of darkness, they might still be able to slip back to Wolfe's Den without being followed too closely, but if the weather turned too wild, he'd get them all killed if he didn't take down his canvas. Calculating that it took his crew only twenty minutes maximum to take down all sails, he knew he still had plenty of time to wait and watch.

The lookout high on the crow's nest shouted out then, announcing an eleventh vessel, possibly French in design but flying no colors. It sliced through the waters about sixteen leagues off the port side, coming up fast.

"French, eh?" Lazar murmured. He had his doubts.

Malik had told him his old friend Domenic Clemente, now Governor of Ascencion, had put a huge price on his head, and with the thousand louis d'ors being offered, Lazar figured it was a bounty hunter—at last. This had been his real concern all along—not the bumbling navies but the cold-blooded mercenaries of his own ilk, well armed, shrewd, hungry, and efficient. In either case, he knew now he was going to have a fight on his hands whether he liked it or not.

"Very well. Let's give 'em a taste of our cannons, boys."

Harcourt grinned at him.

A low murmur ran across the decks as the men prepared the longest-ranged guns.

It began to rain. Within moments, the cold downpour turned to hail, pelting the bareheaded men on the yards. Harcourt roared at them to forget their hides and mind their canvas, but it was hardly necessary. They were the Devil of Antigua's own and pirates all, lusty for battle.

His cheroot promptly soaked, Lazar threw it into the waves

and shrugged into the oilskin Mutt brought him, not bothering to close it.

"Capitán!" cried a high voice from the fo'c'sle.

He turned to see Darius standing by the bulwark, his black hair plastered to his forehead by the downpour.

"Get back below," he told him. "This is no place for you."

"Capitán, no!"

Lazar turned back to him with a dark look. "What did you say?"

"Capitán, please! Do not send me to hide with the old man and the girl! I'm a man! Give me a man's work! You know I can fight!"

"You are as green a pup as ever was born, and a landsman to boot. Now, get below."

"But—"

"You'll be underfoot!" He saw the boy's hurt look and softened. "Don't you care to see your mother's face again?"

"I don't have a mother," he said miserably.

Lazar growled and cast about for a response to this pitiful confession. "Look, it would ease my mind to have a man I can trust to mind my woman. I wager she's terrified, or will be soon. If I know Vicar, he'll soon be too seasick to be of any use to her. Somebody's got to prevent her doing anything foolhardy— not an easy job. Will you watch over her for me?"

Darius heaved a sigh and grumbled a low, "Aye, aye."

Lazar watched the lad slouch through the hatch, then he glanced up at the sky. A bolt of lightning to the south outlined the three nearest ships. They were spreading out in blockade formation. Aye, he would have his battle ere long.

Dark impulse stirred in his breast as he stared at the horizon, fading into inky night. A narrow smile crept over his lips. He tasted the driving salt rain, searched through the telescope, and saw that it appeared he would be saved once again by a storm. He could make out a line of squalls many miles off. The British, too, had seen it. More than half their vessels were dropping anchor and lowering sail to ride out the looming storm, the damned quake-buttocks, but the admiral and the bounty hunter still bore down on them relentlessly.

Thunder crashed overhead, disgorging the contents of a black-marble cloud down upon them, an icy baptism. The sharp scent of lightning loosed something wild inside of him. He roared over the thunder for the gun crews to load. Harcourt strode down the weather-side line to see that all guns were ready. A moment later *The Whale* sent off her first warning fire. Then the pirates began their deep *yo-ho*-ing while the flagons of rum were passed around to fire their spirits.

The admiral's massive first-rate ship of the line loomed off the starboard stern, trying to drift up alongside *The Whale*. The bounty hunter's guns cracked at them from the port side, and the fight erupted.

For the next two hours they did not know the thunder from the deafening roar of broadsides, the wall of waves crashing over the taffrail and the bulwarks from the sleeting rain. Lightning clashed fiery swords with the flare of cannon fire above the ships' mast tops like battling archangels. In the darkness they could scarcely see their hands before their faces. At one point Lazar was forced to grab hold of the capstan to keep from being swept overboard. He noticed a body going by him and reached out to grab the man by the collar, only to find that the bedraggled creature was none other than Darius, the young hero.

"Bloody *Miles Glorioso*!" Lazar muttered. He glared at the boy and, never letting go of his collar, marched across the zigzagging deck and dropped him bodily down the hatch.

"But she said she didn't need me!" Darius protested as he got up from the wet floor, rubbing his backside.

"You're bound for the brig if you don't mind your orders!" Lazar slammed the hatch down and stomped back to his post at the quarterdeck with an ominous sense of foreboding, which there was no time to entertain.

The Whale shuddered with each roar of her guns. There was a gigantic sound of ripping canvas and splintering wood.

He looked up just in time to see the mizzen topsail collapsing over its broken yard a split second before the round slammed down onto the fo'c'sle and smashed through the planks. This was followed a second later by another sickening crack of wood from above. He winced, like any sea captain, feeling his ship's injury in his very bones. The broken yard arm fell, pulling down heavy, drenched canvas and a tangled web of rigging, which slowed its descent by a few precious seconds.

The men swarmed like ants into the waist just before the beam crashed athwart the stern, but Lazar had seen the sea swallow two of his Brethren as they clung to the crumbling rigging.

That did it.

The British bastards weren't following the bloody *Fighting Instructions*, and neither would he. He'd take that damned first-rate and make it his royal flagship! he thought with a Cap'n Wolfe–like laugh.

He bellowed for the sweeps to be lowered and the grappling hooks made ready.

He chased the aft crew out of the waist, back to their sternward posts, with rich oaths, then he ordered the helmsman to swing the ship around five degrees south. He heard the rattle of the giant sweeps being lowered. The great oars splashed down into the water, and the shift in position he'd commanded was soon effected. He shouted for Harcourt, but it was Donaldson whose face appeared before him in the pale blue light of another lightning bolt.

"Harcourt's dead, Captain! The yard fell on him."

Lazar cursed, gripping a shroud as another wave rose over the bulwark. He wiped off the water's cold, salty sting and hung over the quarterdeck, shouting for the lads abeam to hold their fire and those weatherward to shoot faster. They were bearing down on the admiral even as the mysterious bounty hunter did likewise to them.

Blindly, shrouded by pitch darkness, *The Whale* battered the weatherward vessel with everything she had until the other ceased fire. A blaze flared for a moment or two on the enemy's forecastle before the rain and the waves put it out, but it provided light long enough for Lazar to see they had thoroughly disabled her. Her foremast and mainmast were lopped in half like felled trees. Her crew was leaping hopelessly into the longboats.

Lazar's crew sent up a cheer to see it.

Then the rain turned back to hail.

The bounty hunter began firing in their faces. There was nothing to be done but return the volley. Lazar knew his ship was taking a beating, but at the moment he was more concerned about his own hide, especially when a fat round plopped down onto the deck in front of him and went crashing down to the mid-deck. He thanked God the weather was too rough to permit snipers to nest in the rigging, as was usual.

He ordered the helmsman to shift them seven degrees northward. Once the change was accomplished, the gale, he calculated, would drive them quickly out of reach. They passed the bounty hunter side by side and made the passing with everything they had left, the portside's full forty guns, knowing neither how much damage they'd incurred nor how much they'd inflicted, then they caught the wind and were flung out of range.

The enemy did not venture after them, because the squall line hit.

The sea became a witch's cauldron, and Lazar began to wonder if they'd snagged upon an early hurricane. The waters seethed like black, bubbling pitch. *The Whale* teetered up over the crests of twenty-foot waves and plummeted into the troughs, meanwhile swinging side to side with sickening motion.

"Cap, we must drop our sails!" Donaldson cried. "We're gonna broach!"

"*I'll* give the bloody orders!" he shouted back through the roaring rain.

Donaldson looked at him as if he were more than a little mad. God's truth, storms did make him feel a trifle touched, all the element he was made of. It probably was an unnatural passion to love the rage of Nature as he did.

He strode the zigzagging decks to the helm to feel the rudder for himself and found it was a good thing he had, for the big helmsman's strength was spent. Lazar nodded firmly at him and took the wheel.

Immediately he knew it would be a struggle, but he refused to believe it was impossible. If he didn't keep running, the British would catch him easily when the storm was through, thanks to the damaged mizzen, and, the bloody limeys aside, he did not doubt this French bounty hunter was only the first of many to come.

"Come on, big beautiful gal. Steady now. You've got to get me out of here," he murmured to his ship. "Those waves can't hurt you, darlin'. Cap's got you. We love storms, you and I."

Arms burning, he threw all his strength into the wheel, fighting the sea's attempt to turn her broadside and flip her over beneath the massive waves.

"At least let us drag an anchor!" Donaldson demanded.

"All right—one drogue!" he said. "Quake-buttocks."

Just then the lightning swiped at them with its one claw and a wildcat cry, and now their battle was purely with the elements.

He was not sure how long he grappled with sea and sky when the lightning ceased, the winds dipped, and the waves slackened to half their height, still formidable.

By the time the storm was over, the east was gray with dawn, his arms and back and shoulders were numb, and the enemy was nowhere in sight. Russo's, Landau's, and Bickerson's vessels were missing also. Lazar's men lay scattered across the deck, beaten by their ordeal, waiting for the rosy glow of dawn to bloom into full sunlight and dry their clothes.

Ragged with exhaustion, it was all he could do to drag himself across the Swiss-cheese decks toward the hatch, but through his exhaustion came the distant elation of victory. He and his vessel had brazened it out and cheated death again.

Now it was going to be a chore to reckon what quarter the wind had blown them to, for he had no idea where the hell they were. They'd probably run a hundred miles. Before tackling that puzzle, though, first he needed his woman and sleep.

As he picked his way around the half-dead sailors and the holes in the deck where various rounds had hit, Donaldson came weaving across the deck toward him.

"Captain, sir!"

"What is it?" He stifled a yawn.

"My report, sir—"

"Oh, yes," he said, mildly annoyed that this necessary detail would keep him from his bed. "Go on."

"A thirty-two burst on the lower gun deck, port side, amidships. The gun crew was killed. The explosion caused a breach of the hull, but the carpenters plugged it up straightaway, so the water we took on was minimal. As for the mizzenmast, well, er, you're aware of that."

"Indeed," he said, rubbing his neck as he glanced at the mast and all the tattered sails. "Poor old gal."

"Twenty-three dead and fifty injured—" Donaldson stopped and cleared his throat.

A prickle of foreboding crept down Lazar's spine as he noticed for the first time how nervous the shipmaster seemed. "Well? I assume Doctor Raleigh has the situation well in hand? He has enough laudanum and bandages and so forth?"

"Aye, sir, it's just that—" He broke off.

Lazar waited. "Aye, Donny? What do you have to tell me?"

"I'm afraid I have such news, sir, I scarce can think how to tell it."

Lazar's fatigue fell instantly away. "What is it?"

"Sir . . . a, uh, that burst cannon that I told you about—"

Lazar stared at him with his blood slowly running cold.

Allegra.

"Yes?"

"They were in the cargo hold." The shipmaster looked up at him, his eyes stark. "Sir, the cannon burst just below the cargo hold. Sir, Vicar has been grievously wounded—"

"Allegra?" he cried, grabbing the man by the shoulders.

"She is unhurt—the gypsy boy got her out of there moments before it went off. But sir, Vicar is dying—"

Lazar was already reeling away, half stumbling down the companionway.

⊰ CHAPTER ⊱
TWENTY

Allegra met Lazar at the foot of the companionway on the lower deck. She already knew he had not been injured in the battle, but she feared how he would take it when he saw Vicar. The old man's wounds were grievous, his chest seeping with blood that would not stop.

"I'm fine," she told him in answer to his frantic, searching glance. He jumped down from the ladder, he brushed by her and ran to the sick bay. She followed.

"Lazar, wait!"

He didn't.

By the time she turned the corner into the sick bay, a chaos of amputations and loathing and terror, Lazar was standing over Vicar's cot, looking horrified. Quickly she went to him. Then it was as if all the strength went out of him.

"Oh, Jesus." He sank down on the stool beside the cot and sat there, unmoving and forlorn.

The long, wooden space of the sick bay was like the inside of a pine coffin, the rusty lanterns creaking on their hinges with the battered ship's motion. The choking sound of Vicar's breath was horrible. His eyes didn't open.

"Doctor Raleigh did all he could," she told Lazar, laying a hand on his broad shoulder. "The broken ribs have pierced his lungs."

Lazar sat in utter silence, shoulders slumped, his bronzed face etched in exhaustion and grief.

She did not leave his side. Standing behind him, she kept her arms around him as Vicar passed away quietly less than half an hour later. Lazar let the old man's hand go and hung his head in both hands, elbows on his knees.

More losses. How would he ever bear it? she thought.

Tears streamed down Allegra's face for the kind gentleman scholar, but even more so for Lazar's pain. Her mother's suicide had taught her all too well as a child that it was the living left behind who suffered most. She knew no words could help at a moment like this. She caressed the muscled curve of Lazar's back as if she could wipe some of the anguish away from him.

He finally rose, gave his nose a quick swipe on his arm, and turned away without a word. She drew the blood-misted sheet over Vicar's face as Lazar left the sick bay, then followed him at a respectful distance as he walked to his cabin.

The elegant cabin had been wrecked by the battle. The door had been blown partly off its hinges, so he couldn't shut it properly behind him. She had the feeling he would have locked her out if the door weren't broken. She ventured in after him warily with a sense of foreboding.

Still he never turned around or looked at her. In silence, he stood in the middle of the room, looking around with a lost expression at the holes in the floor, the smashed desk, the shattered diamond panes of the stern windows.

Allegra hung back in the doorway, watching him in a mixture of fear and concern.

"What a mess," he said.

"We'll clean it up," she began soothingly.

All of a sudden, he moved like lightning.

He began wrecking the cabin, destroying everything the battle had left unbroken. He threw an unlit lantern through the remaining stern windows so the last glass panels shattered. He hurled the desk chair. It exploded against the wall.

He tore the door off his locker with a roar and punched the looking glass, instantly bloodying his knuckles.

Allegra watched him in amazement, lifting her hands protectively around her head, startled out of her tears. His whirlwind was all around her.

"Why? Why him, too? It's not fair!" he thundered. "*I lost everything!* It's not fair! What did I ever do?" He toppled the washstand; he seized the wooden chair again and slammed it over the desk with a roar. "I want a reason, God damn it! What did I ever do? *Nothing!*"

Shards of wood flew up, a splinter scratched his cheek, and the papers they'd worked on so carefully over the past few days went scattering.

He did not pause until his fury was spent, and all that was left of the chair was a wooden stump in his hand, like a club.

There was a long silence filled with Lazar's ragged panting and the astonished pounding of her heart.

"Get out of here, Allegra. Get far, far away from me," he said in a low, dangerous growl.

"W-why?" she asked, frightened by his display of fury and the bitterness in his face as he stared at the floor.

Running his fingers through his hair, head bowed, he started to laugh with infinite sadness.

"Because I don't love you," he said with a smile at the floor, shaking his head wearily, "and I don't want you."

She stared at him. "You can't be serious."

"Dead serious." He looked over at her with a stare like a lightning bolt. "Get. Out."

When she stood there, unmoving, gazing at him in bewilderment, he lifted the wooden club and stalked toward her. "Get out of here. Get out!" he roared.

She screamed as he chased her all the way out into the passageway as if he would beat her with it.

"Stay away from me, you hear?" he bellowed down the dark, smoky passageway. "I don't want your blood on my hands! I don't want you, not for my wife, not even for my whore! Stay out of my life!"

Sobbing, she fled in terror to the deck, leaving him below.

Later that day, he performed a brief and torturous ceremony, commending Vicar's wrapped, weighted body with the others to the placid green eternity of the sea. Men sobbed. Somehow he refrained. He was their captain. The man in charge, Father and Captain Wolfe both would have agreed, could afford no weakness.

He assigned Allegra the second cabin for her quarters permanently. He avoided her frightened glances and the hurt look in her eyes. She was alive. He had that much to be thankful for. Now all he had to do was find a way to let her go.

Soon, he prayed, she would get over him. He had no wish to get over her, nor any hope of doing so. His only resolve was to stay as far away from her as possible before the curse on him snuffed out her precious life as he had once planned to do himself, incomprehensible as that thought was. Even if he had to make her hate him, he would protect her from the curse that was himself.

The boy came silently to the doorway of the wrecked cabin after supper, tears on his smooth face as he apologized, twisting the knife in Lazar's heart, for having failed to save Vicar. It appeared the child really did have the sixth sense. Darius explained that he had gotten one of his bad feelings about the cargo hold, and though Allegra was willing to come with him, Vicar had refused. Lazar merely sat there in the half light of evening, listening to him, knowing he must be heartless to this lad, too.

"*Capitán,* I tried to save him," Darius whispered. "I-I know I failed, but please don't send me away. I have nowhere to go and no one to go to."

"Sorry," he replied without expression. "I have no use for you."

He could feel the boy staring at him for a moment, then Darius vanished into the shadows.

Lazar sat in the growing dark, staring at nothing.

Now that he had finally shouldered his punishment of solitude, soon, he thought, he would assume the ultimate burden of the crown, his to bear alone.

Well, he could lose himself in work. He was not like Allegra, he reflected as he took a drink of brandy.

Self-sacrifice only made a hedonist like him bitter.

She couldn't believe he had called her a whore. He hadn't meant it. Surely. He had been out of his mind with grief.

But that's all he sees you as, whispered the insidious voice of her conscience. *It's what you've chosen to become, and now you must live with the consequences.*

How could he say he did not love her? Of course he loved her. He had merely been upset.

That night, huddled in her bunk in the second cabin, where Vicar had lived, Allegra was still shaken by the way Lazar had turned on her. She knew he was devastated by the loss of his friend, but his behavior was beyond the pale. He should have turned to her for comfort, not struck out at her. It was so unlike him.

Anxiously she awaited the sound of his light knock on the door, certain he would soon come begging forgiveness, seeking the comfort she knew he needed so much. Though he deserved a good lecture for his behavior, she intended to forgive him the moment he apologized. She felt so lonely, shaken, and hurt by his unwarranted attack that she only wanted to feel his arms around her.

The hours passed, and still she waited. The next thing she knew, she was waking up, and it was morning.

Maybe he knocked and I slept through it, she thought as she quickly dressed.

Sure he did, whore. She flinched at the cruelty of her own bullying conscience and went in search of him.

No doubt by now he had calmed down a bit. He would have come to apologize already, but maybe this morning ship duties kept him away, she thought.

She would not even require a verbal apology of him, she decided. If she could just look at him and see his rueful, crooked smile of apology from across the decks, she could relax in the knowledge that everything would be all right, but she had the iciest feeling in her bones that things were never going to be all right again.

When she went up on deck, she understood at once why he hadn't come to her.

Of course, she thought in relief.

The pirate island, Wolfe's Den, appeared on the horizon just two hazy leagues away, a large, green-shrouded rock baking under the summer sun. They were about to dock, and Lazar was overseeing that task.

The crew was in surprisingly high spirits. Allegra saw Lazar at the rails, peering through his telescope while consulting, and dispensing orders to the men who stood around him. She made no move to approach him.

No, she thought, let him come to me. But she kept him in sight from the corner of her eye.

Mr. Donaldson told her that though the island was partially surrounded by a coral reef, the crew was so familiar with its passage, they could have maneuvered *The Whale* into her berth blindfolded. They cheered from spars and rigging, capstan and lines, as *The Whale* nudged into her home berth at last.

The gangplank crashed down, and the men swarmed onto the dock. Immediately they set about mooring, tying the vessel with huge ropes to the dock's weathered posts. Gulls dodged and swirled overhead. Pelicans got in everyone's way, begging for fish, and were shooed off.

Since Lazar had still obviously not noticed she was there,

she decided to make her presence known. She even had an excuse. She didn't know what he wanted her to do—if there were quarters for her somewhere on the island or if she should leave her things on the ship.

Steeling herself, she joined him on the quarterdeck, standing at a safe distance. "Lazar?"

"May I help you?" He did not look at her. He continued standing at the rails, scanning the crowd of men.

She stared at him without comprehension. Did he blame her for Vicar's death somehow?

"I want to know what I am to do," she said, striving to remain calm.

"Do? I'm sure it's of no consequence to me," he said.

The blood drained from her face. "What's wrong? Why are you treating me this way?"

He finally glanced at her, his face hard as sculpted bronze. "Didn't I mention our affair is over?" He looked away quickly, squinting toward the beach. "Never fear, I shall provide for you. You'll have a house, servants, a carriage. I think it would be best for everyone if you returned to Paris, don't you?"

"Lazar, what are you talking about?"

He clenched his jaw for a moment. "We can't be together anymore, Allegra, not at all. It's over."

She drew back as if he'd struck her. "Why?"

He seemed to consider. "Because it's not what I want anymore."

She reached out and gripped the rails to steady her sudden sense of faintness. "Have I done something to displease you?"

"No, I'm afraid I am merely bored with you. Besides, my wife might not like it. Surely you hadn't forgotten I am to marry Nicolette?" He said the other woman's name like a caress.

"I have not forgotten," she forced out.

"Well, then, what do you want from me? I said I'd cover all your expenses." He glanced at her again. "You don't like the

Paris option. Well, let's see, what else can we do with you? You might allow Captain Landau to become your protector. He has a reputation for satisfying his women—you know the French. That should keep you happy."

"How dare you talk to me this way!"

"How dare I? I'm about to become the king. I can do whatever the hell I want, and I can certainly talk to you any way I feel you deserve. I don't require you anymore."

Her head reeled with disbelief. She could only stare up at him, horrified, flabbergasted.

"Lazar."

"Yes, Miss Monteverdi?" he asked in an annoyed, long-suffering tone.

"What are you doing to me?"

"Getting rid of you, I suppose."

She suddenly felt sick to her stomach. "Why?"

He gave an insolent, one-shouldered shrug. "Oh, I don't know. I guess now that I've had you in every possible position, the thrill is gone. Our voyage together is over, is it not?"

She couldn't speak. Shaking, she looked down at the deck as if the script were there, telling her what she might possibly say.

"Oh, my Lord," she said barely audibly, turning away. "This isn't happening." Closing her eyes, she covered her face in her hands for a brief moment, struggling to collect her composure, whispering to herself in disbelief, "What shall I do?"

"I said I would provide for you."

"I don't want *anything* from you," she wrenched out. "Except to know what I have done that was so unforgivable that you would betray me—"

"Nothing." He studied the open sky. "Please, don't make this any more awkward than it already is."

"Awkward?" she nearly screamed.

"Try to understand this is the way it has to be."

"Is it because of Al Khuum? I would never tell *anyone* your secrets—"

"I know that."

"—because I love you."

Woodenly he nodded as he gazed at the mast. "Aye, I know that, too."

The most horrible thought of all dawned then, the reality of it finally piercing her disbelief.

"Lazar, don't—don't you love me?" she forced out.

He appeared unable to speak, a trapped, desperate look in his sea-black eyes. She stared at his golden skin, his muscled chest and belly she had caressed so many times.

"It's over. I don't want you. Stay out of my life."

Without another word, he crossed the quarterdeck and walked away without looking back.

That night Lazar went walking in the dark tropical forest beyond the clearing in which the pirate village was situated. The teeming, primordial jungle hemmed him in with its palm trees of all shapes and sizes, trees hung with brown-husked coconuts, green bananas, half-ripe mangoes. There were scrubby pines and oak trees overgrown with twisting vines. Birds with long plumage flitted from branch to branch through the darkening canopy, their piercing, raspy calls filling the moist, hot air. The smell of the soil was pungent and heavy in his nostrils.

He felt utterly bereft. His mind was weighted; his muscles ached with a kind of dull constant misery. His heart sat like a lump of charcoal in his breast.

He went up to the lookout point atop some overhanging rocks and leaned against the cannon that was secured there. For a long time he stayed there, gazing out over the dark hillside, the fading sky and calm sea. Below, he could see the village, with its stone kitchen building and smattering of thatched-roof huts. Small bonfires winked to life in the common area as the men huddled together to mull over the uncertain future.

The normal course of events upon returning from a successful mission or raid was for the men to have a huge feast, carouse like lunatics, and drink themselves into a general stupor, but the battle had resulted in heavy losses.

Tonight it was quiet down in the village, the atmosphere tense. Fitzhugh's ship wasn't back yet, Morris said he feared Russo had gone down in the storm, and there was talk that the British were on the verge of discovering the location of Wolfe's Den.

And, Lazar supposed, the men didn't know what would become of them with the way he'd been treating them all since Vicar's death. It was hard to make himself give a damn for his decimated crew and ravaged ship when he had lost the man who had been like a father to him and had had to give up the only woman he would ever love.

He made his way back down the mountain and came to the edge of the village. He meant to skirt around it to avoid the men, with their fearful eyes and their plague of questions, but he heard a conversation that made him pause as he passed in the shadows.

"I want to go home," said the ever-reliable Mr. Donaldson.

The purser sat with Mutt, Andrew McCullough, and Mickey the Bean at the fire. All four swigged from their flasks in dejection.

"Where would you go?" Mickey asked him. "Where could any of us go where we wouldn't be hanged? Our families won't have us. We're doomed, my friends," the redheaded youth said bitterly. "Cap has forgotten us."

"That new admiral wants our blood," Andrew said.

"Aye, and he'll get himself a title and country house for it," Donaldson muttered. "I wish Vicar was here. He'd know what to do."

They fell silent, then Mutt, the head carpenter, spoke.

"You mustn't worry, lads," he said in his low, halting voice. "Cap will stand by us. He always has. No, Cap would never leave us to hang . . . but I confess," he added, " 'twould be nice to have a place to grow old, not here on this old rock. I'd get meself a wife, I would, like Cap done—"

The others started laughing at him.

Lazar gazed at their familiar faces, illumined and etched by the bonfire's glow, with a tug at his heart. They were good, decent men, he thought, loyal men, and they deserved better than this desperate, meager existence. They might choose not to support or even believe him, but the time had come to at least offer them the choice.

He strolled toward them out of the shadows, idly brushing off a mosquito. They greeted him and offered him some rum. He shook his head and put his hands in his pockets.

"Men," he began, "I have something to tell you. It's about Ascencion. It's . . . well, it's a long story, and I guess it's time you heard it. . . ."

He sat down and told them.

He watched the wonder steal over their faces and the fatigue and defeat fall from their shoulders as he told them his story, and before long there were a hundred men listening. By the time he came to the part about the vendetta for which he originally commanded their fleet to Ascencion, the whole company of the Brethren was there, listening in utter silence, watching him intently.

"For me, I've made up my mind," he said. "I must go back. Join me, and if we are victorious—and by God we shall be if we make our stand together—each of you will have my thanks, a proper home, a new start—"

But the thunderous roar of cheers the men had unleashed drowned out his last few words.

They were with him. Lazar stared around in amazement. His spine tingled with the first intimations of what it might be like to rule, truly and legitimately—but then his heart sank.

Without Allegra to share it with him, it was meaningless.

* * *

A week passed, and still she couldn't seem to make herself believe it.

He had betrayed her. The dearest friend she'd ever had. Her Prince and pirate and the husband of her soul and her king. Wolfe's Den was a tropical paradise, but Allegra was apathetic to the lush beauty of its pink beaches and silvery waterfalls, blue lagoons and primordial woods. She was sick, sick, sick to her stomach constantly.

Two of King Alphonse's legendary advisers arrived another week later, but she was in too much of a stupor to care. She only noted that both old men recognized Lazar on sight, weeping with joy to have found him. Father Francesco, the archbishop, seemed a kind, grave soul, but the golden-eyed, hawk-nosed prime minister, Don Pasquale, was cold and insidiously clever. Allegra took the hint swiftly that Don Pasquale intended to despise her forever on account of her father's treachery.

She didn't care. She stayed away from everyone.

Captain Landau often came to sit with her, trying to draw her out. He was friendly, gallant, witty, and attentive, but she was incapable of conversation. How could Lazar have suggested she become this man's lover, do with Landau what she could ever do only with him?

Surely he hadn't meant it. She was half tempted to make him believe she'd taken him up on his suggestion just to try to make him notice she was still alive.

The last week before they left the Carribbean, there was one more new arrival, a lone, mean-looking mercenary whom Lazar had left behind on Ascencion to kill Domenic.

Why exactly Lazar had wanted to kill Domenic was not clear to her. Perhaps for the simple reason that he didn't like him. Or maybe, at the time, he had been merely indignant that Domenic had tried to rape her—rather amusing, in light of what he had done to her himself, she thought.

The rough-looking thug brought back a challenge to Lazar

from Domenic to return and face him, and a demand that he bring Allegra back safely.

Jeffers said Domenic ruled Ascencion with an iron hand and a cruelty to the people worse than Papa had ever enacted upon them. She heard whispers that before the other mercenaries were killed they had been tortured extensively in Domenic's effort to learn more about Lazar.

Apparently, Domenic was out for Lazar's blood, clamoring to bring the Devil of Antigua to justice. She knew Domenic didn't care whatever about her, despite his demands to have her back, but she could well imagine his pride had been wounded by the fact that Lazar had carried off his betrothed and everyone knew it.

Well, she thought dully, if she didn't get her monthly soon, he was going to have even more to be embarrassed about.

Already two weeks late, she forced herself to believe it was merely the effect of all the strain she had been under. The alternative, now that Lazar had cast her aside, was unthinkable. The sensible, prudent, tediously moral Allegra Monteverdi could not become an unmarried mother, surely. She would never be able to face anyone she knew again. No, it was just the shock and worry, she told herself.

As for the king, he looked terrible. Lazar had aged years since Vicar's death. For the few weeks they remained at Wolfe's Den, he was gaunt, haggard, and broodingly quiet, but faster than she would have thought possible, he had his ships repaired and transformed his pirate horde into the first royal navy of Ascencion. At last, the ships were loaded, and the Brethren left Wolfe's Den for good.

Under the green-and-black of the Ascencion flag, Lazar's magnificent warship, festooned with long billowing streamers in every color of the rainbow, led its small fleet proudly in formation as Ascencion's first royal navy crossed the Atlantic once more.

Allegra was surprised that Lazar made her travel with him

aboard *The Whale*. If he thought she was going to resume her former duties as his harlot, he was sorely wrong, but he never approached her. The voyage together was torment. There was no possibility of her attempting to get on with her life at this point, because they were trapped together on the ship, forced to cross paths every day.

She remained in a kind of dull-minded trance, barely able to believe how hard it was to learn not to touch him. She'd grown accustomed to the smallest brush of his hand on hers, a quick hug, a soft caress. All of it, gone. He scarcely even made eye contact with her.

She decided to return to her on-and-off plan of becoming a nun. She had no feelings about it one way or the other, all the emotion wrung out of her like water from a sponge. She only knew she never wanted another man in her life ever, ever again, and she hoped if she stayed close to God, perhaps eventually she could rise above her sense of shame about having been Lazar's whore.

She felt guilty, she felt angry, but she could not escape the sense that in some vague way she had been tricked. Staying away from Lazar was not difficult, since he spent his nights on a simple hammock slung on the stern, sleeping under the stars and the open sky, making the most, she supposed, of his last days at sea.

She tried to divert herself with small tasks, but her time stretched out before her, void hours of staring or sleeping, meaningless, like everything. She felt sick all the time and observed herself with bitter amusement going into a decline over Lazar di Fiore—the man whom she had denied nothing. The man who had taken everything away from her and left her with nothing but perhaps a child in her belly that she did not want.

She was even more stupid than her mother, she supposed. At least King Alphonse had been worth it.

She missed her aunt Isabelle terribly. Aunt Isabelle would have known what to say and do.

Her worry grew. How could she become a nun if she was with child? She would have to throw herself upon her uncle and aunt's charity for the rest of her life, bring home her embarrassment under their roof, for she would rather die than ask Lazar for help.

Yet if she turned to Uncle Marc and Aunt Isabelle, their two little daughters' reputations would be tarnished forever with such a ruined woman in their home. She tried not to go into a panic over the situation, however, because there was still hope that her monthly would come. She prayed. She tried to feel those miserable cramps, but halfway into August, they still hadn't arrived.

Favorable winds carried the fleet swiftly to the mouth of the Mediterranean, where they were met by twelve Austrian ships, which in turn escorted them to moor across the straits from Ascencion in one of Corsica's sheltered bays. From then on, there was an endless procession of visitors who came to pay Lazar homage, all overseen by the eagle-eyed Don Pasquale.

She kept her place in the background, remaining all but invisible while the dignitaries brought the king unimaginable gifts and bowed nigh double before him, not daring to meet his fiery black eyes. And he, she saw with deepening misery, accepted it all as his due, as if he had been born to it, which of course he had.

Maybe he would be a cruel, tyrannical king after all, she thought. She hated him. She loved him. They avoided each other. But she took any chance she could to study him furtively, this man who had wreaked his vengeance on her so thoroughly.

He was grave and dignified; he always seemed to know exactly what to say and do, and his keen gaze missed nothing. The lines of his face seemed hewn of granite, belying his mere eight-and-twenty years. The black of his eyes was as deep and inscrutable as the night sea. He awed all who came to see him.

Already the weight of rule bore down on him, but it would not crush him, she knew, for he was made of rock.

September 3 was the last night they spent aboard, roughly four months since the night of her father's anniversary feast.

It had been a long day, with a steady stream of visitors, and as she finally went into the stateroom on her way to the cabin, she could see the strain telling on the king.

The last of their high-ranking visitors went, bowing backward, out of the stateroom, anxious not to commit the great insult of turning their backs on him, and Lazar let out a wordless, muffled growl as soon as they were gone. He jumped up to pour himself a snifter of brandy.

"You're doing fine," Allegra conceded in grudging reassurance. It had been days since they'd spoken at all.

"I feel like a bloody stage actor," he muttered. "A very poor one, at that."

She wanted to say something bitter, but she couldn't.

She wanted to say she was proud of him, but she wouldn't.

"No," she sighed instead. "It's all real."

He considered this for a moment, swirling the brandy absently in the glass. When he took a drink, she lowered her hungry gaze, remembering with a pang the brandy-flavored taste of his kiss on her tongue.

"I'll be happier when I've got Clemente in custody. I could use a good fight. All this civility is making me lunatic." He sighed as he sat down again and put his head back against the chair, eyes closed.

She stood there, uncertain of what she should do. Fool that she was, half of her wanted to go to him. More than half, really.

"Allegra?"

Hope leaped alive in her heart, and unbearable, immediate desire. She knew that note of longing in his voice. "Yes?"

There was a searing silence.

"What is it, Lazar?"

"I miss you so much," he breathed, holding perfectly still, eyes closed.

"Do you want to make love?" she asked softly, holding her breath, but she could not, would not, go to him.

He swept his long-lashed, midnight eyes open and lifted his head to hold her in a tortured gaze.

Burning all bridges, she crossed the stateroom in five steps. The next thing she knew, she was being lifted in his arms, and they were in his bed, tearing off each other's clothes with feverish, shaking hands. Neither of them spoke a word, then he was inside her, urgent, desperate, and deep. She hooked her arms under his, holding on to his massive shoulders while he took her in a storm of tenderness, grazing her brow with his lips.

She bit her lip until it hurt, rather than tell him she still loved him. Her love was in her every caress of his smooth, warm, golden skin, but she would not give him the words.

When he lowered his head to suckle her breast, she began to weep silently as she lay petting his velvety hair.

Lazar, Lazar, my heart is broken.

When he heard the ragged breath of the sob she fought to steady, he paused. Slowly he came up to her face again and kissed her tears. He cupped her head and kissed her cheeks, her brow. She cried harder at his meaningless sweetness, never making a sound. When he kissed her throat, she closed her eyes and wanted to die.

She didn't know how she could proceed, as if her mind, her heart, were folding in on itself. She was collapsing, though she already lay in his arms. If only he would say he loved her. She would forgive him. She would take him back in a heartbeat. If only he wanted her back.

What a mistake it had been to come into this room with him, she thought as he rode her slowly, gently, as if he could console her with his skills as a lover. All the progress she'd made to forget him was obliterated, the wound of losing him opened afresh.

Yet he made her forget, for the moment. Somehow he brought her body to the edge of a rapture all the sweeter for the knowledge of how fleeting it was, never to return. With a deep, anguished, almost grief-stricken cry, he flooded her womb with his essence.

Then he lay atop her for many hours, not leaving her body or the bed. His head on the pillow beside hers, he stared at her, caressing her skin in the darkness, twining her hair around his fingers.

They never said a word.

⊰ CHAPTER ⊱
TWENTY-ONE

The next morning she woke alone, utterly alone.

She was seized with such dread, she virtually threw on her dress and ran out of the cabin, shaking. There was no one in the stateroom, so she strode out into the passageway, to find herself still all alone. At last, scrambling up the companionway, she came to the deck, which was warm with life, sparkling with dew.

The dawn sky was pearlescent peach, the waves a languid aquamarine. The wind was low. She spied Lazar on the quarterdeck, standing motionless at the rails. Before her pride could stop her, she hurried past the guards and officials to his side.

"Look," he said, nodding toward the east.

The sun was rising behind Ascencion. Huge, magnificent rays of gold fanned out behind the island's crooked bulk, which mounded up, deep violet, from the shining green sea, its jaggedness softened by the incredible light. The sight of it was glorious.

"I want to thank you for this day," he said, staring straight ahead. "I wouldn't be here—none of this could have happened—if it weren't for you. I will never forget you, Allegra."

It was quite possibly the most terrible moment of her life. The words held a burden of such finality.

"So, this is good-bye, then?" she barely whispered.

"Oh, no, nothing like that." He casually stared down at his knuckles, brow furrowed. "I just wanted you to see the sunrise. . . ."

Sunrise.

He stared very hard at his hands on the rail, no doubt remembering, as she did, the sunrise they had once shared.

"Yes," he said. "It is good-bye."

"Oh, for God's sake, look at me," she uttered, fighting tears. "Just once, look into my eyes."

He didn't. He had to study his cuff links.

"What happened?" she cried, not caring who heard anymore. "What happened to us? Is it my fault Vicar died?"

"Keep your voice down," he murmured, staring at his hands on the rail.

"Did you ever love me at all? Were you toying with me all along?"

"Allegra."

"What did I do wrong?"

"I am a curse, Allegra," he said in a taut voice, chafing under his own steely self-restraint. "I don't want you to be hurt."

"You don't want me to be hurt," she wrenched out, incredulous. "And last night? What was that?"

"A mistake." He lifted his chin, standing tall as he always did when he wanted to hold himself remote from her.

She stared up at him, betrayed all over again because she had actually started to hope.

"Good-bye, Allegra."

"You selfish—" She stopped herself, drew a breath. "Your Majesty," she said, "you can go to hell."

Parting words.

She walked away from him abruptly, bumping into someone in her panic as she fled. Stumbling down the companionway, she was reeling with pain. In the cabin, she gathered up the few things that were hers and dropped them into her canvas satchel. She could barely see what she was doing in her effort to hold

back tears. He did not come after her, of course. He had the
business of the kingdom to attend to.

She was so great a fool she stole one of his shirts and stuffed
it into the satchel, one he had worn and that needed washing,
just to keep the smell of him close awhile longer, rum and
smoke, leather and the salty sea.

She wished to God she had never laid eyes on the man.

In an emergency meeting shortly after dawn, the old dons of
the Council broke the news to Domenic Clemente.

"He's here, and he's real," said Don Carlo.

"The pope is on his way for the coronation," Don Enrique
added. "No one can fight *il Papa*. Pius apparently gave Lazar
his confirmation when he was a boy. If *il Papa* recognizes him
as Alphonse's son, we can look to no higher guarantee of his
true identity."

Seated at the head of the long, glossy mahogany table in the
newly repaired great salon, Domenic stared, blank with disbelief that was about to snap to fury.

"Rather than face a battle, Genoa is going to pull out quietly," Don Carlo continued, his lined face impassive.

"And be damned glad for the chance," another muttered.

Domenic slammed his healed right fist onto the table.
"You're not even going to put up a fight?"

"What would be the point?" The old man shrugged. "Ascencion is no longer profitable for us."

"Damn it, that man must be brought to trial! He should hang.
He's a pirate, for God's sake!"

"That was just a ruse," one of the old men said impatiently.
"Don't be tedious, Clemente."

"God's truth," Don Enrique muttered, "if he has survived all
this time, I daresay the lad deserves the place."

Domenic was so enraged, he was barely able to speak. He
had never felt so impotent in his life. "What about me? What
am I to do? This is my whole future you're throwing away!"

The old men shifted uncomfortably in their seats and glanced at one another.

"King Lazar wants to put *you* on trial, my friend," said Don Gian, the most intimidating Councilman.

Domenic sat back in his chair in disbelief.

"Don't worry, Clemente. If he is anything like his father, we can probably get amnesty for you."

Domenic laughed bitterly. "Amnesty." He shook his head, still stunned. He knew that black-eyed savage would never grant him amnesty. "You think I don't see what you're doing? You think me a fool? You're making a scapegoat of me, just as you did of Monteverdi."

Don Gian stared at him keenly. "No one told you to burn villages and allow your soldiers to rape country girls. Nor, surely, did any of *us* advise you to reinstate the practice of burning men at the stake for their crimes."

"Well, it worked, didn't it?" he shouted. "Crime has dropped dramatically."

"There's nothing left to steal." Don Carlo chuckled.

Their laughter was like the rustle of dead leaves. He looked around at them wildly, feeling cornered.

"Don't worry, Clemente. We'll find some position for you in Genoa," Don Carlo assured him, a bold-faced lie, for his eyes said, *You're on your own, boy.* "Go home to your Maria, and wait there while we go to today's conferences. We'll get this matter straightened out. Just lie low for now. You'll have guards to protect you from the rabble."

House arrest, he thought, stunned anew. They could say they were placing soldiers at his heels for his protection, but he knew the truth.

"Yes, the people are indeed in a state of agitation," another concurred.

Don Gian made a dour face. "They should be. Their legend has come true."

Domenic swept to his feet, heart pounding, his handsome face calm. "Gentlemen, I shall take leave of you now, for it looks as though I have some packing to do." He forced a contrite smile. "Forgive my outburst, if you will. It came as rather a shock, but I understand the situation is out of your hands, and I know you will do your best on my behalf."

Don Carlo nodded.

Domenic went on. "While I wait for word of this amnesty, I'll return presently to my country house and get everything in order so I may return to Genoa with you. Feel free to send the guards at your convenience. I'll be there. You have my word as a gentleman," he added. He bowed to them and walked sedately out of the tall, gilded chamber.

After closing the white double doors carefully behind him, he turned and fled.

One word pounded in his brain with every step. *Weakling!* The devil was beating him again. He could not believe the Council was throwing him to the wolves, though why he should be shocked, he did not know. He passed servants and guards who did not yet know they would be ordered in moments to lay hold of him. He stopped on the threshold of the government building, staring about wildly at the square of Little Genoa, where the Ascencioners were already celebrating Lazar's return.

King Lazar. *No!* he screamed mentally. *I will kill you!*

And there was the answer.

All of sudden, he was very calm, even relieved. Though he still had a few minutes to seize the chance to escape, he would not run. No, he was no coward, as his father had always said.

He knew what he had to do. With no king, who would take power? He could have it all back, he told himself. He could even have Allegra back if he wanted her. All he had to do was put a bullet in that pirate's black heart.

Lazar di Fiore was not immortal, no matter what these peasant bumpkins claimed.

Just then the bumpkins noticed him standing there, the hated young governor who had burned three men at the stake—for perfectly justified reasons—and Domenic realized that perhaps he was not immortal either.

Acutely aware of their hostile stares and the way they began drifting toward him in the square with evil looks, he walked slowly, carefully to one of the mounted guards and ordered the soldier to give him his horse and his pistol. He swung up into the saddle, reeled the horse around, and went galloping toward the spot on shore where the so-called king would sooner or later disembark.

Moments later, the Council's soldiers were riding hard after him. *If Fiore eluded them, by God, so can I,* he thought furiously.

The beach was in sight, as were the distant ships, when his tiring horse stumbled.

There was a village overlooking the sea, and Domenic turned in there to take a fresh horse, the best the village had to offer, before he lost his lead on the soldiers chasing him. He had his pistol, and he did not intend to take any insolence.

The whole village looked so poor that perhaps no one here owned a horse, he thought frantically. If no horse was to be had, he would find a place to hide. From somewhere around here, he could shoot the king as his carriage came by, he thought, for the same road went all the way down to the port. Fiore would have to come this way.

But as he rode toward the wealthiest-looking house in the village, the only home that might hopefully possess a horse for him, someone shouted, and he was recognized.

Domenic realized that in his panic he had stumbled into the wrong village—the same lowly place his three burned men had been from.

He screamed as the villagers closed in on him and pulled him off the horse.

* * *

It was late morning when Lazar's men, pirates transformed to royal guards, came to take Allegra away. Men who pitied her. Men whom he had told she was a shrew, she thought, and the last woman on the earth he would ever want to sleep with. They were escorting her to the medieval convent, with its three-foot walls and innumerable hiding places, but she was beginning to wonder what the sisters were going to do with a pregnant nun.

As they rowed toward the beach, she pondered throwing herself into the swirling waters of the Ascencion coast, but she scoffed at herself for even thinking of the melodramatic gesture. She was not Mama, and he was certainly not King Alphonse. She was through martyring herself for that man.

Instead she just sat there, numb, as her heart was slowly torn from her spirit. Once they reached the beach, they hurried her to a waiting carriage, with a second and third carriage ahead and behind for protection.

Perversely, she was almost beginning to hope she *was* carrying Lazar's child. It meant she could not become a nun, true. Indeed, it meant great embarrassment, but at least she wouldn't be alone. At last, she would have someone who loved her and could not leave her.

In the carriage, Darius was staring at her earnestly.

"What is it?" she asked.

He shrugged, kept his thoughts to himself as usual, then looked out the window again.

How hurt the boy was, she thought sadly. Darius didn't understand his idol's rejection any better than she did, but he was too tough to show it.

As their small cortege made its way up the sunny hill, they smelled fire, and moments later heard many angry shouts and screams as they drew near a village. She rapped on the carriage.

"What is happening here? Is the village on fire?"

She realized she knew this village, Las Colinas. She had often brought medicines here for the sick. They pulled alongside the road, but even before the vehicles stopped, Allegra saw what was happening, and her eyes widened with horror.

The people of Las Colinas were burning a man at the stake.

Before even Darius, with his catlike reflexes, could stop her, Allegra jumped out of the carriage and ran toward the mob.

"Stop it! Stop it!" she screamed.

The villagers turned around.

"It's Miss Allegra!" some said in surprise.

"What are you doing?" she demanded. "This is madness!"

They fell back, clearing a path for her.

"She brought our king back to us," she heard some of them murmuring.

"She brought Lazar back. . . ."

"Bernardo said she saved His Majesty's life. . . ."

Two big men came out from a nearby shed, dragging the fighting, swearing victim between them. Her jaw dropped at the sight of her ex-fiancé. She clamped it shut again, casting about wildly for anything she could possibly say. When Domenic saw her standing there amid the people, he began to bawl helplessly.

"Oh, God, God, don't let them burn me, Allegra. Help me!"

One of the big men slapped him, and his shouts broke off. She searched the people's faces around her. When the crowd quieted, there was no other sound but the popping of the blaze they'd made and a jangling harness as one of the carriage horses shook away a fly.

"Did not our Savior tell us to love our enemies, to turn the other cheek?" she asked, breaking the silence.

"This governor burned three of our sons at the stake!" an old woman shouted at her. "He, too, must burn!"

"Aye!" many cried.

Domenic stared at her and formed her name on his lips, too terrified to make a sound.

"You must not do this," she said to the people with all the force she could muster. "Your king would not want this. Do you wish to displease your king? No one here would want to cross Lazar di Fiore. Trust me."

"Aye," one of the ex-Brethren agreed behind her.

The villagers looked around at one another.

Allegra licked her lips and forged on. "This man has wronged all Ascencion, not merely your village. It is the king's right to sentence him, not yours."

She could tell they were considering her words.

"When is he coming?" someone shouted.

"Soon," she told them, heart pounding. "Listen to me. You must let your king deal Lord Clemente his own justice. Rely on it. His Majesty will serve truth—do not forget God has appointed him by divine right. Let my guards take Lord Clemente into custody."

"He must be punished!"

"Not this way, good people," she insisted, glancing around imploringly at all of them. "No more vendettas. If we are ever to know peace on this island, it must begin here. Now."

They looked at one another.

"Oh, God, please," Domenic wrenched out in a loud voice.

She looked over her shoulder at the former Brethren, but they, too, wore evil looks as they stared at Domenic. She realized they were still hungry to get back at him for having tortured the mercenaries whom Lazar had left behind on Ascencion with Mr. Jeffers.

"Gentlemen," she said to them meaningfully.

The men looked at her skeptically, their sun-browned faces gruff under their smart new uniform hats.

"Let us not break any vows today," she said, reminder enough that each had agreed to abide by Ascencion's laws. "Take Lord Clemente prisoner, please, and douse that fire before it catches any houses."

"Right," Sully said. He was the first to march forward, elbowing one of the big village men out of the way.

They brought Domenic to her, and she took him into the carriage with her.

"Allegra," he wept, "you are an angel, an angel."

In the carriage, he laid his head in her lap and stayed like that, his arms around her waist, his whole body shaking, until they reached the convent.

The boy sat across from them and stared at her with a piercing look in his dark Spanish eyes. He glanced down at Domenic in contempt but never said a word. She avoided Darius's steady, reproachful gaze, for she knew what he was thinking.

Capitán would not like it.

These bloody interviews are worse than any hurricane, Lazar thought grouchily.

Outwardly cool, inwardly exasperated, he spent the afternoon enduring the last round of negotiations and questions from a panel made up of Genovese Councilmen, Vatican officials, nobles from the powerful old Ascencion families, and representatives from the nearby Italian states, as well as ambassadors from the Spanish, French, and Viennese courts.

He had no idea how he managed to answer their questions, because all he could think about was Allegra and the unbearable sweetness of loving her last night, for the last time. He would never forgive himself for weakening so until he could no longer brook his need for her, but he had been so lost, so empty. *Her eyes were the color of cinnamon and honey, her skin was ivory, and she had sixteen freckles on her nose. . . .*

Another barrage of questions from the canny old men.

Clearly the diplomats realized he wasn't telling them everything about his past, but they were just going to have to content themselves with what he had decided to reveal, which was very little indeed. He was a king and would not be studied under their microscope.

In any case, he was well aware that all were more interested in how they and their countries could gain from his restoration, so it was to self-interest that he directed his responses, bypassing all direct references to his past mode of living with an urbane deftness that he thought would have made Vicar smile.

At last the formidable, golden-eyed Don Pasquale called the interview to an end.

"Gentlemen," he addressed the Genovese party, "we have presented to you our overwhelming evidence of the authenticity of our claim. The moment has come to decide." Pasquale glanced at his pocket watch for laudable dramatic effect. "Now, it is up to you either to renounce Genoa's claim on Ascencion or fight at dawn."

Lazar kept his face impassive, but he held his breath as the robed dignitaries conferred quietly at their table in the stateroom. As he watched the old men whisper, he wondered if these were the same Councilmen who had sentenced his family to death and had bought Monteverdi to aid them. But he steered his thoughts back to the present. The past was done. He truly did not want more bloodshed. Ascencion had suffered enough.

Finally the Councilmen looked up. "We do not wish to fight. God save the king."

"God save the king!" the others cried, surging to their feet.

"God save the king!" Pasquale shouted, fist in the air.

Well, somebody had better save me, he thought.

Allegra's absence reduced his moment of triumph to tedium, but Lazar lifted his chin, looked stern and composed, and tried not to let anybody see his astonishment.

"Sire, as to the matter of Lord Domenic Clemente," one of the Genovese Councilmen spoke up. "We wish to submit a request for amnesty—"

"Denied," he said. "You shall hand him over to me."

They gave him no argument, to his surprise.

All the men stood when he did, bowing low as he left the room. Lazar found it rather bizarre to be the object of such obeisance. Not bad for a former slave, he thought.

Don Pasquale followed him as he strode down the hall. They congratulated each other on their mutual victory.

"I've just been told Enzo arrived a few hours ago from Vienna with Princess Nicolette's entourage," Pasquale informed him. "Father Francesco is meeting with the bridal party at the cathedral tonight to prepare for the wedding tomorrow. You'll be needed. The royal officer of ceremonies will be on hand, instructing everyone where to sit, stand, kneel, and so forth."

Lazar heaved a sigh. "I suppose we might as well do it right," he grumbled, then he stalked off down the passage, went into his cabin, and pulled the door closed behind him.

Allegra was not waiting there for him anymore. The little room was as empty as the burned-out shell of Castle Belfort.

He sat down heavily in the armchair, rested his elbows on his knees, and lowered his face into both hands. He rubbed his temples in defeat.

Fierce kitten, he thought with that endless ache, *telling the king to go to hell.*

Don't worry, chérie, he thought. *I'm already there.*

When they arrived at the fortresslike medieval convent, Domenic had collected himself considerably. Rather than having any of the men leave to conduct Domenic to Lazar, Sully judged it best to keep the squadron together, for they had not heard if Lazar's takeover from Genoa was final and official yet. Risks could still feasibly arise. There was even a slim chance of battle, which was the reason Lazar had sent Allegra to the fortified convent—the ships might yet be engaged in war. However, there seemed no hurry to bring Domenic to Lazar, for the young governor was so subdued by the horrific fate from which they'd saved him that he was completely docile.

For her part, after those nerve-rending moments at Las Colinas, Allegra needed to lie down. She was tired all the time these days, but that confrontation had completely drained her.

As her traveling trunks were unloaded, she and Domenic walked, surrounded by guards, into the huge convent. They found themselves inside the sisters' dining hall, a dim, drafty vault all of stone, with a hearth at one end as tall as a man. No fire burned there now.

Domenic stood, searching her face with more feeling than she had ever seen him exhibit.

"For your guards, I am stationing men I know can be trusted not to abuse you. Lazar *will* sentence you," she told him. "I don't know what that sentence may be, but he will certainly not burn you. He is not an evil man."

His green eyes flickered with a pained, hunted look. "Allegra, please. If you have any influence over him, I beg you, use it to make him grant me amnesty."

She was silent for a moment, regarding him soberly. "I don't have any influence over him, Domenic, and I'm not sure you should be given more than a partial amnesty at best. But I will say a word in your defense before he sentences you, if you desire."

"Thank you," he whispered.

Just then the plump Mother Superior glided toward her with a kindly expression, one tinged, Allegra thought, with pity.

"Miss Monteverdi, how good to see you again. We are all so glad you've come back safely. Come, I will show you to your chamber," she said in a singsong alto.

"Thank you, Mother," she murmured.

Darius carried her sea chest behind her as she left Domenic with the men and followed the nun across the dining hall to a flight of steps. Allegra glanced back to see how Darius fared under the large trunk. He paused to haul the chest up onto his shoulder. She looked ahead again, only to find at the top of the stone steps that their way was blocked by a quartet of young women richly dressed in light-colored silks, their throats and wrists studded with jewels.

Mother Superior bowed. "Your Highness. Ladies. Good day."

Allegra heard a snuffling growl behind her and turned to find a brown bulldog, like a stocky little gargoyle in a jeweled collar, relieving itself on the stone newel post. Then, dewlaps swinging, it trotted over to a girl in their midst, jumped up to paw at the young girl's knee, and was lifted into her arms with coos of adoration. Allegra realized she was standing face-to-face with the wife.

In spite of herself, she was awed.

Princess Nicolette looked like an angel. She was the first female Allegra had ever seen whose beauty exceeded Mama's. Her hair was the color of winter sunshine, her skin was like fresh cream, her cheeks pale-pink roses, and her large, round eyes were cornflower blue. She appeared as if she had just fluttered down in trembling innocence from Heaven's nursery to sit at Lazar's feet.

God, between two such gorgeous people, their children would look like perfect little cherubs, she thought dismally.

"Is this the mistress?" the princess asked sweetly, addressing Mother Superior.

The ladies-in-waiting crowded closer to Nicolette and glared daggers at Allegra, who in turn recoiled at the way the princess allowed the ugly dog to lick her perfect face.

"Your Highness, an' it please you," Mother Superior said in her soothing tone, "it is His Majesty's command that Miss Monteverdi stay here until the kingdom has been won."

Nicolette blessed the woman with a radiant, dimpled smile. Her voice was candied pins.

"We would never dream of contradicting our lord and husband, but good sister, do see that this person's quarters are situated as far from our wing of the building as possible. And we wish our king to note it is a scandal to our person that we must share quarters with a"—she drew herself up—"a woman of easy virtue."

Allegra stared at her.

"Brigitta, inform the mistress it is bad form to gawk so at a queen."

"Woman," Brigitta dutifully told her, peering down her aristocratic nose, "one does not look into the eyes of a queen. Cast down your gaze!"

"I daresay you are not a queen yet, Your Highness," Allegra murmured.

Mother Superior coughed.

"How common she is!" the third girl said in shock.

"How plain!" cried the fourth.

"There is no accounting for a man's taste," Brigitta murmured wisely.

"Truly, I don't wish to be any trouble!" Allegra exclaimed, recovering from her astonishment by the barest measure. "Perhaps I should stay in the stable."

"Yes, that would suit us well," the princess replied with a gleam in her blue, blue eyes.

Allegra felt her face reddening. Nicolette's angelic smile never faltered. She set her dog down, and it came sniffing at her. Allegra shoved at it with her foot, and it snarled a warning.

"The stable?" Darius growled at last, as if unable to contain himself any longer. "*Capitán* would not like that!"

The princess and the ladies looked over and suddenly discovered him.

They peered at the beautiful youth with great interest. He scowled back at them dangerously. Allegra refrained from rolling her eyes as they ogled him, but it made her almost ill to realize that if they thought Darius was handsome, they were going to swoon when they saw Lazar.

No doubt the king would soon be likewise besotted with his perfect little bride. She wondered if Lazar would whisper to Princess Nicolette, too, that he loved her.

In her drafty stone chamber, Allegra went to the window to look out at the view as she stood, hugging herself about the waist. Far below lay the sisters' neat courtyard. In the distance, green hills spanned the horizon rather than the endless sea. The leaves were beginning to change colors for autumn, and from her vantage point she could see the last remaining tower of the charred, deserted Castle Belfort rising through the trees.

Her heart sank, remembering how they had planned to build the new Belfort over those ruins and on the surrounding land—their city—hers and Lazar's, Ascencion's gleaming new capital.

Now it would be Lazar and Nicolette's shared project. Shared lives, both the joys and sorrows. Shared children.

Traitor, she thought.

They deserved each other.

Standing in the drafty, torch-lit great hall of the convent, Domenic watched the quiet, bristling confrontation between Allegra and the Viennese princess and read in their mutual hostility the means for his escape. It was a long shot, but if Allegra pulled no weight with Fiore, as she claimed, it might well be his only hope. If Domenic Clemente knew how to do anything, he knew how to manipulate women.

He stood staring at the beautiful princess with his most tender, wonderstruck expression, heedless of the guards around him. As the ladies came mincing down the staircase, Nicolette Habsburg saw him. Lips slightly parted, he stared at her, lifted a hand vaguely over his heart, then cast down his gaze quickly, staring at the floor like a lovestruck schoolboy.

He could feel her instant curiosity, that subtle preening of feminine vanity, and he heard the ladies begin to whisper.

"What man is that?"

"He is tall."

"He has a noble air, hasn't he?"

"What fine, golden hair he has."

There was giggling, and he lifted his gaze hesitantly to the princess. Their eyes met. She tilted her head, then came toward him. With a regal nod, she caused his cutthroat guards to back away. The rough, stupid men were so abashed by her beauty, you'd think they had never seen a woman before, he thought, though even Domenic had to admit Nicolette Habsburg was possibly the most beautiful girl he'd ever seen.

He kept his head bowed.

"Sir, what are you called?" she asked. "Are you one of the king's men?"

"No, Your Highness."

"Your Highness, stay back. He is a prisoner," one of his guards started to say, but she cast him a withering look with eyes of ice-blue fury.

"Brigitta," she said impatiently, "inform these creatures they will not speak unless spoken to."

Domenic had to hide his fleeting amusement as Brigitta obeyed. The men around him bristled with resentment.

"Of what crime are you accused, good sir?" the royal beauty asked him.

"The king hates me," he said softly, "for I was once the betrothed of his mistress."

"Miss Monteverdi?" she asked with a flat curl of her pretty lip.

"Yes. He stole her from me, and all I want is to leave this place in peace with her. But he is in love with her and will not let me have her back."

"In love," she repeated. "With her?"

"Oh, indeed, Your Highness. He showers her with rich gifts I cannot match with my poor fortunes. I fear His Majesty will empty half Ascencion's coffers on her."

She folded her arms over her chest and stared frankly at him. "Well, that will not do."

She was easy to read, he thought. He could just see her thinking to herself, *He will certainly not spend my dowry money on that woman!*

Domenic's mind raced with excitement. He was willing to bet the princess had sent Brigitta or someone of her coterie to have a look at Fiore for her and no doubt had heard the finest reports of her new husband's dark good looks and charm. If she had one jot of female jealousy in her pretty, virginal body, he would find it and prey upon it.

"Oh, radiant lady," he sighed, "if only I could leave this place and take Miss Monteverdi away with me, my life would be complete, but alas. Instead I will surely hang for my love."

The ladies sighed behind her.

"Aye," he said woefully, "the king refuses to part with her. He says Allegra Monteverdi is the most beautiful woman since Helen of Troy, with the finest mind and the sweetest temperament."

Nicolette stared for a moment. "We'll just see about that!" She moved closer. "I may be in a position to help you, sir," she confided to him with all the high seriousness of her perhaps seventeen years.

He gave her an incredulous look of thanks. "Oh, gentle lady. Would you, truly? I could never repay you. . . ."

Her perfect, creamy face took on a look of resolve. Oh, this little blue-eyed viper would make the king's life hell, he thought gleefully.

"His Majesty must never know of this, but I believe what the poets always say—true love should never be denied," she whispered. "Tonight while I dine with my husband, I will send my guards to conduct you and Miss Monteverdi to the coast. From there you may sail whither you may. Just don't bring that woman back here. Ever."

"Sweet, radiant lady," he breathed.

Looking tremendously pleased with herself, she gave him her hand.

Domenic knelt and kissed her fingers until she blushed.

⊰ CHAPTER ⊱
TWENTY-TWO

Lazar stood where the priest told him to stand, sat where he was told to sit, walked at the pace that his bride, with her deliberately tiny steps could match. Candles blazed in the cathedral, and there was a party atmosphere among the others, while individually the members of the wedding party learned their places from the old royal officer of ceremonies. Even Don Pasquale was smiling, reminiscing to his Austrian counterparts about a boyhood trip to the Alps.

Lazar stood around with his hands in the pockets of dark blue breeches, an amiable enough look fastened on his face by sheer willpower. After all, he was about to get everything he supposedly wanted—Ascencion, his to cherish and protect. The restoration of Fiori rule. Two million gold ducats. Domenic Clemente taken into custody, awaiting trial for crimes against the people of Ascencion. And a wife it would be easy to keep at a polite distance.

Indeed, his eyes glazed over when he tried to listen to his bride's vivacious chatter, which was exactly what he had wanted.

As for the royal wedding, it was to be a grand production. A lavish show, a giant, sumptuous farce.

He overheard the guests murmuring their various judgments on his quiet mood, some calling him a generally taciturn fellow; some said silence was a mark of wisdom; the courtiers decided he was either dull-witted or seized with a bout of cold feet; the ladies whispered that he was mysterious.

Oh, the joys of public life, Lazar thought dully. It was all coming back to him.

He wanted to leave.

At each round of congratulations he forced a smile, wondering how he was going to endure a lifetime of this without one soul nearby who really knew him and wouldn't make these arbitrary judgments on his every tiny gesture and word. He told himself it would fade. He was merely a novelty to them at this point. Work would be his salvation. God knew there was enough of it to be done.

Upon finishing the rehearsal for the next day's performance, they all piled into the ornate carriages to go take a late supper at the sprawling winter villa of the Duke of Milan. While Lazar waited in irritation for the princess and her ladies to get into the carriage, he glanced up at the cathedral and wondered if lightning would strike him when he stood at the altar and made such hollow vows before God.

He found it difficult to listen to the girls' chatter in the carriage, so he sat, gazing out the window at the dark landscape, missing Allegra so completely his whole body ached for her. This unselfishness business was a great deal harder than it looked.

As he eased out of his melancholia back to the present, the landscape, though dark, took on a sinister familiarity.

"Where are we?" he asked, chills crawling down his forearms.

Just as they reached D'Orofio Pass, Mama gathered little Anna, sleeping, on her lap and sat back against the velvet squabs. "My!" she said. "How that sea tossed! Thank heavens we all are safe."

He slammed his fist against the carriage door. "Driver, halt, damn it!"

The ladies gasped at his obscenity, but the vehicle rolled to a stop.

Heart pounding, Lazar sprang out of the carriage, drawing Excelsior. He looked around wildly, but there were no masked men, no stomping horses or screams, no lightning. Just him, the gleaming royal sword, and the night breeze moving gently through the trees like the sighs of mournful ghosts.

"What is it, sire?" someone asked behind him.

"Let him be," Don Pasquale sagely replied.

The girls whispered nonsense together.

Lazar walked a few steps away. Heart welling, he stared about him at the empty place along the road where his family had been slaughtered. It looked like an ordinary place, but here death twined like a black snake amid the violets. The tiny path through the roadside woods caught his eye as it had almost sixteen years ago, drawing him once more.

Survive, and hold the line.

Dried leaves crunched under his feet as he entered the woods where once a boy had fled, frightened out of his mind. Before long he stood at the edge of a cliff two hundred feet high, the edges of his frock coat billowing in the breeze. He stared down at the swirling, churning waters below.

You poor little bastard, he said to the boy he had been. *Bloody miracle you survived at all.*

He searched the dark, distant waters with the stirrings of a profound realization taking shape in the back of his mind. He felt some twisting emotion he could not name, a bittersweet, exquisite anguish. All he could think was that at last he had kept his promise to his father.

But now he had broken another kind of vow, he thought heavily, one that reached beyond words, branded upon the very ether of his soul.

In my heart I am your wife, she'd said. *That is enough for me.*

Ah, chérie. *What am I going to do with you?*

He looked up at the stars helplessly. Allegra was his compass, the star above his storm who had guided him home. She had saved his soul. She had given him everything, and he had thrown her away. He'd had no choice, for Vicar's death had proved the curse was real.

But how could it be real? he thought achingly. There was a time he would never have dared believe he could have his kingdom back, but his love for Allegra and hers for him had made real the impossible. Perhaps he was equally wrong now to believe he could not have her by his side. *But what if—?*

What if. Always, what if.

Life was a dangerous proposition however you looked at it.

Aye, he thought, one could go stark, raving mad if one dwelt on the mind-boggling fragility of one's own mortality too long, let alone the mortality of one's beloved. Life was so closely braided with death that avoiding one meant avoiding the other; the only way to escape the looming fear of death, he thought, was to embrace death itself, and he had cast away that option once and for all the night he had hurled his silver bullet out to sea.

But to embrace life? He was not sure he had that kind of courage.

For instance, even if he kept Allegra safe from traitors and murderers and such, women died in childbirth half the time, he mused, a bloody affair—the very process of life itself was laced with death. If he gathered her back into his life, children would come sooner or later. He was sure to love his children to distraction, and what if they were taken from him? Babies were more fragile than tiny rosebuds. How could he bear it?

Then there was the fact that Allegra loved to work among the poor, with their filth and their diseases. She had to die sometime. Even if there was no real curse, a day would come when he would have to put her in the ground, for he doubted that God in his munificent cruelty would allow him to be taken first.

Are you really protecting her, or are you trying to spare yourself the pain—running away again to save your own skin?

The waters below and the stars above seemed to hold an answer he was too much of a clod to grasp, one he sensed should be obvious but he just couldn't find it. He searched sea and sky until he grew dizzy there by the cliffside. He knelt on one knee on the windswept rock, steadying himself.

Resting his elbow on his bent leg, the king lowered his face in one hand.

I am damned either way, he thought with a feeling of such despair he didn't know whether to laugh or cry. *We are all damned one way or the other, and such is life. Might as well be happy.*

He began to laugh softly with infinite sadness at his own patchwork philosophy, a peasant's creed, such wisdom as could have come to him from the mouth of any Ascencion grandmother standing before her stove, frying up her garlic in *olio.*

Could life be that simple?

He pressed his eyes shut, longing to believe it. *But she will be taken from me. I cannot bear it. Why were they all taken from me? Why do I lose everyone?*

Then, quite distinctly, he could hear Vicar's voice in his head, his teacher, trying patiently to ingrain some lesson of logic in him to temper his hotheadedness.

Invert the question, lad. Mulehead, you're looking at it backward.

Moments passed, and Lazar didn't move, barely breathing. Perhaps, he thought carefully, he had been so wrapped up in raging against misfortune and asking why it all had happened that he had never considered he might choose instead to be grateful for what he *had.*

He shocked himself by realizing he had much to be grateful for—thirteen good years with a mother who had adored him, a father like a hero from Greek myth. Then came his serious little brother, a little sister with a crazy giggle. By some miracle, he'd been spared the storm and the sea. He'd found friends when he had needed them most. He was alive, he was strong, and because of his enemy's daughter, he'd tasted the most sublime sweetness life had to offer, unconditional love.

She had wrapped him in her love, total and unrestrained, *and that was the gift he'd been given.*

Yes, he thought, staring intensely at the glistening sea.

Allegra *was* alive. Allegra was more miracle than he deserved, and, by God, if there was a curse, their love was strong enough to break it.

He stared down at the swirling waters with a profound sense of humility, and for a moment he bowed his head, his whole spirit moved unto silence.

Thank You, he said, pressing his eyes closed.

Abruptly he rose. There wasn't a moment to lose. He had wasted too much time already.

What if she wouldn't forgive him? The thought was too terrifying to entertain. As he strode back swiftly to the waiting cortege, he assured himself that if she refused him, why, he would simply kidnap her and force her to love him all over again.

She didn't have a chance. He would love her until she couldn't stand it anymore.

He commandeered a thoroughbred from one of the courtier's, gave the princess his briefest regrets, and swung up into the saddle without further explanation. Impatiently, he tore off his cravat and the satin frock coat—*too much damned civility*—and galloped hell-for-leather to the convent with but one goal in mind.

To beg his queen to take him back before they wasted one more precious moment of the time they had to share on this earth under starry heaven.

*   *   *

Allegra sat in the chapel for a long time after vespers were done, huddled into the black broadcloth novice habit Mother Superior had given her. She twirled a length of her hair pensively around her finger and thought about how she must cut it off when she joined the order.

Lazar would not like that.

With that thought immediately came the little invisible needle plunging into her heart again. She sighed, and her eyes watered.

Stop, she thought, squeezing away the tears.

The votive candles flickered over the serene face of the pallid marble Virgin in the alcove, and the ghost echoes of the sisters' crystalline plainchants wafted on the air with the tender scent of wildflowers placed about the small stone altar.

At length she got up from the pew, genuflected wearily, and left the chapel, turning down the dark stone corridor with her mind full of him, inky lashes, sensual laughter, a wicked grin, ecstasy.

Allegra Monteverdi, these are not a nun's thoughts.

She hugged herself as she walked down the hall, awash with a bereft, whole-body misery. When she turned the corner, she found six big Viennese soldiers marching toward her.

One addressed her in careful French, the language of the courts. "Miss Monteverdi, please come with us."

"What for?"

"We have orders to escort you and your fiancé to the coast."

"My fiancé?" she exclaimed, taken aback.

"Darling, at last," Domenic said as he came around the corner just a moment behind.

She stared at him, automatically backing away from the soldiers. She knew that smug look on his face, and, to her horror, she saw he was armed with a pistol.

"What's going on? Where did you get that weapon, and where are your guards? I thought Lazar had you moved to the jail!"

He took her arm firmly above the elbow. "The king is not the only power here, my dear. His queen doesn't want you underfoot," he murmured to her in Italian so the Austrians wouldn't understand. "In exchange for my freedom, I have agreed to get you out of the way so she can have her husband to herself. But you and I, darling, we shall have each other as we intended to from the start."

"I can't go with you! I need to stay here, and you must stand trial for your crimes," she said angrily. "Does the princess know about the charges against you?"

"No more arguing, darling. You are in no danger. I'll look after you from here on in—"

"As you looked after me the night Lazar had to interfere?" she demanded, wrenching her arm free of his grasp.

He clenched his angular jaw for a moment, green eyes snapping sparks.

"Neither of us is wanted on Ascencion, Allegra," he said quickly, his voice taut. "Don't forget you are the traitor's daughter. The dons of the Council have betrayed me just as they betrayed your father. Now, stop arguing—"

"What do you mean by that?"

"There's no time to explain."

"Tell me! How did the Council betray Papa? You're hiding something."

He stared for a second at the ceiling with a look of failing patience, then he looked back down at her. "Will you quit fighting this if I tell you?"

"Fine," she lied.

He spoke swiftly in a low voice. "Your mother's death was not suicide. She was eliminated because she was going to expose the conspiracy against the Fiori. She knew her own life was in danger, so she sent you away to your aunt in Paris. Your father never knew the truth."

She stepped back as she turned white, both hands over her mouth.

"Now, come on, before our escorts here start to question their orders and change their minds."

"I'm not going with you," she choked out. "I belong here."

"You lied? You?" he asked in astonishment. His eyes narrowed, and he gripped her arm harder, turning her about-face toward the exit at the end of the hall. "Your new talents are intriguing, but you fail to understand. You are the key to unlock my cage, Allegra, and time is ticking away." He began dragging her down the hall.

"I cannot leave him!" she wrenched out, fighting him.

He stopped and stared down at her. "You can't be serious. That man is an animal."

"I won't go with you. I love him, Domenic, and you must face justice!"

"This is absurd," he said in exasperation to the wall, then he switched to his condescending patience that she knew so well, placating her like a sulky tot. "Don't worry, darling. You will forget him in time. I care for you, Allegra. I always have."

He reached for her arm again.

"I am carrying his child!" she shouted in French so the soldiers would understand and see they mustn't take her away.

There. She had said it aloud at last, she thought in shaken relief. No longer was her pregnancy a secret she would try to keep from herself.

The Austrians glanced awkwardly at one another, but Domenic's face turned white.

"That is all the more reason the princess will want her gone," Domenic said to the men. He reached for her. "You're coming with me."

"No!" She tried to run, but the big guards caught her.

"I'm afraid he's right, miss," one said. "Questions of inheritance and so forth."

When she drew breath to scream for Sully and the other men of the Brethren, the Austrian clapped a hand over her mouth.

"You disappoint me, Allegra," Domenic murmured, looming over her. "I never thought you'd enjoy being any man's whore. Now I shall look forward to yet another use for you."

She kicked at him to no avail.

As he moved back a step to evade her efforts with a grim smile, far behind him down the hall, she caught a glimpse of Darius. The boy was stock-still, staring at what was happening. Then he vanished silently, unseen by the men, just as Domenic took her from the soldier and half dragged, half carried her down the torch-lit hall.

Riding up to the convent, Lazar sprang off the blowing horse in the cobbled courtyard and tossed the reins to one of the idle Brethren guarding the well-lit front entrance.

"Evenin,' Cap," the man said, then added hastily, "I mean Yer Majesty."

Lazar grinned as he hauled open the huge wooden door and went in. In the vast dining hall he found his men lounging.

"What are you doing here?" Sully asked, but even before he answered, the Irishman's face cracked into a grin.

"Where is she?" Lazar cried in a jolly, booming voice.

"Ach, he's come to his senses!" Sully laughed, clapping his hands together.

"I thought she was a shrew?" cried Donaldson.

"Not if she was the last woman on earth!" guffawed Mutt.

"We all knew you couldn't live without her, lad." Doctor Raleigh chuckled.

"Down that way." Sully pointed to the stone corridor off the dining hall. "Poor little mite's in the chapel. Wanted to be alone, pining over ye. Near about been breakin' our hearts, she has."

Lazar clapped Sully on the back. "My friends, wish me well. I go to grovel for my life," he declared.

He was striding toward the hallway when the stony vault filled with a high-pitched cry.

"Mr. Sully! Donaldson!"

Darius came tearing down the torch-lit corridor, wide-eyed. He skidded to a halt in surprise when he saw Lazar.

"*Capitán!* They've got Allegra! They're taking her away!"

"Who?" he demanded as the men leaped to their feet.

"The foreign guards and Clemente!"

Lazar was already running down the hall, sword in hand, his men a short distance behind him. Heart racing with dread, he turned the corner just as the last Austrian guard was going out the formidable door at the end of the hall, a side exit.

"Halt!" he roared.

The guard turned. "Majesty!"

The man froze as ordered in the open doorway. As Lazar went racing toward him, thunder on his brow, he saw that the other Austrian guards had heard and stopped as well, not daring to disobey him, but he pushed past them with the awful feeling that he knew what he was going to find.

"Stay back!" Clemente screamed at him, pressing a pistol to Allegra's head.

Lazar froze.

Allegra sobbed out his name.

Lazar lowered his sword, gazing deep into his beloved's eyes as he approached slowly.

"It's all right, *chérie,*" he said softly. "I'm here now."

She stared at him for all she was worth, pale beneath her freckles.

"Make him let me go, Lazar, please," she said in a quavering voice.

"What do you want, Clemente? Let her go, and I'll meet every one of your demands."

"You expect me to believe you? You—you pirate?" The viscount laughed at him in bitter hysteria.

"Let Allegra go. What do you want? Amnesty? Granted. Money? Name the sum."

"I want my future back!" he bellowed. "This island is mine!"

"No, this island is mine," Lazar replied. All his concentration on Domenic's face, he switched tactics in response to the fear in the viscount's green eyes. Domenic had only one shot with that pistol.

If he could deflect that bullet to himself, Lazar thought swiftly, Allegra would be safe, then the Brethren would fall upon Clemente instantly.

"What a coward you are, Clemente," he said pleasantly. "Can't you fight your own battles? You need to hide behind a woman's skirts to save yourself?"

"Shut up!" he screamed.

"Quake-buttocks," Lazar answered softly, a mad, wild glint coming into his eyes.

"I am not afraid of you!"

"You should be," Lazar advised him, "because this time I'm not merely going to break your little wrist. I'm going to break every bone in your body, then I'm going to get out my knife and do some carving, as you did on my men."

"Oh, God," Allegra sobbed.

"You like sharks, Clemente? There are many in the waters off our coast. Hammerheads."

"Shut up! I'll kill you."

"You think you can hurt me? Come on, try. Give me that bullet. Let me show you this talent I have for coming back from the dead."

"Lazar, no," Allegra moaned.

"It's all right, *chérie*. Look, little Domenic, I'm only— what—seven, eight feet away? I'll bet you can't even hit me from here."

He bore down on them slowly as Domenic backed away toward the waiting carriage, Allegra in his arms, the gun still pressed to her head.

Completely focused on Clemente's weakening will, Lazar

sheathed Excelsior and held his hands out. "See? Now my hands are empty. Go on—give me that bullet, Clemente. We both know it's me you really want to kill. Wouldn't it be nice if you were rid of me? You could get it all back, couldn't you? Ah, but you're too much of a quake-buttocks to try. You just want to hide behind a woman and run. But you'll never get away."

"You son of a bitch," Clemente said to him, panting now. "I'll shoot her! You'll lose her *and* the baby!"

Lazar stopped in his tracks. He looked at Allegra, stunned.

Tears were streaming down her face.

"Please, Lazar," she whispered.

In the moment that he was distracted, staring in astonishment at her, Domenic took aim at Lazar, but as he pulled the trigger, Allegra shoved his arm upward with an angry cry, breaking free of him. The bullet whizzed over Lazar's head. Roaring, Domenic bolted to the carriage and scrabbled up onto the driver's seat.

Lazar was behind him in seconds. The guards stopped the horses before they'd taken a second step. Lazar pulled Domenic down bodily off the driver's seat and slammed him against the side of it, punching him twice square in the face with all his strength. Then he threw Clemente to the ground and unsheathed Excelsior.

But he did not slay Clemente. He was Lazar di Fiore, and he did not kill in front of women.

Panting, the sword in both hands, he held the tip of the blade to Clemente's throat.

"Arrest him," he growled as his men drew near. "He will hang at dawn. And I want those Austrians held for questioning, too," he added, shooting the princess's men a dark look.

As Sully and Bickerson grabbed the still-dazed Clemente by the arms and clapped him into manacles, Lazar turned away and paused for a second to collect his thoughts, raking a hand through his hair, for he could not remember ever having felt such rage in his life.

When he turned again, Allegra was staring at him, but when he looked at her, she quickly put her head down and began walking toward the door to the convent.

He had tried to get himself shot to save her.

Hugging her waist, Allegra marched woodenly toward the door, concentrating on one foot in front of the other for now, promising herself she could break down for good when she reached her drafty little chamber. She could not face Lazar and his cool indifference after such a nerve-racking experience, let alone his anger at her for not having told him about her pregnancy. She didn't dare hope that the things he'd said to Domenic were anything more than tricks meant to shake the viscount's concentration, but the news about the baby had taken him by surprise.

"Excuse me," she murmured to a body blocking her path.

Head down, she saw black boots. An ornately jewelled sword sheath. She breathed the smell of him she knew so well.

"Please—later," she choked out, staring down stricken at the ground. "I can explain—"

"Allegra," he said softly.

She closed her eyes, for she could not bear to look into his sea-black eyes just now. The fool could have been killed. Two warm, callused fingertips touched her under the chin. She jerked her face away.

"Don't touch me, please," she said, putting her head down again.

"Look at me, honey," he said ever so gently.

Oh, she had never been able to resist him. Slowly she lifted her tear-filled gaze.

The king was staring down at her with a stark, stormy expression she could not fathom. He towered over her, looking haunted and lost. He said nothing.

Still staring at her, heedless of his men and the nuns who had come out at the commotion, oblivious to the worried officials now joining the crowd, Lazar sank down onto his knees in front of her and took her hand.

He pulled her knuckles against his cheek, held her hand to his face.

She stared down at his bent head without comprehension, then she felt him tremble.

"Take me back," he whispered. "Please, please, take me back. Allegra, you are my wife. You know you are. My life means nothing without you."

☆ CHAPTER ☆
TWENTY-THREE

He truly did not know if he was forgiven. Lazar dared, slowly, fearfully, to raise his gaze to hers. She gazed at him, the lantern light on her face. The fear and the wariness in her once-trusting honey-brown eyes was torment to him.

She bit her lip for a moment, then she squared her shoulders.

"It hurts too much," she answered at last. "I am not your wife, and I can't play these games anymore. Find yourself another mistress."

He didn't think he could hurt worse, but her calm, forced words did the trick. He squeezed his eyes shut.

"That's not what I mean." He opened his eyes again and stared up at her. "Allegra, I love you. I want you to be my wife. Marry me."

She stared at him in shock, then tilted her head back and stared at the starry sky. She looked back down at him at last. "Lazar, they are all staring," she murmured. "Get up. You are the king."

"I am your husband," he said with quiet savagery, "and an utter fool."

She lifted her gaze away from his pleading stare, looking very weary.

He tugged on her hand, staring helplessly up at her.

"I love you," he insisted again. "God, Allegra. Say something."

She paused for a moment, gathering herself. "Lazar, it's

been a difficult night. There is no need to do anything rash. Come now. Let's go inside."

He stared at her. It was not what he'd been hoping to hear.

She didn't want him. All his strength fled, but he knew it was only what he deserved for his cowardice. Dumbly he nodded. He had hurt her and disappointed her beyond repair. Now he had no choice but to play the game by her rules.

She straightened up to her full petite height and waited for him. He stood and followed her. They went into the convent and to her chamber. He ached to see the way she held her chin high, though everyone they passed now knew she was pregnant with his child.

His child.

Miracle upon miracle, he thought dazedly. She had to forgive him. They could be a family at last. That was all he'd ever truly wanted.

While he gave a few final orders to some of his men, Allegra went into the chamber.

When he followed her in and locked the door behind him, he found her standing at the open window, staring out at the night. He could read her fear in the very line of her back and in the way she kept her slender arms wrapped tightly around her. He knew that this particular fear had nothing to do with Domenic Clemente. It went deep, and he had done it to her himself.

More chastened than he'd ever been in his life, he waited, head down, hands in pockets, until she turned around to deal with him at last.

Alone, they stared at each other by the light of two candles. She stood at the other end of the room, watching him, her arms still folded self-protectively across her bosom. She looked small and vulnerable and defiant. He was suddenly so unbearably unhappy he went and sat on the bed, as if unable to hold his own weight.

She had to take him back. She had to.

"Well?" she said coolly.

He couldn't stop staring at her.

You are magnificent, he thought. But he put his head down, barely knowing how to begin.

"You have every reason to hate me," he said in a leaden voice. "I wanted your trust, and you gave it to me. I wanted your love, and you gave it to me. You believed in me when I didn't believe in myself. You gave me back everything I once lost, and in return I, ah . . ." He faltered, furrowing his brow as he stared down at his hands. "I pushed you away."

"Got rid of me," she corrected him coldly.

"But I swear to you, it wasn't because I stopped loving you. I never stopped."

The room was silent. He drew a shaky breath.

"You see, I believed I was cursed," he said. How foolish it sounded now. "I thought if I kept you in my life, you would be killed like my family and Vicar. I thought by pushing you away from me, I could save you."

She gave him her most scathing look of skepticism.

He heaved a sigh. "I know. That's why I never told you. I knew you'd say it was absurd, but to me, it was real. Tonight when I came to D'Orofio Pass, I realized . . . I realized that even though I may be a king, God never went to the trouble of cursing me. I think He's got better things to do. Like looking after babies growing in their mothers' wombs."

He looked up at last with tears in his eyes.

"Is it really true? Am I going to be a father?"

She looked as though she was ready to break down, but instead she turned away swiftly. "Don't worry. I shall not plague you. Aunt Isabelle and Uncle Marc will help me—"

He stood up quickly. "No!"

"No?"

Lord, he was botching this.

"I mean— Please be my wife, Allegra. I love you so much it hurts," he whispered. "I'll do anything to have you back. If you could just give me one more chance. Don't make our baby grow up with no father. It's not a safe world out there. He needs someone to protect him, and so do you. Please, Allegra. Please let that someone be me."

"Lazar." She stood fixed in place, put her head down, pulled her arms tighter around herself.

He searched the floor, unable to think what he would do if she said no.

"I am so, so very sorry," he said in a raw, hoarse whisper. "Can you ever forgive me? I swear to you I was only trying to do the right thing and be unselfish for once. Don't you believe me, Allegra?"

"I believe you," she said barely audibly.

"Will you take me back?"

There was a long silence. He shut his eyes, unable to watch. At last he forced himself to face her, whatever her answer might be. He opened his eyes and raised his head.

Collecting herself, Allegra met his gaze from across the room.

"Impossible man," she said, then bit her lower lip as her soft brown eyes filled with tears. "After all we've been through, how can you even ask? When I said I'll love you forever, Lazar, I meant it."

"You'll give me another chance?" he breathed, motionless.

"Sweetheart," she whispered, "a hundred chances, if you need them."

He crossed the room to her before she could move. He pulled her against his chest, vowing never to let her go again.

"Do you really want me back?" Allegra asked so wistfully it wrenched his heart. "You said so many awful things. You said you didn't want me. You called me a—"

"Please, I can't bear it," he whispered, his heart cleaved in two. "I was trying to drive you away before any harm befell you."

"I wouldn't have cared if it had, so long as I could be with you."

He rested his face against her hair and stayed there, so miserable with what he'd done to her that he hadn't the heart to say one more word, hating himself for the doubt in her soft, sweet voice.

"Do you still love me, Lazar?"

"God, yes. Just give me the chance to show you how much. I will never fail you again." He could barely see for the tears in his eyes. Lazar tilted her face upward, her chin between his fingers and thumb. "Look at me, Allegra. Do I look like a man who can possibly survive without you?"

Staring into his eyes for a moment, she somberly shook her head.

He nodded knowingly, then pulled her close again. She hid her face, nestling against him.

"It feels so good to hold you," she whispered. "I missed you so much. I never thought you'd come back to me."

He wrapped his arms around her shoulders and held her tight, laying his head atop hers.

After a few moments, Allegra tilted her head back, gazing up into his face, assessing the man she saw, he supposed.

He awaited her judgment.

She shook her head for a moment, scolding, tender. Then she slid her hand slowly up his chest, cupped her fingers around the back of his neck, and drew him down to kiss her.

He felt life returning with the first, chaste caress of their lips.

"Lazar?" she whispered.

"Yes, *chérie*?"

"Love me."

"I do," he whispered. "More than anything in this world."

She opened her mouth, running her tongue lightly over his lips, then parting them. Instantly he was on fire. He gathered her closer and claimed her with a drowning kiss. She caressed him everywhere. Her hands were all over him, stroking him, bringing him back to his senses. He plundered her mouth with his kiss, dragging her to the bed, never letting her go, but he was astonished when she pressed him back upon the bed, kissing him like a starved woman.

"I love you so much, Allegra."

"Will we be married, truly?" she whispered, panting, pulling off his shirt.

"Tomorrow," he vowed.

"And Ascencion?"

"We will rule together, my wife, side by side. You are what this island needs. You are what I need."

"And our child?"

"Prince of all the land," he whispered, caressing her belly lovingly.

He felt her smile against his mouth. "No, Your Majesty. Princess, I think."

"Is that so?"

"I'm not sure, but I have a feeling," she said softly.

"Wonderful," he told her. "Miracle."

He closed his eyes and gave in to her touch, feeling as though he'd died and gone to heaven. All his pain fled, burning in her white-hot fire.

"Get rid of these, for God's sake," he muttered, tearing at her nun's habit.

She let out a rich, breathy laugh and lifted the dreary robes off over her head in one graceful motion. In a moment, she knelt over him, naked, straddling him. Her touch left him dazed; just to be with her was a magical experience, dizzying as a drug. She bent down over him and kissed his lips, her taut nipples brushing his bare chest.

"I love you." She unfastened his breeches, kissing his belly. "I love you, Lazar," she whispered again. "My Lazar." She kissed his neck, teething him lightly. "My beautiful savage. My husband."

"My wife." He pulled her down flat against him, holding her lithe body as his member throbbed hotly against her belly.

After a deep, sweet, silken kiss, he cupped her face in both hands, staring up soberly into her eyes.

"I will never be worthy of you," he told her. "Never."

She cast him a slow, lazy grin as her hair swung down around his face like a curtain.

"Probably not," she murmured, "but I'm giving you the next sixty years or so to try."

"Scoundrel," he whispered, laughing breathlessly, then she stroked him to raging arousal.

In a few moments, she took him inside her. He let out a sharp groan of torturous pleasure.

"Oh, you *did* miss me, didn't you?" she purred, easing him in slowly all the way, inch by inch.

She sat up, and he watched her ride him, her eyes closed, her face luminous with ecstasy. She tilted her head back.

"You are so beautiful," he vowed.

He pulled her down against him, swearing his love countless times in a fevered whisper, pausing only to kiss her, but words were not enough.

He laid her down on the bed and showed her, offering her everything he was with every stroke, every caress, every breath. She reached for him, and he filled her tenderly, deeper and deeper still, wanting everything, all of her. He wrapped her legs around his hips, glorying in the softness of her skin and the tight wetness of her passage.

"Never leave me again, Lazar. You are my very soul."

His only answer was to gaze deeply into her eyes so she could see for herself that he never would, not for all the world.

Her release when it came was the purest surrender. Sweeter than honey, she flowed for him with anguished cries of passion that floated out to the cool night. Then he let go, clutching two handfuls of her silky hair, gasping her name as he flooded her womb with his essence.

For some time, he lay atop her, stroking her hair as she held him in her embrace, her thighs still enclosing his hips. With a sigh, he braced himself on his elbows and gazed down at her, her lovely face cupped in both his hands.

Her unfathomable eyes swept open under the gold-tipped lashes, and she held him in a gaze that swam with love. "Tell me again that you love me."

"I love you. I love you, Allegra di Fiore. I cherish you and need you, and I am yours completely." He bent his head and brushed her lips lightly with his own. "Thank you, my wife, my dearest friend. Thank you forever for loving me."

Later that same night, hand in hand, Lazar led Allegra down into the secret tunnels of the Fiori, and they climbed out into the cellars of the old, burned Castle Belfort.

They came up through the ruins into the cool air of night and spent hours walking the grounds where their city would stand. Without the two million gold ducats, they would have to build more slowly, but though the job would be harder, Lazar said nothing was impossible for them.

Here would be the senate rotunda, there the new cathedral; in the center of the grand city square would be the monument bronze fountain dedicated to King Alphonse and Queen Eugenia, and a smaller, marble stone commemorating Lady Cristiana, the one person who had tried to get justice for the Fiori and had been killed for it. Where that cluster of pines towered would be the gilded opera house, and on that far hillcrest he'd build the new, majestic Palazzo Reale, where they would grow anew the vine of the ancient royal family in their children and grandchildren.

They joked and debated as always, and kissed often, but as they wandered farther from the vicinity of Belfort, mostly they were silent, walking arm in arm.

"You'll have to talk to Darius," she told him. "His feelings were deeply hurt, you know."

He nodded. "If it's all right with you, Allegra, I'd like to make the boy my legal ward. He has no family."

She smiled up at him with soft pride. "I think that's a splendid idea."

Near dawn, they found a spot on a ridge overlooking an olive orchard, and sitting side by side, they watched the sunrise.

Allegra looked over at Lazar, taking in the sight of the orange morning light softening his rugged, chiseled features.

How much he'd taught her, she mused, and how much he'd grown. His anger had been transformed to strength, his pain to wisdom, his bitterness wiped away by love.

"Lazar?" She linked her fingers through his.

He was the king, but when he turned to her, the roguish sparkle still danced in his sea-black eyes. He drew her hand up to his lips.

"Yes, *chérie*?"

She smiled tenderly at him. "Welcome home."

At noon they walked down the aisle of the sumptuously decorated cathedral. The church was packed with dignitaries from the courts of Europe, and after they exchanged their vows, Pope Pius rested the burden of the thick golden crown on Lazar's head.

In turn, Lazar carefully placed the slender, diamond- and emerald-studded diadem on Allegra's head, then raised her from her kneeling position to stand beside him. When they kissed, all the nobles and dignitaries burst out in thunderous applause that echoed like the roar of the sea beneath the soaring arches of the cathedral.

At last, following the varied ranks of the entourage, the king and queen of Ascencion came out to stand in the sunshine. The air was filled with deafening cheers and applause. Clouds of flower petals rained down on them in the light breeze. Lazar's superbly fitted coat was white with gold braid, and at his side he wore his jeweled broadsword, Excelsior.

They paused on the top step outside the massive open doors of the cathedral, waving to their people. Allegra kept her chin high, though until that moment she had no idea what sort of reception they would give her—Monteverdi's daughter—as their queen.

Though Lazar stood beside her, his white-gloved hand holding hers protectively, for a moment she was truly afraid, longing with all her heart to be accepted by the people and the land she loved.

Suddenly a fat, ill-kempt little man appeared near the front of the crowd and began waving his cap, rousing the onlookers until scores of people were shouting with him, "God save the queen!"

Allegra had to bite the inside of her mouth to keep from laughing at Bernardo's antics.

Lazar winked down at her as if to say, *I told you so.*

Then he embraced her, Ascencion embraced them, and on that tiny island in the jade sea, peace reigned.

If you loved
THE PIRATE PRINCE
by Gaelen Foley,

Turn the page for a sneak peek of
this exciting historical romance

*Darius Santiago was the king's most trusted man, the
champion of honor. She was forbidden fruit. the only
woman he would ever love, and the only one he
couldn't have. . . .*

PRINCESS

⊰ CHAPTER ⊱
ONE

Ascencion, 1805

The sound of her rapid, shallow panting filled the narrow space between the dark green walls of the garden maze. The hedges towered over her, closing in on her, and the pounding of her pulse was so loud in her head she knew they would hear. She inched down the narrow lane, her bare toes creeping silently over the cool, lush grass, her chest heaving. Constantly she looked over her shoulder. Her whole body was shaking, her hand bleeding, maybe broken from punching him so hard, bashing him in his smug, sneering face with the sharp edge of her huge diamond ring, but at least she had managed to throw herself out of Philippe's iron grasp, and had torn into the maze, where she thought she could evade them.

She dared not call out for help because only the three men would hear. No one else was outside on such a night, when the breeze spattered rain from a sky deepest indigo smeared with gold clouds. The cicadas roared in waves, while the wind, as it rose and fell, brought fragments of a tinkling minuet spilling out over the vast gardens and the royal park from the ball in progress. Her engagement party, which her fiancé had been unable to attend.

She jerked her face wildly to the left, hearing movement on the other side of the dense hedge.

He was right there. Her heart pounded. The acid taste of the wine she'd drunk earlier rose in the back of her throat. She could see the shape of him, tall, bedecked in his finery. She could see the shape of the pistol in his hand, and she knew her light-colored silk gown was sure to be visible through the branches. She crouched down and moved silently away.

"Don't be afraid, Serafina," came Henri's mellifluous voice from several rows away in the other direction. "We're not going to hurt you. Come out, now. There's nothing you can do."

They had split up so they could surround her, she thought. She choked back a sob, clawing to keep hold of her fragile control as she tried to decide which way to go.

Clenching her fist so tightly her nails dug into her palm, she huddled against the bush, edging inch by inch down the lane. She heard the lulling splash of the fountain in the tiny center courtyard of the maze, and she used the sound to try to orient herself. She had run around in this maze since she was a little girl, but she was so frightened she had lost all sense of direction.

At the end of the lane, she pressed her back flat against the scratchy bushes, too scared to turn the corner. She waited, trying to gather her nerve, her stomach in knots, shaking, praying.

She didn't know what they wanted. She had been propositioned many times by the gilded, predatory courtiers of the palace, but no one had ever attempted to haul her away before. No one had ever used guns.

God, please.

She would have cried, but she was too terrified. The breeze rose again. She smelled cut grass, jasmine, man.

They're coming.

"Serafina, you have nothing to fear. We are your friends."

She bolted, her hair streaming out behind her. Thunder rumbled, the scent of a summer storm on the wind.

At the end of the lane, she stopped, too petrified to turn the corner again, lest she find Philippe or the blond one, Henri, standing there, waiting to catch her. She kept thinking how her ex-governess always said something like this would happen to her if she didn't mend her wild ways, stop acting so bold. She vowed she would never be bold again. Never flirt. Never trust.

Her chest lifted and fell, lifted and fell.

They were coming. She knew she could not remain where she was for more than a few seconds longer.

I am trapped. There is no way out of this.

And then there came another voice, barely audible, a mystic whisper.

Princesa.

The single word seemed to rise from the earth, or to slip out of the very air.

She nearly sobbed aloud to hear it, wanting with all her heart to believe it was not her panicked brain playing tricks on her.

Only one person called her by that name, the Spanish version of her proper Italian title, *Principessa,* and he was far away on the king's business, no doubt lopping off heads in his leisure time.

"I grow weary of this chase, *ma belle,*" Henri warned. She saw movement through the rows, made out tousled blond curls. She saw the Frenchman stop and cock his head, listening.

Wide-eyed, both hands pressed to her mouth to silence her ragged panting, Serafina began backing away. At a tug on her hair, she almost screamed, whirling to find that one of her long black curls had merely snagged on the grasping bushes.

"Princesa."

She knew she heard it that time! But how could it be? She froze, her gaze darting wildly.

"Make your way to the center courtyard," the dark, airy murmur instructed her.

Again, she could not guess which direction the whisper-soft

voice had come from, almost as if its source was inside her head.

She wanted to scream out to him, but that would only alert her pursuers to where she was.

Calm, she ordered herself as fiercely as possible. If he was here, somehow she must have faith. The possibility gave her a final reserve of strength. Darius Santiago might be an arrogant heathen, coolly insolent to everyone, especially her, but by God, he did not know the meaning of fear, and she quite believed he could do anything.

He was the king's most trusted agent, a master spy and assassin; if ever there was dark work to be done protecting the kingdom and the royal family, he was there to shoulder it without complaint. Serafina lowered both hands from her mouth to her sides. Her chest still heaved with each breath, but she lifted her chin.

"Go to the courtyard, Your Highness. Hurry."

"Where are you?" she breathed, trembling. "Help me."

"I am near, but I cannot get to you."

"Please help me."

"Shhh," he murmured. "Go to the inner courtyard."

"I'm lost, I forget," she whispered, half-choked, blinded now by the tears she had been staving off since the men first seized her. She stared through the dense green lace of the hedge trying to see him.

"Stay calm, be brave," he said softly. "Two right turns. You're very close. I'll meet you there."

"A-All right," she choked out.

"Go now." His whisper faded away.

For a moment, she could not seem to move. Then she pierced the cold fog of fear, forcing herself. She set out for the tiny, brick-laid courtyard, legs shaking beneath her, her scraped knee still burning from before, when she slipped and fell on the grass. The delicate mist-colored silk gown she had been so delighted to wear now had a hole in the knee. Each movement was torturous with her effort to be silent, slowed by her violent, spasmodic tremors of fear, but she painstakingly followed the lullaby of the fountain splashing in its carved stone basin.

With every inch gained, her mind chanted his name, as if she could conjure him, *Darius, Darius, Darius*. She came to the first corner. Steeled herself. Peeked around.

Safe.

She moved on, gathering confidence. Her fists were clenched, while her heart slammed against her ribs. Images flashed through her mind of him watching over her with a look, her stern beloved knight who would always protect her. But when she had finally grown up, nothing had gone according to plan.

Darius, don't let them get me.

Ahead she saw she'd have to slip by a break in the lane. She prayed her pursuers weren't down there to see her pass. At the break in the hedge, she hesitated, her courage faltering.

A bead of sweat ran down her cheek.

Let them put that in the newspapers, she thought madly. *Shocking news! The Princess Royal sweats!*

She shut her eyes briefly, said a prayer, and darted by, stealing a fleeting glance as she went. In the middle of the lane, some twenty feet away, Philippe lay sprawled on his face, unmoving. A length of wire glinted in the moonlight. He had been garroted, she realized, sickened.

Darius had passed this way.

She pressed on with stiff, jerky steps, while cold horror spiraled down to her belly. The cicadas' song stretched to one flat, vibrating note she thought would snap her nerves.

When she reached the end of the lane, she grimaced, fighting a silent, mighty battle for the courage to look around the corner. She forced herself.

Clear! The entrance to the courtyard was in sight at the far end of the corridor. She was almost there. All she had to do was pass the gap in the bushes halfway down the lane, where it intersected another path.

She turned the corner and ran for it.

Her breath raked over her teeth, her bare feet bore her swiftly over the silky grass. The gap was coming, while straight ahead lay the entrance to the courtyard. The sky flung a handful of rain on the breeze into her face. Clouds covered the gold half-moon.

"Get back here, you little bitch!" a deep voice roared.

She shrieked and looked over her shoulder as Philippe tore around the corner behind her.

As she passed the gap, running full force, Henri exploded out of the intersecting path. He caught her in both arms and she screamed. Philippe was bearing down fast, and then Darius was there, lethal silence and grace gliding out of the shadows, attacking with the leap of a black jaguar.

Henri lost his hold on her trying to ward off Darius. She tore free, tackled her way clear of him, heard ripping silk as she pulled, wrenching forward. She sprinted toward the courtyard, sobbing now. She stubbed her toe on the bricks, stumbling into the small enclosure. She passed the leering Pan fountain with its mossy mouth open, trickling water, and flung herself into the shadowed corner. She prayed Philippe would choose to stay and help his friend fight Darius rather than coming straightaway after her, but the prayer was no sooner through her mind when the Frenchman loomed in the entrance between the neatly-trimmed hedges.

Panting hard, he saw her at once, and his sneer turned his handsome face ugly. He strode right to her and hauled her up from her crouched position. She cried out. He hurled her about-face and put a knife to her throat just as Darius came running to the entrance.

She sobbed his name.

Philippe wrenched her. "Shut up!"

Darius stopped short, taking in the scene before him. His fiery, jet-black eyes pierced the darkness with hellfire intensity. The dark, brooding beauty of his face was harsh with icy fury.

The gold, watery moonlight glanced off his body, which was sleek and lean, tall and impeccably attired in black.

Serafina fixed her stare and all her faith on him as she clung with both icy hands to the steely arm around her throat.

"Stand aside, Santiago," Philippe warned him. "You come any closer, she dies."

Danger emanated from him as he sauntered a few paces into the courtyard, and spiked Philippe with a sharp glance, a cold, narrow half-smile on his lips.

She watched him pace casually toward them, her heart in her throat. She stared imploringly at him, but he did not look at her. Her gaze dropped to his sweetly-sculpted mouth, marred on one side by a small, curved scar, like a bitter twist of contempt for the whole world. *Fire and ice,* the palace ladies said of him.

"I thought you were a professional, Saint-Laurent," he said affably, his voice tinged with a Spanish accent. "Is this how you conduct business? Putting knives to young girls' throats? I often wonder how you people can stomach it, serving a man who is without honor."

"I didn't come here to chat with you, Santiago," Philippe ground out. "I'm going now, and she's coming with me."

"I don't think so," he said very softly.

The tension sharpened to a razor's edge as the two men stared at each other for a long, nerve-wracking moment.

Serafina could no longer bear the silence. "Please," she choked out, "let me go."

At her plea, Darius's black eyes flicked to her, and as he gazed at her, a trace of some mysterious emotion softened the dramatic angularity of his face, then vanished, but she could almost swear that, for a fleeting instant, he had faltered.

The keen-witted Philippe had seen it, too.

"What's this?" he asked in smooth amusement. "Have I stumbled upon a weakness? Is it possible the great Santiago has an Achilles' heel?"

Darius's black eyes narrowed on him, glittering in the dark.

"Lower your weapon," he said coldly. "We both know he doesn't want her harmed."

"Ah, but Santiago, you are blocking my path."

"Release the Princess," he clipped out tautly, his teeth gritted. "Surrender is your sole option. Your men are dead, and you know full well I want you alive."

"Hmm. He grows angry. Now *that* is unprofessional." Philippe's next taunting aside was for her. "I think he fancies you, my dear. Look out. They say he is a heartbreaker."

Philippe was not as sharp as she'd imagined, she thought miserably. Little did he know that Darius had naught for her but arrogance and idle mockery, letting her know with Lucifer's own courtesy that he judged her shallow, frivolous, self-centered, and weak. She had no idea what she had ever done to offend him. He used to like her, she thought, when she was a child.

"Don't make things worse for yourself, Saint-Laurent," Darius said coolly, smiling again in his unnerving way. "I'll remember how you annoyed me when you and I have a talk later about your associates and your orders."

"Ah, but my orders don't exist, Santiago. I don't exist. I cannot go back empty-handed, so you see, you'll get nothing from me," Philippe snarled. "Only one of us is leaving this insufferable maze alive, and it won't be you."

Darius started towards them again with slow, wary strides.

"Stay back!"

He paused.

"Move away from the Princess," he said very quietly.

Against her body, Serafina could feel Philippe's heart pounding in his chest. He tightened his hold on her neck. She felt his increasing desperation. She glanced at the knife poised so near her throat, then shut her eyes, praying.

"What do you think of her, Santiago?" Philippe asked in a sudden tone of brittle jocularity. "They say she is the most beautiful woman alive—or in the top three at least. Certainly my patron agrees. The new Helen of Troy, he says. Men fight wars to possess such beauty. Shall we have a look?"

Her eyes flew open as Philippe laid hold of her dress, which Henri had already torn. She gasped as he ripped it open down her back with one lightning-like movement.

"There, there, *ma belle*," he crooned, "don't fret."

She sobbed once, cringing where she stood. She lowered her head, powerless to stop him as he pushed the ripped ends of her dress down to her waist, baring her upper body. Cheeks aflame, she bit her lower lip, fighting tears of rage. She tried to pull her waist-length hair forward to cover her breasts, but Philippe protested.

"*Non, non, cherie.* Let us see what beauty God hath wrought." With his left hand, he brushed her hair softly back again behind her shoulders.

"You bastard," Darius whispered.

She could not bear to meet his eyes.

Hands at her sides, she stood there shaking with humiliation and rage.

Just then the night sky flung down another swift cloud-break of cold rain. She flinched, then shuddered when the first drops hit her bare skin.

She could feel a volcanic force of pure rage building from where Darius stood, but somehow the only thing she could focus on was her pride, her last defense. She held fast to it as if it were a tangible weapon.

She lifted her head high against the crushing shame. Tears in her eyes, she stared straight ahead at nothing.

Philippe laughed at her. "Haughty thing. Yes, you know you are stunning, don't you?" he murmured, running one finger from the curve of her shoulder down her arm. She fought not to sob. "Skin like silk. Come and touch her, Santiago. She is exquisite. I don't blame you—any man would have a weakness for such a creature. We can share her if you like."

Her stricken gaze flew to Darius. But then a cold shaft of

horror spiked down her spine, for he was staring hungrily at her bare breasts.

Her stomach plummeted. Only now did Serafina discover the real meaning of fear.

"Darius?" she said in a pleading whisper.

Philippe's fingers flicked in eager agitation over the handle of the knife, but his smooth, sure voice held a note of triumph. "Really, after all you've done for your king, isn't a taste of her the least you deserve?"

Darius looked up from his intimate perusal of her body, and she caught the flash of white teeth at his cold, wicked smile. Slowly, he sauntered toward them.

"A vision," he agreed. "What do you suggest?"

Serafina's very mind choked. Images exploded in her memory of the last time she had seen Darius, about a year ago, when she had opened the door to the music room in the middle of the afternoon to find him ravishing one of his many lovers against the wall. His loose white shirt had been hanging from his shoulders, brown chest bared, his black breeches clinging upon his lean hips as the woman fumbled to undress him. When she opened the door, he had looked over, locked his gaze on hers for a second. She still remembered the smoldering, mocking look in his eyes as she stood there in the doorway, mouth agape, eyes wide. She remembered the narrow, insolent smile he had sent her before she slammed the door and fled. It was quite the same as the one on his scarred lips now.

Trembling violently, she could not bear to look at him as he stalked slowly toward them.

She lowered her head, heart pounding madly. Darius came to stand perhaps three inches away from her, so close his chest nearly brushed her breasts. She could feel him breathing against her.

She was trapped between the two tall, ruthless men, her breath jagged, her exposed skin racing with shivers, hot and cold.

He was going to touch her any moment, she knew. Cheeks blazing, she wanted to die. Usually she was quick-witted but at the moment she was mute, staring brokenly at a silver button on his coat right at her eye-level. She could not think of one thing to say to save herself, could not find her voice to invoke her father's name or the name of her betrothed, the mighty Russian warlord, Prince Anatole Tyurinov.

Terror wiped her mind blank, and Darius filled her senses. His nearness, the sheer male force of him, overwhelmed her, for she had always been in awe of him, the enigma, the brooding outsider. She could smell the clean, musky scent of him mingled with the smell of horse and leather, the smoke of the cheroots he was always smoking, and the coppery taint of blood. She could feel the heat radiating from his lean, powerful body, feel the thrumming tension coiled in his hard, sinewy form.

Then it all happened at once. He seized Philippe by the throat and knocked her out of his grasp at the same time. Caught off guard even more than Philippe was, she stumbled towards the wall of hedge, landed in a heap near the edge of the courtyard and sat there, immediately pulling the remnants of her silk bodice up over her shoulders with shaking hands.

She looked up in dread when she heard the whisper of metal. Her stare homed in on Darius's ebony-handled dagger, the slim elegance of the blade kissed by moonlight.

Oh, God.

Philippe had dropped his weapon in the scramble. He bolted, but Darius was upon him. He grabbed Philippe by the back of his collar and hurled him around, throwing him down onto the flagstone, blocking the exit.

When Philippe threw up both hands to ward off the first blow, Darius's dagger slashed across both his open palms.

Serafina squeezed her eyes shut tight and turned her face away, but she heard every dragging second of their fight, every gasp and choke and low curse, as Darius savaged him. She longed to run. The cicadas screamed. When Darius swore in some unknown language, she opened her eyes and saw him lift his dagger for the final cut, saw his beautiful face alight with savagery.

Don't.

She squeezed her eyes shut tight as the knife plunged straight down like a bird of prey. Philippe's scream was short, followed by a silence.

Then she heard only the breeze blowing through the junipers until she became aware of the sound of a man's fierce panting. She felt like she was going to throw up.

It dawned on her with sudden hysteria that she had to run. She had to escape from here, get away from him immediately. She could not guess what he'd do next—he was wholly unpredictable. She only knew that the lust-hardened hunger in his face as he stared at her body had been real.

Never taking her eyes off him, she shoved to her feet in one jerky motion as Darius raked a hand through his hair, pushing his forelock out of his eyes, a black, demonic shape against the lesser dark of night. A second later, he wrenched his knife out of Philippe's breast.

She kept watching him, wild-eyed, kept clutching the silk remnants of her bodice together as she inched sideways along the perimeter of the courtyard. She ignored the prickly branches raking the tender skin of her back. He was blocking the only way out, but she would claw her way through the thick hedge if she had to.

Darius rose from Philippe's lifeless body. He took a handkerchief from the pocket of his impeccable coat, the cotton pearl-white in the dark. Wiping the blood off his hands, he paused and suddenly turned, giving the body a vicious kick in the ribs.

Serafina let out a small scream, taken off guard by his swift, tempestuous movement.

He looked over at her, staring harshly at her for a second, as if he were only just remembering she was there.

Then he stood very still, panting, a tall, silent figure looming in the darkness.

"What are you doing?" His voice was unnervingly quiet.

Trapped in his steady, piercing gaze, she froze.

"Jesus," he muttered, closing his eyes for a second.

She said nothing, gathering her torn dress tighter against her in both sweating palms as she calculated the odds of successfully running past him.

He heaved a sigh, shook his head to himself, then went and splashed his face under the cold bubbling fountain.

A moment later, he walked toward her, slipping off his black jacket.

She shrank back against the bushes from him.

He held out the coat, offering it to her.

She didn't dare move even to take it, didn't dare take her eyes off him.

He had killed three men all in a night's work, he was known to do indecent things to women in the middle of the day, he had stared at her breasts, and then there was the other matter, more troubling still, that eight years ago she had been marked with this man's blood.

It had happened in the city square on her twelfth birthday, when someone tried to shoot the king. She had been standing there smiling at her birthday festivities, holding her poppa's hand, when the would-be assassin attacked. And Santiago, this beautiful madman, she thought helplessly, who did not know the meaning of fear, had stepped in the path of the bullet. His body slammed against the king while his hot, scarlet blood splashed on her cheek and on her new white frock.

Since that day, deep down in a primal, illogical place inside of her that responded to things like the warmth of fire and the smell of cooking food, deep down in her blood and bones where she was not princess but simply woman, she knew she belonged to this man.

And the most terrifying thing of all was that she sensed he knew it, too.

His intense, fiery gaze gentled slightly under his long lashes.

She couldn't stop shaking.

Again, he offered the coat. "Take it," he said softly, "Princesa."

Without warning, her eyes brimmed at his gentle tone.

His long lashes flicked downward, as if he had no idea what to do with her.

"I'll help you," he said reluctantly, holding out the coat so she would only have to slip her arms inside the sleeves.

Hesitantly, she let him put it on her like a child.

"I thought," she began. She bit down on her lower lip, unable to finish.

"I know what you thought." His voice was low, quietly fierce. "I would never hurt you."

Their stares locked, clashed, both wary.

She was the first to drop her gaze, astounded by her own unfamiliar meekness. Her ex-governesses would never have believed it.

"Didn't—didn't you need him alive?"

"Well, he's dead now, isn't he?" he said in weary disgust. "I'll manage." One fist propped on his hip, for a moment he rubbed his forehead.

"Thank you," she whispered shakily.

He shrugged and walked away, returning to the fountain.

Finally, now that she saw the danger truly was past, tears overtook her, blinding her.

Serafina sank down where she was, collapsing slowly in a heap on the bricks. Wrapping his jacket tighter around her, she began to weep. When she sobbed aloud, he looked over in surprise. He frowned and came back to her. She could not summon any sense of pride, she just bawled, unable to look up beyond his shiny black boots and gleaming silver spurs.

He crouched down, searching her eyes. "Hey, Princess. What's this? You trying to ruin my night?"

She paused abruptly, staring at him in amazement. *Ruin* his night?

She jumped when he reached out and cupped her cheek, shrinking from his touch.

"What's the matter? You scared of me now like everyone else?"

Her answer was a single, shaking sob that came all the way up from her lungs.

His gaze melted, but he lowered his hand. "Hey, come on, this is me. You know me," he said. "You've always known me. Since you were this big." He held up thumb and forefinger about an inch apart.

She glanced at his hand, then met his onyx eyes uncertainly.

It was a half-truth. Twenty years ago, just before she was born, her parents had saved him from life on the streets as a feral boy-thief. All her life he had been there, in the shadows, but nobody really knew Darius Santiago. He would not allow it, indeed, he saved his most scathing mockery for those who tried to love him, as she had learned.

He lowered his long, thick lashes, and his voice was softer. "Well, it's all right if you're scared of me now. I don't blame you. Sometimes I scare myself."

"You killed them," she whispered. "It was horrible."

"That's my job," he replied, "and yes, sometimes it is horrible. I am sorry you saw it. You should have closed your eyes. Your Highness."

"I did. I could still hear."

He bristled. "He insulted your honor. He got what he deserved."

She dropped her gaze, fearing to provoke him.

There was long, awkward pause, and in the silence the

knowledge hung between them of those moments, and his stare. She heard him let out a weary sigh.

"No more tears, little one," he murmured, wiping her tear-stained cheek with one finger.

"Why did he do that to me?" she wrenched out. "Why would anyone do such a thing?"

For a moment, he appeared as baffled by her naivete as she was by his ruthlessness. Then he shook his head. "It wasn't so much to shame you, *Princesa,* as to try and bait me—distract me into making a mistake. He knew he had no way out, and I went along with it because he was so desperate I thought he might actually cut you."

"Oh, God." She squeezed her eyes shut.

"It's over now. You don't need to be embarrassed with me, all right? We've all had our share of humiliation."

She colored, eyes down, huddling deeper into his coat. "Not you," she answered barely audibly. "No one could ever humiliate you."

He gave a short, unpleasant laugh. "You think not? Believe me," he said.

She stole a curious peek at his chiseled face.

He avoided her eyes as he traced the curve of her cheek with one fingertip, them he laid his hand on her shoulder and gave it a sturdy squeeze. "That man didn't take anything away from you, you understand? It can't hurt you unless you choose to let it."

Her gaze fell. He *was* mad if he thought everyone was as tough and stoic as him.

"You see? That's my secret," he told her. "Now I give it to you."

She glanced up and found him watching her with a faint, teasing smile. She chanced a slight answering smile, then her expression sobered.

"If you hadn't come, what would have happened?"

"Well, let's see." He looked up at the moon, and its light slid downward over his finely-carved, high cheekbones. "You'd have been transported to Milan where you'd have been forced to wed Napoleon's stepson. Your father might have kept his crown but would have lost any real authority, and France would have used our navy to invade England. Beyond that, who knows?"

She stared at him, incredulous.

He tossed his black forelock out his eyes then flashed her an insolent smile. "Such is my life," he said cynically. "Come." He swept to his feet with princely grace and bent to offer her his hand.

Serafina frowned when she saw him sway slightly as he stood. He winced, but the look of pain quickly vanished. It was hard to tell by moonlight, but his sun-bronzed face seemed a trifle pale.

"We've got to go see your father," he continued briskly, "then find someone to babysit you while I catch the rest of Philippe's associates lurking in the palace."

As she reached up to take his outstretched hand, she noticed the dark stain spreading from beneath his black waistcoat onto the left shoulder of his white shirt-sleeve.

Her eyes widened. "Darius, you're bleeding!"

A man bent on revenge
and the beauty who teaches
him to love again . . .

DEVIL TAKES
A BRIDE

by Gaelen Foley

In the quiet English countryside, far from the intrigues
of London, Lizzie Carlisle is devoting herself to her new
position as lady's companion to the Dowager Viscountess
Strathmore—until her peaceful life is turned upside
down by a visit from the old woman's untamed nephew.

Devlin Kimball, Lord Strathmore, has spent years adven-
turing on the high seas, struggling to make his peace with
the tragedy that claimed the lives of his family. But now
he has uncovered the dark truth behind the so-called
accident and swears retribution. He has no intention of
taking a bride—until his eccentric aunt's will forces him
and Lizzie together, and Devlin finds his path to
vengeance blocked by the stubborn but oh-so-tempting
Miss Carlisle. But disillusioned once by love, Lizzie will
accept nothing less than his true devotion. . . .

Published by Ivy Books
Available wherever books are sold